of friendship' *Sunderland Echo*

'I didn't want to put it down ... A must for Catherine Cookson lovers' *Coventry*

'[A] pow ... *Lancashire Evening P*

D0655057

Starlight and Dreams

Benita Brown

headline

First published in 2010 by
HEADLINE PUBLISHING GROUP

First published in paperback in 2010 by
HEADLINE PUBLISHING GROUP

1

Cataloguing in Publication Data is available from the British Library

ISBN 978 0 7553 5290 6

Typeset in Bembo by Avon DataSet Ltd,
Bidford-on-Avon, Warwickshire

Printed and bound in Great Britain by
Clays Ltd, St Ives plc

Headline's policy is to use papers that are natural, renewable and
recyclable products and made from wood grown in sustainable forests.
The logging and manufacturing processes are expected to conform
to the environmental regulations of the country of origin.

HEADLINE PUBLISHING GROUP
An Hachette UK Company
338 Euston Road
London NW1 3BH

www.headline.co.uk
www.hachette.co.uk

To Norman, as ever, and to our family

Prologue

Summer 1939

The sun was bright, but the air was cool. A brisk north wind whipped the waves into small crests. Carol watched the frothy spray blowing in from the sea. Her mother had told her it was called spindrift. She thought that a romantic name.

'Hurry up!' Muriel urged. 'It'll be warmer in the shelter of the dunes.'

Carol's friend forged ahead across the wave-ribbed sand. She was carrying a rug for them to sit on and a net bag containing their sandwiches. Carol's own contribution to the picnic, the bottle of ice cream soda she'd bought with her pocket money, was in her school bag slung across her shoulder. Carol and Muriel had left school two days before and had decided to celebrate the 'last carefree day of childhood', as Muriel had fancifully put it.

Carol paused to watch two small boys lying face down on the rocks exposed by the outgoing tide. They were reaching down into a pool with jam jars, probably trying to catch something, but most of the time they just threw water at each other. Suddenly they tired of their game and scrambled to their feet and ran away. One of them stopped, drew his arm back and threw his jam jar high into the air, aiming for the retreating sea. Carol waited for the splash.

'Carol!' Muriel had reached the dunes and was already spreading the tartan rug under the shelter of some overhanging marram grass.

'I'm coming,' Carol called.

As she turned to go, she noticed the sun glinting on the jam jar the other boy had dropped as he ran away. If it's broken, someone could cut themselves, she thought. She picked it up. It was intact. A set of tiny pincers emerged from the sludge of wet sand at the bottom of the jar, and she almost dropped it in fright.

She must have shouted out, because Muriel called, 'What is it?' and hurried towards her. The two of them peered into the jam jar.

'It's only a baby crab,' Muriel said.

'I know. How cruel.'

'Cruel?'

'To catch it, then run away and leave it to die trapped in the jar. Feel the glass – the sun has warmed it. The poor thing might have cooked.'

Her friend grinned. 'Well, if you want to save its life, all you have to do is tip it into a pool. But hurry up. I'm hungry.'

Muriel trudged back to the little camp she had made, and Carol took the jam jar to the rocks. She knelt down by a pool that seemed deeper than the others, and upended the jar gently until the tiny crab slid out. She watched it hurrying away across the smooth silver sand at the bottom of the pool, then she rose, put the empty jar in her school bag, and went to join her friend.

Muriel spread a clean tea towel on the rug and took the meat paste and jam sandwiches from their separate brown paper bags. She divided them into two equal piles.

'Happy now that you've saved the poor little crab?' She grinned.

Carol returned her smile. 'I don't know how that boy could have been so mean,' she said.

'He probably knows no better. Look at the way he and his pal were dressed – all torn and raggy. They'll be from the Seafield estate, I should imagine.'

'That's where I live, remember.'

Muriel didn't look at all abashed. 'Oh, I know, but you're different. You're not a bit rough and rowdy. If you had been, my mother would never have allowed us to be friends.'

Carol would have liked to ask Muriel what she would have done if her mother had objected to their friendship, but this was not the time for it. Not today. Not when tomorrow their lives were about to take two quite different paths. Muriel was to go to the commercial college to learn secretarial skills, while she, Carol, was going to start working at Rutherford's department store. Muriel would make new friends and a whole new life would open up for her. And what about me? Carol wondered. What kind of life will I have working at Rutherford's?

'Penny for them,' Muriel said.

'What do you mean?'

'You were miles away. Oh, drat it, here comes my brother and that stuck-up Kay!'

Carol's pensive mood faded. She was thrilled to see Muriel's handsome elder brother, Steve, despite the fact that he had brought Kay Blanchard with him. Though she couldn't understand why, for Kay was dressed in whites and carrying a tennis racket.

'What do you want?' Muriel asked.

'I don't want anything, ungracious child. Mum's sent you this.' He handed Muriel a paper bag. 'She forgot to give you the hard-boiled eggs.'

'Thanks. But don't tell me you came to the beach just to give me these.'

'No, I was coming anyway. I wanted to take some shots with my new camera.' Steve patted the leather camera case that hung around his neck on a strap.

'Shots of what, exactly?' Muriel asked.

Steve grinned. 'You know – the sea, rock pools, old couples in deckchairs, kids playing on the beach, that lone fisherman.' He turned his head towards the shore and indicated the man sitting on a camp stool with his fishing line. Then he looked at Carol. 'That would make a good picture. What do you think?'

Carol, startled to be addressed by him directly, felt her throat constrict. 'Erm – yes.'

'It's like a new toy, isn't it?' Muriel smiled at her older brother indulgently.

He grinned. 'Yes, I have to admit I'm excited – but it's important, too. I want to start making a portfolio.'

Carol would have liked to ask him what a portfolio was, but Kay had grown impatient. 'Look here, Steve, you know I'm meeting the others at the tennis club. You said this wouldn't take long.'

'Sorry. We'll get started straight away. See you later, infant,' he told Muriel. Brother and sister smiled at each other affectionately.

Carol watched Steve and Kay walk away and was overcome with envy. If only she could be the girl Steve was smiling at and talking to so easily.

Muriel set about cracking the shell of one of the hard-boiled eggs on a large pebble. 'Look in the bag,' she told Carol. 'Mum won't have forgotten the salt. Hard-boiled eggs are simply foul without a bit of salt, aren't they?'

Carol reached into the paper bag and found a salt cellar with a broken matchstick stuck in the hole at the top. She loved Muriel's way of talking. She was popular at school, where the other girls thought of her as a bit of a lark. Carol often wondered why Muriel had chosen her to be her best friend.

'Drat, I've dropped my egg in the sand,' Muriel suddenly exclaimed. 'Oh well, there's another one in the bag. I'll toss this one down the beach for the seagulls.' Immediately two gulls swooped down, screeching, to fight over the prize. 'Look at them,' Muriel said. 'Funny, that. Them eating eggs, I mean. It's like cannibalism, isn't it?'

'I suppose so.' Carol was distracted. When she had turned to look at the birds, she had glimpsed Steve and Kay along by the steps to the lower promenade. Kay was a little way up them and her head was thrown back slightly as she looked out to sea. Carol thought she looked like one of the film stars in *Picturegoer*.

'She's very pretty, isn't she?' Muriel said. She too was gazing at Steve and Kay. 'But don't let that sweet face fool you. Kay Blanchard knows how to get exactly what she wants.'

Carol looked at the scene a little longer, and then turned back to face Muriel. 'What's a portfolio?' she asked.

'It's a collection of his work. All sorts of arty photographs. Steve hopes it will get him a better job in some big studio.'

'Isn't he happy working for Mr Latham?'

'Not really. All those family groups and little girls in their ballet frocks. And all posed in front of those dreadfully old-fashioned backdrops. Steve says they must have been there since Mr Latham's great-grandfather opened the studio in prehistoric times.'

'But where will he go?'

'Oh, I don't know. London, Paris, Italy. I can't see him staying in this boring old town much longer.'

Carol felt intimidated by the string of exotic names Muriel had reeled off so casually. 'Oh,' she said.

'I hope you've left some sandwiches for me.'

The girls looked up to see Steve standing over them. There was no sign of Kay.

'She's gone.' He answered Muriel's unspoken question. 'She has a date with the usual crowd at the tennis club.'

'Oh, that lot,' Muriel said. 'They swan about in their whites trying to look as though they know one end of a tennis racquet from the other when in reality it's just a social club.'

Steve laughed. 'We all know what an ace player you are, but you'll have to learn to be more gracious towards lesser mortals.'

This talk of tennis and the club meant nothing to Carol. It wasn't part of her way of life – nor that of anyone who lived on the Seafield estate. Tennis was probably the only activity that she and Muriel didn't do together. Carol's parents would never have been able to afford the stylish white skirts and blouses, let alone the shoes and a tennis racquet.

Even if they could have, Carol doubted whether her stepmother would have agreed to it. Look at the row over her elocution lessons. Once a week since she had been seven years old, she had been going to lessons with Miss Grayson. Carol's mother had decided that even though they lived on the Seafield estate, amongst some of the roughest families in town, it didn't mean her daughter couldn't be brought up to speak like a lady.

But her mother had died a year ago, and while Carol was still stunned with grief, her father had found someone else. Six months after Edith Marshall had been laid to rest, Albert had removed his black armband and married Hetty Collins. Hetty was an attractive, but sharp-featured, domineering woman. She took over the running of the household, demanding that Albert hand over his pay packet unopened every week, something that would never have occurred to his gentle and easy-going first wife.

Carol, who had enjoyed helping her mother with the

housework, was now treated like a skivvy. She was given all the dirty jobs so that Hetty wouldn't spoil her hands.

As for her elocution lessons, Hetty had wanted to put a stop to such nonsense, as she called it. Carol had Miss Grayson to thank for the fact that the lessons went on. Miss Grayson had once been an actress whose career had ended after she was horribly scarred in a car crash. She had come back to the town where she had been born and lived modestly, supplementing her savings by taking pupils.

When Hetty had gone to Miss Grayson's house to tell her that Carol was no longer going to come for lessons, the older woman had immediately offered to forgo any payment.

'Don't you know how much promise the child shows?' she had asked an astounded Hetty.

'Promise doesn't butter your bread,' Hetty had replied, but Miss Grayson had pointed out that by encouraging Carol to speak properly, she would be ensuring that she got a much better job when she left school.

'She'll bring more money in,' Miss Grayson had added, although secretly she had other hopes for Carol that would take her away from that grim little house for ever. For she had realised, even from the start, that Carol had not only a lovely speaking voice but also a talent for acting. She wisely didn't mention that to the poor child's stepmother. There would have been no point.

Hetty was talked round. It wasn't just the prospect of a well-paid job for Carol in the future. She had liked the idea of getting something for nothing. Carol had continued with her lessons and Miss Grayson's prediction had come true when she was offered the job in the French Salon at Rutherford's.

Carol brought her attention back to the scene on the beach. She heard Muriel tell her brother, 'We've eaten all the sandwiches. Mum didn't say I was supposed to keep some for you.'

'You weren't. I was just feeling peckish. Anyway, I'd better go. Mr Latham has loaned me the keys to the studio. He says I can use the darkroom. I'm keen to see the results of my morning's work.'

Carol desperately didn't want him to go. Quickly she thought of a question that would delay him. 'Why is your new camera so special?' she asked. 'How is it different from your old one?'

'It's a reflex camera,' he said. 'Stand up and I'll show you what that means.'

Carol stood as she was asked, and Steve said, 'Here. Put your head down and look into this sort of window on the top.'

He had pointed the camera at his sister, and there she was, sitting on the rug and grinning up at them.

'See?' Steve said. 'What you see is exactly what the photograph will look like. My old camera wouldn't be so accurate. This one is German, you know, and the scandal of it is that the man who invented it has had to flee Germany. They say he's gone to America.'

'Why?' Carol asked.

'Because he's a Jew, and it's more than his life is worth to stay there.'

Carol had heard her father and stepmother discussing the situation in Europe.

'Another war!' her father had said. 'I thought the last one was supposed to be the war to end all wars. At least that was what they told us when we were up to our necks in mud in the trenches. And there's many like me that've still got a lungful of gas.'

Suddenly, despite the shelter the dunes afforded, the air had grown cold. They were all silent for a moment, and then

8

Muriel said, 'For goodness' sake, Steve. Don't spoil our last day of freedom with such gloomy talk. I tell you what, before you go, why don't you take our picture? Carol and me on a day to remember.'

'All right,' he said. 'Sit close together and smile up at me. No, wait a moment, I'll kneel down. Look straight into the camera. Do you know, you make quite a pretty picture. Muriel with your dark curls and Carol so blonde and looking like a little angel.'

Carol thought that was a compliment. At least it would have been if he hadn't used the word 'little'. She knew she looked younger than her fourteen years, and she didn't like to be reminded of the fact.

'Muriel!' Steve said. 'Don't grin like that. Try to smile naturally. Carol, that's beautiful. You've got it just right. You're a natural in front of the camera.'

'Am I?' Carol was thrilled, not because she was a natural, whatever that meant, but because Steve had praised her.

After he had taken a few pictures, he left them.

'He'll be in the darkroom for the rest of the day,' Muriel said. 'Sometimes he forgets to eat.'

Carol watched him go. Lean and dark, tall and rangy, he was as good-looking as any film star she had ever seen. 'I wish he was *my* brother,' she said suddenly.

Muriel glanced at her appraisingly. 'No you don't.'

Carol looked at her in surprise. 'What do you mean?'

'I mean, you might want to have a brother *like* Steve, but you wouldn't want Steve himself to be your brother.'

'Why not?'

'Don't you know?'

Carol shook her head, and then was suddenly overwhelmed with a rush of understanding. She held her breath as the wonderful truth dawned on her. She knew what her friend meant, but she neither wanted to admit it nor have Muriel say it out loud. She rose quickly, slipped off her plimsolls and started running towards the sea.

'Come on!' she shouted over her shoulder. 'We can't go home without having a paddle!'

'All right. Race you!'

Soon they were splashing through the frothy waves like children. The tide had turned and the wind was colder, but even so they were the last to leave the beach that day. They hardly spoke as they walked up through the town, Carol lost in her thoughts about Steve. They stopped at the corner of the respectable street of semi-detached houses where the Douglas family lived.

'Well . . .' Muriel paused. 'We've had a marvellous day, haven't we?'

'Yes.'

'And whatever happens in the future, we'll still be friends, won't we?'

'Of course,' Carol said, hugging her friend. 'Nothing will change.'

But she was wrong. Neither of them knew it, but in a few weeks' time, not just their lives but the whole world was going to change for ever. It would be years before either of them would spend such a carefree day on the beach again.

Chapter One

April 1946

Carol gazed doubtfully at the scene she had just created in Rutherford's window. Three of the mannequins were wearing puff-sleeved tea dresses in pastel flower prints; the other three were dressed in the newly fashionable halter-neck frocks made of parachute silk dyed in rich hues. Miss Rawson had told her that the window display must reflect the cheerful mood of the first spring after the war had ended. 'How about some clumps of daffodils and a darling little lamb or two?' she'd said.

'The old girl is losing her touch,' Denise, who worked in the shoe department, had said when Carol had told her what her orders were. And Carol, remembering the days when one elegant gown might have been displayed before a faux-marble plinth supporting a vase with a spray of elegant white flowers, agreed with her.

Now the shop was about to close and Denise was waiting on the pavement outside. Carol sighed and turned to look at her friend. 'What do you think?' she mouthed.

The older girl shrugged as if she couldn't care less, then pushed up her coat sleeve and tapped the glass face of her watch.

'All right. I'm coming,' Carol said.

In the French Salon the lights had been switched off and the only illumination was a watery late sun streaming through the tall windows. Carol was surprised to find Miss Rawson sitting on one of the rococo sofas. The French Salon was like a room in an eighteenth-century French house. Or at least that was what Miss Rawson had intended. She had told Carol that rococo rooms were designed as total works of art, with elegant and ornate furniture, small sculptures, ornamental mirrors and tapestries.

Rutherford's hadn't been able to manage any tapestries or sculptures, but they had come up with two gilt-framed cheval mirrors and some ornate furniture in the form of three red velvet sofas with gold-painted woodwork.

'It looks more like a tart's boudoir than a room in a classy department store,' Denise had once remarked to Carol. 'But then who in this town would know the difference?'

Today the department head was dressed as elegantly as ever, in a black costume with a white silk blouse. Round her neck was draped a leopard-skin tippet that matched her turban-style hat. She wore a pair of large pearl drop earrings and her make-up was perfectly applied, although Carol thought maybe there was a little too much pancake foundation.

'Do you want to come and inspect the window, Miss Rawson?' Carol asked.

'No, that's all right. If anything needs doing, I'll tell you tomorrow.'

To Carol's surprise, because surely she was dressed ready to go home, Miss Rawson remained sitting where she was.

'Honestly, it was weird,' Carol told Denise a short while later as they hurried towards the cinema. 'She actually smiled at me. At least I think she was smiling at me. She had a sort of faraway look. I wonder what's got into her.'

'Elementary, my dear Watson. She's waiting for someone,' Denise said.

Carol smiled at the reference to their favourite movie detective, and then she frowned. 'You mean like a date?' she asked.

'Yeah, but I can't think who would want a date with old Rawbones. I mean, she must be forty if she's a day! But we've wasted enough time in idle chatter. Trevor Howard is waiting for us. Let's go!'

Friday was the night Carol and Denise went to the cinema. Not bothering to go home for a meal, they went straight from work. Sometimes Carol's old school friend Muriel Douglas would go with them, and sometimes, under sufferance, Denise would be persuaded to take her younger sister. She agreed, because despite her protests, she was fond of 'the brat', as she called her, but it definitely spoiled their fun, as her mother insisted that she bring eleven-year-old Ruthie straight home afterwards without making a detour to the fish and chip shop.

Actually, Muriel was a bit sniffy about fish and chips too, so tonight Denise was happy that it was just going to be the two of them. You never knew who you might meet up with in the queue at the chip shop, though annoyingly, Carol never seemed to be interested in any of the local lads and Denise could hardly go and chat to them on her own.

Carol was blonde and sensationally pretty, and many a likely lad had taken a shine to her, but she had spent the whole war writing to Muriel's older brother Steve, who had joined the RAF. And now she was waiting for him to come home.

'Drat it!' Denise exclaimed when they reached the Rialto. 'Look at the length of that queue.'

Carol began to worry that they would not get in before the film began. This was the second and final showing of the night, so they wouldn't be able to stay in their seats and wait until the performance began all over again in order to catch up. And even though the programme started with a supporting film rather than the main attraction, she didn't like to miss any part of the night's entertainment.

'What about the circle?' she asked. 'Look, that queue's moving much more quickly.'

'Can't afford it,' Denise told her. 'Not if we're going to the chip shop afterwards.'

Carol would have liked to tell Denise that it didn't matter about the fish and chips, but at that point several people in the queue ahead of them got tired of waiting and left. Not much later they had their tickets and Carol relaxed. When they entered the auditorium, they peered through the warm, smoky darkness trying to see if there were any good seats left.

Denise sighed. 'It's either right up at the front, where we'll get neck ache staring up at the screen, or we'll have to split up and find single seats.'

'I'll risk neck ache,' Carol replied. 'You never know who you might end up sitting next to otherwise.'

They smiled at each other and laughed. The woman sitting at the end of the row where they were standing turned and hushed them crossly. They managed to reach their seats without annoying anyone else and settled back contentedly, both of them ready and willing to be transported to another world.

The supporting film was an American gangster tale involving a bank robbery, screeching cars and a lot of shooting. It was followed by a trailer for the coming attractions. Then there was the newsreel. Usually this showed four or five filmed reports of the latest world news. Tonight it was mainly concerned with the continuing trial of the Nazi war criminals in Nuremberg, but there was also a report on the massive rebuilding that would have to be done in Europe.

There was a film clip taken from a plane flying over a ruined city. At one stage the shadow of the plane became visible as it flew low across the still smoking rubble. The narrator was silent, and only the drone of the plane's engine could be heard. Carol wondered if that was what Steve was doing now – making films like this. He had spent the war as an aerial photographer, but in his letters home he had never been able to tell her very much. She guessed that most of his work was secret.

'Wake up!' Denise hissed and nudged Carol's arm with a sharp elbow.

'Ouch! I wasn't asleep, I was just thinking.'

'Well stop thinking and watch instead. It's starting.'

Carol stared up at the opening shot of an ordinary-looking railway station. A guard picked his way over the tracks and entered a café. A man and a woman sat at a table looking sad, but the way they were looking at each other made you want to know what it was that was so important to them. The same powerful magic that Carol always experienced in the cinema took over, and soon she was lost in a make-believe world that was almost as important to her as real life.

'Wonderful, wasn't it?' Carol said when the film had finished and they were making for the exit.

'Do you think so?' Denise was surprised. 'I thought it was bloody depressing. Any sensible woman would have gone off with the handsome doctor instead of settling for a humdrum life with that old buffer!'

'Are you serious?' Carol asked.

'You bet I am. That's what I would have done.'

'But what about her children?'

'Well . . .' Denise didn't sound so sure. 'I don't know about that. But fancy giving up a chance of true happiness. What a let-down.'

'No, don't you see? It wouldn't be such a good film if it

wasn't for her sacrifice. It had to end like that. She did the right thing.'

'Silly cow. And anyway, why did she have to be so middle-aged?'

'But she was beautiful, don't you think?'

'Not exactly beautiful. Celia Johnson has style, I'll give you that. But she isn't my idea of a film star.'

They had reached the foyer, and the commissionaire, Mr Benson, was waiting by the double exit doors.

'So what's your idea of a film star?' Carol asked.

'Look around you!' Denise gestured towards the framed photographs lining the walls. 'These are proper film stars. Ignore the men, gorgeous as they are. Just look at the women.'

Carol glanced at the familiar faces: Rita Hayworth, Vivien Leigh, Maureen O'Hara, Margaret Lockwood, Patricia Roc. 'All right, I admit they're very beautiful.'

'That's not the point. They're *glamorous*! It's glamour you need to stand out in this dreary old world. They're film stars because they look more exciting, more romantic and more fashionable than ordinary people. That's the kind of person we want to see when we come to the pictures.'

'Hurry along, you two,' Mr Benson called. 'Though if you're interested in glamour, you might like to look at this before you go.' He took hold of a placard that had been left propped up against the wall, face inwards. 'It's going up tomorrow.' He turned it round to face them.

What they saw was the head-and-shoulders silhouette of a woman with a fashionable hairstyle. The head was superimposed on a scene that looked like a film set, with cameras, scenery and lights. Right in the middle of the head were the words: 'Wanted: A Glamour Girl! Could It Be You?'

'What is it?' Denise asked.

'It's a competition,' Mr Benson said. 'They're looking for a local girl to take part in a film.'

'What!' Denise exclaimed. 'They're going to shoot a film in this dead-end place?'

The commissionaire grinned and shook his head. 'They're not exactly going to shoot it here. They'll film what they call lots of background stuff, but the acting bit will be shot in the studios in London.'

'In London! You're kidding, right?'

'Would I lie to you? Come along tomorrow and get one of the entry forms. It will explain everything.'

'Why can't you give us one now?' Denise persisted.

Mr Benson laughed. 'Because the competition won't be announced until tomorrow.'

'Aw, go on. We won't tell anyone.'

He smiled. 'All right. Seeing as you're such good customers.'

He walked over to the manager's office and vanished inside for a moment or two. Then he came out again and locked up behind him.

'There you are. Don't lose them, because you can't have more than one each.' He held the door open for them and said good night.

As soon as they got outside, Denise stopped and examined the leaflet under the light of a street lamp.

'The old boy's right,' she said. 'They're actually going to make a movie here and there's a part in it for the winner of the competition. The heats will be held down at the Palais, starting next Saturday. A famous film star will be the chief judge, but it doesn't say who.' She gripped Carol's arm. 'Listen to me. You've got to enter.'

'Why should I?'

'Don't be daft. If you win, you'll get a part in a film. You love acting, don't you? You knocked them cold in that little scene you did at the staff Christmas party. Even old Rawbones looked moved when you sang a lullaby to the abandoned baby. But what's more, you're beautiful and you've got a fantastic figure. Dressed up and made up you could look like any of those so-called stars of the silver screen. Looking and talking the way you do, you'd never think you grew up on the Seafield estate.'

'Are you saying I'm a snob?' Carol laughed.

'Of course not. If you were, you certainly wouldn't be pals with me! I'm just saying you're a real class act. Now come on, let's get some chips and batter. We can talk about this later.'

They took their sixpenn'orth of chips and batter to eat on the way home. The chips were hot and salty and the batter crunchy.

'I bet Celia Johnson wouldn't do this,' Denise said. 'She's far too ladylike to walk along eating her supper out of newspaper.'

'But just think what she's missing,' Carol said, smiling fondly at her friend.

Carol was pleased that Denise had let the subject of the Glamour Girl competition drop. She hadn't wanted to admit it, but she was tempted to enter. Denise was right. She loved the movies and had often dreamed of what it would be like to be part of that world. She also admitted to herself that she might stand a chance of winning. Working in the salon for Miss Rawson had taught her a lot about style and grooming, and Miss Grayson had helped her with her speech and confidence.

She wondered what Miss Grayson would think about it. She still went for weekly speech and drama lessons. She had insisted on paying for them once she started work. Over the years, she and the former actress had become more like friends than pupil and teacher. Often Miss Grayson could be persuaded to talk about her career, and Carol loved hearing her stories.

'It was sheer chance,' Miss Grayson had told her. 'Until then, I'd only had stage work. I was "resting" – that means I didn't have an acting job. I was working as a Nippy – a waitress – at Lyons Corner House at Marble Arch, and I was spotted by a film director. It was like a fairy tale. Soon I became quite a movie star, and I might even have gone to Hollywood if it hadn't been for the accident.'

Carol had never met anyone quite like Alice Grayson. Despite the terrible scars on one side of her face, she still had an air of glamour that lifted her above the commonplace.

Denise had finished her chips. She bundled up the newspaper wrapping and put it in a bin. 'Haven't you finished yet?' she asked.

'No – I don't think I can eat any more.'

'Let me see. You've only eaten about half!' she said accusingly. 'What a waste of sixpence! Here, you'd better give that to me. I'll finish it off for you so you won't be conscience-stricken about wasting good food.'

It didn't take Denise long to eat what Carol had left, and after she had disposed of the newspaper, the two girls resumed their walk home. Their route took them past the Waverley, the grandest hotel in town, and they looked up at the lighted windows of the restaurant, where some late diners were still sitting. Even after the lean years of the war, the interior of the Waverley still looked imposing. Maybe the luxurious furniture and fittings were old and just a trifle shabby, but they spoke of a more leisured and prosperous age.

'All right for some,' Denise remarked as they stopped for a moment and gazed through the windows at the glass chandeliers that had been put into storage during the bombing and had only recently been restored to their rightful place in the dining hall. Then she gripped Carol's arm and said, 'Look!'

'Look at what?'

'The table by the end window – it's old Rawbones!'

'No!'

'Yes – and she's not alone, is she? She's with a strange bloke.'

'Strange?'

'Strange in that I haven't a clue who it could be. Have you?'

Carol stared at the man sitting opposite Miss Rawson. He was smartly dressed in a navy-blue blazer. He had neat brown hair and a flamboyant moustache.

'It's the squadron leader,' she said.

Denise looked flabbergasted. 'Don't say old Rawbones has got herself a fly boy!'

Carol laughed. 'I think it might be business.'

'Business? At this time of night?'

'Squadron Leader Wilmot has left the RAF and is working for a firm that makes clothes up from surplus parachute silk.'

'He's a sales rep?'

'That's right.'

'How the mighty have fallen. One minute you're a war hero, and the next you're traipsing round dreary towns selling ladies' wear. And having to take old Rawbones out into the bargain!'

'She's not that bad, you know.'

'I admit she can certainly put on the style. Look at the way she's gazing at him across the table. Do you think she's fallen for him?'

'I haven't the remotest idea. She's certainly impressed by him. That's why I had to make such a fuss with the window. He talked her into displaying some of his gowns along with the new spring fashions.'

'Well at least she's getting a nice dinner out of it.'

'Denise, we shouldn't stand and gawp like this. If they see us it would be embarrassing.'

'Don't worry. They seem to have eyes only for each other. But you're right: we can't stand here any longer. I'm bloody freezing. Let's go.'

Carol linked arms with her friend and thought ruefully of how Muriel would have reacted to Denise's choice of language. Muriel was her oldest friend; Denise had become equally important to her, so Carol took on the role of peacemaker.

Since they had left school, Muriel to go to commercial college and Carol to work at Rutherford's, they had kept up their friendship, although as Carol had feared, Muriel had started mixing with the sort of girls who would never have invited Carol to their homes. The class divide was strong, and Carol lived on the Seafield estate, which was literally on the wrong side of the railway tracks.

Denise was from the sort of family that Muriel called 'rough and rowdy', but she had been the first person to smile at Carol when she started at Rutherford's. It was their mutual love of the cinema that had drawn them together, and now Carol considered Denise to be as close a friend as Muriel was. She often wished that Muriel and Denise could have liked each other more.

Denise insisted on walking Carol all the way home. The older girl didn't live on the Seafield estate; she lived in Garden Square. That sounded grand, but in reality it was the very worst part of the old town. Once, the houses there had belonged to wealthy folk, but as the town grew, that kind of family moved away and the houses were turned into tenements. Some of the tenants did their utmost to keep their modest homes clean and tidy. Some simply didn't care. Carol often wondered how Denise could remain so cheerful.

'Sweet dreams,' Denise said as they parted at Carol's gate. 'And bring that entry form to work with you. We'll discuss it tomorrow.'

'Maybe,' Carol replied.

She let herself into the house and crept upstairs quietly. Her father and stepmother were in bed, and Hetty was a light sleeper. More than once she had flung the bedroom door open and appeared on the landing in her nightgown, her hair in curlers and her face white and pinched, to yell at Carol that she was a dirty stop-out to come home at this time of night when respectable folk were getting their well-earned slumber.

Hetty took every opportunity to find fault with her stepdaughter. Often during one of her tirades she would turn to Albert and demand that he say something. But he never did. 'For God's sake, woman, can't a man have a bit of peace and quiet in his own house?' was the most she got out of him. At least he wasn't supporting Hetty, but Carol longed for him just once to stand up for her, his own daughter.

Carol tiptoed up the stairs and along the landing to the bathroom before going to her own room. She breathed a sigh of relief once she had shut the door behind her. The air in the room was chilly, and she was shivering by the time she put out the light and got into bed. Instead of settling down to sleep, she opened the drawer in the bedside cabinet and took out her torch and the bundle of letters she kept there.

She needed the torch, because if she left the light on, Hetty would look at the meter in the morning and give her a lecture about wasting electricity. Carol didn't mind at all. It was so much more romantic to read Steve's letters by torchlight.

Steve had been eighteen when war was declared. He had left grammar school at sixteen and had been working for two years in Mr Latham's photographic studios. At first he'd loved his job, but it hadn't taken him long to realise that working in a small-town studio was not enough for him. He was already planning a different future for himself when the war had changed everything.

He was a fit young man of fighting age, and it was inevitable that he would be conscripted sooner or later. But he didn't wait to be called up. He volunteered. He chose the RAF because like many young men he was impressed by the excitement and glamour of flying.

His first letter to his parents had been from the reception camp. Its tone was light-hearted as he told them of being met at the railway station and taken to the camp in a truck along with the other new recruits.

And after that we were marched everywhere, he wrote. *Marched to the billet – a wooden Nissen hut – marched to the stores to get our uniforms and marched to the barbers to get our hair cut. And all the time we marched, a fierce red-faced bloke was shouting at us and telling us how useless we were!*

Muriel read the letter to Carol and asked her if she would like to write a little note, which she would enclose with her own reply. And that was how it began.

After that, when Steve wrote home he would enclose a note for the small fry, as he called Muriel and Carol. They would read his letters avidly, relishing all the details of his basic training, or 'square-bashing', as he called it. Then came the letter telling them that he had been posted to the RAF School of Photography at Farnborough to train as an aerial photographer. They could tell how pleased he was.

As the girls grew older, Carol spent less time at Muriel's house and wasn't always there to share the letter-reading. She would ask Muriel about the letters, but her friend would say something like 'Oh, yes, Steve sends regards' or 'He's fine'.

And then one rainy day Carol saw Steve in town. He was in uniform, carrying a small canvas bag slung over his shoulder, and he was walking towards a bus stop on the other side of the road. He must have been home on leave and she hadn't known. Why hadn't Muriel told her?

Ignoring the rain, she stood and watched him. The shock of seeing him without warning made her realise the depth of her feelings for him. She wanted to run after him but it was too late. A bus arrived and Steve boarded it. She watched the bus pull away and backed into a shop doorway as it passed her, sending up spray.

For some reason Muriel had stopped asking Carol if she wanted to write to Steve. Carol wondered if her old friend wanted to keep her brother to herself. One morning, though, she was utterly surprised to receive a letter from him delivered to her home. The post had arrived just as she was setting out for work, so she had stuffed the letter in her pocket and waited until her tea break before she opened it.

Hi, Toots, it began. *The strangest thing: last time I was home I believe I saw you standing in the rain watching the bus I was on. Was that you? If so, why didn't you wave to me? And I've just realised I haven't heard from you lately.*

The letter went on to tell her about the other lads in his billet. The new friends he had made and the awful food: mostly bread, meat and potatoes. He went on to say that he loved his work, although he didn't tell her exactly what that was.

He had ended the letter by telling her that all the lads, himself included, loved getting news from home. Incredible as it seemed, Carol took that to mean that he wanted her to write to him, and she had been doing so ever since.

At first she didn't know what to say. She imagined that Steve's life was exciting, whereas what was going on at home was pretty dreary. The blackout, the rationing, the air raids. Surely he wouldn't want to hear about all that?

So she began to tell him about her own life: her job at

24

Rutherford's in the French Salon, how difficult Miss Rawson could be, and the even more difficult customers, who were having to cope with clothing coupons when they had been used to being able to buy anything they wanted.

'Eleven coupons for that simple little woollen frock!' one of them had complained.

I can't help thinking, Carol had written, *that for many people in this town, clothing coupons don't make that much difference. They're too poor to afford new clothes anyway, and certainly would never set foot in the salon.*

Carol wondered if Muriel knew that Steve was writing to her. Her friend never asked, but then why should she? And for some unexplained reason, Carol didn't want to tell her.

To Carol's delight, Steve started dropping in to Rutherford's to see her when he was on leave. He was so handsome in his uniform that all the girls looked at him. Carol wasn't supposed to have visitors, but Steve knew how to charm even Miss Rawson, who would let them chat for at least five minutes before reminding Carol that she was supposed to be working.

Some of the other girls would tease her, calling Steve her boyfriend, but Denise never did. Carol got the impression that Denise didn't like Steve, but she never actually said anything.

Tonight, the letter that she was interested in was the last one she had received from him. In it, Steve told her jokingly that she'd better get the red carpet out because he was being demobbed. In fact he would be home before the month ended. Annoyingly the torch began to flicker, and Carol realised that she needed a new battery. She shook it a couple of times, but instead of the light getting brighter, it went out completely. She switched it off and tied up the bundle of letters.

Fleetingly, before she slept, she remembered the Glamour

Girl competition. She should have told Denise the real reason why she wasn't interested. Despite all her dreams of being an actress, how could she contemplate going off to London when Steve was coming home?

Chapter Two

Carol and Denise stood in the balcony of the Palais de Danse and looked down on the crowded floor. It was Saturday night, and despite Carol's reluctance, Denise had persuaded her to come along to the first heat of the Glamour Girl competition. 'It's okay if you don't want to enter,' she had said, 'but at least come out of curiosity.'

Carol had agreed. She had gone along to Denise's house and the two of them had got ready together. But no matter what Denise might hope for, and no matter what her own dreams of being an actress might be, she had no intention of entering the competition now that Steve was coming home. So she hadn't minded that the only suitable dress she had to wear was a floral print that she'd had for years. Denise, dressed in a pillar-box-red satin blouse and a black skirt, looked her up and down and said, 'Well, at least let me do something with your hair.'

She got out her curling tongs and turned the ends of Carol's shoulder-length blond hair under into a smooth pageboy. 'You look great,' was her verdict. 'Want to try my new lipstick? It's called Hollywood Starlet.'

'No thanks,' Carol said. 'I've got my own.'

'Let me see. Deep pink. Well, that's more your style, I suppose. Now, let's dab on a bit of Evening in Paris.' She picked up the dark blue bottle and applied the scent generously to her wrists, her throat and behind her ears, then handed it to Carol. 'You too.'

Denise intended to enjoy herself, and Carol was happy enough. After all, she had nothing else to do. She didn't relish the idea of sitting at home by the wireless and listening to *In Town Tonight* along with her father and her stepmother.

She suppressed a niggle of worry about the fact that she hadn't had a letter from Steve since he had written to say that it wouldn't be long before he would be demobbed. Why hadn't he written? Had they changed their minds about letting him come home? Had they sent him somewhere secret and he couldn't say where? There were all kinds of things going on in Europe that were kept from people at home.

'Look,' Denise said. 'Here comes the band.'

The two of them leaned over the velvet balustrade and looked towards the stage. It was still draped patriotically in swathes of red, white and blue. The couples waiting on the dance floor looked up expectantly as the musicians, resplendent in white tuxedos, took their places. When the bandleader, Sammy Duke, appeared, everyone cheered. The mood tonight was extra cheerful. Everyone was prepared to have a good time.

Sammy Duke smiled and announced, 'Ladies and gentlemen, we at the Palais are proud to be taking part in the competition to find a Glamour Girl. The lucky winner will star in a film set right here in Seaton Bay. And just looking around tonight,' he continued, 'I can see it's going to be very difficult to choose just one of all these gorgeous girls.'

'Creep!' Denise hissed.

Carol giggled. 'Mr Smarm personified.'

'Now, ladies and gentlemen, would you please take your partners for the first dance. Let's get "In the Mood"!'

He turned to the band and raised his baton, and a moment

later the chords of the popular dance tune rang out. Soon the floor was filled with couples jiving. Although most were in civvies, there were still some men in uniform. They came from the nearby Canadian airbase, and there was no getting away from the fact that they all looked like film stars and were fantastic movers. The glitter ball shed its patterned light on the dancing couples, and the heat rose with a whiff of mixed scents and hair dressings that wasn't altogether pleasant.

'Let's get down there,' Denise said. 'And if we can't grab one of those Canadians, we'll dance together.'

'Wait a moment,' Carol said. She thought she had seen a familiar face in the crowd. 'Look over there. It's Muriel.'

'I thought she told you she couldn't come tonight.'

'She did. She said her parents needed her at home. Look – she's seen us.'

Muriel Douglas was pushing her way through the dancing couples. She was taller than most, and she had raised her hand to wave to them.

'Let's go down and meet her,' Carol said.

They hurried along the balcony to the stairs. By the time they reached the bottom, Muriel was waiting for them. She had set her dark hair in an up-do, with big fat rolls on the crown of her head, and was wearing a powder-blue crêpe dress with a square neckline and padded shoulders.

'Wow! You look super!' Carol said.

'Very classy,' Denise said. There was grudging admiration in her eyes. 'Are you going to enter the competition?'

Muriel raised her eyebrows as if the idea were ridiculous. 'Of course not,' she said with a hint of condescension. 'We were curious about the competition, but we've really come along to the Palais to celebrate.'

'Celebrate?' Carol asked. She found herself holding her breath.

'Steve's home. He arrived last night. We all talked for hours before we went to bed and we've talked all day today. So Mum and Dad said we should go out and enjoy ourselves tonight, especially as Steve has some wonderful news. Carol . . .'

Carol thought her friend suddenly looked serious, but before she could say any more, Steve appeared. Instead of pushing his way through the dancing couples as his sister had done, he had walked round the edge of the dance floor. And there he was, standing next to Muriel.

'Hi, Toots,' he said to Carol, and she felt her heart miss a beat.

If this were a film, she thought, the music would fade, the people would disappear and Steve and I would be standing on a sort of cloud. He would look at me tenderly, then take my hands and pull me into his arms, and just before he kissed me, he would whisper, 'At last.'

The image was so vivid that Carol found herself reaching out towards him, and she was shocked when Denise seized one arm and pulled her back. Carol looked at her friend questioningly. Denise shook her head almost imperceptibly, and then said brightly, 'Oh look, here's Kay.'

'Kay?'

'Yes. Kay.' Denise was frowning at Carol, almost as if she were trying to warn her about something.

Carol pulled away from Denise and turned her head to look at Steve. Sure enough, Kay Blanchard was standing next to him. She was smiling radiantly and there was no denying how beautiful she was. Her glossy dark-brown hair fell in soft waves to her shoulders. She was wearing an emerald-green strapless dress with a tiny black lace bolero. The outfit couldn't have been bought in Seaton Bay, not even in the French Salon, and it must have cost a whole year's clothing coupons.

'Isn't this fun?' Kay said. 'All these girls thinking they have the chance to become a film star.'

'They do,' Denise said. 'That's what the competition is all about.'

Kay smiled. 'My father says it's just publicity for the film. Whoever wins will have the tiniest of parts, and after that the poor girl will probably sink without a trace.'

'How does your father know anything about it?' Denise asked.

'He's been asked to help – articles in the paper, interviews and the like.' Kay's father was the editor of the *Seaside Chronicle*, the local newspaper.

'But why would they set a film here at all?'

'It's one of these new social dramas. You know, the working class at play by the seaside, but in this case there are some London gangsters involved. Sounds like rubbish to me.'

The first dance had come to an end and the level of noise rose as the couples formed chattering groups round the edges of the dance floor. Kay leaned closer to Steve and said, 'Are we going to dance the next one, darling?'

It was only then that Carol noticed the diamond ring on Kay's engagement finger.

The band was playing a slow, smoochy number and the dancing couples held each other close. Kay looked up at Steve. 'Oh dear, Carol looks heartbroken.'

'What do you mean?'

'Didn't you see the expression on her face?'

Steve frowned but didn't reply.

'I thought there might be a problem. That's why I asked Muriel to go over and break the news to her that you and I are engaged. But I guess she didn't have time.'

'Why should that upset her?

'Think about it, darling. Ever since she was a kid, she was always round at your house.'

'That's because she was Muriel's friend.'

'That's true, though as a matter of fact, I never really understood what Muriel saw in her.'

'Carol was a sweet kid. She was almost like one of the family. At least she was to me.'

'Like a kid sister?'

'Yes.'

'Poor Carol.'

'Kay, you'll have to explain what you mean.'

'Carol Marshall is in love with you. She has been ever since she was a youngster. Ask Muriel. She knew a long time ago.'

'My sister told you that Carol was in love with me?'

'Not in so many words, but I could tell she knew.'

'Well she never said anything to me.'

'She probably thought Carol would grow out of it. But it doesn't seem as if she has.' Kay's eyes filled with concern. 'I hope you haven't been giving her false hopes.'

'What do you mean?'

'Every time you came home on leave, you made a point of calling in to see her at the shop, didn't you?'

'Surely there was no harm in that. I've told you, I like the kid and she didn't seem to have much of a life with that hard-bitten stepmother of hers.'

'You felt sorry for her? Was that it?'

'Yes, as a matter of fact, I did. That's why I sent her amusing letters.'

He felt Kay stiffen in his arms. 'Steve, are you crazy? Any girl getting letters from a guy in uniform would be entitled to think that she meant something special to him.'

'She is special to me, but not in *that* way. Like I said, she's just a kid.'

'Is that really how you see her?'

'Of course.'

Kay looked up into his eyes for a long moment, and then smiled before resting her head on his shoulder. He held her close, relieved that the interrogation was over. Interrogation? That was a strong way of putting it, but that was how it had felt.

Steve glanced over to where Muriel, Carol and that rather strident girl Denise were standing talking under the overhang of the balcony. Denise was the most animated. Muriel looked slightly awkward as she responded politely to what the girl was saying. But Carol didn't seem to be joining in the conversation at all. She stood listlessly between them, and as they were both taller than she was, their chatter was literally going over her head.

Was that why he had thought of her as a child? Because she was small for her age? Or because when you were away from home, fighting in the war, you didn't want things at home to change? For all the years you were away you had a dream of going home and finding life exactly as you had left it.

But it wasn't the same. People at home had had their war, too. They'd had to endure privations and bombing and loss, and throughout it all the pattern of life had continued regardless. People fell in love, babies were born, children grew up and people died. Whether you were there or not, life went on.

He remembered the letters Carol had written to him, letters full of amusing news and hope for the future. And he remembered how much he had looked forward to them. Guiltily he remembered how much more interesting Carol's letters had been than Kay's, even though Kay was his sweetheart, the girl who had promised that she would wait for him.

The music played and Steve held Kay in his arms as they

moved around the floor. Inexorably they were swept closer to the spot where Carol, Muriel and Denise were standing. Kay was right. Carol was no longer a child. She was a woman. A beautiful woman.

Suddenly an image from the past swam up before him: Carol standing in the rain, watching the bus he was on driving away. He remembered how forlorn she had looked, but more than that, his own feeling of regret, which had taken him by surprise as she disappeared from sight.

He blinked to rid himself of the image and realised he was looking straight at Carol. The flickering light of the glitter ball chased shadows across her face. It seemed to Steve that her expression was one of hurt and distress.

Kay lifted her head from his shoulder and for a moment looked at him searchingly. He could not meet the questioning expression in her eyes, so he pulled her close and held her even more tightly. She nuzzled her head against his neck and then whispered in his ear, 'I've waited so many years for this moment. You can't imagine how wonderful it is to have you home at last.'

There was a slightly strained atmosphere as Muriel and Denise watched the floor and tried to guess which of the girls were going to enter the competition. Every now and then they asked Carol's opinion, then carried on regardless when they got no response.

Carol was watching the dancing couples. The floor was crowded and it took her a while before she saw Steve and Kay. They seemed to be talking earnestly. Neither of them was smiling. Then Kay seemed to relax as she laid her face against Steve's shoulder. The music played and Steve and Kay moved around the floor until they were an arm's length away from where Carol was standing. She realised that Steve was looking at her.

And then he pulled Kay into his arms and she whispered something to him. As she did so, she looked over his shoulder and smiled brilliantly in Carol's direction. Carol turned and fled.

'Now look what you've done,' Denise hissed as Carol hurried towards the cloakroom.

'What do you mean, what *I've* done?'

'Carol – she's upset. That's what. You could have warned her.'

Denise was expecting an argument, but Muriel said, 'About Steve and Kay being engaged? I know. I meant to, but I didn't have time. Kay should have held on to Steve for a little longer.'

'Are you saying that Kay asked you to tell her?'

'Well, yes, she did. But I'd already decided to anyway.'

'So Kay knows how Carol feels about Steve?'

'Seems so.'

'Poor Carol. She thought Steve really cared about her,' Denise said.

'He did – he does – but not in the way she wants. I've known for years that she's in love with him and you can't imagine how miserable it made me that Steve didn't seem to realise that. But how could he, when Kay kept such a tight rein on him? There wasn't much I could do except try not to talk about him when Carol and I were together, and once I didn't even tell her when he was home on leave.'

'So what are we going to do?' Denise asked.

'There's nothing we can do, is there?'

'Nope. Don't suppose so. Sometimes I hate men!'

Carol stared at herself in the mirror above the washbasin. She had forced herself to hold back the tears and the effort was giving her a headache. She leaned forward and, taking her lipstick from her pocket, touched up her lips. She thought she looked pale. She didn't have any rouge, so she rubbed a finger gently over the end of the lipstick and applied a little to her cheeks, smoothing it in until it looked as natural as possible. She stared for a moment longer and then, steeling herself to face her friends, went back to join them.

Muriel and Denise looked relieved to see her, but neither of them said anything. 'What is it?' she asked.

'We wondered if you were all right,' Muriel said.

'Why shouldn't I be?'

'You took your time, that's why,' Denise told her, flashing a warning glance at Muriel.

'Ladies and gentlemen,' Sammy Duke announced from the stage. 'The moment we've been waiting for.' There was a drum roll. 'Will all the young ladies who wish to become our very own Glamour Girl take to the floor?' At first only a few girls stepped forward. Sammy called out, 'Don't be shy, girls, don't keep us waiting.'

A few more ventured forward, some of them pushed by their friends, and then they came in a rush, until the dance floor was filled with girls of all shapes and sizes. Ungallantly, one or two of the lads jeered and made catcalls, but they were shouted down by the girls' friends and relatives.

Muriel said, 'Shall we go up to the balcony and watch?'

She was surprised when Carol said, 'You can if you like, but I'm entering the competition. Come on, Denise, keep me company.'

Blinking away a telltale tear and smiling determinedly, she took Denise's hand and pulled her on to the dance floor. Denise grinned broadly, but Muriel's eyes widened in surprise. Shaking her head in what looked like disapproval, she made her way to the balcony.

Denise would have liked to ask Carol why she had changed her mind about the competition, but she had the feeling that she already knew the answer and that Carol might not like to admit it. She looked around at the other girls.

'Some of this lot are complete strangers,' she said. 'I've never seen them at the Palais before. They've just come because of the competition.'

'Why shouldn't they?' Carol asked. 'It's open to all local girls.'

'I suppose so. But just look over there!'

'Where?'

'It's Anne Russell, standing right in front of the band and smirking as if she's already won!'

Carol stood on tiptoe and looked towards where her friend was pointing. 'She's not smirking, she's smiling.'

'You don't suppose it's a fix, do you?'

'What do you mean?'

'Anne Russell is Sammy Duke's latest girlfriend. Maybe it's already been decided that she's the winner.'

Carol frowned. 'I don't see how Mr Duke could influence the judges, do you?'

'With a backhander.'

'You're too cynical.'

'And you're too innocent.'

Carol smiled. 'Well don't let's quarrel, because I think the contest is about to begin.'

The bandleader had been joined on the stage by the manager of the Palais, Mr Gilbert, who looked as smart as ever in his ancient but well-preserved evening clothes. Sammy Duke raised his baton, but before turning to the band, he announced to the waiting girls, 'When the music starts, I want you to start walking around the floor. Don't dance, just move as gracefully as you can. Mr Gilbert here is going to come down and walk amongst you. If he touches you on the shoulder, I'm sorry, ladies, but that means you are out and must leave the floor.'

At this there was a subdued groan.

'But Mr Gilbert's as old as the hills,' Denise whispered to

37

Carol. 'What does he know about glamour?'

'Hush,' Carol replied. 'He may be old, but he's still a man. I'm sure he can pick out a pretty girl.'

'Depends what his idea of pretty is.'

The music started, and Denise pressed her lips together in a moue of discontent. 'For heaven's sake,' she said. 'What on earth are they playing? It's like a funeral march!'

'No it's not,' Carol said. 'It's old-fashioned for sure, but if you move with it, it will help you to be ... well, you know, graceful.' She squeezed Denise's arm, and along with all the other young women, they began to walk around the floor.

Muriel had joined her brother and his fiancée on the balcony.

'Poor dears,' Kay said. 'Some of them haven't the remotest chance, have they?'

'I suppose not,' Muriel said.

'I shouldn't think even half this number will be left when Mr Gilbert has done his job.'

'You're probably right,' Muriel agreed.

This evening should have been a lark, a bit of fun, she thought. If Steve and Kay hadn't announced their engagement, she imagined that she and Carol would be laughing at the whole charade together. She had not thought for a moment that her old friend would want to take part in something so ... well, something that like any beauty contest was not entirely respectable.

It was obvious that Denise had been the moving force in this matter, and Muriel couldn't help feeling that if Carol's dreams about Steve had come true, she would never have entered the competition. She glanced sideways at her brother. His expression was unreadable.

Suddenly Muriel couldn't bear to watch any more. 'I think

I'll go along to the snack bar,' she told the others. 'It's hot in here. I need a cool drink.'

'Good idea. I'll come with you,' Kay said. 'This could go on for a while yet. Are you coming, Steve?'

'Yes, fine. My treat.'

It seemed to Muriel that her brother was as keen to leave the scene as she was. They had the snack bar to themselves, and Kay kept up a flow of amusing chatter. Both Muriel and Steve were grateful.

Carol guessed that Mr Gilbert was trying to drag it out, but already many disappointed girls had left the floor. Some of them flounced off and some drifted away miserably, but there were plenty who hadn't taken it seriously from the start, and these laughed cheerfully as they rejoined their friends.

Those who were left kept a wary eye on Mr Gilbert. If he approached, they tried not to look him in the eye, but that made no difference. If he didn't think they were suitable, he tapped them gently on the shoulder, saying in his gentlemanly way, 'I'm sorry, my dear.'

Gradually the crowd thinned and Sammy Duke told the remaining girls to space themselves out rather than walk in a huddled group, though he didn't mind if they wanted to walk in twos. Carol and Denise weren't the only ones who preferred to stay close to a friend.

'He's coming this way!' Denise whispered hoarsely.

'Of course he is,' Carol replied. 'He's walking round the circle.'

'But what if he stops at us?'

'Then we'll be out of it.'

'I'll be out, you mean. Not you.'

But Mr Gilbert walked on by, and Denise could have sworn he smiled at Carol approvingly. When there were only twelve girls left, the music stopped and Mr Gilbert asked them to go and stand in a line in front of the stage but facing the dance floor. When they were in position, there was a drum roll and the bandleader announced, 'Ladies and gentlemen, may I present the young ladies who are going through to the semi-final!'

There was a burst of applause.

'Look at that,' Denise hissed.

'What?'

'Anne Russell smiling up at Sammy and him looking as pleased as punch.'

'Ssh!' Carol said.

'Well, I still think it's a fix!'

There was a burst of applause and the band began to play 'Lovely Lady'. Sammy asked the girls to walk around the floor again.

'Carol!' Denise said suddenly. 'Do you realise what's happened?'

'Yes. We're through to the semi-final.'

'But that's amazing. I mean, it's not amazing that you got through, but me! I only joined in to keep you company.'

'Stop gabbing and start walking,' Carol said, but she turned to her friend and smiled. 'It's not surprising. You're very attractive, don't you realise that?'

'Well . . . "very" might be an exaggeration, but I suppose I'm not bad looking.' Denise grinned, and then they joined the others in the victory promenade.

Once the successful girls had walked around the floor a couple of times, Mr Gilbert stepped forward and asked them to come to his office.

'I need to take your names and ages,' he told them as they crowded in. 'There'll be a piece in the *Seaside Chronicle*.' When he had taken the details he said, 'Congratulations, ladies. I'm sure you'll do the Palais proud. Now, listen carefully while I tell you what will happen next week . . .'

Back in the ballroom, Connie Walsh, the band's resident singer, was belting out a lively arrangement of 'Five Minutes More'. Carol looked up at the balcony to see if Steve, Muriel and Kay were still there. They had gone. She had been aware of them watching her, and she had held her head up high and tried to smile as if she hadn't a care in the world.

As more and more girls had been tapped on the shoulder and asked to leave the floor, she had begun to wonder whether she had a chance of winning, and if so, what the future might bring. The way she felt now, she knew she had to get away from Seaton Bay, and the sooner the better.

As she and Denise queued at the cloakroom counter to get their coats, two of the successful contestants turned to say good night.

'See you next week,' one of them said.

Denise grinned. 'You can bet on that!'

Chapter Three

There was a cold wind blowing off the sea. The street lamps, dark for so many years during the blackout, now blazed a graceful crescent around the curve of the bay. A sudden gust blew sand-laden spray over the promenade. The grit stung their faces and, heads down, the three of them quickened their pace.

'Hold on tight,' Steve said, and he offered an arm to each girl.

They were thankful when they left the promenade and turned into Ocean View. Halfway up the street, Steve stopped in his tracks, bringing the girls up short.

'What is it, darling?' Kay asked.

'It was only when I saw this earlier that I realised how bad it had been for you.' He was staring at the other side of the street.

'Mum and Dad thought we ought not to tell you everything that happened at home,' Muriel said. 'It would have been bad for your morale.'

'I knew you'd had air raids, of course, but nothing like this. Half the street has gone. Were there many casualties?'

'Most of them got to their shelters in time,' Kay said.

'But a lot didn't,' Muriel added.

They were silent for a moment, and then Kay tucked her arm into his again and said, 'The war's over, and you've come home safely. That's the important thing. And just think what a wonderful future we're going to have.'

The wind strengthened and it began to rain. They started to run. When they arrived at the adjoining semi-detached houses, they found Kay's in darkness while the Douglas house was a blaze of light. Mrs Douglas must have been watching from behind the curtain, for as soon as they reached the gate, she opened the front door.

'Come in, Kay,' she said. 'Your parents are here and a few friends. We thought we just had to celebrate both Steve coming home and your engagement.'

Once inside, Kay vanished to the bathroom to repair her make-up and tidy her hair. Steve took the coats and draped them over chairs in the kitchen, where they began to steam gently. Muriel attempted to pin up stray tendrils of hair in front of the mirror propped up on the kitchen windowsill.

Kay came looking for them. She took Steve's hand. 'Come along, darling,' she said. 'This is the perfect opportunity to break it to them.'

'Break what to them?' Steve asked.

'That I want to be a June bride.'

'Flippin' heck,' Denise exclaimed. 'I'll be soaked through by the time I get home. And you've got even further to go. Tell you what,' she said, 'why don't you bunk in with me tonight?'

'I can't,' Carol said. 'If I stopped out all night I'd never hear the end of it. You know what Hetty's like. She would say it was further evidence of my moral degradation.'

'Crikey! Would she really?'

Carol licked a raindrop from her lips and grinned. 'Well, not exactly in those words. Dirty little slut is what she'd call me.'

'Charming! But forget your wicked stepma for a moment. I want to talk to you.'

'If it's about the Glamour Girl contest, I'm not going on with it.'

Denise gasped. 'What's made you change your mind?'

'How can I? Mr Gilbert said we would need an evening dress. Where am *I* going to get one of those from?'

'We could sort out our best summer frocks and do them up with scarves and some costume jewellery. Anyway, you can't drop out now. That would be a really rotten thing to do.'

'What do you mean?'

'If you hadn't entered the competition in the first place, some other girl would be going through to the semi-final, wouldn't she? You'll be depriving her of her chance.'

'That's true, and it's not that I don't want to. It's just . . . Oh, Denise, please don't go on at me. I can't face it right now. See you at work on Monday.' Carol hurried off into the gloom.

'Yeah.' Denise could barely hide her disappointment. 'See you.'

When Carol reached home, the house was in darkness. She tiptoed across the tiny hall and opened the door that led into the living room. She was met by the greasy smell of a fry-up supper mingled with stale cigarette smoke. She put the light on and straight away saw the note propped up against the teapot on the table.

What time do you think this is? it said in Hetty's angry scrawl. *If you're expecting to make a cup of cocoa, don't. I need the milk for your father's porridge in the morning. If you wake us up, you'll have me to answer to.*

Hetty knew very well that Carol liked to take a cup of cocoa up to bed with her, so this was an act of pure spite. She had probably deliberately made sure there wasn't enough milk left. Besides, even though the next day was Sunday, the milkman would be round before her father stirred.

Carol gripped the back of a chair and closed her eyes. She

remembered how, when she was a child, her mother would bring two cups of cocoa up to her room at bedtime and sit on the bed to either read her a story or simply talk to her until she felt sleepy.

Thoroughly cold, wet and miserable, she went upstairs. Sheer misery washed over her. How could she have been so foolish to believe that Steve was interested in her in a romantic way? Just because he had asked her to write to him and had made a point of visiting her whenever he came home on leave?

She remembered the time he had arrived just as Rutherford's was closing. 'I'll wait for you at the staff entrance in the lane,' he'd said.

'No! Not there!' Carol could imagine the comments the other girls would make.

'Okay. I'll wait in the café at the bus station. I'll treat you to tea and toast.'

Many of the other customers were in uniform, and Carol and Steve watched one or two tearful goodbyes. Steve had been uncharacteristically quiet that day. It was as if he was disconcerted to find himself alone with her – and so close, sitting at either side of the tiny table. At one point Carol had looked up and surprised a slightly puzzled expression in his eyes.

When it was time to go, he'd laughed self-consciously and said, 'Next time I'll take you somewhere a bit more swish.' But for some reason he never had.

Carol imagined it was because every moment of his time home on leave was precious to his family. He had probably forgotten all about his promise the moment they'd left the café.

What was she going to do now? As hot tears stung her face, contemplation of the bleak years that lay ahead consumed her and kept her awake until dawn was lightening the sky.

One of the topics of conversation in the mess during the war was whether you dreamed in colour or black and white. When the subject had first arisen, Steve had thought it odd that there should be a debate at all. Surely your dreams were in colour, just like real life?

His mess mates were evenly divided. Some believed the so-called experts who pronounced that of course dreams were black and white; others swore that their own dreams were in vivid colour. And Gerard Sykes, who was a bit of a boffin, said it was more complicated than that, something to do with the fact that 'things in dreams which aren't relevant are just unspecified'.

Gerard was prepared to go on at length about this but never got very far before everyone groaned and started pelting him with beer mats, empty cigarette packets, cushions, anything that came to hand. It was all good-natured. They liked Gerard, who was a brave and a daring pilot, and there wasn't one who didn't mourn him when he didn't return from a mission one day. He had been photographing shipping movements on the Rhine, a highly dangerous enterprise, and the likelihood was that he had been shot down.

Since then, whatever he had previously believed, Steve's recurring dream had been in black and white, just like the thousands of photographs he had taken during his sorties over Europe. In the dream he was always in the plane, a Spitfire that had had its guns removed and cameras fitted under each wing. A plane that was unarmed and unprotected. He would be flying at as low a level as he dared in order to get the best and most helpful shots of some farm buildings, the cameras' unlikely target.

He had spotted an unusually wide road leading up to an isolated farm, and he hoped that the photographs he took would reveal to the photographic interpreters whether it was tanks rather than cows that had made their way to the barns.

Then some sixth sense would make him look up. A lone Messerschmitt was diving towards him, moving in for the kill. He would see the flash of the guns on the wings of the enemy plane and realise that he was about to be shot down. At that terrifying moment he would wake up covered in sweat. He knew immediately that it had been a dream, but he couldn't quite shake off the notion that one day – next time, perhaps – he wouldn't wake up in time.

He had hoped that now that he was home he would never have that dream again, but as soon as he had fallen asleep it had returned to torment him. Unable to settle, he got out of bed and padded over to the window. The wind had died down and the rain had stopped. The night was quiet. He looked out over the sleeping suburbs and thanked God that the war was over.

And now what?

His former boss Mr Latham had let his parents know that his old job was waiting for him. In fact, better than that, when the time came for Mr Latham to retire Steve would be in charge of the business with a salary to match. The Douglases were delighted.

While the two families had been celebrating the engagement, Kay's father had taken Steve aside and told him of a nice little house just a couple of streets away. It was for sale for eight hundred pounds, a more than reasonable price, and Mr Blanchard had hinted that if it was beyond Steve's means, he would be only too glad to help out. To set them on their way, as he put it.

So he and Kay were to be married. He was a normal man who during the war had lived from day to day, not knowing whether he would survive the next mission. Each time he had come home on leave it had been harder and harder to control his desire, but Kay seemed to know exactly how much to give without surrendering completely.

'Be patient, darling,' she would whisper to him. 'It won't be long now.'

And now that time had come, and soon she would be his. So why didn't he feel more joy?

Looking out at the safe suburban gardens bounded by laurel bushes and neatly clipped privet hedges, he remembered the world he had seen from the air. The unfamiliar country-side with its rivers and canals and ancient farmland, and also the historic cities that he had seen both before and after they had been bombed almost to destruction. His work as an aerial photographer had helped to make that destruction possible.

That knowledge would always live with him. Now that the war was over, he wanted to visit these places again. He needed to know how the people who lived there would rebuild their lives. But that would have to wait. He accepted that for the moment he would have to do what was expected of him, but he determined that as soon as possible he would move on, and Kay, who had waited for him so faithfully, would come with him and discover a whole new world.

On Monday morning there was a rush for the dresses made from parachute silk. No clothing coupons were needed, and it seemed that anyone who could afford one had come along to the French Salon. Miss Rawson was delighted, and so was Squadron Leader Wilmot, who called by at midday to carry her off to lunch.

When Miss Rawson returned, she was in a good mood and told Carol to take an extra ten minutes over her own lunch break.

'Ten whole minutes? Very generous of her, I'm sure,' Denise said when the two of them were settled with their sandwiches in the cubbyhole behind the tall shelves in the shoe department. 'What's in your sandwiches today?'

'Fish paste. And yours?'

'Spam.'

They gazed at each other despondently.

'Bet old Rawbones didn't have to eat boring stuff like this at the Waverley today,' Denise said.

'How do you know she went there?'

'Bound to. Squadron Leader Wilmot is staying there, all expenses paid.'

'How do you know that?'

'My aunt Iris is a waitress there. She told us his firm are putting him up and he's a generous tipper.'

'You ought to work for the gossip column in the local rag,' Carol said.

'I'd like that! The things I hear about would make very interesting reading.'

Denise had made a pot of tea in the staff kitchen, and they talked about nothing in particular as they ate their sandwiches. Carol sensed that her friend was trying to jolly her along, and she knew it wouldn't be too long before Denise brought up the subject of the competition. It came just as she was stirring a spoonful of sugar into her second cup of tea.

'Well, have you made your mind up?' Denise asked.

'If you're talking about the Glamour Girl competition, I told you on Saturday night: I'm pulling out.'

Denise's face fell. 'I thought you might change your mind when you'd had a chance to think about it. I mean, you did think about it, didn't you?'

Carol sighed. 'Of course I did. I lay in bed in my miserable little room and thought about the years I might have to spend in that house with my father and Hetty, and I thought that . . . well, I thought . . .'

'That you should grab any chance of getting away!'

Carol sighed. 'Something like that.'

'There you are, then.'

'But I still haven't got anything to wear.'

'Don't worry. I've got an idea ... Got to go. We'll talk later.'

Denise's time was up. Carol had another ten minutes, so she stayed there and thought about things. She had seen the disapproval on Muriel's face when she had entered the competition. And Kay Blanchard obviously thought it was a very common thing to do. But what about Steve? What would he think? Carol tried to convince herself that she didn't care.

For the rest of the week Carol wouldn't say either yes or no. On Friday, the day after the local newspaper came out, Denise asked, 'Have you seen the *Seaside Chronicle* this week?'

'No. Why do you ask?'

Denise picked up the newspaper that she had brought to work with her. 'You'd better have a look.'

'Look at what?'

'Wait a mo.' She opened the paper and flipped through it before folding it open and handing it over. 'Top of that page ... there.'

Carol stared down at a photograph of Steve and Kay. They were standing in what could be the back garden of Kay's house. Kay's arm was linked through Steve's and their heads were half turned so that they could smile into each other's eyes. The text below the photograph read:

The editor of this newspaper is pleased to announce that his daughter, Kay Margaret Blanchard, has become engaged to Steven Douglas, recently demobilised from the RAF, where he served as a flight lieutenant. Kay and Steve have known each other since they were children, growing up as next-door neighbours. Kay has informed her parents that there was never any doubt that she would fall in love with 'the boy next door', and Steve says that he looked forward to receiving Kay's letters in the war's darkest days. The wedding will take place in June.

Carol wondered how she could feel ice forming round her heart and yet simultaneously burn with rage.

'Why did you show me this?' she asked Denise, her eyes blazing and her voice harsh.

'I . . . I thought you should see it, for your own good. There it is in black and white. He looked forward to her letters and all that.'

'What a fool I've been,' Carol said.

'It's Steve Douglas who's the fool.'

Carol was almost shaking with fury. 'Well, let's not waste any more time discussing it,' she said. 'We've got more important things to talk about than Kay Blanchard's engagement. Like where I'm going to get an evening dress, for example.'

A little later, Denise was trying to persuade a doubtful customer that wedge-heeled sandals would be all the rage this year and a good buy considering you didn't need coupons for them. Unusually for her, she lost the sale. She returned the box to the shelves, then went over to the window and looked out at the street without really seeing anything.

She couldn't shake off a feeling of guilt. Had it been cruel to show Carol the photograph of Kay and Steve? Perhaps it had, but it had had the desired effect. Carol was going to stay in the Glamour Girl competition, and Denise was going to make damned sure that she had a chance of winning.

There were no customers, so she spread the newspaper out on the counter and turned the pages until she found the headline: *Search For A Star*. After a brief description of the event, the piece ended with a list of the names of the successful contestants. Denise had been thrilled to see Carol's name and her own in print, and she had intended to draw Carol's attention to the article. But after Carol had seen the photograph of Steve and Kay, the right moment hadn't arisen.

Even though Carol appeared to be gentle and calm, Denise had always suspected that her friend was a perfect example of still waters running deep. And now she had realised that Carol had a core of steel. If she set her mind on something, she was going to get it. Perhaps she could win the Glamour Girl competition after all.

When Carol got home after work, her father and Hetty were eating their evening meal. They never waited for her. They seldom ate together as a family. Now two pairs of eyes looked up at her. Her father's were troubled, but Hetty's were full of malice. Her lips curled up in a self-satisfied smirk as if she were going to enjoy what happened next.

'Well, well,' she said. 'So that's what you get up to when you sneak out at night.'

Carol couldn't stop herself from exclaiming, 'I have never *sneaked* out in my entire life!'

Hetty, unused to Carol sticking up for herself, scowled and pursed her lips before replying. 'Well, maybe not,' she said. 'But you don't tell us where you go.'

'You know where I go and who I go with. I go to the pictures with Denise or Muriel or both of them. That's about it.'

Carol forced herself to calm down. She saw that Hetty was in the mood to pick a quarrel, and she didn't want to give her stepmother the satisfaction of seeing her rise to the taunts.

But Hetty's next words surprised her. 'Have you seen this?'

Her finger jabbed at a page of the local paper, which lay open on the table. 'Disgraceful, I call it.'

Carol was taken aback. Why should Hetty think that Steve and Kay's engagement was disgraceful? 'Yes, I have.'

'And you didn't think fit to tell us?'

'Why should I? You don't know either Steve or Kay. And why would you think their getting engaged was a disgrace?'

Hetty looked baffled. She scowled and then continued, 'Don't try to bamboozle me, madam. I'm not referring to anyone's engagement and you know it.' She picked up the paper and thrust it into Carol's hands. 'Read that,' she said. 'That's what's upset your father and me.'

Bewildered, Carol focused on the page and saw a piece with the title 'Search For A Star'. The report of the competition at the Palais listed the names of those contestants going through to the next round. Now she realised what Hetty was talking about. She folded the paper and put it back on the table.

'So?' she said, trying to sound casual.

'Don't take that attitude with me!' Hetty said.

'What attitude?'

'As if it doesn't matter.'

'It doesn't.'

'Of course it does. What do you think the neighbours will say when they read this and find out that you're just a common little tart?'

Carol flushed. 'There's nothing common about entering a beauty contest.' She glanced away, not sure of the truth of that statement. After all, hadn't she worried that Muriel would think exactly that?

Her father, who had so far kept silent, cleared his throat. 'I don't like it, Carol,' he said. 'Hetty's right. I mean, film stars and the like. None of them are any better than they should be.'

53

'Oh for goodness' sake!' Carol said. 'How can you say that?'

'You read about them in the papers, don't you? All that carrying on. Divorces and the like. They're not respectable.'

Albert ended his sentence with his usual rasping cough. Hetty pushed a glass of water towards him impatiently and turned back to Carol. 'And in any case,' she said, 'what on earth made you think you had any chance of winning?'

'Well, you ought to know the answer to that!' Carol's attempt at self-control snapped, and she turned on her stepmother in fury. 'You've told me often enough what a little slut you think I am. So considering your low opinion of film stars' morals, I'm a cert to win, aren't I?'

For once Hetty was speechless.

'Don't talk to your stepmother like that,' her father said. 'After all she's done for you, she deserves a little respect.' He paused and took a shallow breath. 'Hetty took you on, a motherless child, and tried to bring you up to be a decent young woman, and you've done nothing but cause her heartache.'

Carol stared at her father in amazement. Did he really believe what he was saying? Did he believe Hetty even had a heart? Suddenly the sheer wretchedness of the life she had been leading since her mother died overwhelmed her, and she saw with hard-edged clarity that she had to get away from this miserable, loveless house before she became as bitter and small-minded as the others who lived here.

She looked at her father and stepmother and realised that she no longer had the heart to fight. 'I'm sorry you don't approve of what I'm doing,' she said. 'But you're not going to stop me. And if I win the competition—'

Hetty snorted derisively.

'If I win,' Carol continued, 'I'll be leaving here and I won't be coming back.'

54

Hetty didn't say another word, but Carol saw from the gleam in her eyes that that would suit her stepmother very well indeed. And perhaps her father, too.

Since her mother had died, Carol had gone on believing that her father loved her, otherwise life would have been unbearable. But now he had sided with Hetty one time too many. And heartbroken over Steve as she was, Carol knew there was no longer anything to keep her here in Seaton Bay. In the resulting emotional turmoil, half-formed dreams turned into genuine ambition, and she realised that she no longer cared what other people would think of her.

Chapter Four

Saturday evening. Rutherford's had just closed and assistants from all departments were leaving by the staff entrance in the back lane. The end of a working week and the mood was cheerful. The younger men and women smiled and laughed as they looked forward to a night out, and the older assistants were simply grateful that they could go home, put their feet up and maybe listen to *Saturday Night Theatre* on the wireless.

Carol, ready to leave, looked down at Denise, who was on the floor sorting shoes into pairs and putting them back in their white cardboard boxes. She looked up and pulled a mournful face.

'What's the matter?'

Denise held up a pair of strappy silver dancing shoes. 'There's been a run on dancing shoes and I didn't have time to put them back in the boxes after each customer.'

Carol knelt down beside her. 'Well, I'd better help you. But I don't understand. Why does everybody want silver sandals?'

'The Glamour Girl contest, of course. Even if they're not going to take part, it seems everyone wants to dress up to impress the famous film star – whoever he or she might be.' She indicated a box set aside on a chair. 'And incidentally, you'd better try that pair on. I kept them by for you.'

'Thanks, but I can't afford them – and I certainly don't

want to use up my coupons when I've already got some dancing shoes.'

Denise pulled a face. 'But yours are ancient! And don't worry about affording them. We're just going to borrow them for one night.'

'Denise, we can't!'

'Why ever not? No one will know. Go on, try them on.'

Carol did so and found they were a perfect fit. She sat on a chair and held one leg up in front of her, turning her ankle this way and that. 'Not too bad,' she said, 'but I still don't feel happy about "borrowing" them, as you call it.'

'Stop worrying, will you? I doubt if we'd ever sell this pair anyway. Not many girls have such small feet as you do. And look, we're done! Let's get out of here.'

Denise's mother insisted they should eat before getting ready. There were five of them round the table: Denise's parents, her sister Ruthie and Denise and Carol.

Carol looked down in dismay at her plate of corned beef hash and peas. 'I'll never be able to eat all this,' she whispered.

'That's all right. Just wait until Mam turns her back for a moment and heave what you don't want on to my plate.'

A moment later Carol did as she was told. 'I don't know how you can,' she said.

'Can what?'

'Eat all that. Especially tonight. My nerves are all a-flutter. Aren't yours?'

Denise frowned. 'Well, in a way I suppose they are, but that's all the more reason to stoke up, isn't it?'

'As long as it doesn't make you throw up,' Carol said, laughing nervously.

She *was* nervous, that was true, but she was also excited. More than she had ever been before. Not wanting to go home, she had agreed readily when Denise had suggested that she should come home with her to have tea and get ready.

'I don't want to wake you up if I come home late,' she had told Hetty and her father at breakfast that morning. 'So I think it's best if I stay with Denise tonight.'

She had held her breath and waited for Hetty's outraged reaction, and had been surprised when her stepmother simply shrugged and said, 'Suit yourself.'

After the meal, Carol got up and started to clear the table, but Denise's mother stopped her. 'Run along and get yourselves ready,' she said. 'Ruthie will help with the dishes tonight.'

'Oh, no,' Ruthie wailed. 'I want to help them.'

'Well they'll just have to manage without you,' her mother replied.

Denise and Carol made their escape. Denise shared her small bedroom with Ruthie. 'I told Mum to keep her out of the way,' she said.

'Poor Ruthie. She's as excited as if she were going to the dance herself.'

'I know. Her and her pals can't stop talking about who the film star is going to be. They've got it into their heads that it's Clark Gable. As if he'd come all the way from America to this godforsaken place.'

'Clark Gable? But he's in the American Air Force, isn't he? Just think, he might be at an airbase in England somewhere.'

'Maybe he is, but he still wouldn't come here to Seaton Bay!'

Carol laughed. 'I was kidding,' she said. 'But I feel sorry for Ruthie all the same.'

'She'd just be a nuisance. I mean, look how small this room is.'

That was true. The two beds had only a narrow space between them. The dressing table was cluttered with combs, hairbrushes and Denise's bottles of make-up. There was one old wardrobe, where both sisters had to hang their clothes. But despite the lack of space and the clutter, Carol thought wistfully how wonderful it must be to have a sister.

She guessed which Ruthie's bed was when she saw the rag doll resting on the pillow. She picked it up and smoothed its yellow wool hair.

'I made that from a pair of old socks,' Denise said. 'Ruthie thinks she's so grown up, but she still takes Daisy to bed with her. Now, let's get on with it. Mum says we can each have a bath if we're careful and don't use up all the hot water.'

A little later, the two of them were kneeling on the hearthrug in the living room, drying their hair by leaning forward and brushing it in front of the fire. Denise was wearing her own dressing gown and Carol had borrowed Ruthie's.

'You look like a schoolgirl in that,' Denise said. 'One minute you look young and innocent, and the next all grown-up and sophisticated. You'll be terrific in films!'

Carol leaned forward and let her hair hang over her face as she brushed it dry. 'My hair will go all fluffy,' she complained.

'Don't worry, I'll get the tongs out. But before we do our hair, we'd better put our frocks on.'

Back in the bedroom, Carol waited for Denise to take her dress from the wardrobe. She had given it to her the day before, and Denise's mother had promised to iron it. She supposed the floral print was pretty enough, but she doubted it could be classed as an evening gown.

'First of all, what do you think of this?' Denise asked. 'I made it myself.' She held a dark-red crushed-velvet dress against her body and smiled at Carol.

'It's lovely,' Carol said. 'But where on earth did you get the material?'

'I did a Scarlett O'Hara. Remember when she wanted to

impress Rhett Butler and she had nothing decent to wear? She—'

'Took the curtains down!' Carol finished her sentence for her. 'You didn't, did you?'

'Yes. I mean, I didn't exactly take them down. They haven't been used for years. The edges were faded but there was enough good stuff to make one dress with.'

'You ought to be a dressmaker.'

'I thought you said I should be a reporter. Obviously I'm a girl of many talents.' They looked at each other and laughed, and then Denise said, 'Now, here's your dress.'

Carol's spirits sank. With Denise looking glamorous in soft clinging velvet, she would look all the more like a schoolgirl in her best summer frock.

'Here you are,' Denise said, and Carol caught her breath.

She stared at the floating silk creation in shades of blue. 'That's not my dress,' she said.

'It is for tonight.'

'Don't say you've "borrowed" the dress as well as the shoes.'

'I have.'

'But you can't. I mean, you shouldn't have done.'

'Why ever not? I looked in the stockroom. The squadron leader has sold old Rawbones so many, she's never going to miss one of them. We'll put it back first thing on Monday morning.' She stared at Carol's doubtful face. 'Look, you want to get through to the final, don't you?'

'Yes, but . . .'

'Well if you do get through we'll buy the dress. Does that make you feel better?'

'Buy it?'

'Those dresses don't need clothing coupons and I'll go halves with you for the cost of it.'

Carol gazed at the halter neckline, the soft folds of silk, the

60

delicate shades of blue. She could imagine it flowing gracefully as she walked.

'But why would you help me to buy it?' she asked.

'Because when you're rich and famous I'll be able to boast that I was the one who started you on your way!'

'You really think I can win this contest?'

'Don't you?'

'Maybe I could.'

'How much do you want to? How much do you want to get away and start a new life?'

Slowly Carol reached out for the dress.

'Who do you think this famous film star is?' Muriel asked Kay. They were getting ready together in Kay's bedroom.

Kay laughed. 'You'll be disappointed.'

'You know?'

'Yes. My father told me.'

'Go on, then.'

'Well, I'm not supposed to tell, but you'll know soon enough. It's Howard Napier.'

'Who?' Muriel frowned.

'Exactly. That was my reaction. Apparently he's some old charmer from the days of silent movies, but he still earns a crust playing character roles. You know, a posh butler, a judge, a retired admiral or the like. You've probably seen him many times without ever registering his name.'

'But no one will have heard of him.'

Kay leaned closer to the mirror while she applied her mascara. 'The older folk will know who he is. Apparently he was quite a heart-throb when my mother was a girl. Here, fasten this for me, would you?'

She held out a string of pearls, then turned round and lifted her hair up out of the way. She was wearing it down tonight, and it fell in soft natural curls to her shoulders. Muriel caught a drift of a sophisticated musky perfume. Kay was always so well presented, she thought. Even when she was just going along to the local shops, she turned out as if she was going off to London.

Muriel was already dreading the wedding. She was going to be a bridesmaid, along with one of Kay's smart friends from the tennis club. Belinda was small and elegant, and Muriel had a vision of herself towering above both the bride and the other bridesmaid. It was so unfair, because she knew she wasn't ugly. In fact she had lovely eyes and good bone structure and was attractive in the way people called handsome. And here she was stuck with a future sister-in-law who was like a fashion plate and a best friend who was as beautiful as any film star.

She felt a pang of guilt. Was Carol still her best friend? She knew she had neglected her lately, but it wasn't entirely her fault. Carol was so taken up with Denise, and even though she always asked Muriel to join them if they were going to the pictures or the Palais, Muriel, sensing the other girl's animosity, often declined the invitation.

Muriel was pretty sure that it was Denise's idea that Carol should enter this silly contest. Surely Carol had too much taste to do something so vulgar if she hadn't been egged on. Muriel didn't know which would be the worst thing that could happen. If Carol didn't win the contest she would be miserable. But if she did win she would go off to London and that might be the end of their friendship.

'It's time to go,' Kay said. 'I'm quite looking forward to this.'

'Are you?' Muriel was surprised.

'Well, it's a bit of fun, isn't it? And we must support Carol, mustn't we?'

'Must we?'

Kay laughed. 'Do you know, Muriel, you have an annoying

habit of answering questions with a question of your own. Of course we have to root for Carol. If she wins this contest she will be whisked away from her miserable little life and maybe she won't ever have to come back here.'

Muriel had the feeling that it was important to Kay that Carol should never come back to Seaton Bay again.

The contestants had been told to go straight to Mr Gilbert's office and wait until they were called. Denise was chattering excitedly to the other girls, but Carol sat apart in a corner by a battered old filing cabinet. They hadn't been told how long they would have to wait, and gradually the chatter faded and nervous tension took hold of all of them. Even Denise.

'Do you think they've forgotten all about us?' whispered a tall, slim girl whose best feature was her amazingly long and shapely legs.

'Of course not,' Anne Russell snapped. 'Sammy will be waiting until everyone is settled.'

At last the door opened and Mr Gilbert entered, ushering another man before him.

'I want you to meet Howard Napier!' Mr Gilbert said.

The man was tall, upright and debonair. Carol thought she detected a gleam of amusement in his eyes as he surveyed the mystified girls. Mr Gilbert had obviously expected an excited reaction from them, and he looked a little disconcerted.

'I think they're overwhelmed,' he said.

Denise suddenly stepped forward. 'Wow! Not *the* Howard Napier?' she said and gazed up at him with wide eyes. Howard Napier raised a sardonic eyebrow and then produced a genuine smile. Carol decided that she liked him.

'I can see it's going to be a hard job choosing which of these charming young ladies will be finalists,' he said.

He's having fun with us, Carol thought. But not in a spiteful way.

'Now,' Mr Gilbert said, 'I'm going to take Mr Napier through and introduce him to our Lady Mayoress while you prepare yourselves.'

'Wait a moment, Mr Gilbert,' Denise said. 'Where do we get ready?'

'In here, of course.'

There were murmurs of protest.

'Why can't we go to the ladies' cloakroom?' Anne Russell asked.

'Because I want to keep you under wraps,' the manager replied. 'I don't want anyone to see you until the dramatic moment when you walk on stage.'

When he and Howard Napier had gone, there was an immediate hubbub of complaint.

'Get ready in here?' one of the girls said. 'But there's barely any room and it's hardly decent, is it, all of us together like this!'

'For goodness' sake just make the best of it,' Anne Russell told her. 'And I suggest we all keep calm.'

'Yes, madam,' Denise muttered, and Anne shot her a cool glance but didn't say anything.

'Hush,' Carol whispered to her friend. 'She's only trying to be helpful.'

'I suppose so. Come on, let's bag that space behind the desk and get a move on. Howard Napier is waiting for us!' She grinned.

'Did you really know who Howard Napier was?' Carol asked her.

'Of course I didn't. But I didn't want him to feel embarrassed that no one had heard of him.'

'That was nice of you.'

'Yeah. I'm all heart.'

They looked at each other and smiled affectionately as they waited for the call.

The floor had been cleared, and halfway back a table had been set up for the judges. There were three of them: the actor, Howard Napier, the Lady Mayoress, Mrs Carshalton, and Ed Palmer, a nondescript-looking man who was introduced as an agent and a talent scout acting for the film company. Howard Napier looked splendid in an evening suit, and Mrs Carshalton was wearing an elegant oyster satin evening gown. Ed Palmer was the odd one out. He looked as if he had slept in his lounge suit.

The balcony was crowded. Muriel stood at the front with Kay, who was still out of sorts. When they were ready, they had gone next door to collect Steve, but he'd said he wasn't coming with them. Muriel remembered the sudden coolness between the newly engaged couple.

'Do you disapprove?' Kay had asked him.

'I'm just not interested,' had been his reply.

'I know it's hard to imagine why anyone would want to enter a beauty contest, but I suppose you could say it's only a bit of fun.' And then Kay had assumed a thoughtful look. 'Although I believe Carol is taking it seriously.'

'Is she?' Steve had looked troubled.

'That's why I think we should go. Show support and all that.'

'You want to support Carol?' he'd asked.

'Yes, why not?'

'Oh, no reason.'

Muriel had seen that Steve was worried about something but didn't want to admit it. Maybe not even to himself.

'Off you go then,' he'd said.

He and Kay had looked coolly at each other for a moment, and then she'd said, 'Well at least will you come along to collect Muriel and me and walk us safely home?'

'Of course.'

'See you in the foyer at ten thirty, then?'

Steve had suddenly leaned forward and kissed Kay's brow. 'Right-ho. Enjoy yourselves.'

Muriel had observed how Kay had forced herself to smile as they left him. She likes her own way, Muriel thought. But she's too clever to push things too far at this stage of the game. She almost felt sorry for her brother, who seemed to be totally unaware of Kay's tactics.

The band had played a medley of popular tunes, and when they stopped there was some half-hearted applause. Sammy Duke turned to face the audience. 'Ladies and gentlemen,' he said, 'this is what we've all been waiting for. The contestants will walk down the steps at one side of the stage, across the floor in front of the judges and up the other steps. I'm sure you all have your favourite, so give them a big hand when they appear!'

He swung back to face the band, and they began to play 'Oh, I Do Like to Be Beside the Seaside'.

Kay raised her eyebrows and laughed. 'What a ludicrous choice of music,' she said. 'Makes the whole event seem more than a little ridiculous, don't you think?'

Muriel agreed, although she wouldn't give Kay the satisfaction of hearing her say so.

Carol, waiting in the wings, allowed herself to wonder whether Muriel and Steve had come tonight. And if they had, what would they think of it all? I don't care, she told herself. Whatever their opinion is, it simply doesn't concern me.

Denise was waiting behind her. 'Why are you frowning?' she whispered. 'You'll give yourself wrinkles.'

'I'm not frowning.'

Denise sighed. 'Suit yourself,' she said. 'If you're worried, there's no need to be. You look sensational. You'd think the dress had been designed especially for you.'

'You don't look so bad yourself,' Carol said. 'In fact, you look gorgeous.'

'Thanks,' Denise said. 'Remember, hold your number up so that they can all see it. That bit of cardboard is your ticket out of here. Don't look at anybody directly except the judges. Now, get out there and darn well smile!'

Thankfully the lights had been lowered so that Carol couldn't have seen the faces of the spectators even if she had wanted to. As each girl reached the bottom step and walked out on to the dance floor, a spotlight picked her up and followed her until she reached the steps at the other side of the stage.

Carol felt as though she was being carried along by the circle of light that surrounded her. When she paused and faced the judges, she smiled and turned round in a complete circle before setting off once more.

When every girl had had her turn, Sammy Duke asked them to go down again and stand in a straight line so that the judges could compare them.

'Oh, no,' the girl with the shapely legs muttered to Carol. 'I'm much taller than the rest of you. I'll stand out like a sore thumb.'

When the judges were satisfied that they'd seen enough, Sammy announced that Connie Walsh, the band's resident singer, would entertain the audience while the judges compared notes.

Back in Mr Gilbert's office, the girls waited nervously. They weren't sure what was to happen next. Eventually the manager came for them.

'You're to line up as before,' he told them. 'Then Mr Duke will announce which four will go through to the final.'

'Only four out of twelve?' Denise asked.

'That's right. I'm sorry.'

This time when they lined up all the lights were on and

Carol scanned the faces of the crowd. She couldn't see him. But that didn't mean that he wasn't here.

A popping sound echoed round the dance hall as Sammy Duke tapped his microphone prior to making the announcement.

'And now, ladies and gentlemen,' the bandleader said, 'it's time to discover who the finalists are.' He turned to bring in the band, who began to play a tune called 'Lovely Lady' very softly. Sammy kept everyone waiting a short while longer, milking the moment as long as he could. Then he said, 'Will the following young ladies please step forward.'

Carol held her breath. She felt the tension knot inside her. He identified the finalists by name, and Carol wasn't at all surprised when the first girl to be called was Anne Russell. She wondered fleetingly if Denise's suspicions could be well founded. The second was Yvonne Pearson, and Carol was pleased to see the tall girl who had been so despondent step forward. She sensed the fading hope in the line of girls remaining. Carol herself was called next. She breathed out and the tension eased. She stepped forward confidently. She had no idea who the fourth girl would be.

Sammy kept them waiting until there were calls of 'Get on with it!' and then he announced the name of the final successful contestant: 'Denise Shaw.'

There were gasps of disappointment from the remaining girls and cries of outrage from their supporters in the audience. Someone shouted, 'I don't believe it!' and Carol glanced round to see if Denise was hurt. She wasn't. She moved forward confidently and winked at Carol.

'Good old Howard,' she said.

Carol wondered if Howard Napier had indeed insisted that Denise be chosen because she had flattered him earlier. She decided that it was likely. She also discovered that she wasn't a bit outraged. In fact she found it amusing.

'You think that's funny?' Denise asked when she saw Carol's smile.

'I do.'

'Well, here's something else to laugh at. One of the other girls told me that Yvonne Pearson is Mrs Carshalton's niece.'

'No!'

'Yes.'

They both started giggling, and then Denise stopped, cast a knowing glance at Anne Russell and said, 'In fact you're probably the only one of us who's got here on her own merit.'

Howard Napier and Mrs Carshalton left the judges' table and came over to congratulate the four finalists. Ed Palmer, the talent scout, ambled over and asked the girls for their names and addresses.

'He's only going through the motions with the rest of us,' Denise whispered. 'You can tell it's you he's really interested in.'

Whatever the truth of it, Mr Palmer took the names, put his notebook in his pocket and left. The judges' table was cleared away and the dancing started again.

Mr Gilbert approached the four girls. 'If you'll come into the foyer, you can have your photograph taken with Mr Napier.'

'And the Lady Mayoress,' Howard Napier added gallantly, earning a smile from the lady in question.

Once in the foyer, although Carol posed obediently for the photographs, she felt a prickle of unease. A small worry had taken root at the back of her mind, but she couldn't work out what it was.

When the photographer had finished with them, Mr Gilbert invited them to go back into the ballroom and join in the dancing. Howard Napier said that he hoped every one of them would save a dance for him. Mr Gilbert had reserved a table for them under the balcony, and a waitress appeared with soft drinks and a plate of fancy biscuits. Anne Russell raised her eyebrows and stared at the refreshments with disdain. 'You'd think they could have managed champagne,' she said.

'Denise laughed. 'Champagne in this dump? That's not very likely.'

Howard Napier courteously led Mrs Carshalton on to the floor first. As the music played and the couples danced past the table where they were sitting, Carol could not help noticing that some of the looks they were given were far from pleasant. She pointed this out to Denise, who said, 'Jealousy, that's what it is. You'll have to get used to that. When you're a famous film star you'll discover that you'll never be appreciated in your own back yard. Small town, small minds. There'll always be people who would rather drag you down than be proud of you.'

'Do you really think that's true?'

'I do. And if I had your looks I'd be out of here as fast as I could go. But here comes Howard, and if you don't mind, I'm going to claim him next. I think he's taken a fancy to me.'

A moment later, as Carol watched Howard and Denise dancing, she thought that might be true. Howard smiled and laughed at whatever Denise was saying. He looked as though he was genuinely enjoying himself. Carol began to wonder if her friend was imagining she'd found her own escape route from Seaton Bay.

'Do you think we should go and congratulate her?' Muriel asked Kay.

'Probably not. She might think we're butting in.'

'What on earth do you mean?'

'Well, look at her. Sitting there in style with the Lady

Mayoress and a real live film star. She might not have time for her old friends now.'

'Carol isn't like that!'

'No? Well go if you want to, but they'll be playing the last dance any minute. I'm going to the cloakroom to get my coat before the rush. I'll get yours too. Don't be too long and meet me in the foyer. Steve will probably be there by now.'

Muriel hesitated, not knowing whether to go right round the dance floor or push her way through the dancing couples. She decided on the latter option, but just then Sammy Duke invited everyone to take their partners for the last dance and a crowd of people took to the floor. Muriel had made the wrong decision. Trapped in the throng, she grew hot and bothered as she dodged and shoved her way through.

Howard Napier looked at the crowded floor and decided it was time to go. However, he was reluctant to bring the evening to an end. Against all expectations he had enjoyed himself, and he acknowledged ruefully that it was because of that amusing girl Denise. He made a decision.

'I wonder if you would like to come back to my hotel for a drink?' he said, smiling round the group at the table.

Mrs Carshalton and Yvonne nodded their agreement. But Carol looked up at Howard and said, 'Thank you for the invitation, but I should go home.'

'You're staying at my house tonight, remember?' Denise said. 'And I'm going to accept.'

'Go on, Carol,' Yvonne said. 'It's not often we get invited to have drinks with a real live film star.'

Carol smiled and gave in.

'Good,' Howard said. 'We'll go to Mr Gilbert's office and phone for a taxi.'

Howard offered Mrs Carshalton his arm and led the way.

Only then did Carol notice that Anne Russell was no longer with them. She had slipped away.

'Other fish to fry,' Denise said, and she placed herself between Carol and Yvonne and linked arms.

As they set off, she began to sing, 'We're off to see the wizard . . .' and they all burst out laughing.

Carol didn't look back, so she didn't see the lone figure standing by the deserted table.

She didn't even notice me, Muriel thought. The strains of the last waltz came to an end and the couples on the dance floor stood still while the band played the national anthem. Kay was right, Muriel thought sadly. Carol won't have time for her old friends now. She felt all the more upset because she knew very well that she could, and should, have done more to nourish their friendship.

Chapter Five

The cocktail lounge at the Waverley had had a busy war. But now the officers from the nearby airbase had moved on and the bar was faded and tired-looking. The only other occupants that night were a couple of salesmen. Nevertheless, Howard made a grand entrance; he couldn't help himself.

Carol hadn't any idea what sort of drink she should request, and was grateful when Mrs Carshalton said that she would have a gin and tonic but that a nice glass of sherry each would do for the girls.

'I bow to your wisdom, dear lady,' Howard said, 'although I was planning to ask for a bottle of bubbly.'

'He means champagne,' Denise whispered in Carol's ear. 'Drat the woman. I've never had champagne.'

Howard ordered a whisky and soda for himself, and after they'd all finished their drink, Mrs Carshalton asked him to phone for a taxi. 'It's time I took these girls home,' she said. And it was plain there could be no arguing with her.

She asked the driver to drop Carol and Denise off first, and when she said good night to them she added, 'We'll see you next week, dears. And may the best girl win.'

The clock on St Paul's church struck midnight as the taxi drove away. This set Denise off giggling.

'What is it?' Carol asked.

'Does Mrs Carshalton look like a fairy godmother to you?'

'What on earth are you talking about?'

'Well she is, you know. Three little Cinderellas and she's got us all home by midnight – and by now she'll have turned the taxi back into a pumpkin.'

'Denise, are you drunk?'

'On one glass of sherry? No, not drunk, just happy. I've had a good time tonight. And I'm not really cross about the party being broken up so soon. Howard looked tired.'

Carol thought that was a strange thing for her friend to say. She would have liked to have seen Denise's expression, but the square was dark and shadowy.

Denise scrabbled in her bag for her keys. 'We'll have to be quiet,' she whispered. 'We don't want to wake Ruthie up or she'll talk all night.'

They undressed quickly, although Carol was careful to fold her borrowed evening dress and replace it in its bag. She was to have Denise's bed, while Denise bunked in with Ruthie.

It wasn't long before the gentle breathing from the other bed revealed that Denise was asleep, but Carol was wide awake. She knew that if she won the competition her whole life would change. She was too realistic to believe that a small part in a film would automatically lead to fame and riches. But once she'd been noticed, anything might happen.

She'd read all the stories in the film magazines about ordinary girls who'd been discovered by talent scouts. Jane Russell had been working as a dentist's receptionist and was signed up with a seven-year contract. Her very first part was a starring role in *The Outlaw*. Lana Turner had been spotted in a drug store.

And her own Miss Grayson had been working as a waitress when she was spotted by a film director. Miss Grayson! Carol suddenly felt guilty that she hadn't told her elocution teacher that she was going to enter the Glamour Girl contest. She hadn't mentioned it because she had still been wavering. But once she had made up her mind to go ahead, surely she ought to have told her. Miss Grayson will have read the item in the local paper, Carol realised uneasily. She might be hurt. I must go and see her as soon as possible.

She began to feel drowsy. The bed was warm and comfortable and the striking of the church clock, instead of being intrusive, was somehow reassuring. As she drifted off to sleep, she went over the events of the night once more. The picture she was left with was that of Denise waltzing away in Howard Napier's arms. It made her smile.

The next morning Ruthie managed to wriggle out of bed without waking her elder sister. She brought them tea and toast, and for her reward she wanted to know all about the events of the night before. She said it was no surprise that Carol had been successful and pretended to be astonished that Denise had been chosen too, although Carol could tell that she had expected no less.

Carol let Denise answer all the questions and do all the talking, and she noticed that not once in the telling did her friend mention Howard, except to tell Ruthie that the film star judge had been Howard Napier.

Ruthie frowned. 'I've never heard of him.'

'Ask our mam. She'll tell you all about him.'

Mrs Shaw had assumed that Carol would stay for lunch, and very soon the flat was filled with the comforting aroma of cooking.

'Rabbit pie,' Denise informed Carol. 'Followed by suet pudding and custard.'

After the meal, Carol helped Denise wash the dishes and told her that she was going to see Miss Grayson.

'Good idea,' Denise said. 'I bet she'll be delighted for you.'

Denise's enthusiasm made Carol uneasy. 'We shouldn't take it for granted that I'm going to win.'

'Howard told me that Ed Palmer was very taken with you.'

'The talent scout?'

'That's the man. Howard and Mrs Carshalton are just for show. Ed Palmer is the one trusted to choose the right girl. He'll be back next week along with someone from the film company. It doesn't really matter who Howard and Mrs Carshalton vote for.'

Carol laughed. 'As ever, you're a mine of information.'

'I can't help it if people tell me things. Now off you go to Miss Grayson's. Leave your stuff here. I'll bring it in to work tomorrow.'

Once lunch was over, Muriel and her mother went next door to the Blanchards' house to discuss the wedding plans. Muriel hadn't wanted to go.

'If you're not there when we discuss the dresses, you'll only have yourself to blame if you hate the one you're given.'

Muriel had to admit her mother had a point, so she went along and tried to look interested while the church, the reception, the flowers and the wedding cars were being discussed.

The Blanchards had booked the Swan Hotel for the reception, but because of the rationing they would have to do the catering themselves. Muriel's eyes glazed over while the two mothers planned the menu, deciding to make use of anything they had stored, such as tinned fruit, and agreeing that they would both contribute coupons for anything they had to buy.

'And I don't want a cardboard model of a cake for the photographs,' Kay said. 'Somehow we must come up with a real one.'

'I'm sure we can,' her mother assured her. 'Although we may not be able to do royal icing.'

What a pity, Muriel thought sardonically, no royal icing for Princess Kay.

'Now, the gowns,' Mrs Blanchard said. 'It's so good of you and Muriel to contribute clothing coupons, otherwise we would have to settle for parachute silk, and that wouldn't be the same as a nice brocade, would it?'

Until that moment Muriel had had no idea that she was giving up some of her clothing coupons, but she supposed that was fair enough as she had to have a bridesmaid's dress. Although heaven knows what I'll do with it afterwards, she thought.

'White satin brocade for my dress,' Kay said. 'And as long a train as we can manage. And as for the bridesmaids, I thought peach crêpe or turquoise satin.'

Muriel was aghast. Peach or turquoise! I'll look hideous in either of those. She stood up so suddenly that the chair she had been sitting on fell over. Three enquiring faces looked up at her.

'What is it, dear?' her mother asked.

'Feel sick. Got to go. No, don't bother, Mother. Dad and Steve are at home. I'll be all right.'

Muriel turned and fled, but she didn't go home. A cool breeze carried the bracing tang of the sea. She ran down through town without stopping, until she reached the promenade, where she clung on to the balustrade and looked out across the waves.

Carol, I need to see Carol, she thought. We could talk over all this wedding nonsense and she would help me put it in perspective and we'd have a good laugh about it. But of course she couldn't talk to Carol. The last thing her old friend would want to talk about would be Steve's wedding to Kay.

★

'I hoped you would come and see me, Carol,' Miss Grayson said when she opened the door.

'I'm sorry I—'

'Don't apologise, dear. There's no need. I understand you must have been nervous and unsure. But do come in.' Miss Grayson stood back while Carol entered and then called out, 'No, not the front parlour, take the next door.'

Carol found herself in what she had imagined would be the dining room but instead was a cosy sitting room. In all the years she had been coming to this house for her lessons, she had never been invited into this room.

'This is my little den,' Miss Grayson said. 'My refuge, my sanctuary. In here I can relive my old dreams and imagine what might have been.' She waved a graceful arm, indicating the theatrical posters and movie stills lining the walls. 'No, don't look sad for me, Carol. It's no good my saying, why me? We were driving too fast. I could have stopped him. I didn't. That's that. Now, do sit down. A friend of mine is in the kitchen making us a cup of tea.'

Carol had just settled herself in the easy chair Miss Grayson had indicated when the door opened and Howard Napier walked in, pushing a tea trolley before him. Carol smiled. 'I wondered if you knew Miss Grayson,' she said.

'Alice Grayson is the reason I'm here in this godforsaken seaside resort,' he said. 'I shall never understand why she decided to come back here.'

'You know why, Howard. I wanted – needed – to get as far away from my former life as possible.'

Howard Napier poured the tea. He handed Miss Grayson and Carol their cups and then sat down. 'I know, my dear. I'm sorry if I've spoken out of turn. But you wouldn't allow any of your old friends to visit you. So . . .' he turned and smiled at Carol, 'when I was asked to be a judge in the Glamour Girl contest and learned where it was to be held, I jumped at the chance.'

'He turned up quite uninvited about an hour ago,' Miss Grayson told Carol. 'I can't say it was unexpected. I'd read the local newspaper.'

'And as Alice didn't relish an unseemly scene on her front doorstep, she had to allow me in. Ever since, all she's done is talk about you.'

'Me?' Carol said.

'Yes, my dear. Alice was keen to discover what your chances were of winning this contest. I told her I think your chances are very good. Your only rival will be Anne Russell. She's a very good-looking girl.'

'Surely not better looking than Carol,' Alice Grayson said.

Howard looked thoughtful. 'They are both attractive. Carol is exquisite, but Anne has a bold beauty, and that may be what the film-makers are looking for. The winner is to play the part of a cigarette girl in a seedy nightclub.'

'But Carol can act any part you want her to – I can vouch for that.'

'Ah, yes. Acting ability. That's important too. The four finalists will be given a short scene to play. That may do the trick.'

The two friends started discussing the old days. They seemed to forget that Carol was there, and soon she was listening fascinated as they recalled other performers they had known and some of the scandals that had surrounded them.

When she took her leave, Howard showed her to the door. 'Alice is very fond of you,' he told her. 'I think she sees something of her young, hopeful self in you. If you succeed in this – as I pray you will – I hope you will not forget her.'

'I won't,' Carol promised. 'Never.'

She was expecting an argument when she got home, but instead she was ignored. Neither her father nor her stepmother looked up as she walked in. They were sitting at each side of the fireplace listening to a comedy programme on the wireless. It was as if she didn't exist. Carol suspected that it was only her weekly contribution towards household expenses and the fact that she helped with the household chores that had prevented her stepmother from asking her to leave long ago.

She went through into the scullery, made herself a cup of cocoa and took it up to her room. She would have an early night.

The next morning she arrived at work to find Denise waiting for her in the French Salon. She was holding something behind her back. She looked worried.

'What is it?' Carol asked.

'The shoes. The dancing shoes we borrowed. I couldn't have been thinking clearly. Look.'

She held out the silver shoes, then turned them over so that Carol could see the soles and the unmistakable signs of wear.

'No . . .' Carol breathed. 'It's not just you. I should have realised too. What can we do?'

'Well, we need to borrow them one more time, of course, but after that I'll be able to bury them somewhere under all the other boxes for a while. Then as soon as we can, we'll have to get the money and the coupons and buy them.'

Another worry surfaced. 'The dress?' Carol said shakily. 'Is the dress all right?'

Denise relaxed a little. 'Don't worry. There's not a mark on it and I've already put it back in your stockroom. That's why I came in early. The only thing is, we'll have to borrow it one more time, won't we?'

'Denise Shaw, what are you doing here?'

Both girls froze at the sound of Miss Rawson's voice.

'Er – just talking to Carol,' Denise said.

'Well just get yourself back to your own department. It's nine o'clock and the store is open.'

That morning brought the usual clutch of better-off women to the French Salon; women who were restricted by the number of clothing coupons they had left rather than by lack of money. Too many were the type of woman who thought shop assistants were of a lower order. Someone to be spoken sharply to and very rarely thanked.

If ever I'm rich and famous, Carol thought, I'll never treat people such as shop assistants or waitresses like that. I'll remember what it's like to work long hours for little pay and I'll smile and be considerate and I'll always say thank you. When the gossip columnists write about me in film magazines, they'll never be able to find anyone to say I was demanding and difficult.

Over the next few days, one or two of the younger staff congratulated Carol and wished her luck; otherwise life went on as drearily as before. Until Thursday, when the local paper came out.

When Carol arrived at work, Denise was waiting for her again.

'What now?' Carol asked.

'Bad news.' She had never seen Denise look quite so shaken. 'Here, you'd better have a look.'

Denise gave her the newspaper. It was folded open to show the entertainments page. Carol remembered her feelings of unease when the photographs were being taken at the end of the contest. She had assumed the photographer was from the film company. But obviously not.

She stared at the photograph in dismay.

'Rawbones is bound to see this, and she'll know that you

didn't buy the dress. There'll be hell to pay.'

'She'll think I've stolen it,' Carol whispered.

'Well you haven't. It's there in the stockroom. We can show her.'

'That won't make any difference. I took it when I shouldn't have done.'

'You didn't. It was my idea. I'll take the blame.'

'No you won't. You may have taken the dress, but I could have refused to wear it. Stay out of this, Denise. There's no point in us both losing our jobs.'

Denise was aghast. 'Do you think it will come to that?'

'I shouldn't be surprised.'

Carol felt sick. What if she was arrested and charged with some sort of crime? If that happened, it would be the end of her chances of winning a film contract. The studios liked their stars to have unblemished records. She'd heard they paid a lot of money to keep them out of trouble, so why would they take on someone who might cause them problems from the start?

'Oh my God, here's Rawbones,' Denise said. 'And she's got a copy of the paper.'

Carol grasped Denise's arm. 'I've told you. Keep out of this.'

Denise held her ground and stood there looking mutinous.

Leaning close to the other girl, Carol said softly, 'If you value our friendship, you'll leave right now.'

Denise stared at her rebelliously, and then gave in.

Miss Rawson waited until Denise had gone before saying, 'Have you anything to tell me?'

'I think you already know.'

'Don't be impertinent.'

'I didn't intend to be.'

'I'll ask you again. Have you anything to tell me?'

'I wore one of the silk dresses at the Palais on Saturday.'

'A dress that you stole from Rutherford's.'

'I didn't steal it. I borrowed it.'

Miss Rawson's eyebrows shot up. 'Borrowed?'

'If you look in the stockroom, you'll find there are exactly as many dresses as there are supposed to be.'

The supervisor's eyes snapped with fury. 'And who do you suppose will want to wear a soiled dress?'

'It isn't soiled. There's not a mark on it.'

'Customers of the French Salon are too fastidious to want to wear something that has been worn by a girl from the—'

'Seafield estate.' Carol finished the sentence for her.

'Quite.'

'I'm truly sorry. I know I shouldn't have borrowed it.'

Miss Rawson looked pained. 'I'm really surprised, Carol. I've always had a high opinion of you. But now I have no choice.'

'Are you going to have me arrested?'

Miss Rawson's glance was scornful. 'And involve Rutherford's in a grubby little scandal? Certainly not. Leave the shop and don't come back. You are dismissed without pay or reference. You won't work anywhere in this town again.'

Just as Miss Rawson delivered this verdict, two young women entered the salon. Carol's friend Muriel, and with her Kay Blanchard.

Chapter Six

'Carol – wait!' Carol was just about to leave by the staff door when Denise caught up with her. 'What happened?' she asked.

'I've been dismissed. Miss Rawson isn't going to take it any further, but she said she'll see to it that I won't be able to get another job.'

'You won't need one after Saturday.'

'I wish you weren't so sure of that. It will just make it worse if I don't win, and how can I now that I'm without an evening dress again?'

'I'll think of something.'

Carol turned away from her friend to stare up at the dense grey clouds. There was a fine penetrating drizzle that soaked her face, and a nasty little wind blew an empty tin along the cobbles of the back lane.

'Where are you going now?' Denise asked.

'I have no idea. Not home. Can you imagine what the reaction will be when I tell them I've lost my job?'

'Go to my place. Here's my key. We'll figure out what to do when I get home.'

'Won't your mother mind?'

'Not her. If she thought you had nowhere to go, she'd take you in like a lost kitten.'

'You're lucky.'

'I know. She never complains, even when Dad is laid off

and she has to find an extra cleaning job on top of the ones she does already. One day . . .'

Denise didn't finish the sentence, but Carol knew exactly what she meant. Her friend had often said that she'd like to make her mother's life easier.

'Go on,' Denise said. 'When Ruthie gets home, you can help her with her homework. And promise not to fret about anything until I get back. We'll worry about it together.'

She squeezed Carol's arm and then hurried back to the shoe department. Carol turned up the collar of her coat and set off for Garden Square.

Meanwhile, in the French Salon, Kay was doing her best to get Miss Rawson to talk about the incident she and Muriel had just witnessed.

'I saw this dress in a photograph in the paper,' she said. 'I thought I really must have one.'

Miss Rawson gave a tight-lipped smile.

'And wasn't that the girl in the photograph? The girl who left just now?'

Muriel squirmed with irritation. Kay knew very well that the girl who had just been ordered off the premises was the girl in the photograph, and that that girl was Carol.

'She looked lovely,' Muriel said loyally, and earned a vexed glance from Miss Rawson. Undaunted she continued, 'I shouldn't be surprised if you get a lot more sales because of that photograph.'

Kay took two of the silk dresses from the rail, one in shades of pink and the other in pale lilac. When she emerged from the changing cubicle with the dresses over her arm, she said, 'I want something nice to take on my honeymoon. There'll be dancing at the hotel.' She looked at the dresses critically. 'I think I'll take the pink one.'

Miss Rawson murmured something about madam having

85

made a good choice as she folded the dress and put it in a bag.

Muriel and Kay took the lift down to the ground floor.

'What do you suppose all that was about?' Kay said.

'What?'

'Don't pretend you don't know what I mean. It looked as though Carol had just been given the sack. What do you think she'd done?'

Muriel didn't look directly at Kay, but she could see the older girl's self-satisfied smile reflected in the mirrored walls. 'Why do you want to know?'

'She's your friend, isn't she? I should think you would be concerned.'

'I am concerned.'

'Do you think she'll tell you?'

'I have no idea. And listen, Kay, I know you don't like her, and I can guess why. So will you just pack it in?'

Muriel was infuriated to see that her outburst had not upset Kay in the slightest. They walked home in silence.

'Would you like Ruthie to take a note home for you? Tell them that you're staying with me again tonight?'

'No, I'd better face up to it.'

Carol and Denise were sitting on the beds in Denise's bedroom, cradling mugs of hot tea sweetened with condensed milk.

'Well if they chuck you out, you know you can come here.'

'Thanks. But what am I going to do about getting another job?'

'You may not need to. You've got to get out there on Saturday and win.'

'I've nothing to wear.'

'Yes, there is that.' Denise looked thoughtful. Then she grinned. 'But at least you'll have a pair of dancing slippers.'

She leaned over and fished in her holdall, bringing out the silver sandals they had borrowed.

'What have you done?' Carol said, feeling panic rising.

'Don't worry. I haven't pinched them. I decided I'd got you into enough trouble and I had to do the right thing and buy them'

'How did you pay for them?'

'I dashed along to the post office in my break and cashed my National Savings stamps.'

'Oh, Denise, you were saving for a new coat.'

'Well I'll just have to make do and mend like they tell you to, won't I?'

'What about the coupons?'

'Ah, well, that was more difficult.'

Carol stared at her friend, hoping against hope that she hadn't done anything illegal.

'No need to worry. I spread the word amongst the girls that you needed a pair of shoes for the final. They want you to win. They came up trumps.'

'They donated their own coupons?'

'That's right.'

'Tell them I'm grateful,' she said. 'Very, very grateful. But that doesn't solve the problem of the dress, does it?'

Denise clasped her mug of tea with both hands and stared into the mid-distance. Then she looked up. 'I have an idea. Just leave it to me.'

Dorothy Rawson was sorry that she'd had to dismiss Carol Marshall. The quiet, well-spoken girl had shown promise from the very first day. Over the years, Dorothy had taught Carol everything she knew about fashion and grooming, and she had discounted suitable clothes for her from the salon. Carol had blossomed from a shy schoolgirl into a graceful and attractive young woman.

Even though Carol lived on the Seafield estate, she had always had the air of someone used to something better. Dorothy guessed that she must be having elocution lessons and admired her for that. There was some indefinable air about her that set her apart from the crowd. And now look what had happened. She had reverted to the sort of behaviour you would expect from someone of her background. Miss Rawson felt betrayed.

After work that day she hurried home to the flat above the hat shop she shared with her widowed mother. She made tea but ate very little herself because Gerald was taking her out to dinner. When she was ready, she tied a paisley scarf around her neck and tucked it into the upturned collar of her camel coat. Her lizard-skin shoulder bag matched her shoes perfectly. She knew she looked stylish in a casual sort of way that was very different from her sophisticated work persona.

She didn't know how old Gerald was – they hadn't got round to exchanging personal information – but she guessed he was younger than she was. However, she knew she didn't look her age, so why dress like a staid matron when in her heart she was still a romantic girl?

The town was quiet and her high heels clicked satisfactorily on the pavement. She walked quickly and easily, like a young woman hurrying to meet her date. Was Gerald her date? Dorothy's sensible self told her no. But her other self, the self that sometimes dreamed of love and marriage and children, allowed her to hope just a little that this handsome, distinguished man was interested in her as a woman and not just as a good business contact.

He was waiting for her on the steps of the hotel. He had

one hand in his pocket and in the other he held a cigarette. He must have heard her coming, because he turned and smiled, then dropped his cigarette, stubbing it out with the sole of his shoe.

'Dorothy,' he said, and came down the steps to meet her. 'Marvellous, isn't it?'

'Is it?' She looked at him in surprise.

'Come along in. I've reserved our usual table.'

The words caused her to catch her breath. They sounded so intimate. Almost suggesting that she and Gerald were a couple.

'Here, let me help you.' Gerald eased her coat from her shoulders and handed it to a hovering waitress, then held the chair for her. 'Don't bother with the menu. I've ordered mixed grill followed by peach Melba. Will that suit?'

'Very nicely,' Dorothy said. 'But please tell me – what's so marvellous?'

'Wait a moment. Let me show you.' Gerald turned to smile at a distinguished-looking gentleman sitting at the table behind him. 'May I borrow your newspaper again, old chap?'

The other diner smiled. 'Certainly. You may keep it if you like.'

The paper had been opened and folded to show a photograph. Dorothy recognised it immediately. She wondered what was coming next.

'This girl, Carol Marshall, she's your assistant in the salon, isn't she?'

'Yes.'

'Stunner, don't you think?'

'Well, I . . .'

'No wonder she's fancied to win the contest.'

'Is she?'

Gerald leaned over the table towards her and lowered his

89

voice. 'Keep it under your hat, but that chap at the next table is one of the judges. He told me that it's a two-horse race and your girl is in with a chance.'

'And that's marvellous?'

'Come on, old girl. Don't be slow on the uptake. She's wearing one of my silk frocks. And if I may say so, she's showing it to great advantage. I'll bet you've had a run on them today.'

'Well, not exactly a run, but yes, the sales have been satisfactory.'

'They'll be even more so if she wins the contest and her picture gets into the newspaper again.' He lowered his voice even more and looked almost conspiratorial as he said, 'Actually, that chap told me that they were all struck by how elegant she looked compared to the other girls. And that's because of the dress, isn't it?'

Dorothy stared at the photograph. 'Yes, I suppose it is.'

'Did you know she was going to wear it at the contest?'

'Actually, no.'

Gerald frowned. 'Didn't she tell you? I mean, you must have wondered why she'd spent her hard-earned pennies on one of these creations. I hope you gave her a discount, by the way.'

'Well . . . no. I didn't.'

Gerald raised his eyebrows. 'Not shop policy?'

'Yes, it is, but in this case I didn't even know she was taking the dress.'

'Taking? I don't understand.'

'She . . . well, in her words she borrowed it.'

'Borrowed?' Gerald frowned.

'That's the word she used, but in my view it was as good as theft.'

'You'll have to explain, old girl. Did she borrow it or steal it? I'm not quite sure what you mean.'

The waitress arrived with their first course. Dorothy stared down at her plate until the girl had gone.

'Well?' Gerald said.

'Carol Marshall took the dress in a most underhand way. She wore it for the contest and then put it back in stock. She was probably hoping that I wouldn't find out, but she was too stupid to realise that her photograph might appear in the local paper.'

Gerald leaned back in his chair, drew in his breath and looked at her through narrowed eyes. 'What did you do?'

'Dismissed her, of course.'

Gerald looked thoughtful. He picked up his knife and fork and started his meal. 'Pity,' he said eventually.

He's annoyed with me, she thought. Suddenly she had lost her appetite for a meal she had been looking forward to all day.

'Look, Dorothy,' he said. 'What if I refund you for the dress? Couldn't you just give it to her?'

Dorothy was astonished. 'Certainly not. What she did was dishonest.'

'Yes, of course it was. But you must admit, this photograph is good publicity for me – and for the salon, too.'

Dorothy nodded mutely.

'And it would be even better publicity if she won the contest.'

'But what she did was wrong. She was lucky I didn't call the police. Don't you think it would be foolish to reward this sort of behaviour?'

Gerald concentrated on cutting into his steak. Without looking up he said, 'I can't argue with you over that. I'm just asking you to be lenient with her.'

'You mean to turn a blind eye?'

Dorothy's tone was sharper than she intended. Gerald

looked at her through narrowed eyes and then sighed. 'Well, if I can't persuade you, that's the end of the matter.'

The room was warm, but Dorothy felt a distinct chill. She looked at Gerald and saw not the war hero she had been having foolish dreams about, but a businessman who would forget all about her once her usefulness was over. She realised with a pang that she did not want that to happen.

'I suppose I could do what you ask,' she said.

He looked up and smiled at her. 'Could you?'

'Mmm.'

'You're frowning. Is there a problem?'

'It's just that I don't want her in the shop again. She might think she'd got the better of me.'

'Well we can't have that, can we? Isn't there someone who could take the dress to her? One of the other girls? A friend?'

'Yes, there is someone. But what would I say? What reason could I give?'

'Nothing like the truth, is there? Tell her that I saw the picture in the newspaper and was so pleased that I begged you to let her keep the dress. Tell her it's very much against your better judgement and it took a long time to persuade you. How about that?'

Satisfied that this would save her pride, Dorothy agreed. Then she gave a self-mocking smile. 'Well, at least you didn't expect me to give the girl her job back.'

'Good gracious, no. And if she wins this contest, I don't suppose anyone in this town will ever set eyes on her again.'

To her surprise, Dorothy enjoyed the rest of the evening. She had set her scruples aside for the chance of hanging on to a man, but she didn't care. If there was any possibility of escaping from living alone with her mother, she would grab it with both hands.

*

Howard Napier had heard enough of the conversation between the squadron leader and his dinner guest to satisfy himself that Denise, the little minx, would be pleased with him. She had phoned the hotel a couple of hours earlier and confessed the whole sorry tale, stressing that it had been her fault. She was only asking him to help because she wanted to make it up to Carol.

'How do you think I can help?' he had asked.

'The sales rep for the firm who makes the dresses, Squadron Leader Wilmot, is staying at the Waverley.'

'I can't very well approach him directly.'

'I don't expect you to. But you could get into conversation about the photograph in the paper, couldn't you? Tell him that—'

'Stop right there. I get the drift. But why do you want to help someone else when you're a finalist yourself?'

She'd laughed and said, 'Go on, Mr Napier. I know I haven't a chance up against Carol Marshall. No one has.'

Howard was touched by Denise's faith in her friend. He hadn't wanted to worry her by telling her that the more obvious attractions of Anne Russell might be better suited to the part of a little tart who worked in a cheap nightclub. Dear Alice had assured him that Carol would be able to act any part she was given. For Denise's sake, rather than Carol's, he hoped his old friend was right.

'Very well, my dear,' he'd told her. 'I'll make sure that the squadron leader sees the photograph in the paper. After that it will be up to his own business acumen. But Denise . . .'

'What?'

'No more Mr Napier, if you don't mind. You know me well enough to call me Howard.'

Chapter Seven

Denise had asked her to stay the night, but Carol knew she would have to face her father and stepmother sooner or later, so she decided to get it over with. When she got home, however, the house was empty. A note on the table said they had gone to Hetty's sister's house for a beer or two and if Carol wanted anything to eat she could see what was left in the pantry.

She found the remains of a plate pie, the pastry soggy and the contents gristly. She spurned the pie and settled for her usual cup of cocoa and a slice of toasted bread. She found a light music programme on the radio and tried not to think of the scene to come.

By eleven o'clock her father and stepmother still hadn't come home. Carol decided to go to bed and face them in the morning. She lay awake trying to think of the best way to tell them that she'd been sacked. The drizzle of earlier in the day had developed into a heavy downpour, and she could hear it drumming against the window. Finally, exhausted, she fell asleep.

When she woke the next morning she was drowsy and confused. She turned her head and looked at the clock on the bedside table and was startled to see that it was half past eight. She had washed and dressed for work before she remembered that she had no work to go to. She paused on the landing, reluctant to go downstairs

Her father would already have left for work as a storekeeper in a builder's yard. She would have to face Hetty alone. Angry with herself for being so spineless, she took a deep breath and opened her bedroom door.

Hetty appeared at the bottom of the stairs. 'You'll be late!' she called.

Carol sped down and, grabbing her coat from the hall stand, pulled it on.

'Not so fast, miss. Aren't you going to have any breakfast?'

Not trusting herself to speak, Carol shook her head.

'What's the matter with you? Cat got your tongue?'

Carol grabbed her shoulder bag, opened the front door and fled down the path.

'What about your sandwich?' Hetty called after her.

But Carol was already halfway along the street. She had flunked it.

Muriel wondered whether she should go to Carol's house and see if she was all right, but she decided she couldn't face Mrs Marshall. She hoped that Carol might come to see her. Once upon a time, if either of them had been in trouble of any kind they would have sought refuge with each other. But not these days. Muriel acknowledged sadly that she and Carol had drifted apart. Carol had become friendly with that Denise. Muriel didn't care much for Denise. She knew the feeling was mutual.

And now Carol had entered the Glamour Girl contest. Muriel was pretty sure that Denise Shaw had egged Carol on to enter it, and she wondered if Carol being dismissed from Rutherford's was tied in with it somehow.

Muriel was sitting at the breakfast table with her second cup of tea when her mother said, 'Why so glum?'

'I'm not glum.' Muriel smiled up at her mother. 'Just thinking.'

'About?'

'Life . . . you know.'

'I think I do.'

'Do you?' Muriel was startled.

'Of course I do. You're a highly intelligent young woman, and here you are, sitting around at home instead of finding useful employment. But don't worry too much, dear. Now that the war is over, I believe there will be many more opportunities for women. You won't have to settle for voluntary work as I did.'

'But you love your work.'

'Yes, I do. And I was so pleased that you decided to help me distribute the clothes bundles and the food parcels from America. But your father and I have decided it's time for you to think of a proper career.'

Muriel grinned. 'So you're going to send me off to the employment exchange?'

'There's no need for that. How would you like to spend a day at the office of the *Seaside Chronicle*?'

'As a reporter?' Muriel felt a surge of interest.

'Well, no, although that might be possible one day. One of the office workers is leaving to get married, and Mr Blanchard was wondering whether you'd like to take her place.'

'I'd love to!'

'You won't get paid much at first, but you never know what it might lead to.'

For the first time for a long time Muriel felt genuinely happy. She got up, hurried around the table and dropped a kiss on her mother's Eugene-enhanced waves, then flew up to her room to make herself presentable. As she hurried through town towards the newspaper office, she was still concerned about Carol, but if Carol wanted to confide in her it was up to her. Meanwhile Muriel had her own future to think about.

★

Carol walked along the links on the headland as far as the lighthouse and then went down the steps cut into the cliff face to the beach. The rain had stopped, but a sea fret painted the sea and the sky an unrelieved grey. Battleship grey, Carol thought. It was hard to tell where the sea ended and the sky began. Ships waiting to enter the river when the tide turned loomed in the mist, and every now and then a foghorn sounded.

Eventually the cold, damp air drove her back towards the string of shops on the promenade. Light spilled from the windows of the Gondola café and glistened on the damp pavement. She decided to go in. As soon as she opened the door, she was greeted by the delicious smell of real coffee and the steamy hiss of the Gondola's new Gaggia coffee machine. Tonio looked up and grinned as he began to fuss over the jugs and levers of his new pride and joy.

'Coffee?' he asked. 'Go and sit down,' he said. 'Pam will bring it over.'

Carol took a table by the window. Not that there was much of a view on a day like this. Pam, who had been in the same class as Carol at school, brought two cups of coffee to her table and sat down opposite her.

'Mind if I join you?' she asked. 'It's time for my break and we're hardly busy.' She didn't wait for a reply, but sat down and took a sip of frothy coffee. It left a faint rim of froth on her upper lip. She licked it off before she said, 'Just think, one day I'll be able to tell my kids that I was at school with the film star Carol Marshall!'

'That's supposing I win.'

Pam sat back in her chair and crossed her arms across her skinny chest. She screwed up her eyes as she thought about it. 'You're bound to.'

'What about Anne Russell?'

'Yeah,' she said. 'Anne's a looker all right, but you've got real class. Take my word for it. Here – let me top up your coffee.' She stood up and took the cup away from Carol.

When she returned with the coffee she said, 'Tonio sent you a sandwich – salmon, a real treat. It's on the house. You take your time over it. Or do you have to get back to work?'

'No, I . . . I've got the afternoon off.'

'That's nice. I'll leave you in peace. No doubt you've got a lot to think about.'

'You mean to say you've just been wandering about all day?' Denise looked at Carol in astonishment.

'What else could I do?'

'And you let your stepmother think you'd gone to work as usual?'

'Yes. I flunked it.'

'Well, I can understand that. But you should have come here sooner. You know what time Ruthie gets home from school.'

'I wanted to wait for you.'

'Well here I am, and I've got some good news for you.' Denise handed her one of the distinctive French Salon bags. 'Go on, look inside.'

'I don't understand,' Carol said when she saw the silk dress. 'Have you bought it?'

'No, it's a gift from old Rawbones.'

'I don't believe you.'

'It's true. Squadron Leader Wilmot was so pleased when he saw your photograph in the newspaper that he persuaded her to give it to you.'

Carol looked searchingly at her friend for a moment, then said, 'I can't help feeling that you had something to do with this.'

Denise laughed. 'Well, don't look a gift horse in the mouth, as they say. And now let me tell you something I've learned about the competition – and don't ask me how I found out.'

When Carol returned home that evening, she saw the net curtains in the front parlour twitch. Before she could put her key in the lock, the front door swung open. Hetty stood there glaring at her.

'And where have you been all day?' she said.

Carol stared at her in consternation. The silence lengthened until Hetty smiled maliciously and said, 'And don't say you've been to work, because that would make you a liar as well as a thief. Well, what do you have to say for yourself?'

She took hold of Carol's arm and pulled her into the hall. Letting go of her for a moment, she slammed the front door shut, then turned to put a hand on Carol's back and shove her roughly ahead of her into the living room. Her father was sitting at the table.

'Here she is,' Hetty said. 'Here's your daughter, although I'm surprised she dared to come home. Well, aren't you going to say anything to her?'

Her father looked up at her, his expression strained, his face grey. 'We know you've been sacked,' he said.

'How did you find out?'

'Hetty took your sandwich to Rutherford's on her way to work.'

'She did what?' Carol was astounded.

'She said that you woke up late and hurried out without even having a cup of tea. She said she thought something was wrong.'

'That's right,' Hetty said. She had folded her arms across her body, and looked as though she was ready for a fight.

'She was worried that you hadn't made yourself a sandwich. So she made one and took it along for you.'

'I don't believe you,' Carol said.

'Are you calling your father a liar?' Hetty asked.

'No. That's obviously what you told him. But I can't believe you were worried about me. And why would you make me a sandwich? You've never done that before. Even when I was at school.'

'That's because you were so fussy that nothing I ever made for you suited.'

'That's what you told my father.'

The two women stared at each other for a moment, and to Carol's surprise it was Hetty who looked away first.

'So why should I believe that you made a sandwich for me today?'

'Because it's true. Ask Miss Rawson. If you dare go back to the shop, that is.'

Suddenly Carol understood. Hetty wasn't stupid, and it must have been obvious that her stepdaughter had been distressed that morning. She had probably worked out that Carol was in trouble of some kind and had used the sandwich as an excuse to go to Rutherford's and find out what was happening.

'Well, I'm sure Miss Rawson has told you everything you want to know, so why are you asking me?' Carol said.

'Because I want to hear it from your own lips. Sneaking off this morning and pretending to go to the salon when all the time you'd lost your job because you stole a dress.'

'I didn't steal the dress,' Carol said. 'I . . . I just borrowed it.'

Hetty sniffed. 'Taking it without asking is as good as stealing as far as I'm concerned. What do you think, Albert?'

'Your mother's right, Carol.'

'She's not my mother.'

'No, I'm not, and thank goodness for that,' Hetty said self-righteously. Then she changed tack. 'So what are you going to do about a job?'

'I don't know.'

'Well, don't expect your father and me to keep you.'

'I don't.' Carol turned to leave the room.

'Where do you think you're going?' Hetty said sharply.

'To my room.'

'Oh no you're not. You still haven't told us what you've been doing all day.'

Carol sighed. 'If you really want to know, I went for a walk on the beach and then I went to Denise's house.'

'Her house again? You might as well live there.'

'May I go now? Or have you anything else to say?'

Hetty stared at her coldly for a moment. 'No, I've nothing else to say to you, and as far as I'm concerned, you can do what you like.'

Once in her room, Carol took her suitcase from the top of the wardrobe, placed it on the bed and began to pack. She chose carefully. She didn't have very many clothes, but even so she couldn't take everything; there wasn't room in the case.

Denise had hung the silk dress in her own wardrobe and had told Carol that they would get ready together again the following evening, and also that if things were hard for her at home, she was welcome to stay with the Shaws for as long as she liked.

'Once my savings run out, I won't be able to pay your mother for my keep,' Carol had said.

'We'll face that when the time comes. But don't forget to bring your ration book!'

As she went downstairs, Carol was relieved to hear the sound of laughter coming from the wireless in the living room. Her father and Hetty were listening to a comedy show.

She put her case down and opened the door of the small front parlour. Hetty kept the ration books in a drawer in the sideboard. Carol hesitated before she took her own and slipped it into her bag.

It's mine, she told herself. I'm not doing anything wrong.

Quietly she closed the front door of the house where she had once been so happy. Her mother had filled her days with warmth and comfort and her father had been cheerful and kind. For a moment the sunlit memories of the three of them together threatened to overwhelm her, and then the other memories flooded in. The nights she had cried herself to sleep knowing that she would never see her beloved mother again. Hetty's cruelty. The gradual change in her father, as though he was forgetting how to be happy.

That part of her life was over. Carol had no idea what lay ahead. She was entering a kind of limbo, but the only way to go was forward. She would never go back.

Chapter Eight

Denise and Carol were sitting in their underwear on the beds in Denise's bedroom. Their recently washed hair was done up in pin curls. Denise leaned over and eased out one of the kirby grips from Carol's hair. She felt the strand of hair between finger and thumb, then pushed the clip back in again.

'Almost ready,' she said. 'Be patient. If you pull the pins out now, your hair will just be a tangle of rat's tails. Once it's properly dry, I'll be able to brush it into nice smooth waves *à la* Veronica Lake.'

'My hair isn't as long as Veronica Lake's.'

'I know, but it's long enough. If we part it as far over to the side as possible, I'll be able to pull one of those seductive little waves over one eye.'

'How are you going to style yours?'

'A victory roll at the front and a snood at the back. Look . . .' Denise leaned sideways and opened the top drawer of the dressing table. She fished out a large hairnet and held it up for Carol to examine.

Carol frowned. 'It's black.'

'Look more closely.' Denise tossed the snood over to her.

As she threw it, Carol saw sparkles of light. Black and silver sequins had been scattered liberally all over the net.

'It's lovely,' she said. 'Where did you buy it?'

'Woolie's.'

'I didn't know Woolworth's sold anything as stylish as this.'

'They don't. Ruthie sewed the sequins on. It took her hours. She's a good kid.'

'You'll look *très* sophisticated.'

'Yeah.'

'No, I mean it.'

'Okay. But I know I'm no scene-stealer. Now, are you ready to get on with what I planned?'

'Denise, I'm not sure. Should we be doing this?'

'Why ever not?'

'Well . . . it's cheating, isn't it?'

'Why do you say that?'

'Oh, come on. You know it is. We're rehearsing a scene that all four of us have to act out during the final tomorrow, and the other two know nothing about it.'

Denise looked defensive. 'We're not exactly rehearsing, are we? Howard didn't give me a script of any sort. He just said it would be a scene where a customer in the club accuses the cigarette girl of short-changing him and she defends herself. So what you and I are going to do now is play a game of pretend. We'll take turns at being the girl and the customer and . . . well . . . sort of get ourselves in the mood. You know what I mean.'

'Yes, I do. Miss Grayson would say that we'd be getting in character.'

'So are we going to do this or not?'

Carol paused for only a moment before she said, 'Okay. You win.'

'Right. Who do you want to be first? The cigarette girl or the customer?'

Steve couldn't understand why Kay was so keen to go to the final of the Glamour Girl contest.

'I thought we should go with Muriel,' she said. 'To keep her company.'

'Muriel wants to go?'

'Of course she does. Her friend is in the final. She wants to support her.'

Steve looked doubtful. 'I had the impression that Muriel didn't really approve of Carol entering the contest.'

'You're right. And now she feels guilty. She wants Carol to win. So do I.'

'You do?'

'She hasn't had much of a life, has she? This could be a great opportunity for her.'

Steve drew Kay into his arms and held her close for a moment. 'You're very sweet,' he said. 'To care about other people like that.'

Kay smiled. 'Now go home and put on your best bib and tucker,' she said. 'And perhaps when the contest is over we can go for supper to the Rainbow Room.'

Muriel was already dressed to go. She smiled when Steve told her that he and Kay were coming too.

'Kay told me that you want to go and support Carol,' he said.

'I do. I thought about it a lot and I decided it would be mean of me not to. After all, here I am about to embark on a new career, and if she doesn't win this contest, what on earth will Carol do? Now go and get ready.'

Steve laughed. 'Yes, ma'am,' he said. 'Orders received. Over and out.'

The Palais was crowded. A queue had formed even before the ticket office had opened, and in the end they had to turn people away. Two of the last people to get in were Denise's mother and her little sister Ruthie.

'It's years since I've been here,' Mrs Shaw told her daughter.

'Not since your dad and I were courting. You know, your father was a very good dancer. A proper Fred Astaire, although I was no Ginger Rogers!'

Ruthie stared at her mother in amazement. 'Dad can dance?'

Her mother sighed. 'It seems so long ago. It was another world then, before the war. But come along, my lass. Let's get upstairs as quick as we can and see if there are any seats left on the balcony.'

Steve looked down from their seats in the first row of the balcony at the heaving mass of dancers. He wondered why any of the couples had even bothered to take to the floor. They could barely move, and as they shuffled round, most of them had lost the beat of the music entirely. The band played on, although it could hardly be heard above the excited chatter.

'I don't know how they can bear it,' Kay said to him. 'All those people, so close to each other. All that cheap scent and hair oil.' She made a moue of distaste. 'But it's quite an event for Seaton Bay, of course,' she added. 'My father says that even one or two of the national newspapers have been on to him for some copy. He says people need cheerful stories in this age of enforced austerity.'

While Steve and Kay were talking, Muriel had been only half listening, but her attention was caught by Kay's remark about the national newspapers being interested in the story. She had loved her day at the newspaper office and had been overjoyed when Mr Blanchard had told her that as far as he was concerned the job was hers to keep.

She'd realised that at first she would probably be a general dogsbody, but it was the whole atmosphere of the place she loved. She'd made friends immediately with June, the copytaker. It was June's job to sit by the telephone and take dictation from reporters who phoned their stories in. Then she would type them up and pass them on to a subeditor.

Seeing how keen Muriel was to learn, the older girl let her have a look at the neatly typed pages before handing them on. She pointed out the differences in style between the various reporters. When Muriel confided that she would like to be a reporter herself, June told her to listen, look and learn. And to have a go at writing up a few stories. June would be happy to give her opinion.

So, why don't I start tonight? Muriel thought as she gazed down at the crowded dance floor. She knew that the junior reporter, Nick Jones, was covering the event, so she would be able to compare whatever she wrote with Nick's report in the paper. It will be good practice, she thought, and immediately fished in her handbag for her diary. It wasn't very big and in no way compared to a reporter's notebook, but it was all she had. I'll take down the relevant facts, she decided, and fill in the atmosphere when I write it up. She thanked her lucky stars that she was proficient in shorthand.

Sammy Duke had given up any attempt to play dance music. He asked the dancers to take their seats while Connie Walsh entertained them with some of the latest songs from the Hit Parade. The trouble was, there weren't enough seats. Many of those who had to stand became restless, and a lot of them decamped to the snack bar, which in turn became overcrowded. Terrific, Muriel thought as she scribbled away. She was already getting the flavour of a story.

Connie was not used to the audience ignoring her, and after a couple of songs she left the stage. Some of the more rowdy young men had been shouting, 'Get on with it!'

Mr Gilbert took the microphone and announced that as soon as everyone settled down, the final would begin. He told them that Mrs Carshalton and Howard Napier were retiring as judges and that their places would be taken by the producer of the film, Donald Cooper, and his wife, the former film star Lorna Lane.

Miss Lane was touching up her make-up in Connie Walsh's dressing room. She looked up from applying her lipstick as the door behind her opened and Connie flounced in. Lorna stared at the singer's reflection in the mirror.

'What's the matter?' she asked. 'Are they giving you a hard time?'

'You can say that again. All they want is to see that bunch of pathetic small-town girls parading around in the best frocks they could come up with.'

'You're not a local girl?'

Connie had the grace to look abashed. 'Well, yes, I am,' she said. 'But I've been singing with the band since I was fifteen. I'm a professional.'

'Of course you are,' Lorna Lane said. 'I expect you'll be glad when tonight is over and all the hoo-ha dies down.'

Connie sighed and plonked herself down in a battered armchair. 'You bet.' She leaned forward and felt for her handbag, which she had stuffed behind the cushion. She opened it and took out a half-bottle of whisky. Unscrewing the cap, she gulped some down, then closed her eyes for a moment and sighed contentedly.

'That's better,' she said. She looked up to find Lorna Lane watching her.

'Sorry,' she said. 'Would you like a shot?' She glanced about her. 'I'm sure there's a glass somewhere in this dump.'

'No thanks. I'm on the wagon.' The former film star blotted her lips on a red handkerchief, then put both lipstick and handkerchief back in her handbag. 'Tell me,' she said, 'do you know anything about the finalists? Anything I ought to know?'

'Not really.' Connie was flattered that Lorna Lane seemed

to be talking to her like an equal. She frowned and tried to come up with some information. 'Anne Russell is a little older than the others. She's attractive in a showy way and she knows which side her bread is buttered.'

Lorna Lane caught the hint of disapproval. 'Why do you say that?'

'She only has time for people she thinks she can get something from.'

'You mean men?'

'Yes, I do.'

'Well, thanks for telling me, but you understand that that wouldn't spoil Miss Russell's chance of winning if she's the girl for the job?'

'Yeah, I know. Her private life should have nothing to do with it.'

Lorna Lane turned to look at herself in the mirror and caught at a stray silver-blonde curl. She smoothed it into place in her upswept hairstyle. 'And the others?' she said.

'Well, I think Yvonne Pearson was pushed into this by her doting aunt,' Connie said. 'She's pretty all right but I don't think she'd have the talent to be a proper actress. As for Denise Shaw, she's a character. She's funny and clever and has a very good figure, but although she's attractive she's not a traditional beauty. You know . . .' she paused and looked thoughtful, 'Denise reminds me of that American film star Lucille Ball.'

'A comedienne, is she?'

'I suppose she is, although she might not realise it. But it was plain that Howard Napier took a fancy to her.'

'Ah. And do you think something is going on between them? Something serious?'

'I don't think so. When this is over he'll move on and forget all about her.'

'And Carol Marshall?'

'Comes from the Seafield estate.'

'And what does that mean precisely?'

'It's where all the raggedy-arsed riff-raff live. But to be fair, she's never been in trouble of any sort and she works in the French Salon.'

'What is the French Salon? It sounds like a brothel with pretensions.'

Connie laughed. 'Well, Dorothy Rawson, the supervisor, certainly has pretensions, but she's not a madam and it's not a brothel. It's a high-class clothes department. At least what passes for high class in this town.'

'So Carol has class?'

'Yes, she has. She speaks well and dresses as well as she can afford. She's quiet and she's ladylike, but . . .'

'But?'

'Well, she's a strange one. You never know what's really going on in her head. It may be a case of still waters running deep.'

Lorna smiled at Connie. 'So you see, you did know quite a bit about the finalists after all.'

Connie shrugged. 'It's a small town. There are others who could tell you what I've just told you.' She looked troubled. 'I have got a conscience, you know. I hope nothing I've told you would affect your judgement.'

'I'll make my own decisions, but I like to be prepared.'

In response to a knock at the door, Lorna Lane rose and said, 'I think that's my call.' She slipped off her fur coat, 'You'll look after it for me, won't you?' she asked.

Connie stared wide-eyed at the black sable. 'Sure,' she said.

Lorna Lane laughed softly. 'You can try it on if you like.'

She smoothed her skirts and, bestowing one last friendly smile on Connie, opened the door and swept out, leaving a delicious aroma of expensive scent behind her. *L'Heure Bleue*, Connie thought.

Connie took up her place at the dressing table and began to touch up her make-up. Suddenly she paused, her powder puff in one hand, and narrowed her eyes. She had remembered a couple of things about Lorna Lane that now made her cringe with embarrassment. The actress's career had ended when she collapsed, totally inebriated, on set one time too many. That Connie had thoughtlessly offered her a drink was bad enough. But even worse was something she had said about Carol Marshall coming from the Seafield estate where all the riff-raff lived. She remembered with dismay that Lorna Lane herself had come from the slums somewhere in London. The rumours were that she had been almost illiterate when Donald Cooper found her singing in the streets at the age of fourteen, took her home, cleaned her up and encouraged her career. He had married her as soon as she was sixteen.

Lorna Lane had become a successful movie actress. She had starred in many major British films. Perhaps too many, because eventually she had not been able to cope with the pace of her working life and had taken to drink. It was very sad. But perhaps her own experience meant that she would be just the right sort of judge to decide which of the finalists could survive being thrust into a world where nothing was as it seemed.

'What are you scribbling, infant?'

Muriel looked up from her diary to find her brother smiling at her. 'Don't call me that. I'm not a child any longer.'

'No, you're not, but you're still my kid sister.'

Muriel placed a protective hand over the page of her diary. Steve laughed.

'Don't worry; shorthand wasn't essential to flying duties.' He paused. 'Well are you going to tell me what you're writing or not?'

Muriel glanced at him, trying to guess what his reaction might be. 'I'm writing a report of the final,' she said. 'As if it were for the newspaper. Do you think that's silly?'

'Of course I don't. I think it's terrific.'

'Thanks. But Steve, don't tell anyone, will you?'

'Not if you don't want me to.'

'Not even Kay. I mean, she might mention it to her father and that would be embarrassing, seeing as I've only just started there.'

Steve put an arm around her shoulders and gave her a fond squeeze. 'I promise, your secret's safe with me!'

'What are you two talking about?' Kay asked brightly.

She was sitting on the other side of Steve and he turned to smile at her.

'Nothing much,' he said, and Muriel saw the swift flicker of annoyance in the older girl's eyes. But Steve had made a promise and she trusted him not to break it.

'Well, whatever it was,' Kay said with an attempt at a smile, 'I think something is about to happen.'

Muriel noticed that all chatter had stopped. She looked down to see that the dance floor had been cleared and a table set up for the judges as before. On the stage, the bandleader was fiddling about with the microphone, which was making ear-popping clicks and screeches. Then he turned to the band and raised his arm for a drum roll.

'And now, ladies and gentlemen,' he said, 'I'd like you to meet tonight's judges.'

The judges walked on to the stage in turn, bowed to the applause, and went down the steps on to the dance floor, where they took their seats at the table. Muriel noticed that Ed Palmer hadn't made much of an effort with his appearance, whereas the film producer, Donald Cooper, looked more like a successful businessman than someone from the world of entertainment.

The loudest applause went to the judge who was introduced last, Lorna Lane. Although she hadn't worked for years, she was still remembered as one of the greats. She was dressed in a halter-necked evening gown of steel-grey silk taffeta. The top of the bodice and the straps of the halter were embroidered with metallic black and silver sequins and pink beads. Muriel knew instinctively that this gown must have been designed in Paris, and wondered how she could work this into her report.

She thought of the four finalists waiting in the wings and wondered if it wasn't cruel to bring someone like Lorna Lane to the Palais. How could any of them, even Carol, ever hope to look like that?

As soon as the judges were settled, the band began to play 'Moonlight Becomes You' and the four contestants came on to the stage, two at each side, and walked down the steps, ending up before the judges' table.

There were catcalls and whistles and Muriel could see Yvonne Pearson flinching unhappily. Anne Russell glanced at the whistlers with contempt and Denise Shaw grinned as if it were all a big joke. Only Carol remained unmoved. Calm and remote, she looked utterly lovely. It was as if she had distanced herself from the world around her and had already entered whatever future lay ahead.

Muriel heard a slight intake of breath and turned her head to see Steve staring at Carol intently. As well as admiration, there was a hint of anguished regret in his expression. If that means what I think it does, Muriel thought, why couldn't he have realised he was in love with Carol before Kay set the wedding date? And my big brother being the honourable bloke he is, I suppose it's too late to do anything about it now. What a mess.

Lost in his own thoughts, Steve was totally unaware of the way Kay was looking at him. Her face was a mask of fury.

I wonder why Kay decided we should all come here tonight, Muriel thought. Whatever her plan was, things are obviously not going her way.

All four finalists stood in front of the judges and twirled slowly as if they were mannequins in a fashion show. By now Yvonne was visibly nervous. On one twirl she managed to trip over her own foot and would have fallen if Denise had not shot out an arm to save her. Carol, on the other side of Yvonne, did not seem to have noticed. If she had, surely she would also have helped Yvonne, Muriel thought. It was not like her old friend to be selfish.

The judges made notes, then Lorna Lane smiled at the girls and told them they could go. Connie Walsh came on stage again, but the audience remained restive. Then to Muriel's surprise, Lorna Lane took the microphone.

'I hope you will be patient,' she said. 'We have to go away and compare notes before the next stage of the competition, so my friend Connie here has agreed to sing for you.' She smiled at Connie, who gazed back at her as star-struck as any fan.

'When we come back, the four finalists are going to act a short scene with Howard Napier.' She paused. 'Lucky girls. When I started out, just about every actress I knew would have felt honoured to play opposite such a distinguished actor.'

Lorna left the stage and Connie sang. The audience had been requested not to dance, but a few unruly couples began to jive around the edges of the floor.

'Can I get you two girls anything from the snack bar?' Steve asked.

'No thank you,' Kay replied. 'It will be like a madhouse in there. I can wait until we go to the Rainbow Room afterwards.'

Muriel would have loved a glass of lemonade, and it was

the first she had heard about going to the Rainbow Room. She wondered if she was included.

The stage had been cleared of music stands and all instruments except the piano. The lights had been dimmed and the pianist sat there playing a medley of music from the Hit Parade. A spotlight played on a table set up with drinks. This represented the nightclub.

Howard Napier walked on and took centre stage. He held up his hand to appeal for silence, and when the chatter had died down he announced that he would be acting a small scene with each of the finalists. It would be the same scene. He would play the part of an aggrieved customer in a night-club and the girls, in turn, would play the part of a cigarette girl, which was exactly the part the successful girl would play in the movie. Then he asked the audience to be quiet and 'give the girls a chance'.

The first finalist to appear was Yvonne Pearson. It's like throwing a Christian to the lions, Steve thought. They had given her a prop of a cigarette tray suspended round her neck on a leather strap. The poor girl was clutching the tray with both hands and was shaking visibly. Howard gave her a kind smile, but that was the most he could do for her. After all, he was playing the part of a disgruntled customer.

The scene began and Howard barked, 'That's not right!' He was looking at some loose change in the palm of his hand.

'Yes it is, sir,' Yvonne said almost inaudibly. She was looking down into the tray, and Steve guessed there must be a script in there.

'No it's not. You've short-changed me. I gave you half a crown.'

Whatever the cigarette girl's response should have been the audience did not discover, because at that point Yvonne fled the stage.

Boos and laughter broke out in the audience. Steve was reminded again of a circus in ancient Rome. He saw that Muriel was scribbling furiously. On stage, Howard held up his hand and with one sorrowful look managed to express his disappointment with the audience's behaviour. The laughter died down, and when peace was restored, Anne Russell walked on to the stage.

She certainly looked the part, Steve thought, and after Howard's line she raised her head and looked at him defiantly. 'No you didn't,' she said. 'You only gave me a two-shilling piece.'

She played out the rest of the scene with confidence, and her supporters in the audience clapped and cheered. The trouble was, Steve thought, that she had a dreadful voice. She was like some of the stars of the silent movies who were dropped as soon as talkies came in because their voices were so awful.

The surprise of the evening was provided by Denise Shaw. She gave a confident performance and she seemed to be enjoying herself. But it was obvious that she didn't take any of it seriously. Steve wondered why she had entered the contest when she didn't seem to care whether she won or not. She was rewarded with a fair round of applause and a few wolf whistles. And then it was Carol's turn to perform.

From the minute she walked on stage, there couldn't have been any doubt that she had real stage presence. Small and delicate as she appeared in real life, she somehow managed to project an aura of steely resolve. Here was no vapid beauty; here was a woman of character who was a survivor in a tough world. How she did this before she had even opened her mouth was a mystery to Steve.

She gave only the barest glance at the script in the cigarette tray, and the way she responded to Howard seemed to draw a real performance from the experienced actor rather than the read-through he had done with the other girls. Steve sensed the audience becoming involved as the scene progressed, and there was a ripple of applause when Howard as the irate customer gave up and walked away.

But then came the moment of genius. Carol must have invented it, because neither Anne Russell nor Denise Shaw had ended the scene in quite the same way. Once the customer had turned his back, Carol threw back her head and shot a swift, contemptuous smile in his direction. Then, taking an imaginary coin from the tray, she mimed dropping it in her own pocket before turning on her heel and leaving the stage.

There was a pause as the audience took in the significance of what she had done, and then there was a burst of laughter mingled with thunderous applause.

Steve noticed that Muriel had stopped writing and was leaning forward staring at the empty stage with a stunned expression. Steve himself was dumbfounded. He had known Carol since she'd been a small child. She'd been pretty and graceful in a gamine way. Recently she had grown into a beautiful young woman. But he had never suspected that beyond this outward appearance there had lain this remarkable talent.

Kay watched Steve's reaction with dismay. She had decided to come to the Palais tonight because she had wanted him to see the vulgarity of it all. And it had been vulgar, with the girls parading like cattle in a market, accompanied by catcalls, wolf whistles and suggestive remarks.

However, to Kay's chagrin, Carol Marshall had risen above it all, her air of detached cool beauty distinguishing her from the other girls so emphatically that no one would ever guess she'd been dragged up at the wrong end of town.

Kay had known from her father that the finalists would

have to act out a little scene with Howard Napier, and she had imagined that that would provide further humiliation. Here again she had been proved wrong. In one short scene Carol had revealed a shining talent that had amazed just about everybody present. Including Steve. Kay had hoped that by the end of this evening he would have recognised Carol for the common little nobody that she was. Instead, from the look on his face, he was seeing her in a whole new light. Kay's only comfort was that if Carol won, as surely she must, she would be leaving town. And as far as Kay was concerned, that couldn't be soon enough.

The four finalists waited in Mr Gilbert's office. Yvonne had collapsed in tears. She was sitting at the desk with her head in her hands, sobbing her heart out. She raised her tear-stained face. 'I'm not going to win, am I?' she said between sniffs and gulps.

'Obviously not,' Anne Russell said. 'Not after the way you bolted from the stage.'

That sent Yvonne into a paroxysm of shoulder-shaking sobs and earned Anne a look of fury from Denise.

There was no point in Denise pretending that Yvonne still had a chance, so she said as kindly as she could, 'Did you really want to win so much?'

Yvonne surprised them by saying, 'No, not really.'

'Then why are you so upset?'

'Because of my aunt. It was her idea that I should enter this contest. She'll be so disappointed with me.'

There was a short silence while Denise thought of something to say. 'If you don't win, she'll be disappointed with the result. She won't be disappointed with you. You did your best.'

She knew this was rather a convoluted argument, but it seemed to cheer Yvonne up. She dabbed at her eyes and said, 'Yes, I did.'

Denise heard Anne Russell sniff, but before she could say anything, the door opened and Mrs Carshalton swept in. 'Have you been crying, love?' she asked her niece.

Yvonne nodded.

'Well don't. Whatever happens tonight, I'm going to take you to the Rainbow Room for a slap-up supper. Now, let me touch up your make-up. You have to look good for the photographs.'

At the mention of photographs, Anne Russell reached for her compact and lipstick. It was only then that Denise realised that since coming back to the dressing room, Carol had said nothing at all. She glanced at her now and saw that she was sitting still and quiet, as if lost in her own thought. She was about to ask her if she was all right, but something stopped her. She sensed that Carol did not want to be talked to. She was away in some world of her own. Denise took her own compact from her handbag and had just finished powdering her nose when the door opened.

'Come along, ladies,' Mr Gilbert called. 'You're wanted on stage.'

The band was playing 'Embraceable You' as the girls took their places. The lights had been dimmed and Carol stared out into the warm darkness as she waited for her future to be determined.

She knew she ought to be feeling nervous, but a strange calm had taken hold of her. She went over the scene in the dressing room. Denise had been kind to Yvonne, but Anne Russell had been a complete bitch. Should I have said anything? Carol wondered. I probably should have, but it's funny how I feel so detached from everything.

The band stopped playing, and Mr Gilbert led Miss Lane on to the stage. The film star said how gracious the other judges were to allow her to make the announcement. 'I won't keep you waiting any longer,' she continued. 'The winner is . . .' she paused, 'Carol Marshall.'

As the audience roared and thunderous applause broke out, Carol stepped forward into the spotlight.

Chapter Nine

Carol lost count of the number of times the light flashed and the camera clicked. They were standing in the foyer of the Palais in front of some weary plants in huge brass pots while the photographer arranged the shots.

The first had been of Lorna Lane and herself both smiling at the camera. The second one was of Donald Cooper shaking her hand. Then a posed shot of Carol in character as the cigarette girl with the tray around her neck, looking up at Howard Napier. Then Carol with the other three finalists.

Ed Palmer stood and watched the proceedings until the photographer was satisfied, then made his way through the watching throng.

'You look as though you need to be rescued,' he said.

Carol looked at him properly for the first time. He was tall and slightly overweight. His face was pale and his hair a little too long.

'Are your parents here?' he asked.

'No. Why do you ask?'

'Your father will have to sign your contract.'

'Contract?'

He smiled. 'Yes, it must be signed before you start work. You're under twenty-one, so we have to make sure we have your father or guardian's permission. Your father is alive, isn't he?'

'Yes, he is. But I'm only a few months short – my birthday's in July. Do we really have to have his permission?'

'I'm afraid so.' Suddenly he looked worried. 'Look, your parents do know you've entered this, don't they?'

'Yes.'

'And they approve?'

'They couldn't care less.'

'Ah, I see. Well in that case, leave it all to me. I'll go and see them and sort things out. You don't have to worry about it.'

'Really? That's kind of you.'

'That's what I'm here for. Now, the reporter from the local rag wants an interview with you, and I've arranged it so that we can have the manager's office. I'll make sure it doesn't go on too long, because Donald's taking us all for supper.'

Carol turned to follow Ed Palmer and suddenly found herself facing Muriel. They looked at each other awkwardly for a moment, then Muriel said, 'Congratulations, Carol. I . . . I'm pleased for you.'

'Are you, really?'

'Of course. But I'm sorry that you'll be leaving town. I'll miss you.'

'Will you?'

'Oh, Carol, don't look at me like that. I know I haven't been a very good friend lately and I'm sorry.'

Muriel looked so wretched that Carol melted. 'It's not all your fault,' she said. 'And I'll miss you, too.'

'We . . . we'll write to each other, won't we?'

'Of course.'

'Carol, I'm sorry to interrupt,' Ed Palmer said, 'but we have to get going.'

'Right. I'm coming.' Carol suddenly stepped forward and hugged her old friend. 'Goodbye,' she said.

'I won't have your address. You'll have to write first.'

'I will.'

Muriel watched Ed Palmer hurrying Carol away. She was glad that they'd had the chance to make up. Not that there had been a proper argument. But now she felt they had parted friends.

'There you are!'

Muriel turned to see Kay frowning at her. 'We wondered where you'd got to. Why did you shoot off like that?'

'I wanted to have a word with Carol. To congratulate her.'

'Will she be leaving for London soon?'

'I didn't have time to ask her.'

'Ah, well, at least you had the sense to get your coat first. The cloakroom's a nightmare. Now come along. Steve has gone on ahead to get a table.'

'Table?'

'At the Rainbow Room. It seems everyone is going there tonight.'

'But I thought it was just you and Steve going for supper. I didn't know I was invited.'

'Whatever made you think that? Of course you're coming with us. I wouldn't dream of sending you home alone.'

Although Kay's smile was disarming, Muriel wondered if it had been Steve who had insisted that she go with them. She submitted without protest as Kay took hold of her hand and pulled her through the crowded foyer towards the exit. After the heat and crush of the dance hall, the cool air was welcome.

As they hurried along the promenade, Muriel could hear dance music leaking out into the moist dark of the April night. The contest was over, but there were still those who wished to dance. After this bit of excitement, their humdrum lives would settle back into the usual routine. But Muriel knew that Carol's life would never be the same again.

The competition made front page news in the *Seaside Chronicle*. GLAMOUR GIRL CAROL! the headline screamed, and there was a beautiful head-and-shoulders shot of Carol that Muriel thought was almost as good as any of the pictures of the film stars lining the walls of the foyer of the Rialto. After a brief description of the event, there was an instruction to turn to a two-page spread in the centre of the paper for more detail, photographs and a personal interview with Seaton Bay's own Glamour Girl Carol Marshall.

Seaton Bay's own, Muriel thought. If only they knew how much Carol hates the place and how much she wants to get away. Uneasily she reflected that no matter how unhappy Carol's childhood had been and no matter how much she wanted to act in films, she might not have wanted to leave if things had worked out differently for her. Steve had a lot to answer for.

She read the interview. Nick had done a good job, asking the right sort of questions and finding out just what the public would want to know. The public! Muriel thought, amused with herself. I'm thinking as though Carol is already a star and this is an interview in *Picturegoer*!

When Muriel had finished, she closed the paper and laid it aside. She wondered if everything Carol had told the reporter was true. Perhaps only the people who were close to her, like Denise and Muriel herself, would suspect she was putting on an act.

Steve had seen the picture of Carol and the headline on the front page of the paper, but he was reluctant to turn to the centre pages to find out more. He was annoyed with himself for feeling so unsettled. He had tried to remind himself that he should be very happy. He was soon to marry Kay, the girl who had been his childhood sweetheart and who had waited for him all through the grim years of the war.

He hadn't been at all put out when, just a few weeks before he was due to be demobbed, Kay had written to him and told him that it would be a romantic gesture to get engaged the moment he came home. Almost delirious with happiness that he had come through safely, as so many of his friends had not, and that now a new life could begin, he had agreed. Kay's next letter had informed him that she knew what men were like about going shopping, so she had already chosen the ring at Samuel's the jeweller's and wanted his permission to buy it. He could refund her later.

Only a little taken aback, he had agreed again. It was only when Kay had announced that she wanted to be a June bride that he started feeling he had been pitched on to a roller coaster. At first he didn't know why he had started having doubts. After all, he had loved Kay for as long as he could remember, hadn't he? And she certainly loved him, otherwise why would she have waited for him? A girl as beautiful as she was could have had any man she wanted, including one of the dashing chaps from the Canadian airbase.

He reflected that perhaps these doubts were normal for anyone who was about to take such a big step and commit themselves to another human being. And maybe he would have been satisfied with that explanation if it hadn't been for Carol.

Carol, the sweet kid whom he'd regarded almost as one of the family. Carol, the girl who had grown into a beautiful woman and who, without his realising it, he had begun to think of as more than a friend. Had he been entirely honest when he had told Kay that he had started visiting Carol at work because he felt sorry for her? Had he been honest with himself when he had tried to deny that he had begun to look forward to seeing her each time he came home?

Sadly, now that it was too late, he knew he'd been kidding himself. But there was no way he could call off the wedding at this stage. Or could he? Tentatively he picked up the newspaper and opened it, turning to the interview with Carol. It was pretty good. The reporter had been tactful about Carol's background, not exactly saying that she'd had a rough time, but mentioning that it must have been difficult for a young girl to lose her mother.

Carol had paid a glowing tribute to her elocution teacher, Miss Grayson, and then gone on to say how much she had enjoyed working in Rutherford's French Salon – could that be true, or was she being tactful here? – and how grateful she had been for the gift of the beautiful silk dress that she was sure had helped her to win the competition. Good publicity for the store, Steve mused smilingly.

His smile faded when he came to the end of the interview.

I put it to Carol that surely a girl as beautiful as she is must have a boyfriend, and what did the young man in question think about her going off to London to be a film star?

'I don't have a boyfriend,' Carol replied smilingly. 'And I certainly don't want one. Nothing could be as important to me as my career.'

Steve was still staring at the page when Kay entered the room. 'Mother needs to start thinking about the invitations,' she said. 'Perhaps you and I should sit down and make out a list.'

'Yes,' Steve said. 'Perhaps we should.'

At ten to ten the following Saturday morning, Carol stood on the platform at Newcastle Central Station. She had a string bag over her arm and her suitcase at her feet. Wherever she looked, there were men in uniform. Some were clustered round the mobile tea bar, some queued for cigarettes at the tobacconist's kiosk, and others sat on their kitbags and waited patiently until their trains were announced. The war had ended, but soldiers, sailors and airmen were still being shunted round the country in seemingly endless and pointless journeys.

Three young women in ATS uniforms hurried past her and were enveloped in steam. Carol was reminded of the scene at the station in the film of *Anna Karenina*, except that she was no Greta Garbo and she had no intention of hurling herself on to the railway track.

'Got some!' she heard Denise say, and looked round to see her friend hurrying towards her.

'Got some what?' Carol asked.

'Chocolate for the journey.' She thrust a bar into Carol's hand.

'Where did you get this? And what is it?' Carol looked down at the unfamiliar wrapping.

'It's a Hershey bar. Army issue. I cadged it from those American soldiers at the tea bar.'

'You're shameless.'

'Yes, I am, aren't I?' Denise grinned.

'You said you were going for a packet of biscuits.'

'I got those too.' Denise fished the biscuits out of her pocket. 'You might get hungry before you reach London.'

'I've got the sandwiches your mother made. Remember?'

'I know. But it's a long journey. Six hours at least, and that depends on whether there are any rail works going on anywhere.'

'If I'd known you were going to fuss like this, I wouldn't have let you take the day off work.'

'Do you think you could have stopped me?'

They smiled at each other.

Just then the station loudspeaker burst into life and informed the waiting passengers that the London train was approaching the platform. Everybody began to move forward. Denise picked up Carol's case.

'Hurry,' she said. 'As the train comes in, try and work out where the nearest door will be. You don't want to have to stand in the corridor all the way to London.'

'It's all right,' Carol said. 'My seat has been reserved.'

'Good. But I wouldn't put it past any of this lot to get there first and remove the ticket from the seat. So hurry up.'

The train slowed down as it entered the station, and as the lettered carriages moved past her, Carol was able to make out the one she should be in.

'There,' she said. 'Look.'

'First class!' Denise said. 'You didn't tell me.'

'I didn't know. Mr Palmer arranged everything for me.'

The train stopped, the doors swung open and for a while there was mayhem as the passengers who were getting off fought their way through the crowd waiting to enter. To Carol's surprise, Denise pushed on to the train ahead of her.

'What are you doing?' she asked.

Denise turned her head and grinned over her shoulder. 'I'm going to see you to your seat and make sure no one pinches it. What's the number?'

Once inside the compartment, Denise lifted Carol's case up into the parcel rack. When Carol had taken her seat, Denise stood and looked at her. There was a noise of train doors slamming.

'I suppose I should go now,' she said uncertainly.

'Denise! Scoot! Unless you want to spend your day off in Darlington!'

Her friend bent down, dropped a kiss on the top of her head, and then almost fell over as she turned and negotiated a way past the other passengers' knees and feet. Carol heard her excusing herself to the last-minute passengers as she hurried along the corridor. And then she appeared, ruffled but smiling, on the platform outside the window.

The guard's whistle shrilled to the accompaniment of a final slamming of doors, then two huge bursts of steam erupted from the engine and the train started to pull away. As it gathered pace, Denise ran along the platform waving madly. When the platform ended she had to stop, but she stood there, a lone figure, waving until the curve of the track meant that Carol could no longer see her.

Carol pressed her face against the cool glass and closed her eyes to prevent the hot tears from spilling over. There was an ache in her throat. Denise, she thought. When am I going to see you again?

'She might have come to say goodbye,' Hetty said. 'After all I've done for her.'

Albert Marshall didn't say anything. He sat at the table studying form in the racing page of the morning paper.

'Mr Palmer seems to think she'll do well,' Hetty said.

Albert remained silent.

'I wonder if she'll show her gratitude.'

'What do you mean?'

'I mean if she starts making a lot of money. Will she remember us?'

'There's no reason why she should.'

'We brought her up, didn't we? She never went hungry. We put up with her airs and graces. I reckon she owes us.'

Albert sighed and laid his pencil down. 'Give it a rest, Hetty. Carol doesn't owe us anything. I shouldn't be surprised if we never see or hear from her again.'

'No, I suppose you're right. Ungrateful little cow.'

'I told you. Give it a rest. We've had a decent enough

payment from Mr Palmer for signing those papers, and that's all we're going to get. Accept it.'

Hetty stared at him mutinously. Albert very rarely argued with her, but when he did, she knew there was no changing his mind. It was true, Mr Palmer had given them a payment – in cash – and he'd been very generous. Hetty had asked him why, and he'd replied that he thought Carol might prove a decent investment.

'And what if she doesn't?' Hetty had asked.

Mr Palmer had shrugged. 'Then she'll come back home.'

Hetty hadn't said anything then and she wasn't going to say anything now. But if Mr Palmer thought she would allow Carol back in this house if she failed to make a success of things in London, he was very much mistaken.

Chapter Ten

Howard Napier sat with his old friend Alice Grayson by the fire in the room she called her refuge. He had brought her a bottle of her favourite cream sherry and a box of shortbread biscuits he'd charmed the chef at the Waverley into selling to him. They sipped their drinks and nibbled their biscuits companionably.

The day was dark and Alice had switched on a table lamp with a pink-swathed shade. In its gentle glow, Howard could see how beautiful she had once been. He marvelled that she had coped so well with the tragedy of her accident. The man who had been driving the car had kept his promise and made sure that she did not suffer financially. It was rumoured that he would have married her – had he not been married already.

But now her one-time lover was old and ill and near to death. His wife and grown children knew nothing about Alice. Howard hoped fervently that he had made provision for her in his will.

'Did Carol come to say goodbye?' he asked.

'Yes. She thanked me for everything I'd done for her.'

Howard could only hope that if Carol Marshall was successful, she would remember this. It was obvious how fond of the girl Alice was.

'She should do well,' he said.

'Do you really think so?'

'I do. There's something about her. I can't define what it is, except to fall back on a cliché and say she has star quality.'

'I know. But she's so young.'

'Meaning?'

'You know as well as I do that she could be exploited.'

Howard sighed. 'As you were.'

'You're wrong. I was in love with him. I didn't embark on the affair thinking he would marry me.'

Howard was surprised that Alice had said so much. Usually her affair with the great film director was forbidden territory. Taboo. Never to be spoken of.

'Would you be able to keep an eye on her, Howard?'

'That will be difficult from Hollywood.'

'Hollywood? You're going to Hollywood at—' She broke off.

'At my age?' Howard smiled.

'At this stage in your career.' She laughed softly.

'I know. It's amazing, isn't it? But the studios over there are in need of old buffers like me to play stuffed-shirt English aristocrats. Not very demanding roles, but the money will be good.'

'I'm very pleased for you. Will you stay there long?'

'As long as my agent can find me the right scripts. So you see, as far as Carol is concerned, I can't be much help.'

Alice asked him to pour her some more sherry, and then said thoughtfully, 'What about Lorna Lane?'

'What about her?'

'For all her troubles she's a decent woman. Do you think if you asked she would keep Carol under her wing?'

'I shouldn't think so. Apart from obliging Donald by doing this sort of thing now and again, Lorna keeps very much to herself at their place by the sea. She very rarely goes up to town.'

'I see.'

'Look, I shouldn't worry too much,' Howard said. 'Denise told me that Carol's life hasn't been easy. She must have learned to look after herself.'

'Ah, Denise. I'm surprised at you, Howard.'

'What do you mean?'

'You've had an exotic love life, but I never took you for a cradle-snatcher. The girl must be young enough to be your daughter!'

Howard laughed. 'I deny everything!'

'That's what you used to say when the press came after you, but it's me you're talking to, remember!'

'All right. I'm very taken with her. She's warm and funny and kind. But I assure you I've behaved honourably. I don't want to get into the newspapers as a dirty old man taking advantage of a provincial shop girl. That would ruin everything.'

'Hollywood, you mean?'

'Precisely.'

'So it's goodbye Denise.'

'Sadly that is so. And now, my darling friend, it's time for you and me to say goodbye. I'm taking the sleeper back to London tonight. I stayed here as long as I could so that I could spend some time with you.'

'I'm glad you did.'

They rose to their feet and Howard took Alice in his arms and held her close. They both knew that they might not see each other again.

The heating must have been full on. The pipes that carried the hot water were under the seats, and Carol could feel the warmth hitting her ankles and the backs of her legs. She glanced at the other passengers in the compartment. The two men sitting on the same side as herself looked like businessmen or civil servants in their smart suits. Each had placed a briefcase in the overhead luggage rack and each had immersed himself in a copy of *The Times*.

Sitting directly opposite Carol was a well-dressed young woman with a black armband stitched to her coat sleeve. She had one arm round a small girl, who was already dropping off to sleep, probably prompted by the motion of the train.

Next to the little girl, in the seat nearest to the sliding door, there was a young naval officer. He was reading a book. Just at that moment he looked up and glanced Carol's way. He saw her watching him and smiled. She looked away in confusion and turned to stare out at the passing country-side.

Soon the warmth and the hypnotic rhythm of the train began to get to her. She closed her eyes. So much had happened in the last few days. Mr Palmer had been to see her father, had got him to sign the necessary papers, made all the travel arrangements for her and given her the money she would need when she arrived in London. He called it an advance. He had also arranged somewhere for her to live.

Since the final of the Glamour Girl contest, one week ago, Carol had been staying with Denise. Apart from going to visit Miss Grayson, she had hardly set foot outside the door. There was nowhere she wanted to go; no one she wanted to see.

She thought about the night of the final and what had happened afterwards. The film's producer, Donald Cooper, had reserved three tables at the Rainbow Rooms. Carol found herself seated with Mr Cooper, his wife Lorna Lane and Howard Napier.

At a nearby table were Denise, Yvonne and Mrs Carshalton. Another table was occupied by Ed Palmer, Anne Russell and a surprised-looking Nick Jones, the local paper's youngest reporter. Mr Palmer had gathered him up after his interview with Carol and brought him along with the rest of the party.

As the meal progressed, Carol noticed Mr Palmer asking Nick if he could see his notes and then making a few suggestions.

Each of the diners was given a menu. Carol stared at hers in dismay. It was all Greek to her – or rather it was in French, and although she recognised the language, she had no idea what the culinary terms meant.

'Shall I order for you, Carol?' Lorna Lane asked quietly. 'I imagine your tastes and mine will be similar.'

Carol was sure that the food must be delicious, but everything tasted like ashes once she noticed who was sitting at a table at the other side of the small dance floor. Steve, Muriel and Kay. She remembered her feeling of desolation.

Now she opened her eyes to discover that everyone else in the compartment was getting up. 'Are we there?' she asked, thinking that she must have been asleep for hours.

'No such luck,' the naval officer said. 'The engine's broken down. We're all off to find a cup of tea. Will you join us?'

Carol looked hesitant, and the young woman smiled at her. 'I think it's best that you do. Without the heating, it's going to get very cold in here.'

'But where are we?' Carol asked.

'York,' one of the smart gentlemen replied, 'and I suggest we find some seats in the tea bar before everybody else has the same idea.'

The young woman took her daughter's hand and prepared to leave, but the naval officer stopped her. 'Look, if there's anything valuable in your case, I would take it with you. You too,' he said, smiling at Carol. 'There are some desperate rogues and vagabonds infesting the railways these days who have no respect for other people's property. And some of them even work for the rail companies.'

He got Carol's case down for her and insisted on carrying it along with his own kitbag, which he slung over his shoulder.

The two gentlemen helped the young woman with her luggage.

When they reached the platform, one of the gentlemen said, 'Look, before we go any further, don't you think it would be easier if we introduced ourselves? First names will do. I'm Austin.'

'Roger,' his companion said, and looked at the naval officer.

'David.'

'Frances,' the young woman said. 'And this sleepy little girl is my daughter Molly. And you?' She smiled at Carol.

'Carol.'

There was an awkward moment when they all just looked at each other, and then David said, 'This sort of thing would never have happened before the war, would it? People like us making friends with strangers. But now we've all learned to get along together, and quite right, too.'

Carol found herself swept along the crowded platform with the others until they reached a café. It was already filling up, but they managed to find two tables next to each other. They stowed the cases under the tables, so there wasn't much room left for legs and feet, but David said it was safer that way.

'Here you are.' Roger had shot off to the counter as soon as they were settled, and he came back carrying a tray. 'I managed to get a glass of milk and a biscuit for young Molly here, but for the rest of us there wasn't even a Chelsea bun left to go with our cups of tea.'

The café had filled up and it was impossible to keep much of a conversation going above all the noise. Carol was pleased about this. Her present companions were what Denise would have called 'posh'. Their clothes were good and their accents were impeccable. She was amused by the fact that they seemed to have accepted her as one of them.

How would they react, she wondered, if they discovered that I grew up on a council estate at the wrong end of town, and that I've never travelled first class before in my life?

Every now and then, an announcement on the station loudspeakers called passengers to their trains. But this never applied to the London train, and after more than an hour, Austin and Roger, who had discovered that they'd served in the same regiment in the First World War, decided to leave.

'We're going to find a comfortable hotel, have dinner in a proper restaurant and get a good night's sleep,' Roger said. 'We'll continue our journey in the morning. How about the rest of you? Would you like to join us?'

'No can do,' David told them. 'I can't risk not getting to Portsmouth before we sail. We're off to Malta to show the flag.'

Carol supposed that 'showing the flag' must mean making sure that everyone knew the British Navy still ruled the waves.

'And the ladies?' Austin asked.

'No,' Frances said. 'My parents are waiting for me at King's Cross. If I'm not on this train when it finally arrives, they'll panic.'

'Carol?'

'I'm . . . er . . . I'm expected.'

That was true, she supposed, although she didn't imagine her future landlady would worry about her very much. And besides, there was no way she could afford a hotel.

Roger and Austin left them with a 'Cheerio!' and a 'Keep smiling!'

'The wartime spirit lingers on,' David said, and grinned. 'Do either of you want another cup of tea?'

Carol and Frances shook their heads, but Molly said, 'I'm hungry.'

'Oh dear,' David said. 'I think they've run out of just about everything.'

'I have some sandwiches,' Carol said, and reached into her string bag, which was on the floor at her feet.

Molly looked doubtfully at the potted meat sandwiches Denise's mother had made, and shook her head.

'Well, how about these?' Carol suggested, and brought out the packet of biscuits. To her dismay, she saw that somehow they had been reduced to little more than crumbs. 'Let's try again,' she said, and brought out the Hershey bar Denise had cadged from the American soldiers.

Molly smiled, but looked at her mother hesitantly.

'That's all right, dear,' Frances said. 'You may take it.' She thanked Carol and then leaned over to pick up something from the floor. 'This fell out of your bag,' she said, handing Carol a copy of the *Seaside Chronicle*.

'Thank you,' Carol said and reached for it, but Frances had paused and was looking at the photograph on the front page.

'Is this you?' she asked.

'Er . . . yes. Shall I take it?'

'But how extraordinary,' Frances said. She looked at the report that went with the picture, and then at Carol. 'I would never have thought . . . I mean . . . Oh dear, I don't know what to say.'

'It's all right. You don't have to say anything.' Carol took the paper from her.

'I've offended you, haven't I?'

'Not at all.'

'Of course I have, and I'm sorry. I implied that you don't look like the sort of girl who would enter a beauty contest, and I've shown myself up, not you.'

'Shown yourself up?'

'For a fearful snob. I hope you'll forgive me.'

David had been listening to the conversation in tactful silence, but now he stood up and said, 'It's getting fearfully

138

overcrowded in here and I think we should get back to the train. Wait here, Carol. I'll take Frances and Molly along and then I'll come back for you.'

'I can manage my own case,' Carol said.

'I'm sure you can, but I want you to watch my kitbag. It weighs a ton.' He paused as they listened to an announcement on the loudspeaker. 'I think that means us,' he said. 'I'll be back in a jiff.'

He was as good as his word, and as he escorted Carol back along the platform he said, 'So you're Carol Marshall, the girl who won the Glamour Girl contest?'

'Yes. How did you know about that?'

'I live in Seaton Bay. Well, just outside. My parents get the local paper. I thought you looked familiar, but I didn't like to say.'

When they reached their compartment, Frances was smiling. 'The heating's working,' she said. 'That must mean that whatever was wrong with the engine has been sorted out. We'll soon be on our way.'

'Don't count on it,' David said. 'We must have lost a couple of hours at least, and if one train is delayed there's a knock-on effect. We'll probably find ourselves waiting outside stations until the signals clear us. I suggest we try to relax and maybe get some sleep.'

Molly was already asleep, stretched out on the seat beside her mother. David took one of the seats vacated by the two gentlemen, and it didn't seem to take very long before he and Frances were sleeping too. Carol remained awake. What a strange day, she thought. It's been almost like one of those films where a bunch of disparate characters are thrown together by some sort of emergency. And then, when it's all over, they go their separate ways and never see each other again.

The compartment warmed up, and after a while she closed

her eyes. She was aware of the train starting up, travelling for a while and stopping again, sometimes at a station, sometimes in open countryside. She lost count of how many times this happened. When the train finally pulled into King's Cross, she glanced at her wristwatch and saw that the journey from Newcastle had taken more than twelve hours.

Chapter Eleven

Molly woke up looking bewildered. David slung his kitbag over his shoulder then picked her up, offering to carry her. Frances smiled her thanks and said a brief goodbye to Carol before gathering up her belongings and hurrying after him.

By the time Carol got to the carriage door, an elderly couple were already hurrying down the platform towards Frances and Molly with smiles of relief on their faces. Carol paused and watched the greetings. David handed Molly over to her grandfather, then stayed to chat. Neither Frances nor David glanced round as Carol began to walk away. It seemed that the friendship they had formed during the journey was over.

The platforms were crowded and all was noise and confusion as people with large amounts of luggage commandeered porters. Others clutched their suitcases and hurried towards the exit. Mr Palmer had told Carol that she must take a taxi to her lodgings, so she followed the crowd to the taxi rank. She was dismayed when she saw the length of the queue.

Most of the people waiting there had had difficult journeys, and tempers were short, although some tried to remain cheerful. Soon Carol noticed that perfect strangers were offering to share taxis if it meant them getting home sooner. As they compared destinations, Carol, who had no idea whether any of the places they mentioned were near the address Mr Palmer had given her, realised that she would simply have to wait until she was at the head of the queue.

She put her case down, and each time the queue shuffled forward she pushed it forward with her feet. Suddenly she looked down and saw an arm sneaking its way between trousered legs and a gloved hand grasping the handle of her case.

'Stop!' she cried, and grabbing the case herself, she tugged it until the hand let go and disappeared.

Clutching her case, she straightened up and scanned the crowd but couldn't see anyone who looked as though they had just tried to steal it. Shaking with shock she looked around at the people nearest to her. Bored faces ignored her. It was as if she were invisible to all, except one young woman, who actually laughed.

'Green, aren't you?' she said. 'You'll have to learn to keep your wits about you now that you're in London.'

An hour after the train had arrived at King's Cross, Carol was on her way again. From the warm darkness of the taxi she looked out at the brightly lit streets. So many people about, she thought. Where can they be going at this time of night? It must be nearly midnight. Right now the streets at home would be quiet and dismal.

She thought back to what had happened while she was standing in the queue, and wondered what on earth she would have done if the thief had got away with her case. She remembered a romantic novel she'd read set in Victorian times. A poor girl who had arrived in London to seek work had her bag stolen, then met a kindly, well-dressed man who told her he would look after her and help her to find a decent job. Instead he led her into the world of prostitution, from which she was rescued by a noble young clergyman. Not only did he rescue her, he even married her.

She remembered how Denise had poured scorn on the

fine-living young hero. She'd said that once married to that sanctimonious prig, the poor girl would pay for her so-called transgressions for the rest of her life.

By the time the taxi reached the address in Ealing, it was after midnight and Carol was worried that her landlady would have gone to bed and would not answer the door. She looked at the price on the taxi meter and was relieved to see that five shillings would cover both the fare and the tip, just as Mr Palmer had told her it should.

With some trepidation she climbed the steps that led to the front door and rang the bell. There was a long silence. Carol began to panic and wonder where on earth she could go until the next morning when the landlady would be up. Eventually, though, the fanlight lit up and the door opened. Carol was confronted by a grumpy middle-aged woman.

'Miss Marshall?' the woman asked.

'Yes.'

'I was expecting you hours ago. Where have you been?'

The landlady, Mrs Evans, was small and thin and her black dress did nothing for her sallow complexion. A cigarette hung from the corner of her scarlet lips and the smoke caused her eyes to narrow as she looked at Carol.

Carol said, 'I'm so sorry. The train was delayed. I haven't been anywhere. I came straight here.'

Mrs Evans sighed. 'This is well past my bedtime, you know.'

'I'm sorry.' Carol wondered how much longer she would have to go on apologising for something that wasn't really her fault.

'Well, you'd better come in.' Mrs Evans stood back to allow Carol to enter. 'Shall I get Mr Evans to help you up with your case?' she asked.

'Oh, no. I can manage.'

'Good,' the landlady said. She closed the door behind Carol. 'Follow me and I'll take you up to your room.'

Throughout the whole exchange Mrs Evans had never once taken the cigarette from her mouth, and now she hurried ahead of Carol, a small woman in dusty black, wreathed in smoke. She led the way up two flights of stairs. On each landing she paused to switch on a dim light bulb without a shade.

'Here you are,' she said when they reached the top. 'A nice little room, a kitchen and a bathroom. You'll find you have everything you want.'

Then, hardly pausing to draw a smoke-filled breath, she went on to explain that actually only the room was Carol's. The kitchen was a sink and an ancient cooker on the landing that Carol would be sharing with the tenant of the other room on the top floor. The bathroom, one flight down, was used by all the tenants.

Mrs Evans opened the door of the room that was to be Carol's first home in London. Barely giving her time to put her case down, she explained the rules of the house. Mesmerised by the cigarette going up and down at the corner of the landlady's mouth, Carol tried not to stare at her as she ticked off each rule on her fingers: leave the kitchen and the bathroom clean, put the bed linen out each Friday, no visitors of the opposite sex, and no playing of radios or gramophones after ten o'clock at night.

The landlady gave her two keys, one for the front door of the house and another for her room, and then, telling her she would see her tomorrow if she had any questions, she left, closing the door behind her.

Carol looked around her. There was a single bed with a faded bedspread set against the wall under the sloping ceiling. A small table stood pressed up against the opposite wall. Two chairs were tucked neatly at each end of it. Well, at least I must be allowed a female guest, Carol thought, but as she knew no one in London, she doubted whether anyone would be visiting her in the near future.

There was a gas fire with a gas ring resting on a trivet in the hearth, and a meter next to it. A set of shelves hidden by a gingham curtain housed a kettle, one pan, a collection of mismatched crockery, a tin opener and some cutlery. A cupboard set into the wall contained a couple of shelves and a rail with a few coat hangers. Not much of a wardrobe, Carol thought, but then I don't have many clothes.

At the end of the bed there was a dormer window, and Carol walked over to look out across the moonlit rooftops. The moon was silver bright and yet the streets below were dense with shadows. It was a strange combination of light and shade, which exactly matched her mood as she tried to adjust to her new surroundings.

Suddenly Carol realised she was hungry. She fished the sandwiches out of her bag, but what could she drink? Without any real hope, she examined the contents of the shelves more closely, and was surprised to find a crumpled packet of tea. It must have been left by a previous tenant. There was also a sugar bowl with about a teaspoonful of sugar left in the bottom.

She shed her coat, tossing it on the bed, and went to fill the kettle at the sink on the landing. But when she knelt to light the gas ring, she realised that she didn't have any matches. And in any case, she thought, I bet I'll have to put money in the meter.

She resigned herself to drinking water. Nevertheless, it felt strangely adventurous to be sitting in this room, which was now her own, and eating sandwiches from a pretty but cracked china plate that must once have been part of a grand set. She could go to bed when she pleased. There was no Hetty to scold or bully her. She was on her own and she decided she liked it.

When she had finished her sandwiches, she rinsed the plate at the sink and got ready for bed. She wondered fleetingly what she would do about buying essential groceries. It was Sunday and the shops would be closed. But in any case she would have to register her ration book with a grocer and a butcher before she could buy anything. She would ask Mrs Evans's advice about that. But she wouldn't starve; thanks to Ed Palmer, she had money in her purse. She would go out and find a nice little café and treat herself to lunch.

Denise crumpled the letter and hurled it across the room. It landed on her sister's bed. Ruthie looked at her questioningly, but Denise shook her head and glared at her younger sister as if to say, 'Don't you dare pick it up, and don't ask!'

None of the Shaw family went to church, even though they could hear the bells summoning them loud and clear. The girls were allowed to sleep late, but Ruthie usually got up first to make tea and toast and bring it back to their shared bedroom. This morning there had been a letter on the tray.

'For you,' Ruthie had said.

'Post on a Sunday?' Denise hauled herself up and took the letter wonderingly.

'There's no stamp,' Ruthie told her. 'Must have been delivered by hand.'

Denise stared at the writing on the envelope. She didn't recognise it.

'Go on then, open it,' Ruthie said.

There was one page of elegant script.

My dear Denise,
When you read this letter I shall already be in London. It has been such fun knowing you. I have enjoyed myself so much that I could not bring myself to tell

you that I was leaving. It may be selfish, I know, but I wanted to enjoy every moment of our last evening together.

You are such a generous-spirited young woman that I know you will be happy for me when I tell you that I have had the call at last. I am going to Hollywood, and after years of banishment to the shadowy edges of the world of entertainment, I will soon be returning to what I immodestly think of as my rightful place in the motion picture firmament.

I hope you will remember me, dear child. I know I shall never forget you.

Yours very sincerely,
Howard

The hypocritical old goat! Denise thought. Holding my hand over the dinner table, saying that he wished he could take me to the best restaurants in London, telling me that nothing was too good for me, and all the time he must have been packed and ready to go.

She remembered the moment when Howard had left the table to have a private word with the head waiter. After a murmured conversation, something had changed hands. She had seen the waiter slip something into the inside pocket of his dinner jacket, and had assumed that Howard had given him an extravagant tip. Well, perhaps that was the case. But almost certainly he had also been giving the man this letter to deliver – probably in the early hours of the morning, when the restaurant staff would be on their way home.

So he was off to Hollywood, was he? Denise reached for a piece of toast. Well of course she had realised that he wouldn't stay here for ever. And to be honest, she had known that once he had gone, she would probably never see him again. But to leave like this – in such a sneaky way! What was he frightened of? Had he imagined that she would make a fuss and cling to him?

She had known from the start that there was nothing serious going on. In fact if anybody had behaved badly it was herself. She had deliberately flattered Howard in order to get him on Carol's side. And he must have known this. He was far from stupid. In a way they had used each other. So why was she so upset?

As she nibbled half-heartedly at her toast, washing each tiny bite down with a mouthful of tea, she suddenly realised that she had actually begun to care for Howard Napier, and, if not broken-hearted, she was more than ordinarily upset that she would never see him again.

Carol was early for lunch so she was able to get a table by the window. She was surprised how quickly the café filled up. From the way some of the diners were greeted by the waitresses, she guessed them to be regulars. In Seaton Bay, somebody new like herself would have attracted attention. Here, no one took any notice of her at all. She imagined that was because there were so many new faces in London. So many people passing through.

She opened the menu card and saw that one side was labelled *À la carte* and the other *Table d'hôte*. It didn't take her long to work out that *À la carte* listed a choice of individually priced dishes, while *Table d'hôte* offered three courses of limited choice at a fixed price. She settled for the *Table d'hôte*.

After brown Windsor soup, lamb cutlets and marmalade pudding, Carol felt as though she need not eat anything else for at least a week. She noticed there was a queue of people waiting for tables, so reluctantly she left the pleasant atmosphere of the restaurant and went out into the street.

She had no idea what to do for the rest of the day. Mr

Palmer had told her that he would be in touch with her about starting work on the film, but he hadn't said when that would be. When she had boarded the train yesterday, she had foolishly believed that her new life was going to begin immediately. But here she was in London with no idea how to occupy herself until she heard from Mr Palmer.

The sun was shining and the air was warm; much warmer than it had been at home. She walked aimlessly for a while, taking in the sights and the sounds, but, worried that she might get lost in these unfamiliar streets, reluctantly she returned to her digs.

Chapter Twelve

When she reached the top landing, she saw that the door to the other room on that floor was open, and a voice called out, 'Hi! Is that you, Carol? Come in.'

Wonderingly Carol stood in the doorway and looked into a room that was pretty much the mirror image of her own. A girl not much older than herself was sitting at the table with one foot propped up on the other chair as she painted her toenails.

'Hi, I'm Patti Lenore.' She looked up at Carol hopefully. 'Maybe you've heard of me?'

Carol was taken aback. 'I'm sorry. I haven't.'

'Ah, well. I thought at least Ed might have told you about me.'

'Mr Palmer?'

'That's the man. But come on in and close the door. The kettle's boiling,' she nodded in the direction of the gas ring, 'and you'll find everything you need to make a pot of tea in the little cupboard there.' She saw Carol hesitate and said, 'You don't mind, do you? It's just that I don't want to walk about until the nail varnish is dry.'

'Oh, of course. I don't mind at all.'

'While you're about it, will you fish six pennies out of that jam jar and feed the meter? If you light the fire we can have some toast.'

'That's kind of you, but I couldn't eat anything. I've just had lunch.'

'Lunch? Oh, dear, I haven't had breakfast yet. But at any rate have a cup of tea with me, will you?'

'I'd love to.'

'Good. Be a dear and make me a slice of toast. The toasting fork's hanging by the fireplace.'

Carol was amused at the way Patti was giving orders, but she didn't mind at all. The girl was cheerful and friendly and would, she thought, make an interesting neighbour. While she busied herself with the tea and toast, she kept glancing at Patti surreptitiously. She saw a very pretty girl with auburn hair and pale skin. When she looked up and smiled, Carol saw she had startlingly blue eyes.

Patti was wearing a light-blue silk robe patterned with exotic-looking flowers. Carol thought it might be a kimono. It was too big for her and she had wrapped it tightly around her slim and shapely body before securing it with a large sash of the same material. When she had finished painting her toenails, she screwed the top back on the little bottle of nail varnish, lifted both feet gracefully on to the chair and wiggled her toes about.

'What do you think of the colour?' she asked.

'I like it.'

'It's crimson. I usually wear pillar-box red, but I thought I'd try to be more subtle.'

Carol returned her attention to the slice of bread on the toasting fork.

'Golly, I'm famished!' Patti said. 'Is everything nearly ready?'

'Just about.'

'If you get me that cushion from the bed, I'll rest my feet on that and you can have this chair.'

Carol got the cushion and wondered how she had so

quickly become a sort of servant to this girl she had only just met.

As they drank their tea, Patti devoured two slices of toast as if she had indeed been starving. Carol noticed that her fingernails were painted the same shade as her toenails but with a white half-moon left at the base and a sliver of white at the tip. That must have taken her ages, Carol thought. I could never do that.

Patti had noticed her glance. 'Like them, do you?' She held out one hand for Carol to admire. 'I'll do yours for you if you like. Have you got any nail polish?'

'No. But I'll get some.'

'Yes, I suppose you'll have quite a bit of shopping to do. Ed asked me to go with you and advise you.'

'How do you know Mr Palmer?' Carol asked.

Patti shook her head. 'Didn't he tell you?'

'Tell me what?'

'That he would find you digs near someone who would look after you?'

Carol frowned as she tried to remember exactly what he had told her. 'He just said he would arrange everything and that I was not to worry.'

'Right. He arranged things for me when I first came up to London.'

'Did he?'

'Of course. He's my agent too, you know.'

'Agent?'

'Yes. Oh Lord, you didn't realise, did you? He played the same trick on me.'

Carol was entirely out of her depth. 'I wish you would explain things,' she said.

'Ed Palmer found me singing in a dance hall in Sheffield. I was only fifteen, but I was well developed, if you know what I mean, so I looked older. He told me he could get me work as a cabaret artiste in London but if I was under twenty-one my father had to sign some papers. Well, my father was dead, poor old soul. He was gassed in the first war and lingered on long enough to marry his childhood sweetheart and father me. He died before my first birthday.'

Carol thought of her own father. Albert Marshall had also been gassed in the war, and although he had survived he had never been truly fit since. 'I'm sorry,' she told Patti sympathetically.

'No need. I have no memories of him whatsoever and my mother and I got along fine. She was thrilled when Ed Palmer promised us the big time. She signed whatever papers he put before her.'

'Didn't your mother worry about you coming up to London at that age?'

Patti grinned. 'Not at all. You see, she came with me.'

'How marvellous for you.'

'Do you think so? I mean, I loved her and all that, but it did cramp my style having her coming round with me and whisking me off home as soon as the show was over. Was I glad a couple of years ago when she fell for that American airman!'

Carol's head was spinning. 'Are you saying she married an American?'

'Yes. He's years younger than she is but he didn't seem to care. And now she's happily settled in Texas. They wanted me to go with them, but I refused point blank. So Ed promised to keep an eye on me, and he has. Tell me, what did he say to your parents?'

'I don't know. I wasn't there. But I thought the papers only concerned a part in a film.'

'Not if I know Mr Ed Palmer. If he suspects he's on to a good thing, he'll have tied you to him for as long as you both shall live!'

'Should I worry?'

'Probably not. He's a good agent. Even if I'm not exactly rich and famous, he's kept the work coming along. And I've no reason to believe he's swindled me, like some do.' Patti had finished eating her toast. She put her cup and saucer on her plate and pushed it aside. 'I'm not working tonight,' she said. 'Would you like to go to the flicks?'

'Now?'

'Well, first we could hop on a bus and I'll show you some of the sights, and then we'll go to the cinema to see *The Picture of Dorian Gray*. Sounds good.'

'I know. I've read the book.'

'Will that spoil it for you? I mean, you'll know what's going to happen.'

'No. I'd love to see it. Especially what happens to the picture in the attic.'

Patti held up a hand, palm outwards. 'Stop right there,' she said. 'Don't tell me any more or you'll spoil it for *me*.'

'Sorry. I didn't think.'

'Don't look so crestfallen. To make up for it, you can wash the dishes while I get dressed.'

Patti stood up, and Carol saw for the first time how tall she was. She undid her sash and shrugged out of her robe. It fell to the floor, revealing that she was completely naked. Carol looked away hastily.

'Have I shocked you?' Patti said. 'I'm sorry. It's just that working in the nightclubs you get used to sharing a crowded dressing room with other girls frantically changing costumes between their acts. Of course some of the costumes are not much more than a G-string and a bunch of feathers with a couple of little spangly stars stuck over your nipples. It's no use being shy if you're in this game.'

Carol didn't think she could ever get used to that, and she hoped she wouldn't have to. She collected the dishes and walked over to the door.

'That's right,' Patti said. 'You've found the sink, have you? I think I've fed the meter enough to get some hot water from the geyser. You'll find a bit of soap on the shelf under the bench. And here's a tea towel.'

It didn't take Carol long to wash and dry one plate and two cups and saucers, but she hesitated about going back into Patti's room so soon. She left everything on the bench and went into her own room to finish unpacking her case. Then she went down one flight of stairs to the bathroom. Earlier today she had been dismayed to find how dark and gloomy it was, with a monstrous geyser, a huge old claw-footed bath and a pulley hanging over it on which some washing was hanging to dry.

When she went up again, Patti was fully dressed and waiting for her on the landing. 'There you are,' she said. 'I've put the dishes away. Let's go.'

Patti insisted that they sit on the upper deck of the bus so that Carol could have a good view. But rather than the imposing old buildings and the fashionable shops, Carol's attention was caught by the amount of bomb damage there was. In the midst of grand terraces there would suddenly be a roped-off area of gaping holes with mountains of rubble filling the former cellars. A profusion of plants had taken root in the ruins.

'They call that fireweed,' Patti said, pointing to the tall reddish-pink flowers that grew in abundance. 'It'll take a while to put things right,' she said. 'Still, we gave as good as we got, didn't we? I mean, I've seen some of those films of German cities taken from above.'

Taken by people like Steve, Carol thought. Men who had helped win the war by pinpointing the targets for British bombers and who then had to fly over the ruins to record what they had done. She wondered how Steve felt about this. She would have liked to have asked him, but she didn't suppose she would ever get the chance now. She realised it was more than likely that she would never see him again.

No matter that the air had been spring-like, Carol suddenly felt cold, and she was glad when Patti announced that they were nearly there and should get off the bus.

'Blast it!' Patti said as they approached the cinema and saw that there was a queue. 'We queue for everything these days, and look how obedient everyone is. It's not a bit like this in France, where everybody just huddles round and it's a bit of a free-for-all.'

'Have you been to France?' Carol asked.

'Bless you, no. And that's a sore point.'

Patti's face suddenly clouded, and Carol wasn't sure what she should say.

'I may tell you about that one day, but I know a bit about it because I was going out with a Frenchman for a while; one of the Free French Army. He went back with General de Gaulle. I mean, that was the point of them, wasn't it?'

Carol wondered if the sore point was something to do with the man going back to France without her.

Patti insisted on buying the tickets. 'You can treat me when you start earning.'

Once they had taken their seats in the warm, dark auditorium, Carol thought she could be at home again and sitting next to her old friend Denise rather than this strange but exciting creature who was like no one she had ever met before.

The film was amazing: George Sanders as sophisticated as ever as Lord Henry Wotton, and Hurd Hatfield handsome as the corrupt young man Dorian Gray who wants to remain young and good-looking for all eternity so sells his soul in order for a portrait to age instead of him.

The audience gasped at the Technicolor film inserts showing the portrait in various stages of decay.

'They're clever these days, aren't they?' Patti said as they made their way out of the cinema. 'You must be excited that you're going to be part of it.'

'I am. But remember, I'm going to have a very small part. I may not even get another one.'

'Don't be silly! With those looks. No wonder Ed has signed you up. One day you could make him a fortune. But talking of looks, you can see why he did it, can't you? Dorian Gray.'

'Not really. Remember, without his soul he couldn't enjoy the life the bargain had given him.'

They had reached the well-lit foyer and Patti's eyes widened in mock horror. 'For goodness' sake, Carol, you're not going to moralise, are you?'

'No . . . it's just that was the meaning of the story.'

'Relax, sweetie. I know that. And you're quite right. It's just that the idea of growing old and ugly is terrifying.'

Carol thought of Alice Grayson, who had once been young and beautiful. What had it meant to her to be so horribly scarred in the car accident that had ended her career? What did she regret most? The loss of her beauty? Her career? Or did she regret the secret affair with the man who had been driving the car?

'Are you tired?' Patti asked.

'No, why do you ask?'

'You went quiet for a moment.'

'I was just thinking about what you said.'

'Sorry, I didn't mean to be a wet blanket.' Patti led the way out on to the crowded pavement. 'Now,' she said, 'there's a marvellous little Italian restaurant in Soho, just a short walk from here. The food is great and it's *the* place to be seen. Do you like spaghetti?'

'I don't know. I've never had it – well, only the tinned sort.'

'Ugh! There's no comparison. Carol, my sweet, it looks as though I'm going to have to educate your taste buds as well as help you buy some decent clothes. Come with me.'

Patti led the way and soon turned in to a narrow side street. Carol followed bemusedly. Until this moment she hadn't realised that there was anything wrong with her clothes. They were certainly more stylish than many to be obtained in Seaton Bay. But this was London, a whole new world, and it seemed she had a lot to learn.

The restaurant was crowded and they had to queue while they waited for a table. Patti seemed to know a lot of people there, and she waved and laughed and talked animatedly. She didn't introduce Carol to any of them, but that didn't matter. Carol was quite happy to stand quietly by and observe everything and everyone.

The framed photographs on the walls were views of places in Italy such as Mount Vesuvius, the Bay of Naples and the Colosseum in Rome. Candles on each table dripped wax down on to their holders, squat wine bottles in straw flasks. Nets decorated with green glass fishing floats and large seashells hung from the ceiling. And somewhere there must have been a gramophone, because evocative Italian music competed with the rising chatter of the diners. Carol breathed in the atmosphere of the place – and loved it.

She observed the people at the tables. All were fashionably dressed, and there were several men and women in uniform. She wondered about their lives.

'And who is this young lady?'

A small, dark-haired, good-looking man had appeared beside them.

'Oh, hello, Mario,' Patti said. 'This is Carol. She's new in town.'

To Carol's alarm, Mario reached for her hand and brought it to his lips, all the time looking into her eyes. 'I'm delighted to meet you, Carol. And why have you come to London?'

'She's got a part in a film,' Patti answered for her.

'I am not surprised. She is very beautiful. As, of course, are you,' he added after a pause during which Patti's eyes narrowed and her mouth thinned. Mario turned to look around the room. 'The guests on the table over there are just about to leave,' he said. 'I shall make sure you get it.' Then, with a slight bow, he took his leave.

'Slimy little toad,' Patti said as soon as he was out of earshot. 'He owns the place, but this . . .' she raised one arm to indicate the photographs on the wall, the nets hanging from the ceiling and the candles in the wine bottles, 'is all sham. He isn't even an Italian; he was born and bred in Southend.'

Carol wondered why Patti came here if she thought so little of the proprietor, but then she remembered that she had said it was 'the place to be seen'. And that was obviously important.

Very soon after that, a waiter ushered them to the vacant table and Patti revealed to Carol the wonders of the menu. 'If I were you, I'd go for the bolognese,' she said. 'It's a good start if you've never eaten Italian before.'

As well as their meals, the waiter brought a bottle of wine.

'I didn't order this,' Patti said.

'With the compliments of Mario,' the waiter said as he proceeded to remove the cork. 'In honour of our new guest.'

Patti smiled brilliantly, but Carol realised the older girl was annoyed. She's jealous, Carol thought. She likes to be the centre of attention and doesn't take kindly to anyone else stealing the limelight.

Carol enjoyed her first Italian meal and her one glass of wine. Patti kept filling her own glass until she had consumed the rest of the bottle. A dish of sugared almonds appeared with the coffee, and the bill arrived on a little silver salver.

'They want us to go,' Patti said as she reached for the bill. 'Look, there are still people waiting for tables.'

Carol opened her handbag and reached for her purse.

'Put that away,' Patti said. 'I'm paying.'

'No, I can't let you. At least let me pay half.'

But Patti wouldn't have it, and Carol had no option but to give in gracefully. As they took their leave, Mario escorted them to the door. Patti thanked him for the wine and praised the food enthusiastically. You would never have thought that earlier she had spoken of him in such a derogatory manner.

Carol wondered how they would get back to their lodgings. Then she saw that, unlike at home at this time of the night, the buses were still running, and she began to look up at the destination boards as they drove by.

'Don't worry about that,' Patti said. 'We'll get a taxi.'

Plenty of cabs passed them, but all were taken. Then Patti saw one approaching that had its 'For Hire' sign lit. 'Quick!' she said and dashed to the kerb waving both arms frantically.

The cab began to slow down and Patti turned to grin at Carol triumphantly. But as she did so, she went over on one of her ankles and would have fallen into the road if Carol had not grabbed her. Completely untroubled, she laughed as she almost fell into the cab. She's drunk, Carol thought as she followed her in.

Patti gave the driver the address, then leaned towards Carol and said, 'I know what you're thinking. But I'm not drunk, I'm only a little tipsy, and you really will have to learn to ease up a little.'

Once home, Patti insisted on paying the taxi fare. 'Just go ahead and get the door open,' she said. 'You go on up,' she told Carol when they were inside. 'I have to make a telephone call.'

Patti fed a couple of coins into the telephone box attached to the wall, then dialled a number. After a slight pause she pushed button A, the coins dropped and she began to talk. She stopped when she saw that Carol was still standing there, put one hand over the receiver and said, 'I told you. Go on up. I'll see you tomorrow.'

As Carol began to climb the stairs, she heard Patti say, 'Yes, of course I have. I made sure your little protégée had a good time, and you'll be pleased to know I've got some change.'

Not wishing to eavesdrop, Carol hurried up to the top floor and into her own room. She had assumed that she and Patti might have a cup of tea together and a gossip as she and Denise would have done after a night out. And there was much she would have liked to talk about: the film they had seen, the restaurant, the sort of people who dined there. But once they had got out of the taxi, their evening out had ended so abruptly that she felt deflated. She looked at the empty shelves and rued the fact that she couldn't even make herself a cup of cocoa.

The bed was comfortable enough, but she couldn't sleep. For the first time since Denise had encouraged her to enter the Glamour Girl competition, Carol realised the full significance of what she had done.

Chapter Thirteen

June 1946

Dear Denise,
Patti and I went to the Victory Parade. She said the Mall would be the best place to go. That's the avenue that leads to Buckingham Palace. We actually went the night before and spent the whole night on the pavement. I got there first and kept a place for Patti, who came along after she had finished work at her club, the Blue Parrot.

Honestly, Denise, it was as if all the people in England had come to a party. People were laughing and singing and dancing and kissing just about everybody in sight. And it went on all night. Nobody slept.

Just after ten in the morning the royal family left Buckingham Palace. The King, the Queen and the two princesses were in a state landau and they were accompanied by the Household Cavalry. Everybody went wild. Then when the armed forces procession came down the Mall to the place where they had to salute the King, the crowd went wild again. You would have loved it.

By the time the march-past had finished, Patti said she might as well go straight to the club and have a rest before starting work. She advised me to get a taxi. Well, there was no chance of that. Those that did make their way through the crowds were full and I even saw one with people sitting on the roof giving the crowds the royal wave as they went by.

Everyone seemed to be going in one direction and it was easier for me to go along with them. Eventually I found myself down by the river waiting for the firework display. When the first lot went off, hundreds of sleeping birds woke up and flew up into the air. The poor things must have thought the war had started all over again. Sometimes it's hard to believe that it ended last year. And particularly today, with all the men and women in uniform in town.

I left the embankment before the end of the display and was lucky enough to get to the underground before it became swamped. As soon as I got back to my room I made myself a cup of cocoa and started writing this letter to you.

Carol paused and looked down at the last words she had written. When Denise had written to her, she'd been sparing with personal details. Carol hoped her old friend wasn't unhappy about something, but knowing how prickly Denise could be, she didn't like to ask. So she bent her head again, and added her love before scrawling her signature.

She hadn't been entirely honest, because this wasn't the first letter she had written after she had got home. The first had been to Muriel, but it wasn't nearly as long as the letter to Denise. It was a duty letter. Carol found it very difficult to write to her oldest friend. Not just because their lives were so different, but also because Muriel was Steve's sister, and when Carol thought of Muriel, she could not help but think of Steve.

Steve, who would be getting married later this month . . .

Carol folded her letter to Denise and put it in an envelope. She knew that neither of the letters was entirely satisfactory, for in neither of them had she mentioned what her friends would surely want to know. What it was like to be a film actress. But she couldn't tell them. In the weeks since she had left home, she had not once set foot in the film studios.

Ed Palmer called by now and then to see if she needed any money, and Patti had taken her to an exclusive second-hand clothes shop patronised by singers, actresses and dancers, and any young woman who was happy to wear garments cast off by the rich. The clothes were the kind that none of them would be able to afford new, and even better, they did not require clothing coupons.

So here she was with a cupboard full of glamorous clothes and not the first idea of when she was actually going to wear them or when she was going to start work.

During the day, she had taken to exploring London, and at night she would go to the pictures. Once she had treated herself to a theatre ticket and had gone to see *Murder on the Nile* at the Ambassadors. The play was by Agatha Christie, based on her own novel, *Death on the Nile*, and was a complicated whodunnit mystery set on a Nile steamer. Carol loved it, even though the reviews in the newspapers had said it was not Mrs Christie's best work.

She ought to have been enjoying herself. But with no firm news of when she was going to start work, she began to wonder if the Glamour Girl competition had been a publicity stunt after all, and that after another few weeks in London the studios would find some reason to send her home.

She looked in her purse and made sure she had enough small change to buy some postage stamps from the machine in the wall outside the post office. Still feeling restless, she went out to post the letters straight away. When she returned, she got ready for bed. There was nothing else to do.

Steve caught the last train from King's Cross and prepared himself for a sleepless night. Every seat in every compartment was taken, and people were standing in the corridors. It was to be hoped that many of those who had been in London for the day would leave the train at places like Peterborough or Doncaster so that he could find a seat.

On the train, the party atmosphere was in full swing. Perfect strangers, people who had never met before and would probably never see each other again, were laughing and joking like old friends. It was many months now since the war had ended, and it had taken all this time to organise this day of celebration. Anyone who could be there had converged on the capital that day.

Steve had come not simply for the celebrations but because he wanted to take photographs — to document what would be an historic event. He had asked for the day off work, and Mr Latham had understood.

'I'll manage with young Peter,' he'd said. 'If I were younger I would be coming with you.'

Kay had not been so understanding. With only a week to go before the wedding, she and her mother had thought it completely irresponsible of Steve to absent himself like this. His own mother had sided with Kay and Mrs Blanchard, but luckily both his father and Kay's understood. 'Wise not to let her keep you on too tight a leash,' his father had said.

Muriel had wanted to come with him.

'Sorry, infant,' he told her, 'but the streets will be crowded as they've never been before. London on Victory Day will be no place for a girl on her own.'

'But I won't be on my own, I'll be with you.'

'And if you are, I'll have to spend the entire day looking

after you. I won't be able to take a single decent photograph.'

'I can look after myself.'

'Even if that's true, as your big brother I would think it my duty to keep an eye on you, and bang would go my chance to get some terrific shots.'

'What about my chance of writing a report for the paper?'

'You're not a reporter. You're just an office junior who sometimes takes copy.'

'Thanks for reminding me! But let me tell you, I intend to be a proper reporter as soon as possible.'

'I'm sorry, Muriel, that was crass of me, but even if you did write a report of the day, the paper wouldn't print it. They'll be taking a piece from an agency.'

Muriel had argued that that didn't matter and that she didn't expect the paper to print her report. She just wanted to practise her style. But Steve had been adamant and Muriel had been in the sulks ever since.

He'd felt guilty about it at first, but from the moment he had boarded the night train to London, he had forgotten all about Muriel, all about the wedding, and even all about Kay as he thought about the best way to get the shots he wanted. In the event, nothing had gone the way he had planned it. He'd had to work in a completely impromptu manner and hope that what he was getting was good. He couldn't wait to get home and into the darkroom.

When the train reached York in the cool hours of the morning, Steve managed to grab a seat, and the motion of the train sent him into a weary half-sleep. At Newcastle he changed trains for the branch line, and arrived at Seaton Bay as the bells were summoning the faithful to church. It crossed his mind that Kay and her mother would be there, but he went straight to Latham's Studios. Pausing only to make a cup of strong tea in the little kitchen, he headed for the darkroom.

Inside an hour he had developed the films and was able to examine the negatives. He began to feel excited. Within another hour he began to print up and his excitement grew. The prints were terrific.

There were shots of various sections of the parade itself, with regimented troops contrasting sharply with the unruly crowd. There were shots of the crowd with their smiles and their flags, the old and the young: children in their parents' arms, some perched on their fathers' shoulders; and old soldiers in wheelchairs, pushed to the front and wearing their medals proudly.

Steve knew that he wouldn't have been the only photographer to take shots of lads climbing the lamp posts and people leaning out of the windows of tall buildings at every vantage point. He'd talked his way into one of those buildings himself to get a view from above.

But of all the pictures he'd taken that day, two of them stood out. One had been taken in a side street, where half a dozen little boys who had no chance at all of seeing the parade had staged a parade of their own. Their clothes were ragged and ill-fitting, but five of them held themselves erect as they marched past with pretend guns over their shoulders and saluted the other lad, who was standing on an upturned box returning their salute as proudly as King George himself.

The other picture was not so obviously appealing, but it had caught Steve at the right moment and had made him smile. A couple of young men and one young woman were sitting precariously on the top of a taxi, each giving the distinctive royal wave with a circling forearm and an elegantly postured hand.

Leaving his prints clipped up on a line in the darkroom,

Steve went home and, ignoring his mother's request that he should join them for lunch, went to bed.

On Monday, Steve was supposed to leave work early and meet Kay at the house that would soon be their home, but when he arrived, there was no sign of life behind the uncurtained windows and the door was locked. He hung around for half an hour before giving up and going to her parents' house.

Mrs Blanchard answered the door. She looked surprised. 'Where's Kay?' she asked. She didn't invite him in. He was still out of favour because of his trip to London

'That's what I'd like to know,' he said. 'I've been waiting at the house.'

'Oh dear. You were supposed to meet at Rutherford's to choose some curtain material.' Mrs Blanchard assumed a worried frown. 'I hope poor Kay isn't still waiting for you.'

'I'll get along there straight away,' Steve said.

As he hurried towards town, he tried to remember exactly what Kay had said. Something about the windows in the room she called the lounge. Once or twice lately, in the sweetest way possible, she had accused him of not listening to her, and to his shame she was probably right.

He found her alone in the drapery department. There were no other customers and no assistants in sight. She was looking intently at some sample books on the counter. He went to join her.

'I'm sorry, Kay,' he said. 'I got it wrong. I went to the house.'

'Well at least you're here now.' Kay tried her best to smile, but Steve could sense her underlying displeasure.

'Am I forgiven?' he asked.

'I suppose so.'

If by her attitude she had intended to make him feel guilty, she had succeeded. She turned to look at the fabrics again, and brightened up immediately. 'What do you think of this one?'

Steve wasn't sure what he thought about it, but he was saved from answering when a young assistant approached with a bale of cloth.

'Is this the one you wanted, madam?' she asked. She put the bale down on the counter and unrolled it a little.

Kay looked at it and frowned. 'It doesn't look quite the same, does it? I mean, it's different from the sample in the pattern book.'

'I know,' the girl said. 'The samples fade a little.'

'Still, I think I like it. What do you think, Steve?'

Steve looked down at the cloth stretched out along the counter. He saw clusters of roses in shades of pink with dark green leaves scattered across a cream background.

'A bit chintzy, isn't it?' he asked.

'Exactly. It will look perfect with the leaded windows.'

Kay's happy expression told him that he'd said the right thing. He thanked his lucky stars that he hadn't immediately gone on to give her his opinion of it.

She opened her bag, which had been lying on the counter, and took out a sheet of paper covered in measurements and diagrams. She seemed to forget all about Steve as she took the girl through the instructions line by line.

Steve felt redundant. He didn't know what to do with himself, so he wandered over to the windows that looked out over the main thoroughfare towards St Paul's church. In five days' time he would be getting married there, and after the reception at the Swan, he and Kay would be heading off for their honeymoon in a hotel in Berwick. Berwick had been chosen because it was easy to get there by train.

Suddenly Kay linked her arm through his.

'What are you thinking, darling?' she asked.

Steve summoned up some enthusiasm. He turned to her and dropped a kiss on her forehead. 'I was thinking that it won't be long now before you will be Mrs Douglas.'

'Were you? How sweet. Now, we'd better go home. You're invited for tea because my father wants to talk to you about taxis and how we're going to get everybody to the Swan.'

Not wanting to make her unhappy, Steve made an attempt to get involved. 'Are you quite happy with your curtain arrangements?'

'Yes. They're going to start making them tomorrow and they'll come to the house and hang them while we're away. My mother will see to all that. She'll have our new home completely ready for us.'

The shop was closing by the time Steve and Kay left. On her way to the staff cloakroom, Denise saw them going towards the lift. Kay's smile was self-satisfied to the point of being smug. Denise was overcome with fury.

Thank goodness Carol isn't here, she thought. With her exciting new life in London, she'll be able to forget all about stupid Steve Douglas. Stupid in Denise's mind not only because he didn't realise what a wonderful girl Carol was but also because he couldn't see what a shallow, manipulating bitch Kay Blanchard was.

The wedding would be the talk of the town. People with nothing better to do would stand on the pavement outside the lychgate and wait for the newly married couple to come out and have their pictures taken. And those pictures would be all over the local paper – naturally, seeing as Kay's father was the editor.

Often when there was a wedding at the church opposite, the staff of Rutherford's would gather at the large windows on the first floor and watch the bride and groom emerge and the people throwing confetti. Well, I certainly won't be

170

watching, Denise thought. And who wants to get married anyway?

On her way home, she saw Muriel coming out of the church. Her instinct was to hurry by, pretending she hadn't seen her. But Muriel called her name and Denise stopped unwillingly. At first their conversation was stilted.

'Hello, Denise.'

'Hi, Muriel.'

'Going somewhere nice?'

'Home. I've been at work all day.'

'Oh yes, of course.'

Muriel looked so miserable that Denise couldn't help saying, 'And you, have you been having fun?'

'Having fun? In church? Oh, you're joking. No, I'm not having any fun at all. I was sent to the church to discuss the flower arrangements for the wedding with Mrs Campbell. You know she always does the flowers. In fact she'd probably kill anyone else who dared to arrange so much as a bunch of daisies.'

'I didn't know. I haven't set foot inside St Paul's since I left school, when they used to take us along to the harvest festival and the carol service. So I'll take your word for it.'

'Strange when you live so near,' Muriel said.

'It's not strange at all. Some folk go to church and some don't.'

'Denise, please don't get snappy with me. I was only trying to make conversation.'

To Denise's consternation, Muriel looked as though she was about to burst into tears. 'Sorry. I didn't mean to be snappy. Just put it down to the fact that I'm a first-rate bitch and I've had a terrible day.'

'Have you?' Muriel sounded surprised. It was as if she couldn't imagine anyone but herself having anything to be miserable about.

'Yes, I have, and I really don't want to stand here discussing it.'

'Oh, sorry. I'd better go now.'

'Muriel, wait! I didn't mean that I wanted you to go. Look, are you going anywhere in particular?'

'Just home for tea.'

'Could you phone them and tell them you're not coming?' Denise indicated the telephone box outside the post office.

'My mother would want to know why.'

'Tell her you've met a friend who has invited you to tea at her house.'

'Are you inviting me to tea?'

'What does it sound like?'

'But . . . but I thought you didn't like me very much.'

'You thought right. No – don't go. I thought I didn't like you, but I realise now that it was because I was jealous. I wanted Carol to myself and you had been her friend since you were kids. Even when the three of us went out together, you always acted as if I wasn't there.'

'I was jealous too. Once Carol started work, she and I drifted apart.'

'That's natural. But we can't stand here talking. Go and phone your mother and tell her you're going out for tea.'

As Muriel hurried along to the telephone box, Denise wondered what on earth had come over her. Why had she invited that stuck-up Muriel Douglas to tea? She supposed she'd felt sorry for her when she'd seen how down-hearted the girl looked. And she was pretty fed up herself. She'd told Muriel that she'd had a dreadful day. In fact it hadn't been much worse than all the days that went before it.

Since Carol had left town, she hadn't been out very much except to take Ruthie to the pictures. And much as she loved her younger sister, she needed someone more her own age to have a good chinwag with and a laugh or two. Was Muriel the sort of girl she could have a laugh with?

Denise cursed the spontaneous impulse that had prompted her to invite the girl to tea. Still, it was too late now to change her mind. It was only when she saw Muriel coming towards her smiling tentatively that she wondered what a girl from Muriel's posh background would make of life in Garden Square.

To Denise's surprise, Ruthie and Muriel got along like a house on fire. Her little sister didn't seem to notice the posh way that Muriel talked, or if she did, she didn't care. It certainly didn't occur to her to feel inferior. While Denise helped her mother in the kitchen, she could hear the two of them talking about the secretarial college that Muriel had attended. Ruthie wanted to know exactly what was taught there and if it cost a lot to get in.

More than we can afford, Denise thought to herself, and then it came to her that if Ruthie wanted to go on with her education and make something of herself, a way must be found to make it possible. She would have to find out if there were any scholarships, and if there weren't, she would have to raise the money somehow. Even if it meant taking on cleaning jobs in offices at night.

After they had eaten, Denise suggested that they should go to the pictures, and they looked at the cinema listings in the local paper. There were three cinemas in town, and while they were trying to make up their minds, Ruthie said, 'I know which film I want to see.'

'Who said you were coming?'

'I'm sorry,' Muriel said. 'I asked Ruthie if she'd like to come with us. I'll pay.'

'There's no need for that,' Denise retorted. 'I can afford to take my little sister to the pictures.'

They glared at each other for a moment, and then Denise said, 'I guess I've got to stop this.'

'Stop what?'

'Behaving like a big kid and taking offence where none was offered.'

Muriel smiled. 'You always did, you know.'

Denise didn't reply while she thought about what Muriel had said, and then she shrugged and smiled and said, 'I guess I did.'

'So what are we going to see?' Ruthie asked.

'I'm sorry, pet,' Denise said. 'I can't take you. It's a week night. You've got school tomorrow.'

Ruthie looked crestfallen, but she had an unexpected champion. 'Oh, go on,' Mrs Shaw said. 'Give the lass a treat. One late night won't hurt. Take her along with you and let there be no argument. I'll pay for her ticket.'

Mr Shaw, who had sat silently with a mug of tea throughout this exchange, suddenly put the mug down and, reaching in his pocket, threw a handful of coins on the table. 'This should pay for an ice cream each. It's worth it if it buys your ma and me a couple of hours' peace and quiet.'

'All right, I know when I'm beaten,' Denise said. 'Let's look at the paper.'

'It's all right, I've already chosen,' Ruthie said.

Denise looked at the listing Ruthie was pointing to. 'Oh no, not that.'

'Please, please, please. It's my treat, Mam said so.'

'But that film is utter rubbish,' Denise said.

'So much so that it might be funny, don't you think?' Muriel asked.

'It's a horror movie. Ruthie's not sixteen. They won't let her in.'

'Yes they will, with a responsible adult, and I'll have two of you.'

'You'll have nightmares.'

'No I won't. I listen to *Appointment with Fear* on the wireless and I haven't had a nightmare yet. Not even when they did "The Monkey's Paw"!'

'That's true,' Denise said. 'But a film might be more frightening.'

'It can't be as frightening as the pictures you make in your head when you listen to a spooky story,' Ruthie said.

Denise stared at her sister in astonishment. 'You're absolutely right,' she said. 'Go and get your coat on. We'll have to get a move on if we don't want to miss the beginning.'

And so, very much against her will, Denise set off with Muriel and Ruthie to see *She-Wolf of London: A Woman Whose Hatred Knew No Bounds*.

Chapter Fourteen

'Do you think they've forgotten about me?' Carol asked.

They were in Carol's room, where Patti had been helping her to get dressed.

'What makes you think that?'

'Well, it's late, isn't it? I mean, Mr Palmer told me to be ready by seven.'

'It's only ten past. And do relax, or you'll break out in a sweat and ruin your dress. Stop walking about and sit down – but carefully, you don't want to get all creased.'

Carol sat down, and Patti stood back and looked at her critically, then frowned and shook her head.

'What is it?' Carol asked, trying to stop a rising tide of panic.

'You know, I'm not so sure we should have swept your hair up. You look better with a pageboy. Well, it's too late now. I haven't time to start all over again. I'll have to go to work soon. I'll just add a little finishing touch. Don't go away.'

Patti shot out of the room, and reappeared a moment later carrying a white artificial flower on a hairpin.

'It's a silk gardenia,' she said. 'Sit still.' She slipped the flower into Carol's hair high above one ear and just below the burst of pin curls on the crown of her head. 'There, that looks just about right. I only wish you had some earrings to match the spray in the centre of the flower. Something glittery.'

'I haven't had my ears pierced.'

'There are always clip-ons. I suppose I'll have to take you shopping again.' She sounded weary.

'I'm sorry I'm such a bother to you,' Carol said.

Patti looked at her in surprise. 'What's the matter with you?'

'Nothing's the matter with me. It's you.'

'Me? I've done everything I can to help you.'

'I know, and I'm grateful, but sometimes you make me feel I'm just a nuisance.'

'Do I?'

'Mmm.'

'Well, I'm sorry. Now don't let's have a quarrel. Ed won't want to have a sulky child turn up at the party. This is an important night for you, you know. You'll be meeting people who can forward your career.'

'I haven't got a career. I've been here for weeks now and I've been nowhere near a film studio. I'm beginning to think the Glamour Girl competition was all a charade.'

Patti shook her head. 'Take my word for it, even if it was just for publicity and they write you out of the film, you will have a career.'

'What makes you so sure?'

'Ed wouldn't have taken you on otherwise. And set you up here and kept you in funds and asked me to keep an eye on you.'

'You mean I'm not being paid by the film studio?'

'Well, I imagine they are giving you something, but not enough to cover what you're wearing tonight and the other gorgeous clothes you have in the wardrobe.'

'I don't understand.'

'It's really very simple. Ed Palmer obviously thinks you have talent and is prepared to take a gamble on you. You can regard yourself as an investment.'

'But he hasn't mentioned any of this to me.'

'No, I don't suppose he has. Listen, Carol, I really have to go. Ed will have told you to be ready for seven because he knows what girls are like. The car will probably arrive about eight.' Patti paused on her way to the door. 'You look terrific, you know.'

'Thanks.'

'For God's sake, Carol, snap out of whatever kind of mood you're in. Do you know, you have the makings of a right little prima donna, and you haven't even been before the cameras yet.'

Carol was mortified. 'Patti – I'm sorry. I really am. And I'm grateful to you for helping me. Will you forgive me?'

The older girl regarded her coolly for a moment and sniffed. 'I suppose so.' She went out and closed the door behind her. A moment later Carol heard her footsteps clattering down the lino-covered stairs, and a thought occurred to her that made her smile. Patti, who normally spoke with a sophisticated drawl, completely lost it when she was really annoyed. When she'd told Carol just now that she had the makings of a right little prima donna, she'd sounded just like the girl from Sheffield that she really was.

Although Patti had told her to sit and relax, Carol got up and started pacing about her room again. She walked over to the fireplace and looked in the mirror above the mantel. Patti had done a good job with her hair. Denise would approve, Carol thought, and she thought not for the first time of how much she missed her friend. The silk gardenia was large and luxurious-looking, with a spray of crystals in the centre. That was what Patti had been referring to when she had wished that Carol had matching earrings.

Carol could only see her head and shoulders. Even when she moved back from the mirror she couldn't get a full-length view. Her dress was made of smoky-blue rayon with padded shoulders and a pattern of deep blue and silver beadwork on the upper bodice. The skirt was slim-fitting, but there was a pleated hip drape that Carol had been a little doubtful about.

'Don't worry,' Patti had told her. 'You're slim enough to carry it off.'

Carol wondered what Denise would have thought of the shoes. They matched the colour of the dress exactly; they had an ankle strap and peep toes and they were the highest heels Carol had ever worn. They were second hand, just like the dress, and from the look of them they had been worn only a couple of times, if that. They must also have been more expensive than anything Denise had ever sold in the shoe department at Rutherford's.

The car didn't arrive until nearly a quarter to eight. Mrs Evans had a habit of knocking on the door and entering without waiting for a response. As usual, a half-smoked cigarette hung from the corner of her scarlet lips. Carol wondered whether the constant flow of smoke was responsible for the fact that her landlady's face was beginning to resemble a wrinkled prune.

'The car's here for Miss Carol Marshall,' she said, putting on a refined accent. Then, in her own voice, 'It's a Daimler. Posh. The royal family has one. And so does Lady Docker. But then Sir Bernard is chairman of the company.'

Carol knew who Sir Bernard and Lady Docker were. They were always in the society pages in the newspapers. And in the newsreels at the cinema, opening something, attending some grand function or having a day out at the races.

'Of course hers is gold-plated and they say it's upholstered with six zebra skins. And her born above a butcher's shop.'

'Fancy,' Carol said.

'Don't just stand there. The car they've sent for you may not be gold-plated, but the driver's dressed in a smart uniform and peaked cap. He's waiting in the hall to see you into the car. And he's not at all bad looking, either,' Mrs Evans added with one of her rare smiles.

'Right.'

'Well, aren't you going to put your bit of fur on, then?' With a nod of the head, Carol's landlady indicated the silver fox bolero draped over the chair. 'That must have cost a pretty penny.'

'Oh, it's not mine.' Carol picked it up.

'Here, let me help you into it.' Mrs Evans took the coat from her and ran a work-worn hand lovingly over the fur. 'Whose is it, then?'

'Patti borrowed it for me. Years ago someone left it at the Blue Parrot. The cloakroom attendant keeps it and lends it out to the girls if one of them has a special occasion.'

'Don't forget your bag.' Mrs Evans nodded towards the blue-sequinned clutch bag on the table.

The landlady waited on the landing while Carol locked her door, and then went with her down the stairs. She stood in the doorway and watched as the chauffeur escorted Carol to the car. Carol thought she had better give her a wave, so before she got in, she turned with one arm raised, but Mrs Evans wasn't looking at her. She was glancing up and down the street, her head jerking backwards and forwards.

The chauffeur smiled at Carol. 'The old girl's hoping that at least some of the neighbours are watching,' he said.

'Why would she hope that?'

He smiled, and she saw how handsome he was, tall and well made. The hair glimpsed under his peaked cap was blond; his eyes were blue.

'It's not often a car drives up to her door, let alone a car like this,' he said. 'It will make her feel important.'

Carol got in and settled down in the luxurious interior. As the car drove off, she realised she had no idea where they were going. She leaned forward and was about to ask him when he said, 'This your first time?'

'First time?'

'At this sort of party?'

'What sort of party?'

'All show-business people trying to impress each other.'

Carol felt a surge of embarrassment mixed with vexation. 'I'm not trying to impress anyone.'

'No?'

'No.'

'Then what's the point of getting dressed to kill and arriving in a car like this?'

'I'm not dressed to kill!'

'Well, dolled up then. You must know that Mr Palmer wants important people – useful people – to see you and take notice of you.'

'Mr Palmer told you that?'

'No, but he's your agent. Stands to reason. He wouldn't hire this car unless he had plans for you. You learn these things in my job. You're a lucky girl. Wish he was my agent.'

Carol was confused. 'Are you an actor?'

'That's the plan. Meanwhile I drive cars, and sometimes escort lonely ladies for a night on the town, and I've been known to star on the front of a knitting pattern like my young friend Roger Moore. Anything to keep body and soul together and pay for acting lessons.' The driver was quiet for a while, and then he said, 'So if you get a break like this, make the most of it.'

Carol sat back. It was only when she saw that they had left the city streets behind that she realised she still didn't know where they were going. She looked at the driver and saw that he was watching her in the mirror.

'Don't worry,' he said. 'I'm not kidnapping you to sell into the white slave trade. The party is at a very nice house in

Surrey. Your host is an industrialist who fancies himself as a film producer, but he hasn't got a clue about film-making. He doesn't know it, but they all laugh at him while they're taking his money.'

'How do you know all this?'

'Because of this job. I learn a lot from my passengers if I just keep quiet and listen. Right, we're nearly there.'

They had just passed through a pretty village. The sky was still light, but they entered a shadowy tunnel formed by the overhanging branches of ancient trees. The car slowed down and turned in through an impressive gateway. Carol couldn't contain a gasp of surprise when she saw what lay ahead at the end of the long drive. The house, which looked as if it had weathered centuries, was bathed in the warmth of the setting sun. The panes of mullioned windows glinted in the fading light.

'What is this place?' she asked.

'Fairview Manor.' The driver laughed. 'He's done well for himself, hasn't he?'

'I wish you'd explain.'

'Jack Rawlins started life as a steelworker and ended up owning the mill and several engineering works. He's never forgotten his humble beginnings but he likes to mix with the rich and famous. His parties are on the vulgar side of spectacular.'

'You've been to one?'

'Yeah. I told you, I sometimes act as an escort to lonely society ladies.'

'You're a gigolo!'

'Where did you learn that word?'

'At the pictures. I saw a film – a comedy – about a man who makes a living doing just that.'

'Just what?'

'Escorting rich women to dinner and dances and the like.'

They had reached the house and the chauffeur pulled up and turned to smile at her. 'I don't know what you mean by "and the like". All I do is escort them. Right?'

Carol nodded, and felt herself flushing. 'Yes, I understand.'

'Sit tight,' he told her as she leaned forward. 'I open the door and help you out. It's part of the job.'

He got out of the car, came round to open her door and offered his hand. 'You look as if you're going to the guillotine instead of a party,' he said, and laughed, but his smile was sympathetic and she realised that he wasn't making fun of her.

'I'm nervous,' she confided.

'There's no need to be. You look terrific and you talk like a lady. You'll be head and shoulders above the other little hopefuls gathered here tonight.'

'You think so?'

'I know so. Look, you want to be an actress, don't you?'

'Yes.'

'Well, start acting right now. Walk up those steps and in through that door as if you've been to dozens of parties like this. Don't let anyone guess it's the first time.'

She had taken his hand when he helped her out of the car, and he had held on to it. Now he gave it a squeeze. 'I'll come back for you at midnight. Will that be okay?'

'Will the party be over by then?'

'Probably not. But I don't think you'll want to stay. If you have any sense, you'll get home and have your beauty sleep.'

He let go of her hand and walked ahead of her to the door. He rang the doorbell, a large bronze antique-looking object, and the door was opened by a superior-looking manservant.

'Miss Carol Marshall,' announced the chauffeur.

The manservant inclined his head and gestured that Carol

should enter. The chauffeur pressed her arm reassuringly and turned to go.

'Wait,' she said.

'What is it?'

'I don't know your name.'

'Ray. Ray Raymond.'

She must have looked surprised, because he grinned and leaned towards her so that only she could hear. 'Actually, it's Ray Rowbotham, but that wouldn't look good up in lights above a cinema, would it?' He raised his eyebrows as if he were surprised at himself. 'I don't know why I told you that. You must promise to keep my terrible secret.'

'Of course I will.'

'Right. I'll be here at midnight, Cinderella. Now off you go.'

While they had been talking, two more cars had drawn up and disgorged their passengers. Carol became part of a crowd that swept into the hall. They were laughing and greeting each other. Nobody took any notice of her. As she stood there wondering what to do next, a maid appeared and smilingly offered to take her coat. Carol gave it to her, and she immediately vanished. Somewhere a piano was playing, but no one seemed to take much notice. They were too busy greeting each other and talking as if they were lifelong friends.

'Ah, there you are.' Carol was relieved to hear a familiar voice and turned to see Ed Palmer coming towards her. He looked her up and down appreciatively and said, 'You look great. Patti's done a good job.'

Carol felt a small prickle of irritation at his words. It was as if he didn't trust her to be able to dress herself. She decided there and then that she would refuse Patti's help in future. She didn't think the other girl would mind. Patti sometimes gave the impression that she was being coerced into assisting her, and would be only too pleased to be excused those duties.

'I'm glad you approve,' Carol said, and she thought that Ed Palmer looked momentarily surprised at the unaccustomed self-assurance of her tone.

She looked at him critically. He was wearing a smarter suit than usual, although it could have done with being pressed. His shirt was clean but crumpled and his hair was as untidy as ever. If he was as successful as Patti had hinted, he certainly didn't spend much money on his appearance.

The hall was getting crowded as more guests arrived. People were making their way through a set of double doors ahead of them and Carol could hear music and high-pitched chatter. No sooner had they entered the room than a waitress approached carrying a tray of drinks. The glasses were saucer-shaped and the pale yellow wine they contained was fizzing.

Mr Palmer took two glasses and handed one to Carol. 'Champagne,' he said. He clinked glasses with her. 'Let's drink to your success.'

Carol sipped the champagne cautiously and discovered that she liked it.

Ed Palmer smiled at her expression. 'There'll be plenty more of that for you in the future,' he said, 'but that's all you're going to get tonight. Hang on to that glass and sip it sparingly. Don't let anyone fill it up. There are some important people here and I want you to remain completely sober. You can eat from the buffet, but don't make a pig of yourself, and whoever you're talking to, you'll make your excuses at midnight and leave. I've told the driver to be waiting for you.'

Carol resented the way he was giving her instructions as if she were still at school, but she acknowledged that it was good advice. She remembered Ray telling her to act confidently, and she started by giving Ed Palmer a dazzling smile.

'Isn't it time you introduced me to some of these important people?'

Carol thought he looked taken aback, but after a moment his eyes widened and he grinned and said, 'That's my girl. We'll start with our host.'

Jack Rawlins was a large, tough-looking man who was wearing an expensive evening suit. His smile was appreciative but there was a hint of a leer that Carol thought distasteful.

'She's a right pretty little lass,' he said to Ed. 'Where did you say you found her?'

'Carol won a Glamour Girl competition. I was one of the judges.'

'You certainly know how to pick 'em! But looks aside, can she act?'

'Yes, she can.'

Carol was annoyed that the two of them were talking about her as if she couldn't speak for herself. As if she was some kind of commodity rather than a real live person.

She surprised herself by her outburst. 'Of course I can act, Mr Rawlins, and I'm very much looking forward to being able to prove myself.'

Jack Rawlins looked at her rather as if something inanimate, a doll or a shop-window mannequin, had suddenly spoken. Nevertheless his next words were addressed to Ed again.

'And she can talk, too. Right posh, I mean. Makes a change from the usual beauty queens, who come over as common little tarts the moment they open their mouths. This one won't need any coaching, will she?'

Carol bridled and she felt Ed grip her arm.

'No, she won't,' he said. 'She looks good and she sounds refined. As I said, she's a winner.' He pulled at her arm slightly, as if they were about to move on, but their host had more to say.

'I've been thinking about that lately,' he said.

'About?' Ed queried politely.

'These lasses who look good but need polishing up a bit.

I thought I might start a sort of finishing school. How to walk, how to talk, how to hold your knife and fork correctly. We could call it a charm school. Do you think it would work?'

'It's worth a try. And you could get lots of publicity out of it. Lots of nice pics and some before-and-after stories.'

'Would you like to be part of it?'

'I might.'

'If you did, I'd be relying on you to find suitable candidates. There's no one better qualified for that job.'

By now Carol had decided that she didn't just dislike their host; she loathed him. It was taking all her acting skills not to show her distaste for the way he talked about women as if they were goods – merchandise. Thankfully he had spotted someone else he wanted to talk to and took his leave of them. As he hurried away, he said, 'Enjoy the party, Ed.'

He had never once addressed a word to Carol.

'Don't let him get to you,' Ed told her. 'There are plenty more like that, and you've got a long way to go before anyone will listen to anything you have to say. If you want to succeed in this business, you'll have to get used to it.'

Carol, even though she was seething, knew it would be useless to argue, so she allowed Ed to guide her round the room. She didn't know what she had been expecting, but the people he introduced her to, although obviously wealthy and influential, looked very ordinary. Producers, directors, writers: Carol had never heard of any of them, and she began to realise how much went on behind the cameras when a film was made.

She had hoped there would be some famous film stars there so that she could write to Denise and tell her all about them, but at first she recognised only one or two supporting actors and far too many young people who were what Ray would have called hopefuls. And then, just as Ed had told her she could go to the buffet, a new surge of guests arrived.

'Here come the leading lights,' Ed said. 'They like to wait and make a proper entrance. There's someone I want to talk to, so I'll leave you now. Remember what I told you. No more to drink, and don't eat too much.' He was gone before she could frame a suitable reply.

Chapter Fifteen

From the look of the refreshments on offer, much of it would have come from the black market, Carol supposed. If you were rich enough, you could have the best of anything that was available. She'd heard that in some places even the policemen knew where to go for black-market food.

She took a napkin and a plate and helped herself to two tiny smoked salmon sandwiches and a couple of vol-au-vents with some kind of creamy filling. While she was doing this, she had put her glass and her handbag down on the table beside her. Before she realised what was happening, a waitress topped her glass up.

Ah well, she thought. I needn't actually drink any more, and if my glass is full, no one will top it up again. The next problem was how to eat while holding her plate in one hand and her glass in the other. And what was she supposed to do with her handbag?

'You look as though you need help,' a man's voice said, and when she turned round to look at him, she almost lost her poise. Tall and dark, with smoky-grey eyes and a slim but powerful physique, Paul Grainger was much more than conventionally handsome. According to Denise, this famous British film star was possibly the most gorgeous man who had ever lived.

Fazed only for a moment by his appraising glance, Carol said, 'Thank you, but I can manage.'

'And how exactly are you going to do that?' He smiled, and Carol saw why women all over the world imagined themselves in love with him. 'Are you going to stand for the rest of the night with your glass in one hand, your plate in the other and your bag tucked under your arm, hoping someone will come along and feed you?'

'Don't be silly. I'll ... erm ...'

He laughed. 'Just wait until I fill my plate and I'll show you where you can sit and eat like a sensible person. I hate these dos where everybody stands about juggling their plate and their glass, don't you?'

'Well, actually I ... yes, I do.'

Carol had been about to say that she had never been to such a do before, but she remembered Ray's advice just in time.

'Come with me,' Paul Grainger said when he had filled his plate and retrieved his champagne glass. He began to thread his way through the guests towards some French windows that opened on to a balustraded terrace overlooking the garden. The sun had set but the night was warm and filled with the delicious scents of unseen flowers. He led her down the steps at the end of the terrace and across the moon-shadowed lawn. Her high heels sank into the grass with each step, and she wondered if she was ruining them. She felt herself wobble, and held on to her plate and glass all the more tightly.

'Where are we going?' she asked.

'We're already there.' They had arrived at a little stone summer house, and he led the way inside.

Carol held back uncertainly, and Paul Grainger laughed softly. 'Don't worry,' he said. 'I only want to eat and drink, and we're in full view of the house. If I do anything to make you scream, people will come running in next to no time.'

'Oh, no ... I didn't think ...'

'I was teasing. Now, where did they put it?'

As her eyes adjusted to the dimness inside the summer house, she saw that Paul had placed his plate and glass on a wrought-iron table and was groping for something underneath the stone bench.

'Here we are.' He stood up and flourished a silver bucket with a champagne bottle resting in it. Ice cubes clinked in the bucket and a white linen cloth was draped round it. 'I tipped one of the caterers to make sure this was waiting for me.'

'But why hide it?'

He laughed. 'Ed gets nervous if he sees me having more than a couple of glasses, so what the eye doesn't see the heart doesn't grieve for – as they say.'

'Ed? You mean Ed Palmer?'

'I do. He's my agent and yours too, Carol.'

'You know who I am?'

'Ed told me you would be here tonight, so I looked for the most beautiful girl in the room.'

'Please don't talk like that.'

'Sorry. But do sit down and relax. What do you want? One of those excruciatingly uncomfortable wrought-iron chairs or this comfortable stone bench?'

'I can't see how the bench would be more comfortable.'

'Ah, but it is. Look, there are some velvet cushions.'

Carol put her plate, her glass and her handbag on the table and took one of the cushions. She put it on a chair and sat down. 'This will do nicely,' she said.

'Have it your own way.' Paul sounded amused rather than annoyed. 'But I'm devastated that you don't want to sit beside me. Now, let's eat up – although you don't seem to have helped yourself to very much. Luckily, I've got more than enough for two.'

The food was delicious, and Carol completely forgot her

promise not to eat too much. Or rather she didn't forget her promise – she just decided to ignore it. She had never had a problem with her weight – much to Denise's vexation. However, she did decide to drink sparingly. She wasn't used to alcohol and this wasn't the right occasion to experiment.

For a while they were silent. They ate and drank and listened to the music that drifted across the lawn. Carol imagined telling Denise that she'd gone to a glamorous party and that Paul Grainger had persuaded her to have supper with him in a romantic summer house.

'And what did you talk about?' Denise would say.

'Nothing in particular.'

She could guess what Denise's response would be to that.

'Nothing in particular!' her friend would exclaim. 'Sitting there alone with Paul Grainger and you talked about nothing in particular? I don't believe you could have been so pathetic.'

'But I didn't know what to say.'

'You should have flattered him. Asked him things.'

'What sort of things?'

'About himself. Most men love talking about themselves. I know Howard did.'

Denise's voice faded wistfully with her last words, and Carol felt a pang of sympathy. 'You really liked him, didn't you? Howard?'

The imaginary Denise didn't say anything, but Carol knew what the answer would be.

'You're very quiet,' Paul said.

'Sorry. I was just thinking.'

'About what?'

'Oh . . .' She thought of Denise's imaginary advice. 'I was thinking how terrible it must have been for you when your ship was torpedoed.'

'For me and the rest of the crew.'

'You were adrift for several days, weren't you?'

'A week.'

'Until your lifeboat was spotted by a passing ship.'

Paul was silent for a moment, and then he said, 'Look, Carol, I don't know why you're bringing all this up. The story of my war has been told many times in the fan magazines. You must know the answers to your questions.'

Carol felt as though her face was flaming. 'I'm sorry.'

'And you don't have to flatter me like any other little hopeful. You've already got the part and I'm looking forward to working with you.'

'*You*, working with *me*?'

'Didn't they tell you? The scenes you and I do together will be shot next week.'

'They didn't tell me anything.'

'That's how they treat the little fish, I'm afraid. They expect them to just swim around, buoyed up by their hopes and dreams.'

'I didn't even know that you were in the film,' Carol said. 'I've been hanging around doing nothing for weeks, wondering if the whole thing was a stunt and I'd be packed off home again.'

'To be honest with you, that could have happened. The director has already dismissed two screenwriters, and the one he's got now wasn't keen on the scenes in the nightclub, but he was talked round. So, let's celebrate.'

Paul reached for the ice bucket and took out the bottle of champagne. 'Time to fill up our glasses,' he said. 'Do you want me to open this the fun way or the sensible way?'

'I don't know the difference.'

'Then let's have fun.'

Paul removed the foil from the top of the bottle, and then the wire cage that seemed to be keeping the cork in place. Holding the bottle so that it was pointing towards the entrance of the summer house, he began to ease the cork up with one thumb. Carol had seen enough scenes in movies to know what would happen next, and she held her breath until the cork finally escaped with a satisfying pop. She laughed as it flew out of the summer house into the moonlit garden and the wine began to fizz out of the bottle.

'Quick, hold up your glass,' Paul said. 'Don't let's waste any.'

'No. I shouldn't have any more.'

'Who said?'

'Mr Palmer.'

'You can't let me drink alone. That's unkind. Just one more glass won't do you any harm; I promise you I'm not trying to get you drunk.'

Was it the moonlight, the scent of summer flowers, the astonishing fact that she was sitting alone with Paul Grainger? Carol didn't pause to consider the answer. She simply held out her glass.

'Let's drink to your future career,' Paul said when he had filled his own glass. 'And to the first film we will make together.'

'We're hardly making the film together,' Carol said. 'I'm only playing a small part.'

'Ah, but when they see how well we look together, the chemistry between us, many more films will follow. I'm sure of it.'

Carol knew what Paul meant by 'chemistry'. She and Denise had often remarked of characters in films they had seen that there was something, some indefinable spark between the leading man and the leading lady that made you believe in the story. If that something wasn't there, no matter how well they acted, the story just didn't come alive.

'How can you know that? That you and I have chemistry?'

'Can't you feel it? I can. Just wait until our scenes together are shot and you'll see what I mean. More champagne?'

'No thank you.'

Carol put the palm of her hand over her glass, but there was no need. Paul, true to his promise, didn't press her to have more. She noticed that his own glass was empty and was surprised at how quickly he had been able to drain it. He sat back and held it up so that a shaft of moonlight caught the bubbles sparkling inside.

'Pretty, aren't they?' he said.

'The bubbles?'

'The bubbles are fun, but I mean the glasses. Did you know that champagne coupes are said to have been modelled on the shape of Madame de Pompadour's breasts?'

Carol, startled, shook her head. 'That can't be true.'

'Maybe it isn't, but it's a nice story. It's said that her lover, King Louis of France, so admired her breasts that he longed to be able to drink champagne from them. So she had casts made and had the glasses crafted as a special gift for him.' He paused, then put the glass to his lips and sipped slowly.

Carol, strangely intrigued by the tale, stirred uneasily.

'Are you shocked?' Paul asked.

She shook her head.

He filled his glass again. 'Of course, the same story is told of Madame du Barry, another of Louis's mistresses. And other courtesans, and even a queen. All nonsense, but a lovely idea, don't you think?'

Paul held the bottle upside down over his glass and sighed when he discovered it was empty. A shadow fell across the table, and Carol looked up to see Ed Palmer standing in the doorway.

'There you are,' he said. 'It's midnight, Carol. Your car is waiting.'

She rose quickly. 'I had no idea. I'm sorry.'

'No need to apologise. Here, I've brought your coat for you.' He helped her on with it and she thanked him. 'Have you enjoyed yourself?'

'Yes thank you.'

'Well, be a good girl and there will be more parties like this.'

Carol felt a surge of irritation at the way he was talking to her, but she was in no position to argue with him.

Paul Grainger laughed. 'You believe in looking after your protégées, don't you, Ed?'

'Of course. They're no use to me if they choose to ruin themselves.'

There was an edge to his voice that made Carol sense that the two men had had similar conversations before. Then he seemed to remember that Carol was still there. He turned to speak to her. 'I'm glad you two have met,' he said. 'It will be easier when you start working together. Now, do you think you could find your own way back to the car? I need to have a word with Mr Grainger.'

After a pause, during which they were no doubt waiting for her to get out of earshot, they began talking again. The words were indistinct, but there was no disguising the exasperation in Ed Palmer's voice and the hint of arrogance in Paul's.

Carol walked towards the house, where the noise level had risen considerably. She paused on the terrace outside the open French doors and nerved herself to dive into the mêlée. Once inside, she had to almost fight her way through the crowd. Chattering groups had spilled out into the entrance hall, and probably into other rooms in the house to judge by the people going up and down the grand staircase and having to climb over other guests sitting there.

She saw that ahead of her the front door was open and Ray was standing there, cap in hand. He smiled when he saw her coming. But before she could take another step, someone called out, 'Going so soon, darling?'

Puzzled, she turned to see a woman tottering towards her. She was wearing a glamorous black satin cocktail dress with exaggerated shoulder pads, and she held a champagne glass in one hand and a long jewelled cigarette holder in the other. Carol looked round to see if the woman could be talking to someone else, but there was no one else approaching the door.

'Yes . . . my car is waiting. I told the − my chauffeur to be here at midnight.'

The woman drew on her cigarette and then flicked the holder so that ash fell on to her dress. The jewels decorating the cigarette holder matched those in her ears and about her throat. She looked at Ray through narrowed eyes.

'Very tasty, I grant you, but let him wait. Come and have another little drink.'

'I'm sorry, but I really must leave now.'

The woman scowled. 'Suit yourself.' She half turned to go, but then turned back. 'Wait a minute − do I know you?'

'I don't think so.'

'Then why have you wasted my time like this?'

'I haven't . . . I mean, you . . .'

The woman's scowl turned into an aggrieved pout, and she turned and tottered away. Carol reached the door without incident and smiled up at Ray.

'Did you hear all that?' she asked him.

'Every garbled word.'

'I didn't realise it at first, but she was drunk, wasn't she?'

'Not only drunk. That white powder on her dress wasn't just cigarette ash.'

Carol had no idea what he was talking about. 'What was it?'

'Coke. Cocaine.'

Carol was shocked. 'But that's a drug, isn't it?'

'It is. You probably don't need me to tell you, but you should steer clear of people like that.'

'I will.'

'Now, madam, your chauffeur is waiting to escort you to your car.'

As they drove back to London, Ray asked her if she'd enjoyed herself.

'I'm not sure,' she replied.

He must have sensed her confusion, because he didn't press her to talk any further. When they reached Carol's digs, he saw her to the door and waited until she had turned the key in the lock.

'Good night, Carol,' he said. 'I'll probably see you again. And don't worry too much about these people. You'll get used to them.'

In Hollywood, the poolside party was just winding down. Howard was pleased to have been invited by his attractive neighbour, Margaret Johns, an English film actress who had married an American director and had settled here.

She had introduced him enthusiastically to her guests as a real British actor of 'the old school'. Howard had mixed feelings about the word 'old', but he was pleased with the way he was treated with respect by her glamorous and successful guests.

A tanned Hollywood heart-throb, once a truck-driver but now one of the highest-earning stars of the moment, had told him, 'We have so much to learn from actors like you. The confidence, the diction, the discipline. I suppose it's the Shakespearean training you had to go through. The spear-carrying.'

'So kind of you,' Howard had replied with a charming air of British modesty and reserve.

He felt he couldn't disillusion the man. He had never been to drama school and he had not started out by carrying a spear as an extra in one of Shakespeare's plays. In fact he had gone straight from a minor public school into the family's office supplies business. He had served his country with honour in the First World War, and come home to find his father bankrupt. So, without an income he had relied on his looks and patrician manner to get him into films.

He had soon become a screen idol, but in truth his acting had not been good enough to keep him at the top of the bill. Until now, when his ramrod posture and very English speech and manner were just what film-makers needed for the plethora of war films they were making. Howard had heard rumours that this year was going to be one of the most profitable ever for the film industry, as people flocked to the cinema to see heroic versions of the war years.

Mostly he was required to play senior army officers, usually British. But now and then he was called on to play a German officer, and that was much more fun. He preferred out-and-out nastiness to the endless portrayal of the stiff upper lip. The parts stretched out in front of him and he was making a fortune. Enough to buy a very nice house instead of renting if he decided to stay here.

That was the problem. Did he really want to spend the rest of his life in this land of eternal sunshine? He missed the softer colours of the English countryside, and even the grey skies and the rain. But that was not all he was missing. To his surprise, in spite of the abundance of shapely young women who would have been only too happy to be seen out with him, he couldn't get a particular rusty-haired girl out of his mind. A girl young enough to be his daughter, and someone his long-dead mother would have regarded as 'too, too common, my dear'.

And what of Alice Grayson, his only true friend from the

old days? He was ashamed to think that he might not have kept in touch often enough over the years, but at least she had been in the same country. The last letter he had received from her had worried him.

She hadn't complained. She never did. But in trying to be cheerful, she had revealed the loneliness of her days. She told him how over the years she had grown fond of Carol. She had been thrilled when Carol had been offered the part in the film, but worryingly, she hadn't heard a word from the child since she had gone to London.

Howard guessed how much it had hurt Alice's pride to do so, but in her letter she asked him if he could find out from his contacts what had happened to Carol. That would be easy enough, he thought. For a start, his agent, who had started treating him with more respect lately, could easily find out what was going on. But Howard had a better idea. There was someone else who would know what was happening to Carol.

He would write a letter as soon as he got home.

Chapter Sixteen

Denise had no intention of going to the window with the other girls to watch the wedding. She couldn't understand why they had started checking the view so early. It seemed to her that most of the female staff were at one window or another, and they took turns to go and look out for early customers.

Determined not to show any interest whatsoever, Denise carried on tidying the shoe boxes on the shelves until eventually she could bear it no longer.

'Hey, you lot, would you mind going and making a nuisance of yourselves in someone else's department. You'll get an equally good view from the French Salon.'

She knew Miss Rawson wouldn't let them anywhere near the windows, but she took a delight in being provocative.

'No room in there,' Eva Smithson from drapery cried over her shoulder. 'Moira gave out tickets.'

Denise was astonished. Moira was the new girl who had been taken on to replace Carol. She was quiet and reserved and had been privately educated at a school in Newcastle until her father had perished on D-Day. Until now she had shown no sense of enterprise whatsoever.

'Moira sold tickets?' Denise asked in astonishment.

'She didn't sell them,' Eva said. 'She gave them to people who had been nice to her.'

'But how did she get away with it? I mean, what did old Rawbones have to say?'

'Miss Rawson will never know,' Eva said. 'Everyone will clear off before she gets in to work.'

'She's not here yet?'

'Well, obviously!' Eva said. 'She's in the church. Honestly, Denise, it's not like you to be so slow. More than one person has remarked that you don't seem to be with it these days.'

Denise thought she understood. Miss Rawson probably mixed in the same social circles as the Blanchards and the Douglases, and old Rawbones wouldn't miss the chance of being at the wedding of the year.

'But what about the wedding breakfast? Won't she be going to that?' she asked.

'No such luck,' Eva replied. 'She told Moira that she would come in straight after the ceremony and that she and the squadron leader would celebrate with their friends after work.'

Denise began to think that the thread of the conversation was untangling. Miss Rawson and Squadron Leader Wilmot were guests at Kay and Steve's wedding, which seemed to have started at an exceptionally early hour. They were going to the ceremony, but instead of the wedding breakfast they were going to attend some sort of evening do. Did any of this make sense? She frowned, and then looked up in surprise when she heard Eva laughing.

'You really don't know, do you?' Eva said. 'You thought we were all keen to see that stuck-up Kay Blanchard's wedding to the gorgeous Steve Douglas, didn't you? Well we are, but that's not until later. Good old Rawbones is getting married herself, and she swore Moira to secrecy. She had to tell her because she was going to be late for work, but she didn't want a fuss.'

'Moira didn't keep her promise?'

'Of course not. And do you know what? I believe old Rawbones knew she wouldn't. After all, this may not be love's young dream, but a wedding day is a wedding day no matter how old you are, isn't it? Now, are you going to stop fiddling with those shoe boxes and come over to the window?'

'You'd better be quick!' another girl shouted. 'The church door has just opened!'

Thoroughly intrigued, Denise hurried over to join the other girls at the window. The sky was overcast and a nippy little breeze worried the branches of the trees at the far end of the churchyard. Not the sort of weather you wanted on your wedding day.

There was a collective 'Oooh!' from the girls at the window when four people emerged from the church. A man in RAF uniform, a smartly dressed woman who could have been his wife, and Miss Rawson and her squadron leader, who was wearing a very smart lounge suit.

'No wedding dress,' Denise breathed. 'Poor old thing.'

'But doesn't she look terrific?' Eva said.

And Denise had to acknowledge that she did. She was like something out of a fashion magazine, wearing a French beige dress and matching jacket. Her hat, a slightly darker shade, was a pillbox, balanced on her upswept hair and secured with a froth of creamy net. The other woman's hat could hardly be seen amongst her extravagantly permed curls. Her two-piece outfit was a very pretty flower print, but she was nowhere near as elegant-looking as the bride.

As the small wedding party lined up outside the door of the church, the young assistant from Latham's stepped forward and took photographs. He didn't take long. There was a confused moment when everybody seemed to want to kiss everybody else's cheek, and a moment of smiles and laughter before the four of them walked down the path and out through the lychgate on to the pavement. There, to their unsuspected audience's delight, the bridegroom took his bride in his arms and kissed her. Denise heard a cheer coming from the French Salon.

The tender moment didn't last long. The squadron leader and the other two walked away, and Miss Rawson – or rather Mrs Wilmot – crossed the road and made towards the alley that led to the staff entrance of the shop.

'Quick!' Denise heard someone shout, and everyone began to move away from the window. Denise remained where she was.

'Aren't you coming?' Eva asked.

'Where? Why?'

'Some of them have confetti.'

'Wedding day or not, Rawbones will kill you if you make a mess in the salon.'

'That's why we want to catch her in the back lane!'

Eva hurried away, leaving Denise staring out of the window. Very soon the guests would be arriving for a much grander wedding. Both fathers, the groom and the best man (a cousin of theirs, Muriel had told her) would be wearing morning suits, and so would the ushers. Ushers indeed! Muriel and the other bridesmaid would be got up like a dog's dinner in peach satin, and as for the two mothers, no doubt they would be dressed like their idea of society ladies.

And would the occasion be any more meaningful than poor old Rawbones' economy version? Denise doubted it. She had been dreading today because of what it would do to Carol. She and Muriel had agreed that neither of them would tell their friend anything about the wedding unless she asked outright.

Denise stared across at the church, where now smartly dressed wedding guests were beginning to arrive. Suddenly, as if it had been saving itself for the more important occasion, the sun broke through the clouds and the air sparkled. Denise turned abruptly away from the window, going over on her ankle as she did so.

'Damn and blast these wedge heels!' she exclaimed, and bent down to rub her lower leg.

She lowered herself gently on to a chair and looked at her ankle. She didn't think she was imagining it, but it was already beginning to swell. Resigned to a day of pain, she felt even more despondent when she heard the applause she guessed was accompanying the new Mrs Wilmot's progress through the shop.

'Bloody weddings,' she muttered. 'Who wants to get married anyway? I'm sure I don't.'

The night before the wedding, Steve and his best man, Duncan, had gone out for a drink, as was expected of them. Settled in the cocktail bar of the Waverley, Duncan had teased Steve mercilessly with the usual risqué jokes.

When he'd realised that Steve wasn't laughing, he'd said, 'What is it, old chum? Aren't you ready to walk the plank?'

For a wild moment Steve considered admitting to his cousin that he wasn't sure if he wanted to go ahead with the wedding, but Duncan hadn't waited for an answer.

'I've heard it's quite normal,' he'd said, 'these last-minute doubts. But the church is booked and the wedding breakfast paid for, and a chap's got to do his duty, hasn't he? Only an utter cad would leave the poor girl waiting at the church.'

Then the next day, when Kay had come to stand beside him in her wedding gown, she had looked so radiantly lovely, so luminously happy, that Steve, caught up and carried along by the sheer goodwill emanating from the congregation, had begun to believe that he could be happy with Kay after all.

When they arrived at the hotel where they were to spend their honeymoon, they had tried not to look like a newly married couple. After Steve had signed the register, a pimply youth in a brass-buttoned jacket carried their suitcases up to their room. Once there, the lad had given them a knowing grin before pocketing his tip and departing.

'Why did he smirk like that?' Kay asked. 'Do you think he knows we're a honeymoon couple?'

'Either that or he thinks we've come for a dirty weekend.'

'Steve! You don't think that, do you?' Kay was horrified.

He laughed. 'No, I don't.'

'How can you be sure?'

'Come here.' Kay walked towards him, and he raised a hand and took something from her hair. He held it out on his palm. 'Look,' he said.

'Confetti!'

'Yes, and there's more, I'm afraid.'

'Why didn't you tell me?'

'I didn't notice until now. It's caught in the net decorating your hat. It doesn't look much different from the blue and pink velvet bows.'

Kay reached up, took out her hatpin, and then lifted the hat carefully from her head. She looked at it critically, then sighed. 'I suppose a mere man wouldn't notice that little bits of paper don't look very much like velvet bows. No wonder those two women on the train kept smiling at us so brightly.'

'Are you cross with me?'

Kay looked up at him, raising her chin slightly and tilting her head back. 'Very!' she said.

'Am I in the doghouse?'

'Yes, bad dog.'

'What can I do?'

'I'll think of something.'

The look in her eyes was so inviting that he pulled her into his arms and began to kiss her, but instead of responding, she struggled to get free.

'What is it?' he asked. 'What's the matter?'

'My hat!' she said. 'Look what you've done to my hat!'

She held the crushed article up for him to see. The net had come adrift and was hanging down secured by only a few stitches.

'Will it mend?' he asked.

'I suppose so.'

She looked so near to tears that he felt himself to be a monster. 'Kay, I'm sorry. If it can't be mended, I'll buy you a new one. I'll buy you as many hats as you want.'

She frowned and suddenly looked like a sulky child. 'Well I'm sure you mean well, but I don't know where you're going to get the coupons from.'

She walked away from him and placed the hat on the chest of drawers. Risking a rebuff, he strode over and took her in his arms. After a moment when she held herself stiffly apart, she sighed and relaxed. 'I'm sorry,' she said. 'I didn't mean to be a crosspatch. It's nerves, I think. Do you understand?'

'Yes, I do.'

When she raised her face to his, he thought she wanted to be kissed. But instead she smiled and pushed him away.

'We've just got time to change for dinner,' she said. 'You first, so I can spend more time in the bathroom. When you're ready, go down and get us a nice table.' She whirled away from him, took off her coat and began to unpack her case.

Steve unpacked his own things as quickly as he could; and washed and changed as she had instructed. He found a table by the window and hoped she would enjoy the view of the sea.

As he sat waiting for her, he thought about all the years he had loved her and wanted to marry her. Now they were man and wife and it was up to him to make a success of things.

He heard an appreciative comment from a nearby table, and looked up to see that Kay had entered the dining room. She was dressed simply in a black velvet skirt and a white tie-necked blouse. She had unpinned her dark hair and it waved softly down to her shoulders, framing her face.

She looked around uncertainly. Steve rose to his feet, and when she saw him, she smiled happily. She had obviously decided to forgive him for ruining her hat. She hurried towards their table, and every man she passed gave her an admiring glance. A waiter appeared from nowhere to hold her chair for her, and she thanked him graciously.

'Isn't this lovely?' she asked Steve as she glanced around the rather grand dining room.

In truth Steve thought the place ostentatious, but as Kay's mother had recommended it, he thought it best to keep his opinion to himself. 'I'm glad you like it,' he said.

She reached across the table and took his hand. 'Perfect,' she said. 'Everything's going to be just perfect.'

If Carol had cherished any illusions that the life of a film star was a glamorous one, they were swept away on the first day on the set. Ed had told her the car would pick her up at five in the morning. She had set her alarm clock for four so that she could make herself a cup of tea and a slice of toast. After this modest breakfast she went down to the bathroom to wash and brush her teeth. She wasn't to bother with make-up, as she would have to be made up properly when she reached the studios. As she left the bathroom, she bumped into Patti, who was coming upstairs, hanging on to the banister rail for dear life.

'Ssh!' Patti said, and she put one finger to her lips and smiled foolishly. 'Mustn't wake the workers!'

As they went up the stairs together, Patti suddenly stumbled. Carol caught her before she could fall over.

'You're drunk!' Carol whispered.

'Just a little bit.' Patti giggled. 'Went on to party with one of the customers. Not supposed to fraternise, you know, but he's fearfully rich!'

When they reached Patti's door, Carol took her key from her and opened it. Patti staggered in and flopped down on the bed, fully dressed. She closed her eyes.

'Are you going to be okay?' Carol asked.

'Don't fuss!'

'I don't mean to. It's just that I worry about you.'

Patti sounded surprised. 'You do? Well, there's no need to. I'm fine, just fine. But be a darling and take my shoes off for me, will you?'

Carol did as she was asked, then left the room, pulling the door shut behind her. As she got dressed, she kept glancing at her wristwatch. She intended to be waiting at the door for the car. She could just imagine Mrs Evans's reaction if the driver rang the bell at this time of the morning.

She was disappointed to find that it was not Ray who pulled up outside the house. She had hoped for a friendly face on her first day of filming. This driver, a much older man, seemed disinclined to chat, so Carol got her script, such as it was, out of her bag and went over it for the umpteenth time.

'Is this all?' she had asked in dismay when Ed had handed her the couple of flimsy pages.

'It's all for the moment.'

'I don't understand.'

'The new scriptwriter seems to change his mind every few minutes. If you're lucky, you'll get the script for the next day's shoot the night before. Just make sure you're word-perfect. Start as you mean to go on.'

Carol was fortunate in that she had no difficulty committing words to memory. She had her years of lessons with Miss

Grayson to thank for that. Now, going over her lines once more as the car sped through the early-morning streets, she felt a pang of guilt as she realised that she still had not written to her elocution teacher.

During her first weeks in London, as she had waited to learn whether she was actually going to be in a film or not, she had been too despondent to write to Miss Grayson. What could she have told her? Here I am in London, getting money for doing nothing and wondering if it was all a mistake and they're going to send me home again. Miss Grayson would have been so disappointed.

I'll write to her tonight, Carol thought. I'll be able to tell her all about my first day. And if I explain, I hope she'll understand why I haven't written before now.

When they arrived at the studio, a brisk middle-aged woman, who said she was called Mabel, swept her off to wardrobe. Not much later, Carol stared into a full-length mirror in dismay. The black satin dress was extremely short, and the scooped neck showed what she thought to be an indecent amount of cleavage.

'I look like ... like ...'

'A tart in a French farce?' Mabel said. 'That's the idea. Look, sweetie, you work in a cheap nightclub, you're probably no better than you ought to be. And if I'd had any say in the matter, I would never have cast you in this part.'

'Why not?'

'You're too damn beautiful, that's why not. Hair and make-up are going to have their work cut out to make you look cheap and rough around the edges. Come here a minute. Your bra strap's showing. Could you manage without it?'

'Definitely not!'

Mabel's machine-gun delivery had Carol's head spinning, but she wasn't going to allow herself to be coerced into taking her bra off.

'Well, we'll have to use a pin or two. There's no time to alter the neckline. You've got a very nice figure, you know, for such a little thing.'

After wardrobe came hair and make-up.

Carol was surprised that it was a man who did the make-up. He introduced himself as Bert, then tied Carol's hair up in a scarf and got on with the job.

'Pity to have to tart you up like this,' he told her as he rouged her cheeks. 'But I must say, you present a lovely canvas for an artist like me to paint on.'

'Ooh, pretentious!' Mabel said. 'Don't take any notice of him, Carol. Next thing he'll be telling you how all the great stars swear he's the best make-up artist in the world and how Greta Garbo begged him to go to Hollywood.'

'Fly off back to wardrobe on your broomstick, you old witch,' Bert said calmly. 'Now, Carol, tilt your head back a little, and keep still.'

Bert gave way to the hairdresser, a willowy young man with an exaggerated way of moving and speaking.

'For God's sake!' he exclaimed when he took the scarf from Carol's head. 'Did nobody tell you to put pin curls in?'

'No. I'm sorry.'

'Well they should have. That's what I told them. I said, "You tell the girl to put pin curls in the night before and keep them in until she gets here." Nobody takes a blind bit of notice of what I say.'

'Tony, you're acting like a drama queen again, and nobody here is impressed,' Bert said. 'Now don't be too long, because she's due on set.'

'I know that. No need to nag. Just go away and leave me in peace. It'll have to be the dreaded tongs, dear,' he said to Carol. 'I'll try not to burn you.'

Tony worked swiftly and deftly, and soon Carol's hair was piled up and arranged in a mass of curls on the crown of her head. When he was satisfied with the effect, he put a couple of sparkly combs below the curls at each side and then yelled for Mabel to bring some earrings. 'And her ears aren't pierced!' he added as though it were a personal affront.

Mabel materialised from nowhere. 'I'd already noticed that,' she said. 'Here you are, dear.'

She handed over a pair of sparkling clip-on earrings, and Carol was just about to put them on when Tony snatched them away from her.

'I'll do that,' he said. 'My job.'

As soon as he had clipped them on, Carol felt that they were too tight. She raised a hand to adjust one of them, but Tony smacked it out of the way.

'Don't fiddle,' he said. 'They're in exactly the right place. And if they're hurting, you'll just have to learn to suffer for your art.'

'Sadist,' Mabel said. 'Come along, Carol. You mustn't keep Mr Grainger waiting.'

Chapter Seventeen

The journey back from the studios was a blur of street lights and traffic noise. It seemed that nobody in London ever wanted to sleep, but after a full day's filming, Carol was so tired that all she could think of was getting to her own little room and falling into bed.

I should write some letters, she thought as she put a small pan of milk on the gas ring. While it warmed, she slipped off her clothes and put on her pyjamas. They were pink and white striped winceyette, and Patti had rolled her eyes in disbelief when she had first seen them.

'Not very film-starry, darling,' she had said. 'We'll have to get you something more glamorous.'

'I don't know why,' Carol had countered. 'Nobody's going to see them.'

Patti had laughed and said, 'If you say so.'

Tonight Patti wasn't here to comment or criticise, and Carol pulled on her old flannelette robe and felt slippers as well. Then she made her mug of cocoa and sat down at the table. Her writing pad and fountain pen were waiting for her. The pen had been a present from Muriel for her sixteenth birthday, but it was Denise she intended to write to first.

How shall I begin? she wondered. How could she explain to her friend that for a lot of the time, working in films could be very boring? She had spent much of the day just sitting around waiting to be called, and had been surprised at how tiring that could be.

The first scene with Paul Grainger had been exciting. Just as Mabel had said, he was waiting for her and ready to begin. The set representing a nightclub was pretty much what she had expected. It reminded her of the shady little clubs she had seen in other films. There were people sitting at the tables pretending to chat and drink. They were what were called extras, and they didn't have proper speaking parts in the film.

Paul had looked pleased to see her, and there were a few surprised glances from the crew when he had greeted her by name and personally introduced her to a fierce-looking man with a shock of white hair. This was Max Preston, the director. In spite of his English-sounding surname, Carol was surprised at his accent.

'Another Hungarian,' Paul whispered to her. 'They're taking over the film industry!'

The scene was almost the same as the one she had acted in the Glamour Girl competition. She was a cigarette girl, but this time the customer was played by Paul Grainger. Paul was dressed in a smart chalk-stripe suit, but something about him suggested that he wasn't a gentleman. His shirt was black, his tie white, and his hair was slicked back with a little too much hair cream. He was good-looking in a dangerous sort of way.

The script had been written to show that he hadn't been taken in by the cigarette girl. There was a shot of him smiling as he watched her pocket the change she had robbed him of. The cigarette girl was unaware that he was observing her, and when Carol watched them shooting a close-up of his sinister smile, she felt a frisson of alarm even though she knew he was acting.

Nothing was straightforward. Someone or other kept

stopping the action. The director, the sound engineer, the lighting cameraman. Each time the filming began again it was called a 'take', and this went on until Max was satisfied.

At one stage Carol sat around and watched as Paul acted scenes with other characters. When she was called again, the director took one look at her and shouted, 'Your hair! It's falling down. Fix it.'

Carol was rooted to the spot with consternation, but thankfully Tony appeared at her side with a brush and a comb and did a quick repair.

'Sorry, darling,' he said quietly. 'I should have told you to check hair and make-up after each shot. You look so at home here that I forgot you're new to this game.'

The only other scene she was required for that day involved another girl who worked at the club, the hat-check girl, who was warning her not to tell anyone what she'd seen or her life might be in danger. This was intriguing but puzzling as, because the scenes had not been shot in sequence, Carol had no idea what she had seen that she shouldn't have.

This scene took even longer to shoot because the other girl, Joan, kept muddling her words up. The first time it happened everybody laughed, but when she went on getting it wrong, patience ran out and tempers were lost. Finally she got it right and Max shouted that that would have to do. Then, in a lightning change of mood, he came over to Carol and said, 'Very good, darling. You ought to give that young woman some lessons.'

The look in Joan's eyes told Carol that she'd made an enemy.

Max's assistant, Rafe, gave her the next day's script and told her she could go. 'Make sure you know your lines,' he said, 'even if you have to stay up all night.'

Carol looked round for Paul, and was disappointed to discover that he was nowhere in sight. But of course there was no reason why the star of the movie should wait to say goodbye to a bit-part player. She returned to the dressing room, cleaned her make-up off and changed into her own clothes. Mabel, who was already preparing costumes for the next day, looked up from the ironing board and said, 'Your car is waiting, Carol. The driver's just been in to ask for you. See you in the morning.'

On the way out, Carol saw Joan standing smoking in the doorway. Even when Carol said, 'Excuse me,' the other girl didn't move, so Carol had to squeeze past. As she did so, Joan took the cigarette from her mouth and tapped it so that a column of ash fell on to Carol's coat.

'Oh dear,' she said. 'That's what you get for barging past people.'

Carol was incensed, but she was too weary to argue.

Joan watched through veiled eyes as Carol walked towards her car. 'It's all right for some,' she said. 'Other people have to get the bus.'

She threw her cigarette down and ground it viciously with her foot before walking towards the entrance gates.

Now Carol stared at the blank sheet of paper on her writing pad. She hadn't written a word. It was nearly midnight, and the car would be coming for her at five the next morning. Her eyelids felt heavy and her eyes scratchy. She was bone weary and she hadn't yet looked at her script. She closed the writing pad and pushed it away. Her letters home would have to wait until another day.

At the end of his first day back at work after the honeymoon, Steve made his way home through respectable suburban avenues. He looked at the neatly clipped privet hedges, the lawns, the rockeries, the birdbaths, and here and there a garden gnome. He had grown up in such a street, had been perfectly happy there. But even as a boy, he had dreamed of moving on. He'd had plans that the war had interfered with.

Why had he not made that clear to Kay? Had he believed that once they were married she would be happy to go anywhere with him? He supposed he had. But now he was not so sure. Her obvious delight in their new home, the easy way she fitted into the small-town society she had always known, made him more and more uneasy for their future.

When Steve entered the house, he was met by delicious cooking smells. He could hear the clink of glasses and the rattle of cutlery. Smiling, he entered the dining room, then stopped in dismay. The table was set for six.

The tablecloth was peach damask, as were the napkins. The set had been a present from Kay's great-aunt, and from the look of the box it came in, Steve suspected it had been one of her own wedding presents, never used. Other presents – the crystal water and wine glasses and the silver-plated cutlery – only just found enough room around the small table. A crystal bowl in the centre held roses from their own garden. Kay was in the act of putting candles in the silver candelabra that had also been one of their wedding gifts. She looked up and smiled at him.

'If you're hungry, you can have a quick Spam sandwich,' she said. 'But just one. Then you'll have time to go up and have a wash and brush-up before our guests arrive.'

'I didn't know we were having a party. What's the occasion?'

'It's a thank-you to Mummy and Daddy and to your parents, too. For everything they've done for us.'

She looked around the room happily. The French windows looked out on to the pretty little garden, where the rose bushes seemed to repeat the pattern on the curtains. The pink of the roses exactly matched the pink glass bowl of the hanging lampshade above the table.

'Oh, Steve – everything's just perfect, isn't it?'

Kay's pleasure in her home was endearing. He could see how hard she must have worked to make this occasion special.

'Perfect,' he said.

He took her in his arms. She smelled deliciously of her favourite gardenia perfume. She responded to his kiss briefly, but then wriggled out of his embrace and pushed him away.

'Steve, don't. They'll be here at eight and I've still got so much to do. Go on into the kitchen. There's a bottle of beer in a bucket of cold water on the floor of the pantry, and I've already made your sandwich.'

The fact that she was so busy preparing for her first dinner party and yet had still found the time to make him a sandwich and think to chill his beer was touching. He sat at the kitchen table as he'd been told and watched Kay as she came to check on the progress of her cooking.

'What's on the menu?' Steve asked.

'Mock oysters, followed by mock goose, and we'll finish off with treacle tart.'

'*Real* treacle tart?' Steve asked laughingly.

'Yes. Real treacle tart. Mummy donated a tin of golden syrup and a tin of custard powder. Now, if you've finished that sandwich, go and get ready.'

As Steve went to the door, he stopped and frowned.

'What is it?' Kay asked.

'The table's set for six,' he said.

Kay had just picked up his empty plate and glass from the table. She looked up at him. 'That's right,' she said. 'What's wrong with that?'

'Isn't Muriel coming?'

'I asked her, but she said she'd already made arrangements to go out straight after work. She's going for tea at that girl Denise's place and then they're going to the pictures. Goodness knows why they've suddenly become such pals.'

218

'Perhaps they both miss Carol,' Steve said.

Kay shrugged, and turned to put the used plate and glass in the sink. Somehow the temperature in the kitchen had dropped. Maybe she was offended that Muriel had chosen to spend time with Denise rather than come to her dinner party.

'Well,' Steve adopted a conciliatory tone, 'she doesn't know what she's missing.'

Kay still didn't speak. Steve decided to withdraw before the atmosphere chilled any further. As he climbed the stairs, he tried to figure out why her mood had changed so suddenly. Was she angry with Muriel? Ought he to have a word with his sister and tell her that she had upset Kay and she must try to make it up to her in some way? Maybe that was part of it, but he sensed there was more than that. It was when he had mentioned Carol that he had lost any chance to lighten the mood again.

He had only just washed and shaved when Kay appeared at the bathroom door. 'I've put a clean shirt on the bed, darling, and if you don't mind, I've chosen a tie.'

She hurried into their bedroom and drew the curtains. In the pink glow shed by the bedside lamps, she started to undress. Steve, still shirtless, moved towards her. When he wrapped his arms around her from behind, she jerked away.

'Not now, Steve. I've got to get ready.'

He let go of her and stepped back quickly. She had made him feel like a bothersome child. Kay took her robe from the hook on the back of the door and hurried to the bathroom.

'When you're ready, would you go down and get some drinks sorted out?' she called before she closed the bathroom door. 'There are a couple of bottles of wine in the cocktail cabinet. Would you take the corks out? Daddy says you've got to let the wine breathe.'

Kay was the perfect hostess. Both sets of parents complimented her. After the meal, they moved next door to the room Kay called the lounge and settled down for a comfortable chat over coffee. No one seemed to notice that Steve took very little part in the conversation. Not even Kay.

Much later, in bed, she snuggled up to him and said, 'That went well, don't you think?'

'Very well.'

She yawned contentedly and turned away from him. 'Well, now that I've practised on the parents, I feel confident enough to give a proper dinner party.'

'Proper?'

'People from the tennis club. You know, the right sort of people. Oh, Steve, now that the war is over, life is going to be wonderful, isn't it?'

Steve lay awake for hours. He had planned to tell Kay tonight that he didn't want to be manager of Latham's Studios. That the job wasn't right for him. He had believed that, as she had loved him enough to marry him, she would be happy to go with him wherever his work took him.

He suppressed a groan when he realised how blind he had been. Tonight he had seen her more clearly than he had ever seen her before. She loved her comfortable suburban life. The tennis club, the dinner parties and mixing with what she called the right people.

How could he ask her to up sticks and follow him wherever the job he really wanted might take him? But equally how could he stay here facing a future of family portraits, beautiful babies, weddings and works dinners? He would never survive the tedium of such a life.

Steve fell asleep eventually, but in a neat little house only a few streets away, Alice Grayson sat wide awake in an armchair in the room she called her refuge. On her lap lay the letter that had been delivered that morning.

The love of her life was dead. He had died several weeks ago and they had only just got around to telling her. The letter was from his firm of solicitors. From the grandson of the man who had been responsible for arranging her allowance all those years ago.

After a brief paragraph informing her of her former lover's death, he had gone on to tell her that although she had been provided for in the will, the deceased's family intended to challenge what they thought of as the extravagance of the allowance. Especially as they believed that the deceased had only provided for her in the first place because she had threatened blackmail.

'But you know that's not true!' Alice had cried out when she read those words. 'I didn't ask for anything. He insisted.'

Alice Grayson wept as she had never wept before. Not even when she had woken up in hospital to find her face irreparably scarred and her career over had she wept like this. But the only people there to hear her were the long-dead film stars portrayed on her collection of playbills and framed portraits.

She had sat there all day hardly moving and making no attempt to find food or drink for herself. The sun that had flooded the back garden with light moved round and then sank lower in the sky. The shadows lengthened and the moon rose, but Alice did not see the silvered beauty of the old trees. The letter fell from her lap and the faces on the walls went on smiling into the camera.

Chapter Eighteen

Carol studied her script every night, fell exhausted into bed and responded to the alarm clock with a groan each morning. One morning as she waited on the front doorstep for her car to arrive, a taxi drew up and Patti staggered out. Her hair was rat-tailed and there were dark smudges under her eyes.

'You look dreadful,' Carol said.

Patti bridled. 'Thank you very much. You don't look so hot yourself.'

'I didn't mean to offend you.'

'Didn't you? God help me when you do, then.'

'Patti, don't let's quarrel. It's just that I'm concerned. You've been coming home later and later, and I don't think you're getting enough sleep.'

The older girl stared at Carol belligerently for a moment and then grinned. 'Pot and kettle. Neither are you.'

Carol couldn't argue with that. 'You're right, but I can't help it. I work long hours and I've got to be up bright and early the next morning.'

'Whereas I'm simply having a good time.'

'Are you? Are you really?'

'I certainly am. I've already told you. He's very, very rich.'

'Maybe. But is he . . . does he . . . I mean, are his intentions honourable?'

Patti hooted with laughter. 'Carol, have you any idea what you sound like? Of course his intentions aren't honourable. But what do you take me for? I wasn't born yesterday. I can look after myself, so for goodness' sake stop worrying about me and get on with your own life.'

Carol's car drew up and Patti pushed past her and went into the house, slamming the door behind her. Imagining what Mrs Evans would have to say about the noise, Carol was pleased to hurry into the car. The driver seldom spoke and she took advantage of this to close her eyes and relax. Patti was right. She wasn't getting enough sleep, but there was nothing she could do about it.

At work, she catnapped whenever she could, or at least tried to relax while she was sitting around waiting to be called. It was during her brief moments in front of the camera that she came alive.

The writer was still infuriating everyone by changing his mind just about every day, although it wasn't entirely his fault. Max Preston was mercurial. He would suddenly, for reasons known only to himself, demand a rewrite. Members of the cast would groan or cheer when they were handed their new scripts.

Weekdays merged into the weekend, and after her seventh day at the studios, Carol took the next day's script and stuffed it into her holdall bag without comment. She went to the dressing room she shared with all the female bit players and sat before the row of mirrors to clean her face. The only seat left had been next to Joan Summerfield, who pointedly ignored her.

'Nice day out tomorrow, then,' Mabel said when she came to collect Carol's costume.

'Day out?'

'Haven't you looked at your script?'

'No . . . I haven't.'

Mabel undid the zip at the back of Carol's frock and helped her take it off. 'Go on, take a look,' she said.

By now, Carol was completely unselfconscious about standing around in her underwear. She wiped her hands on a clean rag and reached for the script she had stuffed in her holdall. As she looked at it, her eyes widened.

'What do you think of that?' Mabel asked.

'We're going to the races!'

'That's right. Out on location for two or three days. Bit of excitement for all concerned. I'll be here all night loading up the wardrobe trailer.'

'What will I be wearing?'

'A very pretty summer two-piece. And Tony's going to let you have your hair down. You're supposed to look vulnerable rather than like the little tart you are at the club.'

Carol laughed. 'So I'm a nice girl after all.' She put her script back in her bag, which she left on her chair as she walked over to the rail where her own clothes were hanging.

'Maybe you're as sweet as pie, or maybe you're a sour little tart,' Mabel said, 'but why should you care, when you're going to have all those scenes with Paul Grainger? And speaking of Mr Grainger, you haven't found out where he hides it, have you?'

'I don't know what you're talking about,' Carol said.

'Don't you? Everybody else does. Why do you think he vanishes smartly to his dressing room whenever he's not needed on set? And why do you think that agent of his, Ed Palmer, is always looking around in there?'

Carol remembered the night of the party. The champagne waiting for Paul in the summer house. She remembered how vexed Mr Palmer had seemed when he found them drinking there, and how he had dismissed her quickly.

Paul had laughed and said, 'You believe in looking after your protégées, don't you, Ed?'

And Ed Palmer's answer: 'They're no use to me if they choose to ruin themselves.'

At the time, Carol had imagined that Ed wanted people like herself to watch what they ate and drank and have early nights. But now she understood the true meaning of his words. And she understood the significance of the raised voices echoing from the summer house as she walked back across the lawn.

'Paul likes a drink?' she asked Mabel, although she already knew the answer.

'That's putting it mildly. Until lately, he's always managed to turn up on time and say his lines, but more than once recently he hasn't been too steady on his feet. Somehow he's managing to bring alcohol to work with him, and it's like a battle of wits between him and Mr Palmer as to where he's hidden it.'

'But why did you think that I would know where he puts it?'

'I got the impression that you two were pals. I mean, the way he greeted you the first day and introduced you to Max.'

'I'd only met him once. At a party. We're not pals.'

She heard Joan snort but did her best to ignore it.

'Well, you certainly have that extra something when you act together,' Mabel said. 'Folk can't help thinking . . . well, you know . . .'

'Thinking what, exactly?' Carol asked nervously.

'That you and he are friends.'

Carol knew by the way Mabel's eyes slid away from her that the wardrobe mistress really meant that she and Paul were more than just friends.

'Is that what people think? That Paul and I are *friends*, as you put it?'

'Listen, Carol. If you say there's nothing between you, I'll take your word for it. But you'll have to get used to this sort of thing. Some of it is just spiteful gossip, and some of it is jealousy. In your case I would say that the green-eyed monster has been having a busy time.'

'Why?'

'Because you're so damn good, that's why. And if you're going to get any further in this business, you'll have to grow another skin. Now stop worrying over it and go home and learn your lines.'

Carol decided to take Mabel's advice and stop worrying. After all, there was nothing she could do about the gossip. On the way home, there was a heavy shower and she sat back in the car and closed her eyes. The noise the tyres made on the wet road was somehow soothing, and it helped her to relax, to wind down.

Back in her room, which she now regarded as home, her own little eyrie at the top of the house, she dumped her holdall and her coat, and even though it was not strictly necessary, she lit the fire. It made things cosier. She made herself some tea and toast and, sitting down at the table, pulled the holdall over and reached down for the script. It wasn't there.

Even though it was quite obvious that there were no sheets of paper in the bag, Carol turned it upside down and emptied the contents on the floor. She stared at them miserably. She was sure she had put the script back in the bag before dumping it on the chair. She closed her eyes and visualised the scene. Yes, she could see herself stuffing the script into the soft leather holdall at an angle. And she also saw something else. Joan Summerfield staring into the mirror as she combed her hair.

Joan had taken her script, Carol was sure of it. The older girl knew how important it was to study the lines before turning up on set, and this was an act of pure spite.

That night, Carol got no sleep at all. She lay in her bed wretchedly contemplating what she would do.

When she reached the racecourse the next morning, it looked as though the circus had come to town, with the trailers pulling in to their places and the film crew setting up the equipment. Carol sought out Rafe, the assistant director, and told him that she had lost her script.

He was furious. 'Did you lose it before or after you learned your lines?' he asked.

'Before.'

'How on earth did you manage to do that?'

'I don't know.'

Carol had no proof that Joan had taken her script, and even if she had, she had no intention of telling anyone what had happened.

'I hadn't figured you for a dumb blonde,' Rafe said.

Carol kept quiet.

'All right. I just happen to have a copy you can have. Now go away and study it. One mistake and you'll never work on a film I have anything to do with again.'

Carol took the script and was about to walk away when Rafe stopped her. 'Carol,' he said. 'I know you're only here because you won a beauty contest, but I believe you show great promise. Max does too. If you want a career in films, you'll have to learn to be more professional. Don't make a mistake like this again. Believe me, not many people in this business are as forgiving as I am.'

'I won't.'

'Luckily for you, you won't be needed until this afternoon. So as well as studying the script, I suggest you try to find a quiet corner and have a nap. You look dreadful.'

Carol didn't manage to find anywhere to sleep, and she had no appetite for any of the hot meals on offer at the catering van. Once she was dressed and had been to hair and make-up, she sat and shivered on a canvas chair while she waited to be called. The sun was bright but the air was cool. The little cotton two-piece that Mabel had promised was pale blue with a white trim, and her shoes, hat and gloves were white. Tony had told her how divine she looked, but secretly Carol thought the effect was rather common.

She gazed around at all the paraphernalia needed for location work. Trailers full of costumes and equipment, trailers for dressing rooms, and a catering van dispensing tea, sandwiches and a selection of hot meals. The film company now seemed more like an occupying army than a circus, but to her surprise, Carol found that the racing went on as though they weren't there.

By now she had pretty much worked out the storyline of the film. The title was *A Safe Bet*, and the hero was a gambler who had to go on the run to a northern seaside resort after annoying some dangerous people. He'd taken refuge there, but sadly he hadn't learned from his past mistakes and had got into more trouble.

None of the cast had actually been to Seaton Bay. The film crew had taken background shots of the crowded beach, the amusement arcades on the promenade and the busy funfair. These shots would be intercut with the action shots, and no one would know that the actors were not really there.

Today, Lewes racecourse was standing in for Newcastle, and it amused Carol that no one seemed to notice that the accents of the crowd were completely wrong. Or if they did, they didn't care.

Paul was playing the hero – or rather the antihero: the central character in the story who was neither traditionally brave nor good. Carol was sure that women filmgoers would fall for him anyway and believe that even though he was a hardened criminal, nothing that happened was really his fault.

Her own part had grown since it was first written. After observing the cigarette girl give short change to several customers, Paul's character blackmailed her into helping him rob the nightclub. However, a brittle sort of romance had developed between them, and in the closing sequences of the film the gangster took the cigarette girl to the races. She thought it was a day out and didn't realise that he had another reason for going there.

Today there was a sequence of the two of them arriving at the races, and then another where they were having a drink and talking in the bar. Carol managed to be word perfect in both scenes, and when Rafe told her she could go, he said, 'You got away with it, Carol. Now go home, learn your lines for tomorrow and get some sleep.'

Carol treated herself to a relaxing bath and took her script to bed with her. When she was satisfied that she had done all she could, she switched off the bedside lamp and settled down. Despite her upset at what had happened, she slept well. Pure exhaustion, she supposed the next morning when she woke at the usual time.

On location there was the usual cheerful banter and the usual sitting around waiting to be called. She enjoyed herself more than she had the day before for obvious reasons, and also because Joan Summerfield was not required in any of the scenes at the racecourse. Mabel told her that there were to be no more scenes at the nightclub, so Carol guessed that Joan had already left the cast. Carol hoped she would never see her again.

Her first scene with Paul today was one where he told her he was going to place a bet and then disappeared. After a close-up of her looking worried, she went looking for him and found him arguing with another shady character behind the stables. Knives were drawn and the other man was killed.

229

All very exciting, Carol thought, though she didn't believe the average filmgoer would have any idea how many separate takes were involved and how long it took to put this bit of the story together.

Paul looked more handsome than ever and even more dangerous in a sharp suit, black shirt and white silk tie. His enemy was played by a burly, broad-shouldered actor who looked as though he'd been recruited from an American gangster movie. He had an incredibly battered face, but he ruined the illusion for Carol when he opened his mouth and produced a phoney Italian accent.

How Miss Grayson would laugh at him, Carol thought, and immediately suffered a pang of guilt when she remembered that she still hadn't written to her former elocution teacher. But when I do find time, I'll have so much to tell her that I'll write screeds and screeds, she thought. And I'll thank her from the bottom of my heart for making this possible for me.

In her final scene, the cigarette girl was shown realising how evil her gangster really was. There was a close-up of her face that seemed to last for ever, and the watching crew actually applauded when Max called, 'Print it!'

Then she was shown hurrying away towards a uniformed policeman. Carol would have to wait until the film was released to see what happened next and what the final outcome would be.

When Paul said goodbye to her, he spoke slowly, as if he was having to concentrate. 'It's been a pleasure working with you, Carol,' he said. 'I'm sure we'll meet again.'

They were standing beside the catering van, and Carol noticed his hand shaking a little as he sipped a cup of coffee. His eyes were glassy.

He noticed her looking at him curiously and said, 'I'm dead beat. It's tiring working outdoors, isn't it?'

Suddenly he stumbled and grabbed at Carol for support. In doing so, he spilled his coffee all down her jacket and skirt.

Carol stared down in dismay.

'Oh my God, Carol,' Paul said. 'Mabel will kill you!'

'No I won't.'

They both spun round to find the wardrobe mistress observing them coolly.

'It's you I'd like to kill, Mr Grainger. I saw what happened and I don't blame Miss Marshall at all. Now, if you'll come with me, Carol, I'll try to get that stain out straight away. It's just as well the costume isn't needed again. At least not for this film.'

'I'm truly sorry,' Paul said. 'I couldn't help it.'

'I know you couldn't, Mr Grainger.'

She hurried Carol away. Once inside the wardrobe trailer she said, 'Sad, isn't it?'

'Sad?'

'They say he never had a problem until what happened to him during the war. He was a real hero, you know. But I guess he saw too much. Maybe he drinks to forget, but if he goes on like this he's going to ruin himself. There's already a director or two who has doubts about hiring him. Yes, it's very sad.'

By the time Carol was ready to go home, her car was waiting and she sank into the leather seat in a strange mood made up of both elation and disappointment. Elation that everything seemed to have gone well, and disappointment because her work on the film was over.

She was worried, too. Everyone had seemed to take it for granted that she would find more work, but Mr Palmer hadn't mentioned anything. Her spirits rose when, just as the driver was about to pull away, Mr Palmer himself appeared and stopped him.

'Wait a moment,' he said, and he climbed into the car next to Carol. Taking out his wallet, he peeled off a ten-shilling note, then leaned over the seat and asked the driver to go and buy him some cigarettes.

'Get yourself a cup of tea and a bun while you're about it,' he said. 'And you can take your time. I have to talk to Miss Marshall.' When the driver had gone, he smiled at Carol. 'You've done very well,' he said. 'You were lucky to win that competition and get a proper part in the film. Most young hopefuls would have to start by playing walk-on parts, mostly uncredited. But now and then someone comes along who lights up the screen, and it seems that you are one of those people. You're a natural and worth every penny you've been paid.'

'I've been paid?'

'In cash.'

Ed took a long, slim envelope from his inside pocket. He handed it to her and watched as she opened it. There was a bundle of crisp white five-pound notes and a payslip. She looked at the payslip first, and gasped. 'One hundred pounds!'

'That's right. Ten pounds a day. Even for the day you just sat and waited to be called.'

'But that's wonderful!'

'For a start, maybe. But once this film is screened and they see what you're capable of, they won't get you so cheaply.'

'That's cheap?'

'In this business it is.'

Carol looked at the money.

'Go on, count it,' Ed said.

'No . . . it's all right. I trust you.'

Ed laughed. 'Touching, I'm sure, but I want you to count it.'

Carol did so, and then she looked at Ed and frowned. 'There's only forty pounds here.'

'That's right. And every penny of it is yours to keep.'

232

'But the rest?'

'Listen, and I'll explain. I get ten per cent of everything you earn, so that's ten pounds gone for a start. Then there's the money I've been advancing you. Your rent, money to buy food, clothes, the hire of the cars.'

'The cars?'

'You didn't think the film company had sent them?'

'I suppose I did. And I thought the money you gave me came from them too.'

Ed laughed. 'Not them. Oh, they paid your train fare to London. That was part of the deal when you won the competition. But after that they expected you to fend for yourself. Maybe they even wanted you to give up and go home. But I made sure that they didn't – the scriptwriter owes me one – and I also made sure that you had enough to live on while you waited for the call.'

'Thank you. But why?'

'Because you're going to be a big star and I want to represent you. Remember, as long as you're with me, I'll do the very best I can for you. And in return, you've got to promise to keep your nose clean.'

'Meaning?'

'No scandals, no stories in the gutter press. So long as you're a starlet, you've got to live like a nun.'

'And when I'm a star?' Carol said jokingly.

Ed smiled. 'Then you learn to be discreet. And if you slip up, we pay people to keep it out of the papers. Now look after that money. You and I are square. I won't be subsidising you any longer, but I think you've got more than enough to see you through to the next job.'

Carol looked down at the large white five-pound notes. She had handled one now and then when taking payment from a customer in the French Salon, but she had never owned one.

'Maybe you should open a bank account,' Ed told her.

'I will.'

'But for the next few days, I want you to relax and enjoy yourself. Buy yourself a birthday present.'

'Birthday?'

Ed laughed. 'You're a funny kid. It's your birthday next week. Your twenty-first birthday. Had you forgotten?'

'Yes . . . I had.'

'What would you be doing if you were at home in Seaton Bay? Would your folks have a party?'

'You've met them, haven't you?'

'All right. So they wouldn't be celebrating. But you'd be going out with your pals, wouldn't you? Out for a drink, maybe a meal at the – what was it called? The Rainbow Room?'

'Perhaps I would.'

How could she have forgotten her own birthday? Suddenly she felt bereft. There was no doubt that Denise and Muriel would have made a fuss of her. Guilt kicked in. She still hadn't written to them to tell them about the filming. Fine friend she was.

'Look, Carol, I've got to go and see Paul. But I've saved the best news until last. Do you think you could do a French accent?'

'Yes. Why?'

'Because I've got you an audition for a part in another movie. It's a war story, set in France. They need a beautiful young woman to play a member of the Resistance. It's small, but it's a great part.'

'France?'

'If you're asking whether you'll be going to France, the answer is no. It will be shot right here in England. There are plenty of bombed buildings around to stand in for a town in France. But wherever they shoot it, aren't you pleased?'

'Yes, I am. Why do you ask?'

'Most young actresses would be throwing themselves at me and thanking me profusely for a chance like this, but you just sit there coolly keeping your own counsel.'

'I'm sorry. I am grateful. Truly I am. It's just that I have so much to think about.'

He looked at her for a moment, then said, 'Here's your driver. You'll be hearing from me soon, and before you go for the audition, I want you to sign a new contract. Once you're twenty-one, we won't need your father's consent any more.'

Chapter Nineteen

Carol woke up and glanced at the clock on the bedside table. Four o'clock. She hadn't set the alarm the night before, but this was the exact time she had been getting up for the past ten days. She turned over, pulled the bedclothes up over her shoulders and tried to get back to sleep.

For a while she luxuriated in the fact that she didn't have to get up. She lay in a drowsy, contented state, replaying the filming in her mind and marvelling at how easily she seemed to have taken to the work. She also ran through the more unsettling memories. Unfortunately, it had not taken her long to make enemies. Joan Summerfield had disliked her from the moment the director had praised her and suggested that she give Joan lessons.

She had no idea who her other enemies were, but Mabel had warned her that there was a lot of jealousy and malicious gossip about her and Paul. Would she be able to get used to it? She knew she would have to. Because now that she had actually worked on a film, she was even more sure than she had been before that this was what she wanted to do.

She gave up trying to get back to sleep. Knowing that there was no hurry, she yawned, stretched and got out of bed. The kettle was empty. She reached for her robe and eased her feet into her comfortable old slippers, then opened the door of her room and went out on to the landing.

As she filled the kettle at the small sink, she noticed with distaste that Patti had dumped her dirty dishes there as usual. She had not even rinsed them. Patti didn't do much cooking, which was just as well, as she must have run out of clean plates long ago. The cheesy smell of the unwashed pots and the whiff of gas from the geyser mingled unpleasantly with the smell of the polished lino on the stairs.

Suddenly Carol knew that she had to get away from this house. She decided she would work hard and as soon as she was earning enough to pay rent on a decent flat she would go.

She set the kettle to boil on the gas ring in her room and lit the fire so that she could make a slice of toast. Ed had told her that he would get in touch about the audition soon, and that she should relax and enjoy herself for a few days.

When she had finished her toast, she reached for her bag. She took out the envelope with the money inside and spread the five-pound notes across the table. She had never had so much money in her life. She had no idea what to do with it – except to open a bank account and start saving as Ed had suggested.

A ray of sun eased through the gap in the curtains and slid across the faded carpet. Carol swung round in her seat and stretched her legs out. She kicked off her slippers and wiggled her toes in the warmth of the sun. She had left the window slightly open, and the curtains billowed a little in the slight breeze.

The draught of air carried with it the fresh smell of a summer morning that hadn't yet been tainted by traffic fumes. The electric whine of a milkman's float and the rattle of his crates echoed up from the street below. Carol was suddenly filled with the urge to get ready and go out.

Maybe she would walk in the park and buy a cup of tea from the stall and a bun to crumble up and throw to the birds.

Then later she could go back to the little restaurant and sample anything she liked from the *à la carte* menu. Or maybe she should head straight up to the West End and do some serious shopping. Yes, that was what she would do.

Denise was eating her sandwich lunch in her hidey-hole behind the shelves of the shoe department when Ruthie appeared.

'What is it?' Denise asked. 'Is Mam all right? Is it Dad?'

Ruthie shook her head and smiled. 'Don't worry, they're both fine.'

'Then what are you doing here? You're not playing truant, are you?'

'Of course not. A letter arrived for you after you left for work this morning, so when I went home at lunchtime, Mam asked me to bring it to you on my way back to school.'

Denise frowned. 'What's so important about this letter?'

'Look . . .' Ruthie opened her satchel and took out a flimsy blue envelope.

Denise stared at it. 'An airmail letter,' she said.

'Yes, and it has an American stamp on it. The sender's address is on the back. Mam thought you'd like to have it straight away.'

Denise turned the envelope over. 'It's from Howard,' she said.

'Well go on, open it.'

'Not with you here.'

'I had to gobble my dinner down to bring that letter to you.'

'Well . . .'

'Aw, go on. Don't be a spoilsport.'

'All right, then.'

Denise was annoyed to find that she was shaking. She had tried to tell herself that Howard was not important to her and had accepted that she would never see him again. So what was he doing writing to her like this? She slit open the envelope and began to read.

Dear Denise, the letter began.

I hope you don't mind my writing to you like this, but there is no one else who can help me.

Suppressing her disappointment that the letter was obviously not going to be what she had been hoping for, Denise read on to the end. Then she frowned.

It was Ruthie's turn to ask if something was the matter.

'Maybe there is and maybe there isn't,' Denise replied. 'I'll tell you later. But I want you to take a message to Muriel for me before you go back to school. Have you got a piece of paper?'

Ruthie opened her satchel again and ferreted around until she found an old spelling test. 'What about this? You could write on the back.'

'That'll do. Have you got a pencil?'

Ruthie found her one and Denise scribbled a note. 'Here you are,' she said. 'Take it to the newspaper office and give it to Muriel. Go on, get a move on!'

Ruthie made no attempt to go. 'Can I read it?' she asked.

'Yes, you can read it. Not that it will tell you very much. Now off you go.'

Ruthie, not wanting to appear to be nosy, waited until she was in the lift before she read the note. Denise was right. It didn't tell her much.

Albert Marshall had asked the foreman on the building site if he could leave work a little early. On the way home, he called into Woolworth's. Hetty would be finishing work at the laundry round about now and she might be doing some shopping, so Albert found himself glancing over his shoulder apprehensively. All he wanted was a birthday card, and he was angry with himself for feeling guilty. Hetty had made it clear that they would not be acknowledging Carol's twenty-first.

The subject had come up only the night before, when Hetty had said, 'Well she's not getting a key to this door, not if I have anything to do with it.'

'I shouldn't think she wants one,' Albert said, and earned himself a furious glare.

'Just you wait,' Hetty said. 'Once she's come of age and hasn't got us to look out for her, it will all end in tears, I'm sure of it. And she needn't think she can come crawling back here.'

'When did we last look out for her, Hetty?'

Hetty was outraged. 'How can you ask that? Haven't I looked after her since she was a little girl, and didn't you sign those papers with that Mr Palmer allowing her to go gallivanting off to London to act in a film?'

'We did well out of that. I sometimes think it's almost as if we'd sold her.'

'What a disgusting thing to say! We did no such thing. We . . . we made it possible for her to be a film star. To make money and be famous.'

'If you really think that, why did you just tell me that it will all end in tears?'

For once, Hetty had not been able to answer him. She had glared at him speechlessly, her small eyes becoming even smaller as she screwed her face up into an expression of fury. Then she had grabbed her coat and handbag and flounced out, saying she would spend the night at her sister's house and that Albert had better be ready to apologise for upsetting her when she came back. *If* she came back!

Once, Albert would have hurried after her. But he was tired. More than usually tired of late, and he simply couldn't face another of Hetty's rages. He went into the kitchen and took a spoonful of his cough syrup, and then a large spoonful of milk of magnesia to try and ease the pain that had been troubling him for weeks now. Then he went to bed.

Hetty had returned early the next morning. Albert hadn't apologised, and neither of them had mentioned Carol's birthday again. But that didn't mean that he was not going to send his daughter a birthday card.

After leaving Woolworth's, he went to the post office and bought a stamp and a postal order for twenty-one shillings, which he enclosed with the card. He did not have Carol's address, but he had already worked out what he was going to do. He would drop the card off at her friend Denise's place and ask her to post it.

After work, Muriel was waiting at the staff entrance to Rutherford's, just as Denise's note had requested. 'What's this about?' she asked. 'I mean, your note was fairly cryptic.'

Denise glared at her. 'If you mean mysterious, why don't you just say so?'

'I'm sorry. But I'm sure you didn't ask me to meet you just so we could quarrel.'

'Sorry.'

It was so unlike Denise to apologise that Muriel was taken aback. 'Is it something serious?' she asked. Then, panic rising, 'Is it about Carol? I haven't heard from her for ages. Is she okay?'

Denise's smile was vinegary. 'I have no idea whether she's okay or not, because I haven't heard from her either. So no, it's not about Carol. I've had a letter from Howard. He's worried about a friend of his. She hasn't replied to his letters and he thinks she might be in trouble. She hasn't got a telephone, so he wants me to go and check up on her. I was hoping you'd come with me.'

Muriel thought it must be an indication of how worried

Denise was that she had actually asked for her company. 'Of course I'll come,' she said.

'Thanks. Let's go.'

By the time they got to Alice Grayson's house, Denise had told Muriel as much as she could. Muriel already knew that Miss Grayson had been Carol's elocution teacher, but she had not known that she and Howard Napier were friends.

'Howard's worried because he thinks Miss Grayson may be upset about something: something to do with an old friend – a man friend – dying. It was someone she was very fond of,' Denise said. 'And there's more to it. She may be hard up.'

Now they stood at the gate and looked up the short drive towards the front door. The sky had clouded over and the house was in shadow from a large tree in next door's garden. Denise shivered involuntarily. 'Well everything looks okay from the outside,' she said.

'Why shouldn't the outside of the house look okay?'

'No milk bottles on the step.'

Muriel caught her breath. 'Surely you didn't think that . . . that she'd died?'

'It did cross my mind, but only because Howard seems to be in a blue funk.'

'I suppose that's because he's so far away. He must feel helpless.'

Denise opened the gate and strode up to the front door. She rang the bell and waited. And waited. Then she knocked on the door, but there was no answering sound from within the house. No doors opening, no footsteps across the hall or coming down the stairs.

'Do you suppose she's gone away?' Muriel asked.

'Where would she go? Howard says she has no family. Nobody.'

'Well what are we going to do?'

'Follow me.'

Miss Grayson lived in a semi-detached house. At one side there was a tall gate that led to the back garden. Denise opened the gate. About halfway along the path there was a door that probably opened into the scullery. It was locked. She knocked on it loudly, but again, there was no response from inside.

'What shall we do now?' Muriel asked.

Without answering, Denise followed the path along to the back garden. 'Look,' she said, 'French windows. I thought there might be.'

The two girls leaned close to the window panes and peered in. The sky had darkened further and there was a smell of rain to come. Inside the house it was dim and shadowy.

'You'd think she'd put the lights on,' Muriel said.

'If she's there.'

'Should we go in?'

Denise tried the door. 'It's locked,' she said. 'But we've got to get in somehow.' She took off one of her shoes, and before Muriel could stop her, she had aimed the heel at the small square of glass nearest to the door handle. It took two or three blows, but eventually the glass smashed and Denise reached in gingerly and found the key. A moment later they had entered the house.

'Miss Grayson?' Denise called. 'Miss Grayson, are you here?'

The only answer was the steady tick of the ormolu clock on the mantelpiece.

'I feel like we're being watched,' Muriel said.

'What do you mean?'

'All those pictures – those people on the wall – they're watching us.'

'Don't be daft. But I know what you mean. I feel like a housebreaker.'

'Well we've done it now. We're in. So we'd better search the house.'

Denise led the way into the entrance hall and, finding a switch on the wall, turned on the light. They heard a small sigh, and looked up to see Alice Grayson sitting at the top of the stairs, her upper body hunched over her knees like a child trying to curl up small and hide. She was wearing a cream silk robe embroidered in bright colours with exotic birds and flowers. Her hair, a faded blond with grey roots, was unpinned, and it fell forward, obscuring most of her face.

Miss Grayson raised her head wearily. Her arms were folded across her slim body. 'I hoped you'd go away,' she said.

Denise and Muriel stared up at her, not knowing what to say.

'I heard you, you know. Shouting and banging on the doors fit to wake the dead.' She sighed. 'But now that you're here, who are you?'

They spoke simultaneously.

'I'm a friend of Carol's.'

'I'm a friend of Howard Napier – and Carol, too.'

Alice Grayson looked at Denise. 'I saw your picture in the paper. You're Denise, aren't you? And I know about you and Howard. I mean, he told me how sweet you were.'

'Did he?' Denise suddenly sounded despondent.

'Yes, he did. And you,' Alice Grayson's gaze rested on Muriel, 'you must be Muriel. You've been friends with Carol ever since you were children.'

'Yes.'

'Have either of you heard from her? Do you know if she's all right?'

'No, she hasn't written for a while,' Muriel said.

'She must be busy,' Alice Grayson said.

'Too busy to write to old friends?' Denise asked.

'I remember what it was like. Early mornings, late nights, learning your part. Don't worry. I'm sure she'll write soon. But why did you come here?' Miss Grayson asked. 'Why did you break into my house? I heard the glass shatter.'

'I'm sorry about that,' Denise said. 'And please don't worry; I'll get my dad to fix it. But we had to get in and see if you were all right. Howard wrote and told me he was worried because he hasn't heard from you. And . . . and he knows you may have had some bad news lately.'

Miss Grayson sighed. 'Yes, I've had bad news.'

Her head dropped and she relapsed into silence. Muriel and Denise looked at each other, unsure of what to do.

'Is there . . . I mean, can we help in any way?'

Alice Grayson reached out an arm and grasped the banister rail. She pulled herself up and raised her head as she stared down at them. Both girls' eyes widened as they saw for the first time the extent of the scars on one side of her face.

'No, my dears. I don't need help. Please tell Howard that I can manage perfectly well. But what am I thinking of? I should offer you a drink. Will you stay and take tea with me?'

Without waiting for an answer, she began to come down the stairs. On her feet she wore a pair of embroidered boudoir slippers with Louis heels that must have been fashionable twenty years ago, Muriel thought. She started forward as she saw the heel of one of them catch the hem of Miss Grayson's robe. But she was too late. With a cry of surprise and terror, Alice Grayson fell headlong down the stairs.

Chapter Twenty

Alice Grayson lay frighteningly still. Her eyes were closed.
Denise was nearer to the bottom of the stairs, so she hurried
forward and knelt down. Muriel pushed her aside.

'Don't touch her!' Muriel took hold of Miss Grayson's
wrist while she felt for a pulse. 'She's alive,' she said. 'Find the
nearest house that has a telephone and call an ambulance.'

Denise opened the front door and went out, leaving it ajar.
Muriel watched as the wind blew rain into the hall. She was
just about to go and find a rug to keep Miss Grayson warm,
but as she got to her feet, the door opened and Denise walked
in.

'Did you call an ambulance?' Muriel asked.

'Better than that.' Denise stepped aside, and a middle-aged
man entered. He was wearing gold-framed spectacles and a
smart suit, and was carrying a small leather bag. 'This is Dr
Mason,' Denise said. 'He lives two doors away.'

The doctor took charge of the situation straight away. 'I'll
deal with this,' he said. 'Why don't you two go into the
kitchen and put the kettle on? You're both as white as
parchment, so I prescribe hot sweet tea for the pair of you.
Don't worry,' he added. 'My wife is calling the ambulance.'

The kitchen was small and sad-looking. It was the kitchen
of someone who lived alone and probably didn't eat very
much. Denise put the kettle on. They had hardly had time to
pour their tea when Dr Mason appeared in the doorway.

'The ambulance is here,' he said. 'No, don't get up. You'll just get in the way. I'm going to follow them down to the hospital.'

'How is she?' Denise asked.

'I don't think it's too bad, but I'll know better when she's had an X-ray. I believe she's been very lucky. She needs to be in hospital, though. I've convinced her of that.'

'You've convinced her? Does that mean she's come round?'

'Yes, and she's most reluctant to leave the house. Her main concern is a broken window.' Dr Mason looked at them quizzically.

'Tell her not to worry,' Denise said. 'I'll get my father to fix that tonight. And tell her I'll leave Muriel in the house to guard it while I go and get him. He'll board it up until he can get a piece of glass.'

'Good girl,' the doctor said. 'Now, I must be off.'

They heard him giving instructions to the ambulance crew as they lifted Miss Grayson on to the stretcher. A few moments later the front door closed.

'Well, thanks for that,' Muriel said.

'Thanks for what?'

'Saying that I would stay here.'

'I didn't think you'd mind.'

'I don't, but my parents will be worried by now. Would you call at the house and tell them what's happened?'

'Sure. Will you be all right here?'

'Of course.'

When Denise had gone, Muriel washed their cups and then opened her shoulder bag and took out the notebook and pencil that went with her everywhere these days. She went back into the little sitting room and, examining the intriguing faces on the wall, started to make notes.

★

The rain had settled into a steady downpour, and by the time Denise got home, she was soaking wet. The family had already eaten, and as soon as Denise walked in, her mother got up from the table.

'I've kept your meal warm, pet,' she said.

'Thanks, Mam, but it will have to wait.'

As Denise explained what the problem was, Ruthie watched and listened, wide-eyed. Before she had finished talking, her father had already risen from his seat.

'I think I've got something that will do to board the window up, but it's at the allotment. So is my tool bag. Give me the address and I'll meet you there.'

'Thanks, Dad, you're a prince.'

'That's what your mother keeps telling me.' Bill Shaw grinned as he took his jacket from the back of his chair.

Denise gave him Miss Grayson's address, then said, 'You'll need your mackintosh. It's raining cats and dogs out there.'

'Won't you at least have a cup of tea?' her mother asked.

'No. I feel guilty leaving Muriel there on her own. I'd better get back.' She took her own raincoat from the peg in the tiny entrance hall. 'Blast!' she said.

'What is it?'

'I promised Muriel I'd let her parents know what's happening.'

'I can do that,' Ruthie volunteered.

'You'll forget what to say.'

'I won't!' Ruthie was indignant. Then she grinned. 'But why don't you write it all down?'

'Good thinking, Watson!' Denise smiled at her younger sister affectionately, and hastily scribbled a note to Muriel's parents.

When both her daughters had gone, Mrs Shaw remembered the card that Carol's father had left earlier. She didn't suppose it would matter if Denise posted it tomorrow.

★

It didn't take Bill Shaw long to remove the remaining shards of glass from the window frame. He began to board it up. 'I can get some glass tomorrow,' he told Denise. 'But who will pay for it?'

'I will.'

'I will.'

The two girls spoke simultaneously again.

'It should be me. I broke it,' Denise said.

'But I didn't stop you, did I?'

Denise smiled. 'I don't think I gave you the chance. We'll go halves, shall we?'

'Okay. Did you tell my mum where I was?'

'I sent Ruthie round with a note.'

'Good.'

As they smiled at each other, the doorbell rang.

'Who on earth can that be?' Denise asked.

They both hurried into the hall, and Denise opened the door. She stood back quickly to allow Dr Mason to enter. Raindrops shone on his hair. He took off his spectacles and reached into his pocket for a clean white handkerchief to wipe them.

'It's getting worse out there,' he said as he put his spectacles back on. 'And it's not too warm in here. Miss Grayson is in the best place tonight, I think: a warm hospital bed.'

'Is she all right?' Denise and Muriel said, once more in unison.

'She'll survive,' Dr Mason said. 'Nothing's broken, but she's going to be badly bruised. But for all that, perhaps it's just as well this happened. She's obviously been neglecting herself, and in hospital they'll keep an eye on her and build her up again.'

'Thank you for coming to tell us,' Denise said. 'Is there anything we can do?'

'Yes. That's why I'm here. Miss Grayson has recovered enough to be very unhappy with the hospital nightgown. She's dictated this list for you.' The doctor handed Denise a piece of folded paper. 'She would like you to pack a little bag for her. You could take it in tomorrow. Is that all right?'

'Of course it is.'

'She'd also be very grateful if you would keep an eye on the house. Have you got a key?'

'There's the key to the French window.'

'Hang on to it, then. Now, I must go before my wife gives my dinner to the dog.' He said good night and hurried out into the rain.

Denise looked at the list she had been given, and she and Muriel went upstairs to find a small case and pick out the items of clothing.

'Oh no,' Muriel groaned suddenly.

'What is it?'

'Dinner . . . my mother . . .'

'Surely she'll keep it warm for you?'

'Of course she will. It's not that. Steve and Kay are eating with us tonight, and Kay's bound to think I've done this on purpose.'

'That's crazy. If it's anybody's fault, it's mine for asking you to come here.'

'It's no use telling her that. She'll just say I shouldn't have agreed.'

Denise's father called up the stairs. 'We'd best get back,' he said. 'While you're up there, why don't you see if there's a coat Muriel could borrow? Otherwise she'll get soaked.'

'Good idea,' Denise said.

'Do you think Miss Grayson will mind?' Muriel asked.

'Of course not.'

But before they could do anything about it, the doorbell rang once more.

Thinking that Dr Mason must have forgotten something, Denise hurried downstairs, with Muriel following. But when she opened the door, it was not the doctor standing there. It was Steve Douglas.

'Oh, you,' Denise said.

Steve raised his eyebrows, but there was a hint of a smile on his lips. 'That's not a very cordial greeting. Are you going to let me in, or do you want me to stand here in the rain?'

Denise moved back. Steve entered quickly and shut the door behind him.

'We got your note,' he said, 'so I came to see if there's anything I can do.'

'Why would you want to do that?' Denise scowled at him.

'Concern? Courtesy? Good manners? Will any of those do? And why are you being so hostile?'

Denise would have liked to tell him it was because she simply didn't like him. That she hadn't liked him for years because she was convinced that he had just been stringing Carol along, and that just as she had feared he had broken Carol's heart. But she could hardly do that with his sister standing so close.

She had discovered lately that she rather liked Muriel. She wasn't half as snobbish as Denise had once thought, and a huge point in her favour was that she obviously disliked Kay as much as Denise herself did.

Muriel hurried forward. 'Steve! Have you brought my raincoat?'

'Better than that. I've brought Dad's car.'

'Thank goodness.'

'Are you finished here?'

'Yes. I'll just get Miss Grayson's case.'

'Well then, I'll take you home. You as well, of course,' he said to Denise.

'No thank you. My father and I can walk.'

'Why would you do that when I'm offering you a lift in a nice dry car?'

'Yes, why, Denise?' her father asked.

If she'd been on her own, Denise thought she would have died rather than get into a car with Steve Douglas, but it would be really mean to make her father walk home in the rain just because of her own dislike of Muriel's brother.

'Okay,' she said. 'We'll accept your offer.'

If Muriel noticed what an effort it had been, she didn't remark on it. After checking each room carefully to see if any lights had been left on or any windows open, Denise pocketed the key to the French windows and they let themselves out of the front door. They pulled it closed behind them, then hurried towards the car.

Steve dropped them off right outside their door, even though this would mean an awkward manoeuvre to get out of Garden Square again. Denise's father saved her the task of thanking him, and they hurried upstairs to where her mother had her hot meal waiting.

After the meal, Mrs Shaw gave Denise the birthday card that Carol's father had left, together with a request that she should post it. That reminded her of the twenty-first card she herself had bought for Carol. She would post them both the next day, she thought. Even though she was more than a little angry with her old friend.

It was weeks now since Carol had written to either her or Muriel. And as for poor, lonely Alice Grayson, it didn't seem as if Carol had written to her at all.

The rain had thinned to a penetrating drizzle by the time the Douglas family had finished their delayed evening meal. Mr Douglas offered to run Steve and Kay home in the car, but

Steve, with a mind to saving his father's petrol coupons, said they would walk.

Kay clung on to his arm as they hurried home through the wet streets, dodging the drips from overhanging tree branches. She laughed when she stepped in a puddle and the cold water splashed her stockings.

'They'll wash,' she said, and clung on to him all the tighter.

It was moments like this that made Steve remember their happy times together when they had been teenagers.

After an initial coolness when Muriel had arrived home late, the evening had gone well. Muriel had seemed a little distracted at first, but after gentle prompting from their mother, she had told them why she and Denise had gone to Miss Grayson's, and what had happened there.

The only slightly chilly moment was when Kay had said, 'It was very good of you to agree, Muriel, but I can't understand why Denise expected you to go with her.'

Muriel had hesitated before answering. 'Perhaps she was worried about what she would find there.'

'But why ask you?'

Steve thought his sister's expression was bordering on truculent when she replied, 'I suppose because we're friends.'

'Friends? Really?' Kay said, sounding astonished. For a moment she looked as though she wanted to say something more, but thankfully, perhaps warned by Muriel's incipient scowl, she let the matter drop.

When they got home, Kay told Steve how much she had enjoyed the meal and what a wonderful cook his mother was. She began singing 'Run Rabbit Run', and broke off to say, 'I must ask her how she does it, but I thought it tasted like chicken, didn't you?'

In bed she came willingly into his arms, but when it was

over and Steve wanted to hold her close, she smoothed her silk nightdress down and said, 'I think you ought to put an end to that friendship, Steve. Muriel is too naïve. That girl is just taking advantage of her.'

He didn't answer her; simply turned away and pretended to sleep. He felt completely hollow.

Chapter Twenty-One

Mrs Evans brought the post up for her. She didn't usually do this, but from the look of the envelopes, they contained birthday cards, and the landlady was curious.

'Special day?' she asked, her cigarette dangling from her lips and her eyes squinting through the curling smoke as she handed them over.

Carol had only just got out of bed. She pulled her robe around her and fastened the tie. 'Mmm,' she said. 'Twenty-first.'

She had no idea why she'd told her landlady this. Maybe it was because the woman was smiling for once. She had actually removed the cigarette from her mouth to do so.

'Doing anything particular? To celebrate?'

'I hadn't planned anything.'

'Shame. I sometimes wonder whether it's worth it.'

'Whether what's worth it?' Carol asked.

Mrs Evans put the cigarette back in her mouth and took a long drag before she answered. 'You young girls. Coming up to London. Chasing rainbows. And nine times out of ten it ends in tears.'

'Yes ... well ...'

Carol started to shut the door, but Mrs Evans showed no sign of wanting to leave. 'Just think,' she said. 'Here you are, all alone on your twenty-first birthday, and you could be at home with your family. Wouldn't you like that?'

'Not at all.'

Mrs Evans was taken aback. 'Fancy not wanting to be with your folks on your birthday!'

'You haven't met my folks,' Carol said. 'But thank you. It's very kind of you to bring my cards up.'

She shut the door, then went to sit at the table. There were three birthday cards. The first one she opened was from Muriel. On the outside there was a silver key and the number twenty-one, also in silver. Inside the card, below the words 'Many Happy Returns!', Muriel had written that she wished her a very happy birthday. She had added: 'Please write again soon.'

The second card was exactly the same, but Denise had simply written: 'From Denise.'

When Carol opened the third envelope, she was bemused to discover that the card was identical to the other two. Perhaps that had been the only twenty-first card available in Woolworth's. But this one contained a surprise. When she opened the card, a postal order fell out. Carol examined it. It was for twenty-one shillings. She stared at it for a moment, and then looked at the card. It was from her father. Inside, on the blank left-hand page, he had written:

Dear Carol,

I wish you a very happy twenty-first birthday. I want you to know that I'm sure your mother would have been very proud of you. As I am. Please spend the enclosed on something nice for yourself.

Love,
Dad

Carol felt like crying. She remembered what a fuss her

mother used to make of her on her birthdays when she was a child, and how when her father came in from work he would say, 'How's my birthday girl?'

Hetty had never acknowledged her birthdays with so much as a card. She said birthday cards were a waste of hard-earned money. Her father had gradually stopped sending them.

So this year, even though it was her twenty-first birthday, Carol had not expected even a card from her father, let alone a gift of money. She wondered what her stepmother had to say about this, and decided that Hetty probably didn't know.

She was about to put the cards up on the mantelpiece, but before she did, she looked at them again. Muriel's message was just about what she would have expected, but Denise's was a jolt. No best wishes, only the words 'from Denise', and unlike Muriel, she hadn't signed it with love.

Carol was hurt. Did Denise no longer want to be her friend? Then she looked at Muriel's card again and realised what the matter was. I haven't written to them for ages, she thought. They must think I've forgotten all about them. She put the kettle on and made herself a cup of tea, and then, still wearing her comfortable old dressing gown, she took the new rose-scented letter paper she had treated herself to from her top drawer and sat down to write the letters she ought to have written long ago.

She had barely sealed the last envelope when there was a knock at her door. Thinking it would be Patti come to cadge tea and toast from her as she sometimes did, Carol prepared herself to listen to the older girl's confidences about her gentleman friend and how she was playing him along.

But it wasn't Patti. It was Mrs Evans again.

'Phone message for you. Mr Palmer.'

Carol looked down at her dressing gown and her old slippers and hesitated.

'He says he's in a hurry. You'll just have to come down like that.'

'Right-ho. Thank you.'

'I don't usually take phone messages,' Mrs Evans said.

'I know. I'm sorry.'

'Sounded important.'

Carol hurried downstairs to the telephone in the entrance hall.

'Good news,' Ed Palmer said as soon as she got through. 'You're going for that audition I told you about.'

'When?'

'Today. I've ordered a car. It's on its way.'

'What will I have to do?'

'Screen test, sound test. The usual.'

'Will anyone else be auditioning for the part?'

'Yes. But listen, you haven't time to chat. Dress well and pay attention to your make-up and your hair. I want to see you after the audition. The car will bring you to my office.'

Ed Palmer hung up and Carol hurried up to her room, her heart racing. This wasn't going to be anything like the Glamour Girl competition. This was a proper audition and there would be other girls trying for the part; girls with more experience than she had. It was all right Mr Palmer telling her that she didn't have to worry. She *was* worried. But she was also determined to succeed.

She was dressed and ready and waiting at the front door just seconds before the car arrived. When it drew up and the driver got out, she was pleased to see it was Ray. She hadn't seen him since the night he had driven her to the party.

'You look great,' he said as he held the door for her. 'Word is you're on your way.'

'How can you say that?' Carol asked.

Ray smiled and walked round to get in the driver's seat. He checked the rear-view mirror and then pulled away. 'It's a small world,' he said. 'Everyone in the business knows everyone else, and as I told you before, I hear a lot just by sitting here and keeping my ears open and my mouth shut. And Carol Marshall is the name on everyone's lips.'

'Ray?'

'What?'

'Would you mind if we didn't talk?'

'Who am I to mind? I'm only the hired help.'

'Please don't say that. It's just that I want to ... want to compose myself. To think about the part. You're an actor yourself. You must know what I mean.'

'Well, thanks for that "actor yourself" bit, and yes, I do know what you mean. I won't disturb you.'

He was so understanding that Carol felt guilty. 'Actually, I don't know very much about it except that I'm a member of the French resistance. I wonder if ... if you could drop me any hints.'

If Ray guessed that she was trying to soothe any hurt feelings he might have had, he didn't show it. 'Think yourself into all the war pictures you've ever seen,' he said. 'Or better still, think what it must have been like for the real heroines of the resistance, risking everything – even their lives. Try to do them justice.'

After that they didn't talk. When they arrived at the studios, Ray parked the car and opened the door for her. Then, to her surprise, he threw his chauffeur's cap and jacket into the car and reached in for an ordinary sports jacket. He smiled when he saw her questioning glance.

'I didn't tell you. I'm auditioning too.'

'Really? That's wonderful.'

'Well ... I shouldn't think there's much hope of getting a speaking part.'

'I don't understand.'

'It's a war picture, isn't it? They need lots of young fit guys who'll look good in uniform. And what's more know how to wear one. As I did until a few months ago.'

'You'll look more than good, I'm sure of it.'

'I know. No false modesty with me. The only question is will I be wearing a British or a German uniform.'

'Will you mind?'

'Of course not. Now let's go. You future is waiting for you.'

Once inside the large, echoing studio, Ray pointed Carol in the direction of a young woman with a clipboard and then vanished. The young woman scrutinised a list, ticked Carol's name off and gave her a copy of the script. She told her to go and sit with the other girls until she was called.

To her dismay, Carol found that Joan Summerfield was there. She looked up as Carol walked towards them and nudged the girl sitting next to her with her elbow. For a moment both their heads leaned close together as Joan whispered something. Then they moved apart and stared at Carol scornfully.

Carol chose a seat as far away from them as possible, smiled briefly at the girl sitting nearby and began to study the script. There wasn't much of it, just a couple of scenes involving the young resistance fighter and a wounded British soldier. She read it through once or twice, and became aware that the girl sitting beside her was reading the words aloud very quietly. She looked up and saw Carol watching her, and gave an embarrassed smile.

'I'm practising the accent,' she said. 'I'm not sure if I can do it. What about you?'

'I'll try my best.'

'I'm Noreen, by the way.'

'Carol.'

'Are you nervous?' Noreen asked.

Carol considered the question and decided that she was. But it was a special sort of nervousness; an excited building up of tension that would spur her on to do her best. She didn't think she would be able to explain this, so she just said, 'Yes, I am.'

'Me too. And it's even worse that it's going to be Paul Grainger, isn't it?'

'What's going to be Paul Grainger?'

'Well, it's usually a stand-in for an audition, but Paul Grainger said he wanted to do this himself. That girl over there . . .' she pointed towards Joan, 'said it was probably all a fix.'

'What do you mean?' Carol had already guessed what the answer would be.

'She said it would go to a girl who had been obliging to Mr Grainger – you know what I mean?'

'Yes, I know what you mean.'

'I've been looking at the others and trying to work out who looks cheap enough. What do you think?'

'I think it's just malicious gossip and that Joan Summerfield should keep her evil mouth shut! And furthermore, you shouldn't repeat such insulting slander.'

Carol had not meant to be so vehement, and she watched Noreen's eyes widen with comprehension and dismay.

'I'm sorry. I didn't know.'

'Didn't know what, exactly?'

Noreen quailed before Carol's furious gaze, but she glanced over at Joan and said, 'That you were the girl. I mean . . .'

'Listen, Noreen, I know what you mean, and let me assure you that Paul Grainger and I are not having an affair.'

Noreen was speechless with embarrassment. Carol heard sniggering and glanced round to see Joan and the girl next to her covering their mouths to hide their foolish smirks. The

261

other two girls were pointedly studying their scripts and trying to pretend that they hadn't heard anything.

Carol picked up her chair and angled it so that she didn't have to look at Noreen or anyone else. She tried to concentrate on her part, but she found herself wondering why Paul had insisted on doing this screen test. She stared down at the script again.

In the first scene, the girl found a wounded British soldier and knelt down to see if he was still alive. The soldier opened his eyes and looked at her. Something passed between them.

Am I supposed to fall in love with him on the spot? Carol wondered.

She helped him get up and supported him as she took him into a nearby barn. The final scene showed the girl settling the soldier down in the straw – she would have to imagine the straw – and saying, 'You'll be safe here for a while. When night falls, I'll come back for you.'

Then he murmured, 'My angel.'

Carol knew she would find it hard not to laugh at that point. It would require all her acting skills to remain looking suitably angelic. She read the script through a few times, and then became aware of a shadow falling across the page. She looked up to see Paul smiling down at her.

'Why did you come here today?' she asked him.

He raised his eyebrows. 'That's a nice greeting, I must say. Aren't you pleased to see me?'

Carol clutched her script as she rose to face him. 'No, I'm not.'

'For goodness' sake, what's the matter? You look like one of the Furies in a Greek drama.'

'You didn't have to come. A stand-in could have read the lines.'

'I know, but a stand-in might not have made sure that you got the part of the French girl as I will.'

'And why would you do that?'

Carol was aware that Noreen was listening to every word.

'Because you're just right for it.'

'Then surely I don't need your help.'

'Maybe not. But I wanted them to see not just that you're good but that there's a certain chemistry between us.'

'Oh, that again.'

'Yes, that again and don't dismiss it. You must have seen pictures where the stars are brilliant but there's no spark. You know what I mean, don't you?'

'Yes.'

'And because of that, the picture isn't quite as good as it should be. Do you agree?'

'Yes.' She knew he was talking sense.

'Well, I don't want any picture I'm in to fall into that category. It's box office, Carol, box office. My career could suffer. Don't you understand?'

There was a long pause while Carol considered his words. Eventually she said, 'Yes, I do, but the part of the French girl isn't very big, is it? I mean, whoever plays it won't be anything like a star.'

'That's true. But the character is important to the story. The sad, sad story.' Paul smiled, and Carol saw immediately why so many female film fans thought themselves in love with him.

'How is it important?'

'The soldier never forgets her, you see. He never forgets the way she sacrificed her life to save him. It makes a better man of him.' As he said this, he looked into the distance with an expression of sorrow.

'The girl dies?'

''Fraid so.'

'Oh.'

'You'll have a lovely death scene.'

He smiled again, and Carol couldn't help warming to him.

'So are we friends?' he asked.

'I didn't know we were enemies. It's just that you've made things very difficult for me.'

'How?'

'Look at these girls behind me. What are they doing?'

'They're listening to every word we say.'

'Exactly. And every one of them will think that if I get the part it will be because, as one of the girls so eloquently put it, I have been "obliging" Mr Grainger.'

Paul's eyes widened and he burst out laughing. 'Oh, Carol, surely you can't take any of that guff seriously? It's just empty talk. Something to keep small-minded people of little talent happy.'

'Why should they be happy at my expense?'

'Because if it's not you it will be some other gifted actress, or actor for that matter. You'll just have to get used to this sort of thing.'

This echoed Mabel's advice, but Carol remembered something Ed Palmer had said on the night of the party. 'But what if anything got in the newspapers?'

Paul's expression became serious. 'Publishing false statements about somebody that damage their reputation is against the law. In this business, reputation is important. Now promise me you won't let this upset you. When you're called, give it all you've got. I think we're about to begin.'

Behind them, the floor manager had approached the seated girls, and now he started reading out the running order. Carol discovered that she was to be last.

Chapter Twenty-Two

When she made her way back to the car park, Ray was waiting for her. He was grinning broadly. 'Guess what?' he said.

'You got a part!'

'I certainly did. A speaking part.'

'Ray – that's marvellous! What is it exactly?'

'I'm a German soldier. They say I look just right.'

Suddenly Ray's whole body tensed. He looked up, scanned the sky anxiously and then pointed to the far horizon.

'*Achtung!* Spitfire!' he said.

He threw himself face down on the ground and covered the back of his head with his arms and hands. He lay there for a moment and then rolled over and smiled up at Carol, who began to laugh. Ray, not a bit offended, joined in.

'Hammy enough?' he asked.

'Oh, Ray, you'll do marvellously. They're right. You do look the part.'

'Two words,' he said. 'But it's a start, isn't it? Mind you, as there will be a lot of action going on at the time, I'm not sure if anybody except my mother will notice me.'

'I'll notice you,' Carol said.

Ray got up and dusted himself down. 'What about you?' he asked.

'I don't know. They said they'd tell my agent.'

'But you must have a feeling about how it went?'

'It went well, I think.'

'I hear Paul Grainger was there.'

'He was.'

Ray, puzzled by her reticence, waited for a moment, but when she made no further comment, he said, 'Okay. Let's go. I've instructions to take you to Mr Palmer's office.'

Ray, perhaps still full of his own success, was happy to drive in silence. Carol replayed her audition on the screen in her mind. It had been a long day and most of it, as usual, was spent sitting about waiting. But once her turn came, she had enjoyed every minute of it. Afterwards the cameraman had told her she looked great no matter which profile she presented and that the camera loved her.

The sound engineer told her that her voice was clear and strong and that she articulated her words beautifully. He was also of the opinion that her French accent was convincing.

'You should have heard one of the other girls,' he said. 'Joan Summerfield. She sounded like a comic turn in a French farce.'

Carol was glad that Joan was not there to hear that. It would surely have spurred her on to even more spiteful behaviour.

She knew that it had gone well. She knew that Paul was right and there was some kind of magnetism between them. But when the test was over, she had noticed that Paul's hands were shaking.

'That was good, Carol, but I've got to go. Urgent appointment. See you around.'

The change in his mood might have puzzled her if she had not suspected that the urgent appointment was with the bottle of vodka waiting in his dressing room.

She was roused from her reverie when Ray said, 'Wardour Street. Nearly there.'

Carol looked out of the window and saw that the streets

were already busy with people coming into town for a night's entertainment. Ray pulled up, put one arm along the back of the passenger seat and turned towards her. 'These cars are expensive, you know, and you don't really need to be taken to the film studios in such style, do you?'

'Mr Palmer wanted me to make an impression.'

'Well I suppose there's sense in that, but you've made your initial impression and you're probably on your way. Until you reach the top, why go on paying for chauffeur-driven cars? You could make your own way to the studios on the bus or the tube like other young hopefuls. Diana Dors does.'

'Who's Diana Dors?'

'I've heard she's another name to look out for.' Ray paused, and then, as if about to impart a secret, he lowered his voice and said, 'Mr Palmer has a good deal with the hire company, you know. And I bet he isn't paying for the cars himself.'

Carol remembered the list of expenses Ed Palmer had presented her with. 'No, he isn't. I pay.'

'And some.'

'What do you mean?'

'I mean that Palmer will be getting his cut.'

'He's dishonest?'

Ray smiled. 'No, he's not a crook. But I don't think he can help himself. He likes money. God knows why, because he never seems to spend any. I think he just feels impelled to amass a fortune.'

'What shall I say?'

'Don't fall out with him. You can't afford to. Just tell him that you're grateful that he's made things so easy for you up until now, but you'll make your own arrangements in future. And don't repeat this conversation. In spite of my heroic role in the coming war picture, I'll probably need this driving job for a little bit longer.'

Carol laughed. 'I won't say anything. Don't worry.'

'Well, so long for now, Carol. I hope we'll meet up now and then.'

'Aren't you waiting to take me home?'

'No. He told me not to wait as you had some business to talk over.'

Ray got out of the car and opened the door for her. He pointed out the building that housed Ed Palmer's office. 'You want the first floor,' he said.

'Thanks.'

Carol paused in the doorway and watched as Ray drove away. Then she turned, went along a narrow passage and climbed the stairs to Ed Palmer's first-floor office. This was the first time she'd visited him here, so she did not know what to expect.

The passage and the landing were dark, but she could make out a door with a frosted glass window and the words: 'E. Palmer, Theatrical Agent' painted on it in gold letters. She could hear talking. She knocked on the glass and a voice shouted, 'Come in.'

The office was hardly what she had expected. It wasn't exactly shabby, but it was merely functional. The windows needed cleaning and the carpet was old and faded. The walls, however, were livened with beautifully lit head-and-shoulder shots. Carol recognised a picture of Paul, and guessed the others were all Mr Palmer's clients too.

Ed himself was sitting behind a cluttered desk. He was on the phone. At first he ignored Carol as he went on talking into the receiver. Then he gestured with one hand, indicating that she should sit down on the chair at the other side of the desk.

She wasn't sure whether it was rude to listen to his side of the conversation, but she was sitting so close that she could hardly help doing so. Not that she learned much. The person on the other end of the line seemed to be doing most of the talking, and Ed's answers didn't give much away. But he didn't seem to be agreeing with what the other person was saying.

Eventually he said, 'That's better.' He smiled and gave the thumbs-up to Carol with his spare hand. Then he said, 'It's a deal,' before replacing the receiver.

'They want you,' he said. 'And they're prepared to pay a proper price.'

Carol asked him what a proper price was.

'Just leave the details to me, but I know you'll be pleased. Now, what are your plans for tonight?'

'To go to bed early. I'm tired.'

'Aren't you hungry?'

Carol, who had eaten no more than a couple of biscuits with a cup of tea from the studio canteen, said, 'Actually I am.'

'Then let me take you for a meal first.' As he spoke, he tidied the papers on his desk, locking some in a drawer. 'You deserve a treat.'

Carol was surprised. She had been told of her agent's reluctance to spend money, and yet here he was offering to take her out to eat.

'Are you coming?' he asked. 'We're going to a really good restaurant.'

Carol looked down at the dress she was wearing. It was pretty and stylish but not exactly suitable for evening wear. 'But . . .' she began.

'Don't worry about your clothes. We're not going to the Ritz. We're going to a little French restaurant in Soho. The usual clientele are a rather bohemian lot. You might even be the best dressed there.'

'Bohemian?'

'Actors, writers, artists, costume designers. You'll like the place, it's full of atmosphere. It's where the Free French who were in London during the war would gather. Some of them still go there. You might pick up some tips for your part.'

Carol thought of going back to her bedsitting room and spending the night alone. On her birthday spending spree she had bought some books at Foyles and a portable radio at a little shop in Tottenham Court Road. She could make herself beans on toast and then sit by the popping gas fire with a cup of cocoa and a book. Either *Sparkling Cyanide* by Agatha Christie, or, if she wished to escape into historical times, she could read *The Turquoise* by Anya Seton. Or she could just find a music programme or a drama to listen to on the radio.

But there had been far too many nights on her own since coming to London, and she decided that she needed company.

'Thank you, I'd love to come,' she said.

'Good. We'll walk there. It isn't far.'

As soon as they entered the restaurant, a waitress approached them. 'Mr Palmer, good evening. Please follow me.'

She led them towards a large round table where a group of people were waiting. One of those people was Paul Grainger. He rose when he saw them coming, as did the only other man in the party. Carol thought she recognised him as someone she had seen at Jack Rawlins's party, although she had not spoken to him. He was about the same age as Ed, maybe older, and he was the only man wearing formal evening clothes.

'Sorry about the penguin suit,' he said with a smile. 'I'm going on to supper at the Savoy.'

Ed introduced him as Cecil Everett, the girl with him as Elsa, and the woman seated on one side of Paul as Phyllis Greenwood. Carol had recognised her straightaway. Phyllis Greenwood was one of the most successful film actresses of the moment. She was slim and beautiful in a very aristocratic English way, and she played all kinds of parts from high comedy to near melodrama.

Phyllis, along with Elsa, was eyeing Carol speculatively. Phyllis did not even try to hide a faint antipathy and Elsa merely looked bored and a trifle sulky. On inspection, Elsa, despite her voluptuous figure and heavily made-up face, looked about sixteen.

The two vacant chairs were next to each other, and Carol found herself sitting between Ed and Paul.

'I've already ordered,' Cecil said. 'Might as well make things easy for the chef.'

Paul leaned close and said smilingly, 'That's the trouble when you accept an invitation from Cecil. He doesn't give you any choice. But then I suppose he's so rich that he doesn't have to observe the minor niceties.'

So that was it, Carol thought. We are Mr Everett's guests. Ed isn't paying for the dinner. Bearing in mind all she had learned about her agent's frugal lifestyle, she couldn't help smiling.

'What is it?' Paul asked quietly.

'Tell you some other time,' she replied equally quietly.

'Amusing conversation, darlings?' Phyllis Greenwood asked. 'If so, why don't you share the joke with us?'

To Carol's dismay, everyone at the table turned towards them. But Paul passed it off with a laugh. 'We are only remembering how hopeless one of the other girls was at the audition today.'

'And who was that?' Phyllis asked.

'Oh, you'll have seen her around. She turns up for everything. She's desperate to succeed. It's—'

Paul broke off when he felt the pressure of Carol's hand on his arm. He turned to look at her and saw the entreaty in her eyes and the slight shake of her head.

'Let me think . . .' he continued. 'No, it's no use. I just can't remember her name.'

Carol whispered, 'Thank you.' She had no wish for this conversation to get back to Joan Summerfield and add to her hostility.

Two waitresses started bringing the food and wine to the table, and to Carol's relief, Cecil started talking to Phyllis about the part she was going to play in *Salute the Brave*. It took her a few moments to realise that they were talking about the film she herself had just won a small part in.

From listening to the conversation, she gathered that Phyllis was to play Paul's wife, a brave woman who looked after a houseful of refugees in London, survived the Blitz and, in the expression of the day, 'kept the home fires burning'.

She also learned that Cecil Everett was putting money into the film, and that Elsa was to have a part in it too. Elsa remained silent throughout the meal. Phyllis had a lot to say for herself, and she had the air of someone who was used to being listened to.

The talk was mostly business, and Carol began to wonder why she had been invited, although every now and then Cecil Everett would glance her way and ask her opinion politely. As the meal progressed, she noticed that Ed was keeping a nervous eye on the amount Paul was drinking. Each time his wine glass was filled, Paul raised it towards Ed as if making a toast, and this only deepened the scowl lines on the agent's face.

As soon as the coffee was served, Cecil rose to leave. 'Got to go,' he said. 'All sorts of trouble from Diana if I'm late. I've already settled for the meal. Come along, Elsa, Uncle Cecil will find you a taxi. Anyone else need one? But you'll have to be quick.'

'I do,' Phyllis said. 'Good night, Mr Palmer; see you on the set, Paul,' she said as she got up from the table. She hurried after Cecil and Elsa without bothering to say good night to Carol.

There was silence as the staff began to clear the table. Carol heard the chatter of the diners at the adjoining table and realised they were speaking French. She glanced round and tried not to stare. The two men were young, and one wore a patch over his left eye. There was only one girl, and, although she was not truly beautiful, Carol thought she was incredibly sophisticated in a continental way.

She watched fascinated as the three of them punctuated their speech with extravagant gestures. She wished she knew enough French to be able to understand what they were talking about. She found herself repeating their words under her breath and trying to get the accent exactly right. She became aware that she was even imitating the girl's facial expressions. She could have sat there for much longer, but Paul rose and said, 'Good night, Ed. Come along, Carol,' he added. 'I'll take you home.'

She looked at him in surprise, but took his hand as he helped her rise. As they left the restaurant, she glanced back and saw their agent sitting at the table gazing into the mid-distance. She thought she had never seen anyone look so lonely.

Chapter Twenty-Three

The moist air promised rain to come and the breeze was chilly. As they waited outside the restaurant to hail a passing cab, Paul noticed that Carol was shivering. Her navy and white linen dress and cropped jacket were designed for warm summer days rather than evening chills.

'Cold?' he asked.

'Just a little.'

'Come on,' he said. 'I know where we can warm you up.'

'I thought you were taking me home.'

'Don't worry, I will.' Not giving her time to object, he took her hand and hurried her away. 'It's not far,' he said. 'A little club just off Leicester Square.'

When they reached their destination, Paul stopped and hung back a little. Three young women, brightly but cheaply dressed, were pleading with a burly doorman who stood in the open doorway of the club.

'Sorry, ladies,' the doorman said. 'Members only.'

The girls gave up and turned to walk away. Paul pulled Carol back into the shadows.

'What is it?' she asked.

'Don't worry. I just don't want them to recognise me.'

'Why?'

'Because they might ask for my autograph and then I would have to stay and talk to them and send them away thinking what a wonderful bloke I was.'

'And you're not?'

Paul responded laughingly, 'Of course I am, but sometimes wonderful blokes just want to be anonymous.' He turned his head away as the three girls walked by.

'We'll just have to hang about and ask a member to take us in,' one of them said. 'We'd better split up. No one will want to take the three of us.'

As soon as they had moved on, Paul said, 'Right! The coast is clear!' He put an arm around Carol and hurried to the door.

The doorman, a large man whose muscles strained against his dinner jacket, said, 'Good evening, Mr Grainger,' and let them enter.

Paul held on to Carol's hand as they made their way down the narrow, dimly lit stairs into the warm alcohol- and tobacco-laden atmosphere of the basement club.

'Well, what do you think?' he asked her when they reached an arched doorway at the bottom.

He watched as she gazed round, her grave blue eyes taking in the scene. Stylish young women in fashionable square-shouldered dresses and open-toed wedge-soled shoes. Men in dapper double-breasted suits who looked just a little too smart to be entirely respectable. The small stage at one end of the room where a spotlight encircled a girl vocalist. She was singing 'Sentimental Reasons' and accompanying herself on the piano. A few couples were circling the small dance floor.

'It's like a nightclub in an American film,' she said.

'Great minds,' Paul said. 'That's exactly what I think, although I don't believe it's deliberate. Perhaps Lenny's seen too many movies.'

'Lenny?'

'He owns the club. Ah, here he is.'

A tall, dark-haired man wearing a white tuxedo approached

and said, 'Good evening, Mr Grainger. Let me find you a table.'

Paul noticed Carol's eyes widen as she looked up into the man's scarred face, and he gripped her hand tightly. When they were seated at the table and Lenny had left them with a menu, Paul said quietly, 'I know, he looks like something from a horror movie. A shock when you first set eyes on him, but you get used to it.'

'Did it happen in the war?'

Paul smiled. 'Well, those scars could be called war wounds but he got them many years ago in a different sort of war. Lenny was born into one of London's criminal families. His scars are the result of gang warfare.'

'He's a gangster?'

'If he is, nobody can prove anything. This is a legitimate business. Although I wouldn't like to answer for the probity of some of his customers.'

'Why do you come here?'

'The food is good, the entertainment first class. Lenny makes sure no one bothers me. And perhaps I come for the thrill of mixing with some dangerous people. A taste of real life quite different from the make-believe world of cinema.'

A waitress came to their table. 'Ready to order, Mr Grainger?'

Paul looked at Carol. 'Sorry, I should have asked. Are you hungry?'

She shook her head.

'Just a plate of canapés,' Paul said. 'And a bottle of the cat's piss that Lenny claims is the best champagne.'

He said this with a smile and the waitress shook her head but obviously wasn't offended.

As the girl walked away, Paul saw that Carol was trying to conceal a smile.

'What is it?' he asked.

'The dress she's wearing. The black satin with the scooped neck and the little white pinafore. It's like the costume I wore as a cigarette girl.'

'So what's funny?'

'Well at least my skirt was long enough to cover my stocking tops. No one got a glimpse of my suspenders!'

The champagne was brought to their table in a bucket of ice. Lenny himself opened the bottle and poured the drinks. 'Enjoy the cat's piss,' he said with a lopsided smile.

'Why the champagne?' Carol asked when they were alone.

'A toast to your success, and also I thought you needed cheering up.'

'Why do you think I need cheering up?'

Paul had drunk his first glass of champagne as if it were fizzy pop and was already pouring his second. 'I got the impression that you didn't enjoy the meal at the restaurant at all.'

'I enjoyed the meal very much. But you're right in that I didn't enjoy the occasion.'

'Phyllis Greenwood is a first-rate bitch.' He grinned. 'Although I have to admit that she's a talented first-rate bitch. I hope you weren't upset by her cavalier attitude.'

'Not at all.'

Paul looked at her thoughtfully. 'No, you weren't, were you? So what was the matter?'

'I wasn't sure why I'd been invited.'

'Didn't Ed tell you?'

'No.'

'I'm guessing Cecil wanted to have a look at you. He may give the appearance of being the complete dilettante, but he's a shrewd businessman and his interest in where he puts his money isn't in the least superficial. Ed's probably been telling him how you're the next big star, and Cecil would want to see you for himself. I think he liked what he saw, although thankfully I imagine that you're a little too old for him.'

'What do you mean?'

Lenny appeared at the table with another bottle of champagne. 'Are you ready for this now, Mr Grainger?'

'Yes. Thank you.'

The bottle of champagne was opened and both their glasses filled despite the fact that Carol tried to tell them she didn't want any.

'What do you mean, I'm too old for him?' she asked as soon as they were alone.

'You saw Elsa. What do you think?'

'His niece?'

'Carol, surely you can't be that naïve. I thought you must have guessed that Cecil's interest in Elsa isn't avuncular.'

Even in the dim light he saw Carol's expression of distaste.

'She's young enough to be his daughter,' she said.

'Yes. How old do you think she is?'

'Sixteen . . . seventeen.'

'She's fourteen if she's a day.'

The distaste changed to revulsion. 'How do you know that?'

'Ed told me. Cecil wants him to take her on and find enough work for her to keep her happy. And quiet.'

'And Ed agreed?'

'Of course. Why not?'

'Because it's wrong. Immoral.'

'Finding work for the girl isn't immoral.'

'You know what I mean.'

'It's a dirty business, Carol. Didn't you know that?'

Carol stared into her glass of champagne. Paul had no idea what she was thinking.

'Don't worry,' he said. 'Not everyone is like that. There are men and women, serious professionals, who wouldn't dream of compromising their principles. I'm only telling you about the other sort because I want you to be aware of what you've got yourself into.'

Carol remained silent.

'You're not having second thoughts?' he asked. 'You're not going to give up and go back home, are you?'

The look of cool resolve she shot him was impressive. 'Of course not.'

The club had filled and every table was taken. The girl pianist had been replaced by a small dance band, and the noise level was rising. At the next table were two dangerous-looking men in sharp suits. Paul noticed that the girls with them were two of the group that had been trying to get into the club earlier. He caught Carol's eye and gestured towards them with his head, then leaned across the table so that she could hear him and said, 'They found someone to bring them in.'

'Can you see their friend anywhere?'

Paul scanned the tables. 'No, I don't think so.'

'Poor girl.'

Paul looked at the two men again and said, 'From the look of those two characters, perhaps she's the lucky one.' He caught Carol trying to suppress a yawn. 'You're tired,' he said. 'Let's get out of here.'

He rose and began to lead the way between the tables. When they reached the door to the street, they discovered that the rain that had been threatening had started. The slick wet pavements were reflecting the city lights. They waited in the doorway while the doorman found them a taxi. Even in the short distance from the doorway of the club to the taxi, Paul was noticed.

279

'Isn't that Paul Grainger?' a woman said

The man with her turned his head and replied, 'I think you're right. I wonder who the girl is. She's certainly a looker.'

The inside of the taxi smelled of cigarette smoke and cheap perfume. The rain streamed down the windows and the streets became a blur of shimmering lights. Carol had leaned closer to the window on her side and was gazing out at the rain-drenched world.

'What are you thinking?' Paul asked.

'Nothing much. Just taking things in. The people hurrying through the rain. Wondering who they are, where they're going. Wondering about their lives.'

'That's what you do, isn't it?'

'What do you mean?'

'You watch and listen and take things in.'

'Yes, I suppose I do.'

'And what do you make of it all?'

'Nothing ... everything ... I can't explain.'

When they reached the house where she lived, he offered to see her to the door.

'There's no need for us both to get soaked,' she told him. She thanked him for taking her to Lenny's, then left the taxi and made a dash for her front door.

As soon as she was safely inside, Paul instructed the driver to take him back to the club. He glanced at his wristwatch and smiled. He would be there in good time to join an interesting game of poker in the room reserved for special members. He sank back on the seat and automatically reached for the silver flask he kept in his inside pocket, then unscrewed the cap and took a much-needed swig. He'd be playing for high stakes tonight, and there was nothing as good as vodka for steadying his nerves.

★

When Carol reached the top of the stairs, she found that Patti's door was open.

'Is that you, Carol?' Patti called.

'Who else would it be?'

'Jack the Ripper? The She-Wolf of London?'

Carol laughed. 'Of course it's me. And why are you not at work?' She entered Patti's room to find the other girl sitting up in bed looking pale and ill.

'They sent me home,' Patti said. 'Feel dreadful. Would you be a darling and make me a cup of tea?'

Carol was tired and she longed to get to bed, but Patti was so obviously distressed that she agreed.

'Wait a mo while I get out of these damp clothes,' she said. She hurried to her own room, where she stripped off quickly, rubbed herself down with a towel and put on her pyjamas and robe. Then she took her hair grips out and towelled her hair.

'You took your time,' Patti said crossly when she went back to her room.

Carol, who had become impatient with the older girl's self-absorption, bit back a sharp response. Patti really did look ill.

'Shall I put the fire on?' she asked.

'If you've got any change for the meter.'

'I suppose that means we can't use your gas ring either?'

'Of course. Don't be stupid.'

'I wasn't being stupid, I was being sarcastic.'

Patti opened her eyes wide and then she saw that Carol was smiling. She smiled in return. 'Honestly, Carol,' she said, 'you've certainly changed since you first arrived here. I hope you're not letting your success go to your head.'

'What success?'

Patti's voice was sharp when she said, 'Oh, don't pretend

you don't know that everyone is talking about you. I hate false modesty.'

Carol glared at her, and after a moment Patti said, 'I'm sorry.'

'That's okay.' Carol went back to her own room to get her purse. After feeding the meter, she lit both the fire and the gas ring and made a pot of tea.

'I haven't any milk,' Patti said apologetically.

'That's all right. I have some left. Would you like a biscuit or a slice of toast?'

Patti, sitting hunched over her cup of tea, shook her head. 'Nothing to eat, darling, but I wouldn't mind a teaspoonful of whisky in my tea. There's a half-bottle in the cupboard. Do you mind?'

Carol got the whisky.

'Do you want a drop in yours?' Patti asked.

'No thanks.' Carol didn't think the whisky would mix very well with the champagne she had been drinking earlier.

Patti closed her eyes while she drank her tea laced with whisky.

'Do you want me to go now?' Carol asked.

'No!' The alarm in Patti's voice startled her. The older girl seemed to make an effort to control herself before she said, 'Why don't we have a nice girlie chat?'

Carol longed to go to bed, but she couldn't leave Patti in such a distressed state. 'Okay,' she said. 'But just for a while.'

'Bless you. Now what shall we talk about?'

Carol stared into the hissing gas fire. She was bone weary and she didn't particularly want to talk about anything at all.

'I know,' Patti said. 'Tell me where you went tonight. You were all prettied up if a trifle damp when you came home just now.'

'Well, since you ask, I had an audition today.'

'And did you get the part? Of course you did,' Patti added without waiting for an answer. 'But surely the audition can't have gone on this long?'

'I went out for a meal.'

'With people you met at the studios? With a man? Someone gorgeous?'

Carol shook her head. 'Not gorgeous at all. Mr Palmer took me out to dinner.'

'Ed?' Patti looked astonished. 'Old Ebenezer himself? He took you out for a meal?'

'Yes. But he didn't pay for it.'

'Don't tell me *you* did?' Patti looked indignant on Carol's behalf.

'We were guests of Cecil Everett.'

'Wow! Big time. What was he like?'

'I didn't like him.'

'Hope you kept that to yourself. He's so influential.'

'Yes. Well . . .'

'Well?'

'Maybe I did let Paul know.'

'Paul as in Paul Grainger?'

'Yes.'

'When exactly did you let Paul Grainger know?'

'Paul was also a guest. Afterwards he took me to a club – Lenny's – and then he brought me home.'

Patti stared at Carol for several seconds, and then smiled wryly. 'Maybe I should start being nicer to you.'

'Maybe you should. Not because of the people I mix with, but simply because we're housemates and it would make life more pleasant.'

'Have I been a bitch?'

'Sometimes.'

'I can't help it. I'm sorry. When Ed asked me to keep an

eye on you, I thought you'd just be here until you'd played your little part in the film and then you'd be back off home. I thought you were just another girl he was taking a chance on and that he would soon move on to the next young hopeful and forget all about you.'

'Did he forget about you, Patti? Is that why you don't like me?'

'I've never said I don't like you.'

They were silent for a moment, neither of them wishing to pursue the subject.

Then Patti said, 'To be fair, he didn't forget about me. It just didn't work out. He promised me Paris, you know. The Bluebell Girls, no less. But when it came to it, I wasn't tall enough. Half an inch too short. Half an inch! Miss Kelly won't take on any girl who is less than five foot eight, but Ed must have been hoping that we would get away with it.'

Patti looked so miserable that Carol's irritation with her melted away.

'But he's kept you in work, hasn't he?'

'Oh, yes. Plenty of work. One second-rate little club after another. But never fear – I won't have to put up with this life much longer. Not if my ship comes in.' Patti laughed. 'The bloke I'm seeing is a shipping magnate, you know. Greek. Rich as Croesus. I'll be sailing away into the blue yonder any time now. Just wait and see.'

To Carol's consternation, Patti suddenly began to cry. Huge racking sobs that seemed to speak of utter misery. Carol went over to the bed and put an arm round her shoulder, but Patti shook her off.

'It's okay,' she said. 'Don't know what come over me. You go along to bed and get your beauty sleep.'

Despite her worries about Patti, it didn't take Carol long to get to sleep. She'd had a tiring day; a strange sort of day. She was overjoyed to have got the part in the film but disturbed by all the undercurrents of jealousy and outright spite. She was confident enough in her own talents to know that she had been the best of the girls who had auditioned that day, but she had come to realise that there would be those who would never accept that.

Paul had told her to ignore the gossips and she had resolved to follow his advice. She had not enjoyed the dinner at the restaurant, but she knew she would have to learn to appear at ease in the company of such people. As she drifted off to sleep, she knew that another step had been taken towards the future she dreamed of.

Ed Palmer went back to the semi-detached house in Wimbledon where he had been born. After his mother was widowed relatively early, he had lived there alone with her. She neither sought nor wanted any kind of social life.

He had gone straight from school to work for his uncle, a theatrical agent, and had taken over the business when his uncle retired. He knew that people thought him strange – a loner, they called him. And secretly he despised them. Except that every now and then someone special came along.

When he had been younger, he had fooled himself that one of these beautiful creatures might even fall in love with him. But not one of them ever had. And Carol, who could prove to be his brightest star, would be no different from the others.

Chapter Twenty-Four

Denise picked up the envelope that lay on Miss Grayson's doormat. It was pale pink and gave off a faint scent of roses. She herself had received an identical envelope that morning, containing a letter written on rose-scented paper. And when Muriel had called into the shoe department at Rutherford's during her lunch hour, she had told Denise that she had received a letter from Carol too.

She put the letter into the shopping bag along with the books she had just collected and the neatly wrapped parcel that was already there. It contained newly washed underwear and a nightdress. Denise had visited Alice Grayson in the cottage hospital each evening after work and taken her washing home to her mother, who had been only too happy to help.

When she arrived at the hospital, Muriel was sitting by Miss Grayson's bed, scribbling something in her notebook. Denise knew that as soon as Muriel saw her, she would put the notebook in her handbag. She was being annoyingly secretive about what she was writing.

Miss Grayson was sitting up in bed. Over her nightdress she wore a matching silk eau de Nil bedjacket with a fluffy white marabou feather trim. She had draped a bead-trimmed chiffon veil, the same colour as her bedjacket, round her head and shoulders and had pulled one side of it forward to partially cover her scarred face.

When they noticed Denise, Muriel put her notebook away as predicted and smiled a welcome, although Denise could not help feeling that she had interrupted something. But there was no mistaking how pleased Alice Grayson was to see her.

'How can I ever thank you and your mother for being so kind to me?' she said as Denise put the books and the clean clothes in her bedside locker.

'You can thank us by doing what the nurses tell you and getting better. Then you'll be able to go home.'

Miss Grayson suddenly looked bleak. 'They don't want me to,' she said. 'Sister thinks I won't look after myself. She says Matron wants to put me in a home.'

'Surely not,' Denise said. She was shocked.

'Miss Grayson is making it sound worse than it is,' Muriel said. 'The matron means a nice convalescent home. I don't think she means her to stay there for ever.'

'But I want to go to my own home,' Alice Grayson said. 'Please, Denise, tell them I would thrive much better there.'

Denise wondered when exactly she seemed to have been given the authority to arrange Miss Grayson's life. 'I'll see what I can do,' she said. 'But now here's a letter for you.'

Miss Grayson held the pink envelope to her face and sniffed it. 'It's scented,' she said. 'What a luxury. I wonder who . . .' She glanced at the postmark. 'London! But of course! Carol. How marvellous!'

She opened the envelope and, taking out the letter, began to read it eagerly. After a moment or two she looked up and said, 'How rude of me! I'll read it after visiting time is over.'

She folded the scented pink pages and began to put them back in the envelope, but Denise stopped her. 'No, please read it, we don't mind.'

'Really? That's so kind. I know, I'll read it aloud, shall I?

I'm sure that as Carol's friends you'll want to know everything she has been doing.'

'But we already—' Muriel began.

'That would be marvellous,' Denise said.

She shot a warning glance at Muriel, who, after a moment of wide-eyed incomprehension, suddenly nodded as if to say she understood.

Miss Grayson glanced at the first page briefly. 'Poor Carol,' she said. 'She apologises for not having written before, but she was downhearted because nothing seemed to be happening and she didn't want to upset me.'

She began to read the letter aloud, her trained actress's voice bringing the words alive. It wasn't much different from the letters Denise and Muriel had received, but they listened with appreciative expressions, as if the news of the filming and the people she had met at the studios was all news to them.

'Isn't it wonderful?' Miss Grayson said when she had finished. 'What an exciting time for her. And how different her life must be now.'

Denise was grateful that Carol had written to Miss Grayson only about the good things. Not that anything she had put in Denise's letter had been very bad. She had only mentioned the jealousy and bitchiness of some of the other hopeful starlets, but added that she was learning to deal with it.

Just as Miss Grayson replaced the letter in the envelope, the bell rang to tell them that visiting time was over. Denise and Muriel said good night to Miss Grayson, who asked them if they would be visiting again next day.

'You bet,' Denise said.

'And listen, my dears. I don't want you to tell Carol I'm in hospital. I don't want to upset her and have her rushing back here and perhaps missing a part in a film.'

Denise and Muriel took the bus back into town together.

They both got off at the bus station, and just before they said goodbye, Muriel said, 'Do you think Carol would come back if she knew Miss Grayson was in hospital? I mean, she's changed, hasn't she?'

Denise thought about it for a moment. 'Yes, I think she has. But not that much. If she thought Miss Grayson needed her, she'd be on the next train home.'

Steve arrived home from work to find Kay sitting sobbing at the kitchen table.

'What is it?' he asked.

She raised a tear-stained face and looked at him accusingly. 'You're late home,' she said.

'Is that all? I thought it was something serious.'

He made the mistake of laughing, and she rose to her feet in a fury.

'*All?*' she said. '*All?* The dinner's ruined. Burned to a cinder! That's *all!*'

Despite being annoyed at the way he was being taken to task, Steve couldn't help feeling sorry for her. She was making such an effort to be the perfect housewife, and he had behaved thoughtlessly.

'Kay, I'm truly sorry. I was working late in the darkroom and I forgot the time. You have every right to be angry with me.'

Kay was silent for a moment. Then she said petulantly, 'You could have telephoned my mother. She would have come and told me you were going to be late.'

'Yes. I should have done. I didn't think. I promise you that next time I work late, I will. As for the ruined meal, why don't I take you to the Rainbow Room and we'll treat ourselves to the best they have to offer?'

Kay's scowl vanished. 'Really?'

'Yes, really. Go and put your glad rags on.'

'And you'll wear your suit?'

'If you say so.'

'And Steve?'

'What is it?'

'I'm sorry.'

'What do you have to be sorry about?'

'Making a fuss when you've been working hard all day. I mean, I should be pleased that you were prepared to work late, shouldn't I? It proves that you want to make a success of your job at Latham's.'

'I still should have told you.'

'Never mind. I forgive you.'

Kay smiled radiantly and hurried upstairs, leaving Steve racked with guilt. Of course he should have let her know that he would be late home, but that wasn't the reason he felt guilty. He hadn't stayed in the darkroom to complete work for Latham's. He had been working on a project of his own. Something he couldn't tell Kay about because he knew that if he pursued it, it would cause problems between them. Maybe the sort of problems that couldn't be resolved.

Later, when they had taken their table in the Rainbow Room, Kay's mood had changed completely. She loved getting dressed up and dining out. Tonight was made even better for her when she looked around and saw some of her friends from the tennis club.

'Look, there's Sarah and Jessica,' Kay said. 'But I'm not sure who they're with.'

Steve knew the Harland twins slightly. Their father owned a chain of grocery shops in the north of England, they lived in a grand house overlooking the links, and they had been in the same class as Kay at her girls' private school in Newcastle.

Kay glanced surreptitiously at her friends again, and her

eyes were wide when she turned back to look at Steve. She leaned across the table and spoke in an awed voice. 'I do believe that one of the men is David Fellowes!'

'Should I know him?'

'Fellowes! Woodford Hall!'

'Oh that Fellowes,' Steve said, and he smiled, although he was a little irritated by Kay's propensity to be impressed.

'I don't know who that good-looking chap with them is,' Kay said. 'I suppose he could be a friend of David's. Someone from the navy.'

'Fellowes is in the navy?'

Kay looked at him exasperatedly. 'Honestly, Steve, don't you know anything?'

'Apparently not.'

Kay gave him a sharp glance when she caught his tone, but he was saved from reprimand by the arrival of the menu. Still feeling guilty about the ruined evening meal, he said, 'Don't even glance at the prices.'

Kay laughed. 'I had no intention of doing so.'

She studied the menu, told Steve what to order for her and then rose and said she was going to the powder room. As he watched her go, he saw Sarah and Jessica preceding her. A little later, the three girls came back together. They were smiling and talking animatedly. It occurred to Steve that Kay had seen the other two girls leave their table and had followed them deliberately. This feeling was reinforced when Kay came back but didn't sit down.

'Sarah and Jessica want us to join them,' she said. 'They're going to get the waiters to put two tables together.'

Steve wondered what David Fellowes and his companion thought of the arrangement, but he could hardly make a fuss, so after a short period of activity he found himself sitting with Kay and her friends and two men he had never met before. During the introductions he learned that the other man, Rupert Penfold, had indeed served in the navy with David Fellowes throughout the war.

The meal went well enough. Most of the talking was done by the girls, with the men exchanging long-suffering but amused glances now and then. During a pause while the girls caught their breath, David asked Steve about his war. That was how he put it: 'What was your war like?'

Steve told him briefly about his years in the RAF as an aerial photographer, and he saw how pleased Kay was when the others seemed to be impressed.

'Damned dangerous job, that,' Rupert Penfold said. 'If you were in it from the start you were lucky to survive, eh?'

Steve remembered his messmates who hadn't survived and answered briefly, 'Yes. I was lucky.'

'Of course you had an entirely different view of things, didn't you?' David Fellowes said. 'Literally, I mean.'

Steve thought of the beautiful countryside and the fine old cities he had flown over, and how most of those cities were now reduced to rubble. He tried not to think of the people who had lived in them. They had been at war. And English towns had been destroyed too. Steve knew what he wanted to do. He wanted to record and photograph the heroic efforts to rebuild those cities both in England and on the continent. As if by doing so he could make things right again.

'My goodness, haven't we gone serious,' Jessica Harland said. 'I suggest it's time for another bottle of wine and some more cheerful conversation. David, you have an interesting little story to tell us, don't you?'

'Have I?' David looked puzzled.

Jessica looked around and addressed the table in general. 'David met Seaton Bay's very own Glamour Girl. You know, the girl who won that cheap little beauty contest. Carol Marshall. He met her on the train going up to London.'

It was hard to tell what Kay's expression was. Her eyes had widened and then her lips thinned into an unattractive line. Steve himself had gone icy cold.

'Furthermore,' Jessica continued, 'she was trying to pass herself off as a lady.'

'She always did try to make out she was better than she was,' Kay said. 'We all know she grew up on the Seafield estate.'

'Now wait a moment,' David said. He seemed annoyed. 'Jessica has put an entirely different slant on things.' Suddenly he looked embarrassed. 'Perhaps I did say I was surprised when I realised who she was, because – God forgive me for being an utter snob – I had taken her for what Jessica here would call "one of us". But whatever background you say Carol Marshall comes from, the girl is a perfect lady.'

Jessica Harland wasn't at all put out by David's rebuke. She made an amused moue with her scarlet lips and Sarah controlled a giggle by turning it into a cough and reached for her water glass. Kay tried her best to remain impassive, but Steve could see from the way she was clutching the stem of her wine glass that she had been mortified by David's reprimand.

Throughout the entire exchange Steve had found himself gripped by cold fury. How dare anyone talk about Carol like that! All the feelings he had been trying to suppress rose to the surface and threatened to overwhelm him. He picked up his water glass and drained it, imagining the cool liquid soothing the emotional turmoil within him. He looked around the table. Jessica and Sarah Harland were shallow creatures whose views were not worth bothering about, but Kay had revealed herself to be an utter snob and he felt ashamed for her.

He was relieved when the waiter came to the table with a pot of coffee. Everybody fell silent as the cups were filled.

He glanced at Kay, saw how uncomfortable she looked and immediately, despite his anger, felt sorry for her. He knew her evening had been ruined and he cursed the wretched Harland girls for inviting them to join their party.

Rupert Penfold, although unmistakably upper class, seemed to be innocuous, though as an officer in the Royal Navy, he must be more intelligent than he looked. And David Fellowes was obviously a decent sort. But neither of them were men Steve would choose as friends.

Steve glanced at his wife, who was now talking to Rupert Penfold. It wasn't Kay's fault if he was discovering that she wasn't exactly what he had imagined her to be. And if he was unhappy, it was his own fault for giving up so easily when Carol had gone to London.

He remembered his cousin Duncan's words the night before the wedding.

I've heard it's quite normal, these last-minute doubts . . . a chap's got to do his duty, hasn't he? Only an utter cad would leave the poor girl waiting at the church.

Steve had felt compelled to do his duty. On his wedding day, he had truly believed that he could make a go of things with Kay. He looked at her now. She had recovered her composure, mainly thanks to Rupert Penfold's attentions, and Steve felt a familiar niggle of guilt. He was the one who should have been comforting her.

The rest of the meal went without incident, and Kay was delighted when Sarah and Jessica urged her to keep in touch.

'You and Steve must come to dinner some time,' Jessica said. 'Mummy and Daddy are pretty good at finding interesting dinner guests.'

'Oh we'd love to,' Kay replied, and Steve found himself hoping that Jessica was only being polite and that the invitation would never come.

★

On the way home, Kay tripped and grabbed Steve's arm to save herself from falling. She giggled, and Steve wondered whether she'd had too much wine. When he thought about it, he remembered that Rupert Penfold had seemed eager to fill up her glass. She kept her arm through his and they walked home companionably enough.

There was a cloudless sky and a bright moon. Steve stopped and looked at the silver path the moon had trailed across the sea. A bomber's moon, he thought. During the war, the brighter the light of the moon, the easier it was for pilots and crews to see potential targets, so the night of a bomber's moon often brought a large number of raids. Since coming home, Steve had learned that Seaton Bay had suffered its heaviest air raid on a night like this.

The bomber's moon could also work against pilots. They could see the ground very well, but people on the ground could also see them, allowing them to target anti-aircraft guns at approaching aircraft or even send up fighter planes.

'Is something the matter?' Kay asked.

'Why do you ask?'

'Well, I'm getting cold standing here and I want to go home.'

'Sorry. Let's go.'

Kay, suddenly animated, started talking about the dinner invitation. Steve didn't say much, and eventually she asked him, 'Aren't you pleased?'

'Should I be?'

'Of course you should! I hate it when you seem so . . . so detached. If you're going to make a success of life, it's important to get in with the right crowd.'

'And these people are the right crowd, are they?'

'You must know that they are. I mean, David Fellowes! Woodford Hall!'

'It's not Fellowes who has invited us,' Steve said. 'And I'm not sure that he will.'

Immediately Kay's cheerful air of exuberance vanished. She removed her hand from the crook of his arm. Steve knew he'd been a brute to remind her of her faux pas, but he couldn't for the life of him think of anything to say that would put things right. They walked the rest of the way home in silence.

Kay took longer than usual to take her make-up off and hang her clothes away. Is she hoping that I'll be asleep before she comes to bed? Steve thought. Not wanting to upset her any further, he lay still and kept his eyes closed. His wife slid into bed gently and kept her back turned to him. Soon her even breathing told him that she was asleep.

Steve lay awake, going over the day. Things had begun to go wrong the minute he had decided to work late in the darkroom. He ought to have let Kay know, there was no question of that, but he had been so keen to see the results of his work that all else seemed to be forgotten.

One of the services Latham's offered was home visits by a photographer to take pictures of infants who might be too overwhelmed to come to the studio. In other words, Mr Latham was not really keen to have squalling infants putting off other clients. Neither was he keen to take these photographs himself, so when Steve had returned from the war, he had been only too happy to hand that job over to him.

Mr and Mrs Simpson had welcomed Steve into the front parlour of their terraced home, where baby Brian lay in a sturdy perambulator.

'He should be in a good mood,' Mrs Simpson said. 'He's been fed and changed and he's just having a little rest.'

'I've put the chairs near the window,' Mr Simpson said. 'That's what you want, isn't it? A north-facing light.'

'Perfect,' Steve said.

Mrs Simpson lifted Brian from the pram and, holding him in her arms, took her seat alongside her husband. 'I know every mother probably tells you this,' she said, 'but he really is a beautiful baby.'

Steve agreed that he was. The trouble was that Brian, too well fed perhaps, to make sure that he would be contented, refused to open his eyes. Mrs Simpson spoke softly in an attempt to awaken him, but the baby slept on.

At last he opened his eyes.

His parents sighed with relief and smiled at the camera, but just as Steve pressed the shutter release, Brian closed his eyes again.

'Oh no,' Mrs Simpson said. 'I'm so sorry.'

'Don't worry. I always take more than one so that you'll have a choice.'

But the baby was asleep again. Mr Simpson went to get a rattle from the pram.

'No!' his wife said. But it was too late.

Brian opened his eyes and began to howl with indignation. While the parents rocked the baby in their arms and tried to soothe him, Steve packed his camera away.

'Look,' he said, 'I'll come another day. Just call in to the studio and make an appointment. Maybe you should wait a month or two, when Brian will be more aware of what's going on. And don't worry,' he said, 'this happens all the time.'

Steve felt sorry for the young couple. They had been looking forward to having this photograph taken. But he had spoken the truth when he'd told them that this sort of thing happened all the time. Eventually Brian would co-operate, the Simpsons would get the photograph they wanted and they would be happy. But will I be happy? Steve asked himself. How can I possibly bear to do this sort of thing for the rest of my working life?

He decided not to go straight back to the studio. Ocean View, where the Simpsons lived, led down to the promenade. Steve thought he might walk down and have a look at the sea. However, just a short way further along the road, he came to the houses that had been destroyed during the town's worst air raid.

He stopped and looked up at the gaunt outlines of the walls that were still standing. Whole rooms had collapsed exposing fireplaces, wallpaper, even pictures and mirrors still hanging on the walls. The damaged houses had been cordoned off and demolition work was in progress. There were men there erecting scaffolding.

The foreman noticed Steve and said, 'This is just to keep things standing until we can demolish everything properly. Sad, isn't it? I mean, people's homes.'

Looking up, Steve had noticed that on the mantelpiece in a room on the second floor of one of the houses there was a clock and a pair of candlesticks. Instinctively he reached for his camera.

He stayed there for more than an hour, taking shots of the ruined buildings and the men working. He persuaded the foreman to let him cross the barrier, and lying on the ground, he took shots pointing up through roofless walls towards the sky. During the war he had taken photographs of houses just like this but so far below him that they had looked like a tumble of children's building blocks rather than real homes of real people.

When it was time for the men to finish work for the day, the foreman asked him politely to leave. He hurried back to the studio, grateful to find that Mr Latham had already gone home and Peter, the young assistant, was waiting to lock up.

'I'll see to things,' Steve said. As soon as he was alone, he had gone into the darkroom. And had completely lost track of time.

That night the dream began as it had always begun. He was alone in the Spitfire, flying at as low a level as he dared in order to get the best and most helpful shots. Below him he saw the wide road, the farm buildings and the innocent cows.

Then, as always, he looked up and saw the Messerschmitt diving towards him, guns blazing, moving in for the kill. But this time, even in the moment of panic, he knew it was a dream. And he knew that he was going to survive and return to the girl he loved.

Still sleeping, still dreaming, a sense of elation carried him home over the Channel to the green patchwork of English fields. When he landed, the airfield was deserted. There were no other planes, no men in uniform. No one at all save for one figure waiting for him. He climbed out of his plane and began to walk towards her. She stood perfectly still, but as he got closer, he saw the love and hope shining in her eyes.

He woke to feel tears pricking his own eyes and a hollow emptiness where his heart had been. The girl in his dream had not been Kay.

Chapter Twenty-Five

Carol sat in front of the mirror and watched her appearance change subtly as Bert applied her make-up. Her personal opinion was that she looked impossibly glamorous considering that she was supposed to have been hiding out in the ruins of a city that had been destroyed by German tanks.

'Shouldn't I have a bit of soot or something on my face?' she asked. 'And how on earth have I managed to keep my hair so fashionably waved?'

Bert laughed. 'Remember we're not dealing with real life here. The filmgoers want to see handsome men and beautiful women. They identify with the actors – so why shouldn't they be allowed to escape from their drab selves for an hour or two?' He stepped back and admired his handiwork. 'You'll do,' he said.

Carol took the protective cape from her shoulders and rose to go. The door opened and Paul appeared.

'Ready for our big scene?' he said.

'Yes.'

He grinned, then reached for her hand, adopting a serious expression as if about to say something of great significance. 'Come with me,' he said. 'Today, cinema history will be made!'

At the end of the day's filming, Paul did not immediately go off to his dressing room as he usually did. Seeing his thoughtful expression, Carol asked, 'Is anything wrong?'

'No,' he said. 'Far from it.'

'Then why are you looking at me like that?'

'I was right. We're going to be a great screen couple. After this film is shown, Ed won't be able to cope with the offers; people wanting you and me as a team.'

'So what's wrong with that?'

'Nothing at all.'

Carol looked up into his eyes, and seeing her puzzled expression, he made an effort to smile. 'I'm tired, that's all. And I need a drink.'

He walked away leaving her feeling utterly confused. Joan Summerfield, who by sheer persistence had landed herself a non-speaking part as a fellow resistance fighter, had watched the exchange along with a small group of other bit players.

'Lovers' tiff?' she said to Carol.

One of her pals sniggered.

Carol turned on her in fury. 'Bugger off, Joan,' she said. 'And unless you stop this constant bitching, I'll see to it that you never work on the same film as me again.'

She strode off, leaving Joan wide-eyed with outrage. Carol herself was shaking. I can't believe I just said that, she thought, but she was unrepentant. A small group of actors still in their film costumes moved apart to let her pass, and she looked up to discover that one of them was Ray.

'Oh . . . hello,' she said.

'Hi, Carol.'

'I suppose you heard that?'

'Yes.' There was no trace of his usual friendly smile.

She hesitated, not knowing whether he would want to talk to her, but he couldn't meet her eyes. After an awkward moment or two she walked on.

Gazing in the mirror as she removed her make-up, she had to fight to stop the tears flowing. Today should have been wonderful – today *had* been wonderful. Her scenes with Paul had brought applause and respect. So what had gone wrong? Why had his mood changed? After working so well together, why had he become so subdued? He needed a drink. That would be it. But Ray? She'd thought Ray was her friend, yet he didn't seem to want to talk to her.

She cleaned off her make-up, changed back into her own clothes and slipped quietly out of the studios. She had never felt so alone.

Paul climbed into his car and reached for the flask he kept in the glove compartment. He unscrewed the cap and took a long swig of vodka. He knew he should be careful how much he drank when he was driving, but he'd needed that. It would keep him going until he got home.

He didn't start the car immediately. He needed to think. Today's filming had shaken him. At first he'd been elated when he realised he'd been right about Carol. They looked good together and they interacted well. But as the day wore on, he'd grown uneasy. It was dawning on him just how much potential she had, and somehow that worried him.

Carol knew that if she was going to be any good at all at work the next day, she needed to wind down; she needed to find some way to relax. She wondered if that was why Paul relied on alcohol. Whether a drink or two soothed away the tensions of the day and helped him prepare himself for the day to come. Except that it didn't prepare him. It made him stumble and forget his lines. Drink wasn't the answer.

What I need is a good old gossip, she thought. I need to talk to someone. If only Denise and Muriel were here. As she climbed the stairs to the top floor, she heard a wireless playing light music. The sound was coming from Patti's room. Patti will have to do. I'll make her a cup of tea and have a gossip with her while she's getting ready to go to work.

She frowned when she saw that Patti's door was slightly ajar. Apart from the music, there were none of the usual sounds of her housemate getting ready.

'Patti?' Carol called. She knocked, but there was no reply. Perhaps she's asleep, Carol thought. I'd better wake her up or she'll be late. She pushed the door open. The curtains were closed and the room was shadowy. At first she thought there was no one there. And then she saw that Patti was lying in bed with the blankets pulled up almost over her head.

Not wanting to startle her, Carol walked quietly over and placed a hand on Patti's shoulder. 'Time to wake up, sleepyhead.'

'I'm awake. I hoped you would come in.'

The older girl sounded so unlike herself that Carol was alarmed. 'What is it? Are you still poorly?'

Patti didn't answer the question. She struggled to sit up. 'Do you think you could be a darling and make me a cup of tea? And put a good shot of whisky in it?'

'Of course.'

Patti smiled faintly. 'I haven't actually got any tea.'

Carol smiled. 'So what's new? And I don't suppose you've got any milk or sugar either?'

'Just the whisky.'

'I'll make the tea in my room. Don't go away.'

Patti laughed faintly. 'No chance of that. And before you go, turn that damned wireless off. I only left it on so that you would hear it and come in.'

Carol made the tea as quickly as she could. When she returned to Patti's room, she propped her up with the pillows and placed the cup on the bedside table before adding the whisky. When she got the bottle from the cupboard, she discovered that there was very little left.

Patti groaned with disappointment. 'Tip it all in,' she said.

'Are you hungry?' Carol asked. 'Would you like some toast? Biscuits?'

'God, no. Couldn't eat a thing.'

Carol sipped her own tea and watched the other girl anxiously. Her skin was paper white and there were deep dark smudges under her eyes.

'Do you think I should get a doctor?' Carol asked.

'No!' There was a note of panic in Patti's voice. Carol began to feel really frightened.

Suddenly Patti flung her cup aside, the hot liquid narrowly missing Carol's face, and clutched her abdomen with both hands. The sound she made was unlike anything Carol had ever heard before. She realised the other girl was trying to get up.

'What is it?' Carol asked.

'Bathroom. Need the bathroom. You'll have to help me down the stairs. Oh God. It's too late.'

As Patti struggled to rise, Carol pulled the bedclothes aside. She stared with horror at the blood flooding from Patti's body and staining the sheets.

'What have you done?'

'Isn't it obvious? Botched job. She must have left something behind.'

'How could you?'

'Don't be bloody stupid. How could I not?'

'I'll phone for an ambulance.'

'No . . . don't.'

'It's no use, Patti. I'm not listening. If you don't go to hospital, you'll die.'

Mrs Evans appeared at her doorway and watched through the usual spirals of cigarette smoke as the ambulancemen carried Patti down the stairs on a stretcher.

'What's the matter with her?' she asked Carol.

'Bad case of food poisoning, I think. She's in absolute agony.' Well at least that last part is true, Carol thought. She could hardly tell their landlady the truth. If Mrs Evans discovered that Patti had had an abortion, she would throw her out.

'I'm not surprised,' Mrs Evans said. 'Look at the way she leaves her dirty dishes in the sink until they're covered in mould.'

At this point Patti groaned and Mrs Evans's critical gaze softened. 'Still, I don't like to see the poor girl suffer like this. Will you be going with her in the ambulance?'

Patti suddenly reached out for Carol's hand and held it as if she didn't intend to let it go.

'Yes, I'm going with her.'

'Let me know how she is when you get back. If it's past midnight, just slip a note under my door.'

Once inside the ambulance, Patti seemed to slide in and out of consciousness. Carol watched her anxiously as the ambulance raced through the streets, sounding its warning bell. This is like something in a film, she thought, and I don't know if there's going to be a happy ending.

At the hospital, Patti was wheeled away down a brightly lit corridor that smelled of disinfectant. One of the ambulancemen took pity on Carol and directed her to a gloomy high-ceilinged room furnished with uncomfortable-looking chairs and a large polished table. He said she could wait there.

Carol thanked him, but he lingered in the doorway.

'It's against the law, what your pal has done.'

'I know.'

'There'll be questions. I thought I'd better warn you, the hospital might call the police.'

'Let them. I won't be able to tell them anything. I came home from work and found her like that.'

The ambulanceman stared at her for a moment and then smiled. 'You know what? I believe you. I've got to go now, but I know a nurse here who will find you a cup of tea if I ask her nicely.'

'Thank you, you're very kind,' Carol said.

When he had gone, she sat down at the table. It didn't take long for the nurse to appear with her cup of tea. 'Try not to worry,' she said. 'Whatever she's done we'll do our best for her.'

Alone again, Carol sipped her tea and tried to blank out the image of Patti's frightened face as they'd wheeled her away. It had been hard to tell from the brisk expressions of the attendant nurses whether they thought it a matter of life or death. The nurse who had brought Carol her cup of tea had told her not to worry and that they would do their best for Patti. Despite this reassurance, Carol's tears began to flow.

The voice was brisk. 'Your friend will live. You can go now.'

Carol had fallen asleep at the table, her head resting on her outstretched arms. She came up groggily from a dark place and looked up to find a severely starched senior nurse looking at her as if she were something the cat had dragged in.

'Oh, but can't I see her? I've been so worried.'

'Visiting time was over long ago.'

'Please.'

The nurse looked at her with pursed lips. 'Very well. I'll take you along.'

The ward was dimly lit. The nurse led her to Patti's bed and pulled the curtains round it. 'Keep it quick and keep quiet,' she said. 'The other patients are sleeping. And no sitting on the bed. Use the chair.' She left them alone.

Patti smiled up at Carol wanly. 'Thanks for staying.'

'Patti . . . why did you do it?'

'Have the abortion? What else could I do? Go off to a home for fallen girls and then hand the baby over to be adopted?'

'Well, that would have been an option, but I meant why did you get yourself pregnant in the first place? You told me you wouldn't.'

'Did I? I don't remember saying any such thing.'

'Not in so many words, but you said you were going to be careful. You led me to believe you were trying to get him – whoever he is – to marry you.'

Patti smiled ruefully. 'That was the plan.'

'So what happened?'

'He told me he loved me. I trusted him.'

'Oh, Patti . . .'

'I know. You'd think I'd be the last person to fall for that old line. I still don't know what came over me. I think it was because I was getting desperate.'

'Desperate?'

Patti lay back and closed her eyes. 'I'm sick of it all. Working at that cheap little club every night, and knowing that that's as far as I'm ever going to get. You'll never see my name in lights in the West End, you know. I'll just go on until I'm getting too old for London and then it will be some jolly little end-of-the-pier show in a run-down seaside resort and pantomime work in the winter months. What kind of life is that? Surely you don't blame me for trying to find a way out?'

'No, I don't blame you. But what will you do now? Go back to the club?'

'I've told you, I'm sick of it all. I never want to work there or any other tawdry little club again. And anyway, the hospital's got my address. Maybe it's better if I vamoose before the cops come. I can't give the old girl away, can I? She would go to prison.'

'She nearly killed you.'

'Whatever she did, I can't turn her in. It just isn't done.'

'When will you go?'

'As soon as I'm able to get out of this bed and walk.'

'Is that wise?'

'No, but you won't change my mind.'

'Is there anything I can do?'

'There is, as a matter of fact. You can bring my things to the hospital.'

'Which things?'

'As much as you can cram into the old suitcase under my bed. Choose the best stuff, obviously. And bring the shoulder bag that's on a shelf in the cupboard. All my papers are in there – and my money.'

'All right. I'll bring them after work tomorrow.'

'That'll be too late. I need them now.'

'Now? But . . .'

'I'm sure you'll be able to talk your way in. You just won that old battleaxe round, didn't you?'

'But where will you go?'

Patti laughed bitterly. 'As far away from London as I can. Wherever the fancy takes me – so long as a hundred pounds will cover it.' She managed a rueful smile.

'That's a lot of money. Is it your savings?'

'Savings? Me? Don't be daft. When I told lover boy I was pregnant, he gave me the money for the abortion plus a hundred smackers and told me he didn't want to see me again. And – wait for it – he claimed that I must have known that he was married. What a prince!'

'I'm so sorry.'

'Don't be. Just do what I've asked.'

'What about Mrs Evans?'

'I'm paid up until the end of the month. She'll easily find someone else to take the room.'

'But what shall I tell her?'

'Tell her anything you like. Tell her I've kicked the bucket. But for God's sake stop dithering and go and get my stuff.'

Carol stared at Patti. She heard the desperate edge to her voice and saw that nothing would change her mind. As she rose to leave, Patti called her back.

'What is it?' Carol asked.

'I'm sorry I'm being so obnoxious, but believe me, this is the best thing to do. I need to start again somewhere, and at least the money will give me a chance to sort myself out. And you've got to promise me something.'

'What's that?'

Patti produced a ghost of a smile. 'Promise not to snitch on me.'

'Snitch?'

'Don't tell old starched knickers at the desk out there what I'm going to do.'

Chapter Twenty-Six

Carol arrived at the studios the next morning having had no sleep whatsoever. She had packed Patti's belongings, then removed the bloodstained sheets from the bed and wrapped them in a clean towel. She intended to take them to the laundry before returning them to Mrs Evans. She was still working out what she was going to say when their landlady met her at the bottom of the stairs.

Mrs Evans eyed the suitcase Carol was carrying. 'She's not ... I mean ...'

'No, she's all right but very weak. She's decided to go home to her family.'

'I thought her mother was in America.'

'There's an aunt in Blackpool. She ... she isn't coming back. She said to say sorry.'

Mrs Evans looked at Carol through narrowed eyes. She took the cigarette from her mouth and removed a bit of tobacco from her tongue with the fingers and thumb of her other hand.

'Pull the other one, Carol.'

'What do you mean?'

'I believed you last night when you said it was food poisoning. That's because you've got a sweet innocent face and big blue eyes. But it was all tripe, wasn't it?'

'Yes. I'm sorry.'

'She's had an abortion, hasn't she?'

Carol nodded.

'Well, good riddance to her. But I'm surprised at you. A nice girl like you getting mixed up in this sorry affair. I thought better of you.'

'What did you think?' Carol said angrily. 'Did you think a nice girl like me should just walk away and refuse to help? And if I had just left her there, what would you have done if you'd found her dead in bed the next morning?'

Mrs Evans stared at her as if she was seeing her through new eyes. 'Well, well,' she said. 'You've changed since you came here, Carol. Do you know that?'

'Maybe I have. But helping Patti was still the right thing to do.'

Carol was aware of her landlady staring after her as she left the house. Thankfully a cruising taxi came by within minutes and she told the driver to take her to the hospital and wait for her. She had her story ready for the nurse who tried to stop her entering the ward.

'Her landlady's put her out,' she said. 'I thought I'd better bring her things before the old harridan tossed them into the street.'

She must have been convincing, because the nurse, although far from pleased, let her in.

Patti was sitting up in bed, reaching round to untie the tapes on her hospital gown. Wordlessly Carol helped her. Patti suddenly clasped the younger girl's hands.

'I'm sorry if I've been a bitch,' she said.

'You, a bitch? Surely not.' Carol smiled.

'I think I was jealous. But you've proved a true friend and I'll never forget you.'

'That sounds as though we're never going to see each other again.'

'We both know that's the case.' For a moment Patti looked utterly forlorn, then she sighed, let go of Carol's hands and grinned. 'Be a darling and get some decent underwear out of my case, will you? And then you'd better go before I act completely out of character and start crying like a baby.'

Carol hadn't wanted to go back to her room and possibly face Mrs Evans again. In any case, she knew she wouldn't be able to sleep. She asked the taxi driver to take her straight to the studios, where she sat in the cab until the canteen staff arrived to start on the breakfasts. She paid the taxi driver and gave him a generous tip. Once inside, she drank two cups of hot strong coffee and tried to prepare herself for the day ahead.

She noticed that other supporting players were avoiding her. Not in an unfriendly way; it was just that they were treating her differently, as if she were not one of them. Neither was she one of the stars. She wondered if she had changed as much as people said she had. She knew the only person she could trust to be honest with her was Denise. But the only way she would be able to see Denise would be to go back to Seaton Bay, and she'd promised herself she would never do that.

But no matter how tired she was, no matter how upset she had been by recent events, as soon as she got in front of the camera, the everyday world fell away and Carol Marshall no longer existed. She became Yvette, a French resistance fighter. She spoke, she moved and she even thought the way Yvette would think.

By the time the day's work was over, she was exhausted but at the same time exhilarated. This is all I want to do, she thought. So long as I have this, nobody and nothing else matters.

Muriel's ambition to become a journalist was stronger than ever. One evening, on the way home from work, she hurried along to Latham's. She had phoned and asked Steve to wait for her. She didn't think he'd mind, because he was always working late these days.

After letting her in, Steve closed and locked the door. 'That's it for the day, thank goodness,' he said. 'Why don't we go through to the staff room and I'll put the kettle on.'

When they were sitting at the table with their tea, Steve said, 'Now, why are you here? Do you want a studio portrait to send to your boyfriend?'

'I haven't got a boyfriend and you know it. No, I want you to do me a favour.' She moved the tea things aside and put the folder she had brought with her on the table. Then she opened it up and turned it round so that it was facing Steve. 'Is it possible for you to copy these photographs?' she said.

'Yes, it's possible,' he said. 'I can prop them up, light them, put my camera on a tripod and photograph them. But have you got permission?'

'Yes, I have.'

'And are you going to tell me what this is for?'

'Not yet.'

'Am I allowed to guess?'

'No. And when you're done, may I have the negatives?'

'Of course. And if you want any further prints, just let me know.'

Denise went straight home from work. She intended to have a bite to eat before going to the hospital. She entered the old apartment building in Garden Square and found Ruthie sitting halfway up the stone stairs.

'What is it?' Denise asked.

'Mam said I had to stay here and warn you.'

'Warn me? Has something happened?'

'No. Well, yes. Nothing bad's happened. You've got a visitor.

Mam wanted you to comb your hair and all that considering it's a film star.'

Carol!

Denise made to push past Ruthie and then stopped. She needed to sort out her feelings. Was she pleased to see Carol? She had been cross and hurt when Carol seemed to have forgotten all about her old friends. But now that she was here, Denise knew that she was ready to forgive her anything.

'Get up then,' she said to Ruthie. 'Unless you want me to step on you.'

'Wait a minute – me bum's numb,' Ruthie grumbled, but she grinned as she got up and moved out of the way.

Denise raced up the rest of the stairs to the Shaws' landing.

'You haven't combed your hair or fixed your lipstick,' Ruthie called after her.

'Don't be daft,' Denise called back. 'Carol won't mind.'

'But—'

Whatever Ruthie was going to say, Denise didn't hear it. Their front door had been left ajar. She pushed it open and rushed through the tiny lobby into the kitchen-cum-living-room, then pulled up short when she saw who was sitting drinking tea and chatting with her parents. Howard Napier.

When Steve got home that night, he found a note on the dining table.

Steve,
Had you forgotten that we were invited to go to the Harlands' for dinner tonight? Rupert Penfold came to collect us in his car. We waited for a while and then Rupert decided that we'd better go. I shall give

Mrs Harland your apologies and tell her that you had to work late. There's a tin of tomato soup in the pantry.

Kay

Steve, not *Dear Steve. Kay*, not *Love, Kay*. He deserved it, he supposed. Fancy forgetting something that Kay had been so excited about: an invitation from the Harlands. They were definitely the sort of people she believed they should mix with if they were going to get on in life. What Kay meant by getting on in life was being able to afford a comfortable home in the right part of town and becoming part of the right crowd. Whatever that was.

So now what was he going to do? Open the tin of soup and sit by himself and listen to the wireless? He supposed he could go and visit his parents, but his mother would want to know why Kay wasn't with him. He looked at his watch. The Silver Grid would be open. Kay probably wouldn't approve, and she would curl up with embarrassment if anyone saw him and told her. But drat that. He would go and get himself some fish and chips.

Howard looked so at home sitting at their table talking to her mother and father that Denise was uncharacteristically speechless. Ruthie had followed her in and, trying not to be noticed, sat in the armchair at one side of the fireplace.

'Sit down, Denise, pet,' her mother said. 'I'll pour you a cup of tea.'

Wordlessly Denise sat down and stared at Howard across the table. An ache came to her throat when she realised how much she had missed him, and how pleased she was to see him.

'Why have you come here?' she asked.

'I had to see Alice,' Howard said.

315

If she had hoped for a different answer, Denise did a good job of hiding it. 'Are you going to come to the hospital with me tonight?'

'I've already been.'

'They let you in even though it wasn't visiting time?'

'Of course they did,' her mother said as she put a cup of tea on the table in front of her. 'I mean, who could refuse Howard Napier!'

'Miss Grayson must have been surprised to see you,' Denise said.

'She was,' Howard said. 'But I didn't just walk in. I asked one of the nurses to tell her first. If she'd seen me arrive out of the blue, she might have thought that her last hours had come and she was hallucinating.'

'I doubt it,' Denise said. 'For all her film-star ways, Miss Grayson is a very sensible woman.'

'Yes, she is, isn't she? She's also very stubborn.'

'About not going to a convalescence home, you mean?'

'That's right. Even when I came up with a solution that would suit her better, she still argued over the details. But I can be equally stubborn. I made it plain to her that unless she agreed to my plan, I would side with the matron.'

'And what is your plan?'

'I told her that I would arrange for her to employ a respectable couple. The woman would come in every day to cook and clean and the man would come along at the weekend to do the odd jobs and the garden.'

'You can find such a couple?'

'I've already found them.'

Denise became aware that everyone was smiling.

'My parents?' she said.

'None other.'

'And I'm going to help too.' Ruthie spoke up from the depths of the armchair. 'I can go and have my dinner in Miss

Grayson's kitchen after morning school so long as I make myself useful and run errands.'

'How on earth did you persuade her to let herself be taken over by the Shaw family?' Denise asked. Then she added, 'Can she afford it?'

'To be honest, no,' Howard said. 'Until recently, she was well provided for, but the situation has changed and her pusillanimous solicitor has advised her not to make a fuss. So I told her I would pay your parents' wages.'

'And she agreed?' Denise was surprised. In the short time she had known Alice Grayson, she had learned how independent she could be.

'Only after a great deal of wrangling. She gave in when I told her she would be doing me a favour.'

'And how is that?'

Howard shook his head. 'I'll tell you later. Now I'd like you to get your glad rags on and come out for dinner with me.'

Denise looked at him levelly. When he had gone to America, she had believed that she would never see him again. To her surprise, that had hurt, but she had gradually got used to it. And now here he was expecting her to get up and go out with him as if nothing had happened in between.

'But Miss Grayson will be expecting me at visiting time. And Muriel isn't going tonight.'

'That's all right, pet,' Mrs Shaw said. 'Ruthie and me will pop in to see her.'

'Please come,' Howard said.

There was something in the way he looked at her that made her smile and say, 'All right. I'll be ready in a tick.'

Howard was staying at the Waverley, and as they walked through town together they attracted curious glances. When they passed the Silver Grid, a man came out holding his fish and chips wrapped up in newspaper.

'Denise? Is that you?' he asked. 'And Mr Napier?'

Howard nodded politely.

Steve looked surprised to see Howard, Denise thought, but then his visit was pretty surprising.

'Hello, Steve,' she said. 'Slumming it tonight, are you?'

He was taken aback by her curt tone, but he grinned and said, 'There's nothing wrong with fish and chips.'

Won over by his refusal to take offence, Denise smiled. 'No, there isn't,' she said. 'Hope you enjoy them.'

She and Howard began to walk on, but Steve called them back. 'Have you heard from Carol lately?' he asked.

'She writes now and then.'

'And how . . . I mean, are things going well for her?'

'Very well. The best thing she did was to leave this town behind her, believe me. But surely Muriel could tell you? Carol writes to her too.'

'Yes . . . well, good night, then.'

Steve watched them go. Suddenly his parcel of fish and chips had lost its appeal. Muriel made no secret of the fact that she was receiving letters from Carol. But neither did she offer to tell him anything that was in them. And Steve knew there was no way he could ask her, not his own sister. It was too close to home.

The head waiter at the Waverley greeted them with a smile. 'Lovely to see you again, Mr Napier. And you, Miss Shaw. Would you like a table by the window? There's a grand view of the sea.'

'Thank you, but we'd like something a little more discreet,' Howard said. 'The view may be lovely, but it also means that we can be seen.'

'Of course. You don't want your fans staring in at you, do you? Follow me.'

The waiter seated them at a table for two conveniently

half obscured by a pillar, then brought the menu.

'Good of him to mention my fans,' Howard said. 'He must know I'm a forgotten man.'

'No you're not,' Denise said, 'and very soon you'll have a whole new bunch of fans, won't you? I mean, all these films you're making in Hollywood.'

Howard smiled ruefully. 'True. But I'm not the romantic hero any more, am I?'

She fought down the urge to say something really soppy, like, you are to me. Instead she looked at the menu. 'He remembered me too,' she said. 'The head waiter remembered my name.'

'How could anyone forget you?' Howard asked with a grin, and suddenly they found themselves smiling at each other radiantly.

Denise allowed Howard to order for her, and as the meal progressed, she realised she hadn't been so happy since ... oh, since the last time she and Howard had dined together.

Over coffee and ratafia biscuits, she reminded him that she had asked him how he had persuaded Miss Grayson to let him pay for her to have help at home, and that he had promised to tell her later. She was surprised to see how solemn he became.

'What is it?' she asked. She was alarmed at the change in his expression.

Howard remained silent for a moment, then he squared his shoulders as if he had made his mind up.

'I told her she would be doing me a favour,' he said.

'So you said, but I don't understand. How is it doing you a favour to let you pay for my parents to work for her?'

Suddenly Howard lost his actor's poise and sounded both self-doubting and apprehensive. 'I told Alice that I loved their daughter very much, and that despite the fact that I'm probably older than her father, I was going to ask her to marry me. And if by some miracle the girl accepted my proposal, I would be whisking her off to Hollywood, so I wanted to make sure that she wouldn't have to worry about her parents.'

In the silence that ensued, Howard reached across the table and took Denise's hand. Now that he had spoken, he had recovered some of his sangfroid, and he smiled at her before he raised her hand to his lips and kissed it. Looking into her eyes, he grinned as he said, 'Don't worry. They'll still get the job even if you refuse me.' Then he paused and with the slightest hint of panic said, 'Well . . . tell me. Shall I order the champagne?'

'Yes, Howard. Order the champagne.'

When Kay got home, she was nervous but smiling. Steve expected to be scolded, but instead she came up to where he was sitting in the armchair and sank on to the floor, resting her arms on his legs.

'You're not cross with me, are you?' she asked.

'Why should I be cross with you?'

'For going without you.'

'No, I'm not cross. I deserved it.'

'Yes, you've been a naughty boy.' Kay started giggling and put her head in his lap.

Steve took her head gently in both hands and raised it, forcing her to look at him. 'Have you been drinking, Kay?'

She lost her dreamy smile and scowled petulantly. 'What's wrong with that?'

'I'm not criticising you. I'm just surprised, that's all.'

She looked at him for a moment and then started laughing again. 'Yes, I've been drinking. We've all been drinking. Naughty Jessica didn't say her parents wouldn't be there tonight. Rupert just kept on filling my glass up. He said it would do me good. Make me feel better. And not to worry, because he would see me safely home.'

'And did it? Make you feel better?'

Kay didn't answer, and Steve realised that she'd fallen asleep. He moved her aside and got up without disturbing her, then he picked her up gently and carried her to bed.

Chapter Twenty-Seven

Meg, the new tenant in Patti's room, was a woman in her forties who worked as an engineer at the BBC. She was quiet but friendly, and over a cup of cocoa one night she told Carol that she thoroughly enjoyed her job, although the male engineers had not at first been very welcoming. She worked peculiar hours at Bush House, the headquarters of BBC overseas broadcasting, so Carol only saw her occasionally, often passing her on the stairs.

One morning Meg arrived home at the same time as the postman and brought Carol's mail up for her. Carol opened the door in her dressing gown.

'Sorry, did I wake you?' Meg said. She handed over two envelopes. 'I thought you'd be getting ready to go to the studios by now.'

Carol's smile turned into a yawn. 'My part in the film is in the can, as they say. I'm out of work.'

'Oh dear. Will that be a problem?'

'I hope not. My agent has assured me that I'll get more work soon, and I've enough money put by.'

In fact Carol had more money in the bank than she had ever dreamed of. And she wasn't quite sure what to do with it.

'Are you coming in for tea and toast?' she asked Meg.

'Kind of you to ask, but I'm exhausted. We had no end of trouble with the Post Office line to Daventry, and I just want to get to bed. Anyway, you'll want to read your letters.'

Carol made herself a cup of tea and took the letters back to bed. She had recognised the handwriting on both of the envelopes, and smiled at one then scowled at the other.

Propped up amongst her pillows and with her tea on her bedside table, she opened the letter from Denise first. Her eyes widened in surprise at its contents.

Dear Carol,

Who would have thought I would get to Hollywood before you! No, don't worry; I'm not going to be your rival. You know very well that I can't act for toffee. Carol, you'll never believe this – Howard and I are married! And before you ask, I'll tell you – yes, yes, yes, I really do love him. And it seems that he loves me. He told me that even if he hadn't had to come back to England he would have written and asked me anyway.

Now, I'm not sure how to tell you this and I hope you won't be cross, but the reason he came to Seaton Bay was because Miss Grayson was taken ill. I know I should have written and told you, but Miss Grayson absolutely forbade me to. She didn't want you worrying and maybe coming back to see her when you should be concentrating on your career. Carol, she's so proud of you.

And you're not to worry. She's out of hospital now and back home. Howard has arranged for my mother to help her in the house and Dad will do odd jobs and the garden.

I feel dreadful that I didn't invite you to the wedding, but it all happened in such a rush. Howard got a special licence so that we could tie the knot before he returned to America. Nobody came to the church except my parents, Ruthie, Muriel and Sidney Jessop, the head waiter from the Waverley. Ruthie and Muriel were my bridesmaids and Sidney Jessop acted as Howard's best man.

If there were few guests, there were plenty of onlookers. Everybody who could squeeze near the windows at Rutherford's was smiling and waving when we came out of the church. I'm not sure how they knew about it, I had asked for a day off work for personal reasons; I didn't mention a wedding. From the way she was giggling and waving back to everybody, I suspect Ruthie told them.

Miss Grayson was still a little frail so she didn't come to the church, but we went to her house for a small reception. Howard had organised Mr Jessop to bring salmon sandwiches, champagne and a fruit cake – a real fruit cake with icing!

And as for a honeymoon, we spent one night in Howard's suite at the Waverley and then he had to go back to America. He's about to start work on a big movie. A war movie, and just about everybody who is anybody is in it. All the top stars, including Clark Gable! Howard's part is quite important. He will play a double agent of some sort – the story sounds terribly complicated, so I'm not sure whether he's a goodie or a baddie. But he's so pleased not to be acting the friendly old buffer for a change.

He so much wanted me to go back with him. He said a few days on an ocean liner would be like a proper honeymoon, but I have to stay and organise things like a passport and other official documents. And guess what? I've decided to do the right thing and stay working in the shoe department until they can find a replacement for me, although I've told Mr Rutherford to get a move on.

And when at last I can join my husband – get that, *my husband* – I may be sailing on the *Queen Elizabeth* from Southampton. Howard says they're working on it now to turn it back from a troop ship into a luxury liner. They claim it will be one of the grandest luxury liners of all time. And your friend Denise will be travelling on it first class. Howard will meet me in New York and then we'll fly to California. Me – flying. Does this sound like one of the films we've seen together? I'm having to try very hard to keep my feet on the ground.

I'm sorry if this letter has been mostly about me. I would so much like to see you before I sail. Perhaps I could stop off in London on the way to Southampton? But whatever happens, I know that I'll see you again. Howard's agent told him that everybody says Carol Marshall is going to be the next big star, and Howard predicts that it won't be too long before you come to Hollywood too.

Well, must close. I've so much to do. Whatever happens, we must always keep in touch.

Much love,
Denise

Carol folded the pages and put them back in the envelope. Her hands were trembling. Tears streamed down her face and she couldn't say for sure whether they were tears of sadness or of joy.

The next letter, however, brought tears of rage.

Dear Carol,
No doubt you will be surprised to get a letter from me,

but I thought you ought to know that your dad is very poorly. He hasn't been to work for weeks now and it is very hard getting by on the money I earn at the laundry.

I am at my wits' end knowing what to do for the best. If I go to work, your poor father will be alone all day without anybody to look after him, but if I give up work, what are we going to live on?

You ought to know, Carol, that there are those who are very surprised that you are not doing anything to help us. Especially after the way I looked after your dad and yourself after your mother died. Sometimes at night I can't help going over it all and thinking that this is all the thanks I get.

I got your address from that stuck-up friend of yours, Muriel Douglas. I could tell she didn't want to tell me where you lived and I suppose you've told her not to, but when her mother heard what it was about she made her write it down for me. I can tell you, Mrs Douglas was very surprised that things have turned out like this.

Well, Carol, that's all I have to say.

Yours truly,

Hetty

By the time she had finished reading, Carol was fuming. She could just imagine the sort of poison that Hetty would have poured into Mrs Douglas's ear. No doubt she's painted me as a cruel, selfish, ungrateful daughter, she thought. And who were the people who Hetty said were surprised that she wasn't doing anything to help? And how was she supposed to have known that help was needed in the first place?

At this point she felt a twinge of guilt. She had deliberately cut off communication with her father and stepmother, and even when she had written to thank her father for the birthday card and postal order, she had not given him her address. But if her father needed help, why hadn't Hetty written straight away, instead of spreading evil gossip all round town?

Carol screwed the letter up and hurled it towards the waste-paper basket. It missed. She leapt out of bed, scooped it up and took it out to the sink on the landing, where she lit a match and burned it. Then she turned the tap on and washed the ashes away.

There was no point in going back to bed; she would not be able to sleep or even to relax. She had an appointment with Ed this morning and he had told her to be as smart as possible, as someone important wanted to meet her. She decided to wait until the other lodgers in the house had left for work and then go down to the bathroom and have a long, hot soak.

She would put a shilling into the meter that supplied the gas geyser and ignore the line painted round the inside of the bath that marked the five inches of water allowed in order to save fuel. She would soften the water with rose-scented bath crystals and lie there until she had soothed her anger away. The only problem was that other lodgers often hung their washing over the bath, and she didn't fancy being dripped on by a collection of shirts and underwear. I'll dump them in the washbasin, she thought. As long as I peg them up again when I'm finished, no one will ever know. She gathered up her towel and her sponge bag and headed downstairs.

Carol called in to the bank as soon as it opened. The clerk recognised her and was only too pleased to give her advice. After she had made her arrangements, she headed for the hairdressing salon. Ed had asked her to look her best, and besides, she could afford to pamper herself.

By the time she emerged from the salon, she looked every inch the film star. Her hair, parted at the side, fell in soft golden waves to her shoulders. She'd had a manicure, too, and the deep pink nail varnish matched her lipstick. She had bought her outfit at the pricey second-hand shop, where she was now a valued customer. It consisted of an off-white sleeveless rayon dress and a short rayon jacket with a nipped-in waist. The jacket had two black buttons and black velvet trim. She had thought long and hard about wearing a hat, but although it would have been more fashionable to do so, she found most hats ageing. She had completed the look with a black handbag and a pair of high-heeled black peep-toe shoes.

She knew she was attracting admiring glances as she stood at the edge of the pavement to hail a taxi. She saw one coming and raised her hand, but before it reached her, another cab on the other side of the road did a nifty U-turn and pulled up smartly.

'Hop in, love,' the driver said with a grin. 'I'll take you anywhere you want to go!'

When she walked into Ed's office, he got to his feet quickly, knocking a pile of papers off his desk as he did so.

Carol moved forward immediately and began to pick them up.

'No, that's all right . . . leave them,' Ed told her. 'I'll do that.'

But she had already gathered them together and put them on his desk. A ray of sun shone through the grimy window like a spotlight, enclosing Carol in its dusty warmth. Ed held his breath. She was getting more beautiful every day.

'Erm, sit down, Carol,' he said. 'Would you like something? A cup of tea?'

Carol, remembering previous cups of tea, served in chipped cups with tea leaves floating on a swirl of condensed milk, declined the offer politely.

'Or something stronger, perhaps?' he said. He opened his top drawer and brought out two glasses and a bottle of whisky.

Carol smiled and shook her head. 'What's the matter, Ed?' she said. 'Has this job offer you mentioned fallen through? Are you trying to put off the moment of breaking the news to me?'

'Not at all.' Ed stared at her and marvelled at how confident she had become. 'Far from it, in fact. The part is as good as yours. All you have to do is go along and meet Mr Daniels and we'll clinch the deal.'

'Mr Daniels?'

'The producer, Monty Daniels. He'll be sending a car for you.'

'But I thought that whoever I was to meet was coming here.'

'I don't think I told you that. And we can't expect a man as important as Monty to leave his luxury office suite and come along here, can we?'

'He's important?'

'Very. He was behind some of the biggest-grossing films before the war, and this one he's setting up could be even bigger. Paul will be the male lead. Just think, you'll be co-starring with one of the biggest stars of the moment.'

'Co-starring?' Carol's eyes widened.

'That's right. It's a starring role. Your name will be second only to Paul's on the credits. It's a fantastic chance for you. I . . . erm . . . I had to work hard to convince them that you're ready for this.'

'I'm grateful – very grateful.' Carol looked overwhelmed for a moment, and then she seemed to bring her emotions under control. 'Can you tell me anything about the film?'

'The title is *Dangerous Dreams*. It features murder, mystery, suspense, betrayal. And it's also a love story.'

Carol smiled. 'Strong stuff.'

'It's a costume drama set in the eighteen eighties. You will play Violet, a cockney maid who falls in love with the master of the house. He falls in love with you too, but the problem is he has a wife; an older woman who is rich and holds the purse strings. What will the star-crossed lovers do?'

'It sounds like melodrama to me.'

'It is. But it will be nothing like a melodrama acted on the stage. Just think of the close-ups, the moody lighting, the music, the sound effects, the fog! And think how wonderful you will look with the hairstyles and costumes of the day.'

Ed looked at his watch and then rose and went to the window, where he peered down into the busy street. 'The car's here,' he said. 'I'll walk you down.'

The chauffeur got out and held the door open, but just before Carol got in, Ed said, 'Carol . . . ?'

'Yes.'

'Remember, this is a very important moment in your career. Your future depends on it.'

'I know.'

'You have to . . . to impress Mr Daniels.'

'I'll do my best.'

'Don't . . . don't do anything to upset him.'

She looked surprised. 'As if I would.'

Back in his office, Ed sat behind his desk and stared morosely at nothing in particular. He had known from the first moment he saw Carol in that tatty little Glamour Girl contest that she had star potential, but he hadn't expected success to come quite so quickly. He had envisaged a period when he would be guiding her, teaching her.

She hadn't needed his help. She seemed to learn as she went; taking everything in and forgetting nothing. She was a natural. She had listened to him politely when he talked about clothes and hairstyles and make-up, but he soon learned that she had an inbuilt sense of style.

How quickly she was learning her way around the world of films. How quickly she had acquired a level of quiet self-confidence. The little incident when she had told Joan Summerfield where to go had got back to Ed, and it had astonished him. Carol, fresh from a small town in the north of England, was already showing signs of becoming a diva. But had she learned enough? She was still very young, and despite her new air of self-assurance, she was relatively unsophisticated.

But one thing was crystal clear – she was motivated by a fierce ambition. He hoped to God that ambition was strong enough to make her do whatever was necessary. She mustn't mess things up now. Not when starlet Carol Marshall had been given the chance to become a real star.

Ed sat back in his chair and wondered whether he still had the stomach for this. He reflected that he had never actually chosen to be a theatrical agent. It had just been convenient for him to go into the family business. He had been judged unfit to be a fighting man, and had spent the war making as much money as possible and putting it away for ... for what exactly?

Ironically he was a good agent. He had the knack of spotting talent and he knew how to foster it. Look what he had done for Paul Grainger. Paul was good-looking, but more than that, he had charisma. When Ed had first seen him working in Simpsons in Piccadilly before the war, he had known immediately that he could make him a star whether he could act or not. It had been a tremendous stroke of good fortune to discover that he could. He was soon being offered starring roles.

Even the interruption of Paul's war service in the navy had worked out well, because he came back a hero. But that was when things had started going wrong. Ed had looked after him, tried to curb his drinking and, more worryingly, his growing gambling habit. Ed hated to even think of the amount of money Paul was throwing away in the back room at Lenny's club.

And then there were the dangerous people he was mixing with. He'd have to be very, very careful. The film-going public liked their heroes, even the ones who played villains on the screen, to be clean-cut and scandal-free. Unless Paul did something to refresh his image very soon, he might end up throwing his starry career away. And that was the last thing Ed wanted. For the richer Paul had become, Ed as his agent, had benefited as well.

But now he wondered if it was worth the effort. Perhaps it was time to retire from the business and move abroad. The trouble was, he hadn't the remotest idea where to go.

When Carol was shown in to Monty Daniels' inner sanctum, he was sitting behind a large mahogany desk. He was not what Carol had expected. She had imagined that she would meet another anonymous-looking businessman. Instead she found a flashily dressed man who once must have been extremely good-looking but had gone to fat. The fleshy rolls at each side of his face and under his chin looked as if they were attempting to swallow up his features. His expensive suit strained to confine his bulk.

His secretary left discreetly and Monty Daniels rose to greet her. As he did so, he took a large cigar from his mouth and laid it across a heavy brass ashtray. He came round the desk and took her hand. His palm was sweaty and Carol had to control a shudder of distaste.

'Lovely! Lovely!' he said. 'Absolutely enchanting!'

Carol wasn't sure how to respond, but fortunately he didn't seem to expect a reply. He dropped her hand and moved back a little. He eased his immense bottom on to the edge of his desk, folded his arms across his vast stomach, cocked his head on one side, narrowed his eyes and looked at her.

Carol found the ensuing silence unnerving. She wondered if he would ask her to sit down.

Eventually he unfolded his arms and twisted his body to reach round behind him for his cigar. As he picked it up, about an inch of ash fell off. The cigar had gone out. He took the box of matches from the ornamental matchbox holder in the centre of the ashtray. The business of lighting his cigar left him breathless. When he had recovered, he drew on it deeply, removed it from his mouth and closed his eyes in satisfaction.

When he opened them again, he said, 'Miss Marshall . . . or may I call you Carol?'

'Please do.'

'Carol, I wonder if you would oblige me and take your jacket off?'

'Whatever for?'

'This film has been a project of mine for a long time. Originally another actress was cast to play the part of Violet. That actress was – how shall I put this? – somewhat voluptuous. You, on the other hand, though very attractive, have the body of a young girl. Now, much can be done with costume, but maybe the part will have to be rewritten. The master of the house could be attracted by your youth and seeming inexperience. But I must see for myself what is to be done.'

Carol placed her handbag on the only other seat in the

room, a velvet-covered chaise longue, and removed her jacket, which she placed next to her handbag. She stood there uncertainly, unnerved by his silence.

'That's a good girl,' he said at last. 'Now turn around – like a mannequin in a fashion show. Slowly . . . that's right.'

Suddenly he placed his cigar in the ashtray, pushed himself up from the edge of his desk and waddled over to the chaise longue. He sat down, breathing heavily. Carol noticed with disgust the trail of fallen ash on his waistcoat.

'So far, so good,' he said. 'Lovely rounded buttocks and pert little breasts that would fit nicely into a man's hand. I think maybe you'll do, little lady.'

Carol was suffused with embarrassment. She felt the heat creeping up her neck, and yet deep inside she was icy cold. She wanted to grab her things and run, but to her horror she saw that Mr Daniels was sitting on her jacket and her handbag had fallen to the floor at his feet.

He seemed to be completely unaware of her reaction. 'We'll have some lovely costumes made up for you. They'll emphasise your figure and reveal just enough of your cleavage to whet the appetite.' He closed his eyes and they vanished into folds of flesh. He appeared to be thinking. When he opened them again he said, 'What are your legs like?'

'I beg your pardon?'

'Your legs.'

'Does that matter?'

'Of course it does. There's a scene where you're putting on your garters. Nothing salacious; just a chance to show a nice bit of stocking. I'd better have a look. Lift your skirt up.'

'No.'

Mr Daniels looked surprised. 'No?'

'That's right. No.' Carol looked at him with loathing. 'And if I can have my jacket and my bag, I'll go now.'

The film producer looked astounded. 'I don't think you understand,' he said.

'I understand very well, and I don't intend to give you a cheap thrill just to get a part in your film.'

'And how else did you think you were going to get a part in my film? Or in any film? A cheap little beauty queen like you. Don't you realise there are plenty of girls who would show me much more than their stocking tops for a chance like this? A starring role when you've had next to no experience. Now come here and do as you're told.'

'No.'

'I only want to look, not touch.' He sounded exasperated. 'There are others in this business who would expect more than a peep show. You should be pleased it's me you're dealing with.'

She stared at him coldly. 'Please just give me my coat and my bag.'

He stared back as if he couldn't believe what he was hearing. Then he heaved his bulk up and slid her jacket out from under him. 'Here you are,' he said. 'But you're a very silly girl talking to me like that. I promise you you'll pay for it.'

As Carol reached for her jacket, he lurched forward and grabbed at her skirt. 'I only want a look,' he panted as he pushed it up.

The feel of his clammy fingers on her legs filled her with revulsion. Shocked and humiliated, she leapt back so suddenly that she stumbled and began to fall. To her horror, Monty Daniels had leaned too far forward, and as she went down, he lost his balance and fell towards her.

As his mass loomed over her, she tried to roll out of the way, but she was too late. He fell on top of her, crushing the breath from her lungs. Stunned, she lay on the expensive oriental carpet, trapped by his inert weight. At first he lay still, and then, wheezing and panting, he pushed himself up far enough to leer down at her. She felt the bile rising in her throat.

'Well this is a nice surprise,' he said.

She looked up at his engorged face and the spittle trailing down his chin. Then to her horror she felt one of his hands moving over her body. Gathering all her strength, she brought both her hands up and, fingers like claws, her nails digging into the rolls of flesh, she scratched his face as hard as she could.

Monty Daniels roared with pain and rolled sideways, clutching his cheeks. Blood oozed between his fingers. 'Bitch!' he screamed, 'Leading me on and then suddenly going all coy like any common little prick-tease.'

Stung, Carol gasped, 'I didn't lead you on. That's an outright lie.'

She scrambled to her feet. To reach her bag and jacket, she would have to step over Monty Daniels' bulky figure.

'So why did you take your jacket off and stick your tits in front of my eyes?' He raised himself on one elbow, reached into his pocket for a handkerchief and began to dab at his cheeks. 'Why were you happy to twirl around and wiggle your buttocks for me if you weren't leading me on?'

'It wasn't like that. You said you wanted to see if I was suitable for the part.'

'And I'm sure you knew what I had in mind.'

'Of course I didn't,' Carol said.

'Then you're more stupid than you look. A stupid little small-town glamour girl who thinks she's got what it takes to be a film star. Well let me tell you, you haven't.'

Monty Daniels began hauling himself to his feet. It was painful to watch. He staggered round his desk and collapsed in his chair, wheezing painfully. For one horrified moment, Carol thought he might be going to have a heart attack. But the wheezing subsided and he drew himself up and looked at Carol coldly.

'You can go now, Miss Marshall,' he said. 'I shall tell your agent that you're definitely not suitable for this part. And I hope you know you're finished in this business. Now get out!'

Chapter Twenty-Eight

Hetty was suspicious of envelopes that had typewritten addresses on them. Inside there would be something she didn't want to see, like a bill or a final demand for payment. She decided to deal with it later.

'Was that the postman?' Albert asked when she took him up his cup of tea.

'No. What made you think that?'

'I thought I heard something come through the letter box.'

'Well, you thought wrong. Now here's your tea. I haven't time to make any toast, but you always leave most of it anyway.'

'Do you think she'll write to us?'

'Who?'

'Carol.'

'Why should she?'

'Didn't you write and tell her I was poorly?'

'Yes, I did, but she obviously couldn't care less. Now I must go. I don't want to be late for work. Someone in this house has to earn some money.'

Downstairs, Hetty stood in front of the mirror that hung above the sideboard and tied her scarf turban-like round her head to hide the curlers. She wanted her hair to be nice for tonight. She was going along to her sister and brother-in-law's house to have a drink or two with them and their lodger, the foreman who was working on the demolitions. Well, you had to have a bit of fun now and then, didn't you? Life was no joke these days looking after Albert.

When she was ready to go, she picked up the letter. She was about to stuff it in the top drawer of the sideboard when she changed her mind and put it in her pocket. You never knew with Albert these days. He had started going through the drawers and cupboards looking for old letters and photographs. The letters were from his brother who had gone to Canada before the war, and the photographs were mostly of his first wife and Carol. One day Hetty had found Carol's school reports spread across the table. School reports, for God's sake. She'd put the lot on the fire.

Just to be safe, she decided to take the letter to work with her. She didn't want Albert finding it and opening it and discovering that she'd fallen behind with the tallyman, if that was what it was about. And it very well could be.

When Steve got to work, he found a middle-aged woman waiting for him in the doorway. She explained that her son had eaten something that had disagreed with him and wouldn't be coming in today. Steve told her not to worry and that he hoped Peter would get better quickly.

Peter's absence meant he would be on his own today. Mr Latham was taking a day off. He was happy to leave everything to Steve.

Once inside, Steve picked up the letters from the doormat. Amongst them was the one he'd been waiting for. He went into the small office and sat down slowly, but made no move to open the letter. He simply stared at it. Finally, accepting that they could only say yes or no, he picked up the letter-opener and slit the envelope open. The letter was brief, but it told him all he wanted to know.

His sense of elation was marred by the fact that he had no one to share the news with. He certainly couldn't tell Kay, not until he had thought very carefully how he was going to explain what he wanted to do. And the same thing went for his parents. His father would worry and his mother would be upset. But he had to tell someone. Someone he could trust to keep quiet for a while.

While he was thinking about it, the door opened and Muriel walked in. She was smiling broadly. 'Can you keep a secret?' she said.

'I can if you can.'

When it was time for the morning tea break, Hetty took her cup outside to sit on the wall overlooking the railway track. Despite the sunshine, there was a chill wind blowing in from the sea, so she'd slipped her coat on. Resting her cup on the wall beside her, she reached into her pocket for her packet of Woodbines and came across the letter.

She looked at it cautiously. It was only then that she noticed the London postmark. Well she certainly didn't owe money to anyone in London, so who could have sent it? Carol, she thought. But why was the address typewritten?

The letter was from a firm of solicitors. Hetty began to read.

Dear Mrs Marshall,
Your stepdaughter, Miss Carol Marshall, has asked me to inform you that she has arranged for you to be sent a weekly money order for six pounds. She wants you to know that this money is to enable you to look after her father, and she will continue to send funds so long as you write to her, care of the address supplied below, informing her of her father's progress.

You will shortly receive the first money order and

a letter from the bank, who will advise you how to cash it.

The letter ended with the address of the office Hetty was to send her reports to. She lit a cigarette and drew deeply on it.

Six pounds. That was more than she and Albert had earned together when he was working. If Carol could afford to send them six pounds a week, that must mean she was earning much more than that. Hetty wondered if there was a way to get more out of her. She could say that Albert needed a holiday, perhaps. She'd have to think about it.

Brother and sister stared at each other across the desk. Muriel was clutching the latest edition of the local paper, and she could hardly contain her excitement.

'Who's going first?' she said.

'I suppose it should be ladies first.'

'All right.' She pushed the newspaper towards him.

'I take it you want me to read something.'

She nodded. He thought she looked too excited even to speak.

He began to turn the pages. 'Where shall I look? Hatches, matches and dispatches? Have you got engaged to that secret boyfriend of yours?'

'No, I haven't got engaged, and I wish you'd stop that. I haven't got a boyfriend and I don't want one. I'm not one of those girls who just sit around waiting to get married. Girls like that are history. I want a career. Just give me the paper back. I wanted you to be the first to know, but now I'm not so sure.'

She reached across the desk for the newspaper, but Steve took hold of her hand. 'Muriel – I was teasing.'

She snatched her hand away. 'I know you were. That's the

trouble. You still think of me as a little kid. You thought the same about Carol. When are you going to realise that while you were away we grew up?'

'I'm truly sorry,' he said. 'My only excuse is that while I was away I wanted to think of everybody at home being just the same – never changing. It was more comforting that way. But now ...'

Muriel looked uncomfortable. 'I'm the one who should be sorry,' she said. 'I should have understood how difficult it is for you and all the others coming back from the war.' They were both silent for a moment, and then she grinned. 'Right. That's that settled,' she said. 'Now get on with it before I burst.'

Steve carried on turning the pages.

'Further on,' Muriel said. 'Past the news ... it's in features. There! What do you think?'

Steve stared at the paper. 'This is marvellous – a double-page spread. Congratulations.'

'Thanks, but read it and tell me what you think.'

The feature bore the headline 'Our Very First Star', and over the two pages there were three photographs of Alice Grayson in her heyday and one of Carol taken at the Palais on the night she won the competition. Steve glanced at them quickly and then read on:

We are all justly proud of local girl Carol Marshall, who won the Glamour Girl competition and as a result now has a promising career in films, but how many of you remember another local girl who became a very big star indeed?

Alice Grayson could have gone to Hollywood, but after a tragic accident she chose to come home to the town she loved ...

The article went on to describe the highs and lows of Miss Grayson's career and the famous film stars she had worked with, and eventually got round to the fact that she had befriended and encouraged Carol Marshall.

When Steve had finished reading, he put the paper down on the desk and looked at his sister. 'This is very good indeed.'

'Do you really think so?'

'I do. You must have spent ages on research.'

Muriel smiled. 'Not really. Miss Grayson was only too pleased to talk to me, and she's still as sharp as a needle. She can remember locations, dates, everything.'

'And she gave you permission to write this?'

'Yes, but on condition that I let her read it first. Also she refused point blank to give me any details of the car accident that ruined her career.'

'I see you managed to work in the fact that Howard Napier, who was one of the judges in the Glamour Girl contest, was also an old friend of Alice Grayson's.'

'Yes – and I began and ended the piece with a reference to Carol. Nice touch, don't you think? Gives it a proper shape. And thanks for copying Miss Grayson's photographs for me. The paper already had this one of Carol.'

'Well, it looks as though you're on your way to Fleet Street.'

Muriel laughed. 'Not for a while yet. I haven't been promoted to reporter yet, not even a junior one. But Mr Blanchard says he'll be willing to look at anything else I come up with.' She glanced at her wristwatch. 'Golly, I asked if I could slip out for a moment, but I've been here far too long. I'd better be going.' She got up hurriedly and made for the door, where she paused and said, as if she'd suddenly remembered, 'Oh no! You had something you wanted to tell me, didn't you?'

'That's all right. I don't want to make you late. Can't have you getting the sack just as you've got your foot on the ladder.'

'But ...'

'No, run along. I'll tell you all about it later.'

After Muriel had gone, Steve picked up his letter, which had been lying unnoticed on the table, and slipped it into his inside pocket. He opened the appointment book and checked the work for the day. There wasn't much, and he would easily be able to manage without Peter or Mr Latham, but his heart sank at the sheer repetition of it all.

I must shake off this apathetic mood and do my best for these people, he thought. After all, for most of the customers this was a once-in-a-year occasion when they dressed in their Sunday best and came to have their lives recorded for posterity. Making a huge effort of will, Steve put his own concerns aside and went to prepare the studio for the first customer.

At lunchtime, Steve was about to turn the card in the window to Closed when Denise Shaw arrived in a hurry.

She looked at him through the glass panel and mouthed, 'Can I come in?'

Steve opened the door. 'What can I do for you?'

'I need some passport photographs. If you don't mind, that is.'

'Why should I mind?'

'Well, I haven't been altogether friendly in the past, have I?'

'No, and I always wondered why.'

'Oh ... nothing really. Maybe I thought you and Muriel were a bit toffee-nosed. But once I got to know your sister better, I realised that basically she's all right.'

Steve didn't believe that was the complete truth, but nevertheless he agreed and invited her in.

When he had taken the photographs, Denise thanked him. 'I'm really grateful,' she said. 'I hope I've left you time to have something to eat.'

'Don't worry. I've got a sandwich, and it doesn't take long to make a cup of tea.'

'Why don't you make that two cups?' Denise asked. 'I've got my sandwiches in my bag and I really don't fancy going back to the cubbyhole behind the shoe department. The other girls mean well, but they can't leave me alone. They keep asking daft questions about what it's like to be married to a film star.'

Steve smiled. 'And what do you tell them?'

'That he's a man like any other man.'

'Come on then. I don't know if our little staff room will be any more comfortable than your cubbyhole, but at least I won't ask you daft questions.'

As Steve boiled the kettle and made the tea, he realised that he liked this girl a lot and he was pleased that she and Muriel had been able to get over any differences they'd had in the past.

When they were sitting with their sandwiches, Denise told him, 'I've seen today's paper by the way. You must be proud of your sister.'

'I am. Did you know she was writing it?'

'No. But I should have guessed. All those notes she was taking when she was talking to Miss Grayson and the way they both clammed up as soon as they saw me.'

'I suppose she didn't want to tell you in case the paper didn't accept it.'

'Yeah, I realise that. But who would have thought it?'

'You've lost me.'

'Who would have thought that in such a short time Carol has become a film star, Muriel is a proper reporter, and I am going to live in Hollywood!'

'Who indeed.'

'What's the matter?'

'Matter?'

'You should look pleased for us. Well, for your sister at least.'

'I am. I'm pleased for all of you. It's just that the three of you are moving away – moving on – and I'm stuck here.'

'But isn't that what you wanted? You're married to Kay, you have a lovely home, and you've got a good job. What's wrong with that?'

'Perhaps that's not really what I wanted after all.' He saw Denise raise her eyebrows and added hastily, 'The job, I mean.'

Denise rose from her chair and filled the kettle. 'I'll make us another pot of tea, shall I? And then you can tell me why on earth you look so miserable.'

He looked at her guardedly. 'In confidence?'

Denise drew a finger across her throat. 'Cut my throat and hope to die.'

And so, to his surprise, Steve found himself confiding in Denise Shaw.

'Latham's is an old and respected firm,' he said. 'I was only too pleased to get a job here when I left school, but now I know that this isn't what I want to do.'

'You don't want to be a photographer?'

'More than ever. But not here, not this kind of work. I want to be a photojournalist. I want to use my camera to report what's happening not just in this country but all over the world.'

Denise smiled. 'Who would you work for? Some big newspaper?'

'Maybe, but I'd have to prove myself first. I'd be what they call a freelance.'

'And do you think you could make a living that way? I mean, you've got a wife to think about.'

'I think I could. I've made a start. Look at this . . .' On impulse he took the letter from his inside pocket and handed it to Denise. 'Go on, read it,' he said. 'Read it and tell me I'm not dreaming.'

'*Picture Post*?' Denise said. 'My dad likes that magazine.' She scanned the letter quickly, then looked up and smiled. 'But this is marvellous. They've accepted your photo-feature. What's it about?'

'Rebuilding – renewal – and the men and women who are working to put this country together again.'

'Sounds important.'

'I believe it is.'

Denise looked back at the letter. 'And not only are they paying you for this, they want to see more of your work. So what's the problem?'

'The problem is that if I'm going to do this properly, I can't stay here in Seaton Bay. I'll have to travel. I might be away from home for weeks, sometimes months at a time. I'd have to give up this job, and I'd be letting Mr Latham down.'

'I suppose you would. But he'd find someone else. There are plenty of men back from the war who are still looking for jobs, you know. And some of them must be photographers. But that's not all, is it? I'm guessing Kay won't stand for it. Is that it?'

'Denise, I'm not going to talk about Kay.'

'No, of course not. Ever the gentleman. But that's your real problem, isn't it? And it's all your own fault.'

Steve looked at her in surprise. 'What do you mean?'

'You married the wrong girl, that's what I mean. I never thought I'd hear myself say this, but I actually feel sorry for you. Especially when I think of what might have been.'

There was a moment's silence as they looked at each other, each wanting to say more but not daring to. Then Denise said, 'Thank you for taking the photographs. My mother will come and collect them.' She offered her hand hesitantly, and he took it. 'Goodbye, Steve. And good luck.'

When Hetty got home, Albert was sitting in his pyjamas at the table with the local paper spread out in front of him.

'Come and read this,' he said. 'It's about Carol and her teacher, Miss Grayson.'

'That's nice,' Hetty said. 'I'll read it after I've made the tea. But Albert, what are you doing down here without your dressing gown? Can't have you catching a cold, can we? Tell you what, I'll go up and get it for you.'

Albert looked up in surprise. 'That's very kind of you, Hetty.'

'Well, I've got to look after you, haven't I? And just wait until you see what I've got for your tea.'

A short while later, as she was frying ox liver and onions, Hetty was trying to work out how she could tell Albert about Carol's generosity without letting him believe the girl was a plaster saint. Maybe she'd suggest that Carol felt she had to do it to stop people talking. But one thing was for sure. She really would have to look after Albert, because the letter had made it quite clear that if anything happened to him, the money would stop, and then Hetty would have to go back to work.

Chapter Twenty-Nine

Carol could feel her cheeks burning. She was convinced that everyone who looked at her could tell what had just happened. She stood on the kerb waiting to hail a taxi, but in one of those inexplicable lulls, none came by. Knowing that she was attracting attention, and imagining it to be for the wrong reason, she decided to take the bus. The bus queue was more anonymous. Everyone in it was concerned only with their own journeys, their own lives.

Once on the bus, she climbed the stairs to the top deck and sat at the back. For a while she gazed miserably at nothing, and then she began to look at the passing scene. The crowded pavements, the imposing buildings and the fashionable shops. Well-dressed people leaving grand houses and hotels. And then, in stark contrast, the cordoned-off bomb sites.

Carol looked down at the craters and the plants growing amongst the ruins. Rosebay willow herb and buddleia, and flowers she could not name. People said the seeds were blown there from London's gardens. New life growing where people had lived and dreamed and died. She felt like weeping at the stark beauty of it.

Was her own life ruined? Surely it must be. Her dreams of stardom had come to nothing. A lifetime's hopes had been destroyed by one repulsive man. She found herself replaying the whole sordid episode and wondering if there was any way it could have ended differently. But she knew there wasn't. She could never have gone along with what he wanted her to do.

So what was she going to do now? She could not go back to Seaton Bay. She could imagine the derision of the sort of people who were glad when someone failed. And yet had she been happy there, she knew she would have been strong enough to deal with those people. No, despite her friendship with Muriel and Denise, she had never been truly happy since her mother died.

Memories of her miserable life with her stepmother were bad enough, but more devastating even than that was the fact that Steve was there. The man she loved and who had married someone else. That was enough to keep her away for ever.

Once she was back at her lodgings, she ran a deep bath and tried to soak the memories away. She scrubbed at her skin, trying to remove the feel of Monty Daniels' hands. Back in her room she bundled up the clothes she had been wearing and made a parcel of them. She would take them down and put them in the bin. She never wanted to wear any of them again.

'Leaving already, Mr Grainger?' Lenny appeared from the shadows as Paul rose from the gaming table.

'Got to get my beauty sleep, you know.'

'Perhaps I can tempt you to stay with another bottle of champagne. On the house.'

Paul gave a sardonic smile. 'Do you want to clean me out completely?'

'Certainly not. If you stay a little longer maybe your luck will change. I hate to see a friend of mine losing so much money.'

'Are you my friend, Lenny?'

'Of course.'

'Then if you don't mind, please step out of my way and let me go home.'

Lenny didn't budge. He stared at Paul for a moment, and then shrugged and stepped sideways. 'Maybe it's just as well. You've had a long losing streak and I'm beginning to worry whether you'll be able to pay me. Because, friend or not, your debts will have to be settled sooner or later. I let you play here because of who you are. Your name attracts the people who like to be mixing with celebrities. But even *your* name isn't worth what you owe me at the moment.'

'Don't worry, Lenny. I promise you, you'll get your money.'

In the taxi on the way home, Paul wondered how the hell he was going to keep his promise. Christ, what a mess he was in. Thank God this film was in the offing. The sooner work started the better.

He knew it would be a success whoever played the female lead, but with Carol Marshall in the role, and the chemistry they had together on screen, it should smash all box-office records. And Ed was negotiating for a healthy percentage of the box-office takings for Paul rather than a payment up front. If Paul was going to keep his friend Lenny happy, much depended on the success of *Dangerous Dreams*.

The next morning the telephone rang, splitting his head with its shrill sound. Paul, who had had too much to drink even before he had refused Lenny's offer of a free bottle of champagne, pulled the bedclothes up and tried to get back to sleep. But the phone went on ringing and in the end he sat up and reached for the receiver. The caller was Ed Palmer.

Paul listened for a moment and then yelled, 'You what! You let her go there on her own? What were you thinking of?'

'That's the way Monty likes it.'

'And we all know why!'

'Look, Paul, he only ever wants to have a look. As far as I know, he doesn't want to touch. I thought Carol would be able to handle that. But something went wrong, and not only does he not want Carol in his film, but he's threatened to make sure she never works again.'

'And that won't suit you, will it, Ed? I'll bet you imagined she was a dead cert to make you even richer than you are.'

Ed didn't respond, and after a moment Paul, now thoroughly awake, said, 'Leave it to me.'

Monty Daniels looked up from his desk as Paul Grainger, ignoring his secretary's protests, walked into his office.

'Ah, Mr Grainger. What a pleasure, although I do not remember you making an appointment.'

'I didn't.'

'So ... erm ... why are you here? And won't you sit down?' He waved a podgy hand at the chair on the other side of his desk. 'You're making me nervous glaring down at me like that.'

Paul sat down, but took his time before answering the question. 'Carol Marshall has the makings of a great star, and I'm not going to let you take that away from her.'

Monty Daniels flushed. 'I'm not having that little slut in my film. Didn't Ed tell you how she led me on?'

'Yes, he did, but I don't believe it. And anyway, it doesn't matter what the truth of it is. If Carol isn't going to be in this film, then neither am I.'

Paul saw the flash of uncertainty in the other man's eyes before he said, 'Good riddance then. There are plenty of other guys who can take the lead. Big names.'

'Are there?' Paul asked. 'Big names that are available right now? Big names that haven't gone to Hollywood to be in the latest big-budget war movie?'

'I can wait.'

'No you can't. I know how much you've gambled on this film. I know how much money you've already put into it and I'm pretty sure the money is running out. You need me, Monty. You need my name on the billboards. And if you want me, you have to take Carol.'

Monty Daniels opened a box of cigars and took one out. Instead of lighting it, he played with it nervously.

'I see what this is about. You've promised to get your girlfriend a big part in a movie.'

'What makes me think she's my girlfriend?'

'I've heard rumours. People talk.'

'Let them. When they see the film, they'll know she could have got the part without any help from me.'

The producer glared at Paul, his voice filled with venom as he said, 'Okay, you win. But I don't want her blackening my name.'

'That goes both ways.'

Monty managed a sickly smile. 'I won't breathe a word of what happened. Your girlfriend's reputation will remain untainted.' Then, as Paul rose to go, Daniels whined, 'I only wanted to look, you know. I never want more than a look.'

Paul stared at him for a moment, then said, 'You disgust me.'

On leaving the film producer's office, Paul went straight to see Ed Palmer and told him what had happened. 'And before I sign that contract, I want you to screw that fat bastard for as big a percentage as you possibly can.'

'Goes without saying. And for Carol too.'

Paul laughed. 'Of course. Now perhaps you'd better break the good news to her.'

'I will. But Paul, we need to talk.'

'Go on.'

'There are rumours.'

'What about? My drinking?'

'Yes, that, though up until now I've managed to keep your worst excesses out of the papers.'

'Worst excesses? That sounds bad.'

'Don't joke, Paul. Drink has ruined many a star. Remember Lorna Lane?'

'Before my time, old boy.'

'For God's sake, be serious. It's not just your drinking I'm worried about; it's the gambling as well.'

'Gambling?'

'Don't act the innocent. And it's not just the gambling; it's the company you keep. Mixing with crooks and shady underworld figures is not good for the reputation of a leading film actor. If the public stop admiring you, your career will be finished. Paul, you've got to change your ways. Find new friends.'

'Easier said than done.'

Ed suddenly looked uneasy. 'What do you mean?'

'Some of my old friends might not want to part company.'

'Exactly what kind of trouble are you in?'

'Who said I was in trouble?'

His agent sighed. 'All right, Paul. You don't have to tell me. But we'll have to think up some way of getting you a new image – a nice wholesome image – before the truth gets out.'

'Fresh and clean and new, eh?'

'Why are you smiling?'

'Because that might be easier than you think.'

When it became obvious that whoever was banging on the door was not going to go away, Carol got out of bed and opened it. Mrs Evans stood there, wreathed in cigarette smoke as usual. Her eyes narrowed when she took in Carol's state.

'You look bloody awful,' she said.

'Thank you.'

'I mean to say, you've just got out of bed, haven't you? And it's well past lunchtime.'

'Is it?'

'What's the matter with you?'

'Nothing.'

Her landlady eyed her suspiciously. 'You haven't got yourself pregnant, have you, like that fine friend of yours?'

'No. What do you want?'

'Gracious, I must say. Mr Palmer is here to see you. He says it's very important. He's waiting in the parlour.'

Carol giggled. 'Come into my parlour . . .' she began.

'For God's sake, are you drunk?'

'No.'

'Well there's something the matter with you, and I haven't time to stay here and find out. I advise you to wash your face, put some clothes on and comb your hair. Mr Palmer says it's urgent.'

Carol's heart sank. She wondered if she could face him. She thought she knew what he would have to say.

'Are you coming down or not?' Mrs Evans asked.

For one wild moment Carol contemplated saying, 'No, tell him I don't want to see him,' but she knew that would be cowardly.

'Yes. I'll be down as soon as I'm ready.'

'Then get a move on.'

Ed Palmer sat in Mrs Evans's dingy parlour, rehearsing what he would say. Paul had warned him that Carol might not want to see him. That she might pack up and go. After all, she must have a nice bit of money saved up, more than a girl like her could have earned in a lifetime working in a shop. She could go back home and live it up a little until she found a new job.

When she walked in looking tired but composed and as beautiful as ever, Ed stood up and went forward to meet her. 'I'm sorry, Carol,' he said.

'Why are you sorry? It's me who messed things up. Presumably Mr Daniels told you what happened?'

'Yes, but I want you to forget all about it. He's agreed that you should play the part after all.'

Carol looked stunned. 'What changed his mind?'

'Paul went to see him. He said that if you weren't offered the part, he would walk out.'

'Paul said that?'

'He did.'

'Why?'

'Because he thinks you're the best for the part. As I do. And don't worry, you won't ever have to see Mr Daniels again or have anything to do with him. You can put this behind you.'

After Ed had gone, Carol went back to her room and put the kettle on. For a while she took pleasure in simple things. Making tea and toast and tidying her room and not thinking too much. She had spent most of the night wondering what she was going to do, and by morning she had still had no idea.

But now, thanks to Paul, she didn't have to worry any more. He had given her back her hopes and her dreams. She wasn't sure why he had risked his own part in the film for her, but she would always be grateful.

Chapter Thirty

Howard kept his word and managed to get his new wife a passage on the *Queen Elizabeth*'s first peacetime voyage, setting sail in October. Denise enjoyed the sort of luxury she had only seen in films made in Hollywood. It was champagne and caviar all the way, and an ecstatic welcome when the largest ocean liner in the world sailed into New York with all flags flying. Howard was waiting for her, and after a night at the Waldorf-Astoria, they flew to California and the beautiful home he had bought in Canyon Drive.

Denise had tried to contact Carol to arrange a meeting before she left for America, but there had been no reply to her letter. When she broke her journey to Southampton to call at Carol's address in London, a sour-faced woman with a cigarette dangling from her thin scarlet lips said that Carol had moved out and hadn't left a forwarding address.

Denise didn't know if she believed that last bit; she got the impression that the woman was just being spiteful, but she could hardly shake the information out of her, so she had to go. She could only hope that Carol would get in touch with Muriel and Miss Grayson and let them know where she was.

Agnes Evans watched the young woman get into her taxi and drive away, and felt a niggle of guilt. Mrs Napier, as the girl had introduced herself, had seemed nice enough, and although she had a distinctly northern accent, she was respectably dressed. But if Agnes had given her Carol's address, she would have had to admit that she hadn't bothered to forward any of her mail, not that there had been much. She had, in fact, just thrown the letters into the bin.

The trouble was, the landlady had not forgiven Carol for the manner of her leaving. The Evanses had been having a bite of supper while they listened to a ghost story on the wireless. They'd heard the front door opening and footsteps going up the stairs. Two sets of footsteps; and as all the other lodgers had returned, even the woman who worked for the BBC, that could only mean that Carol had invited a friend in.

That wasn't against the house rules, so long as the visitor wasn't a man. But even if the friend was female, she shouldn't be visiting at this time of night. Just as Mrs Evans was deciding what to do, she heard a burst of laughter. Male laughter. She shot out of her chair, hurried to the door and flung it open, in time to see Carol Marshall turn to face the man who was following her upstairs and place a finger across her lips.

'What's this, my girl?' Mrs Evans said. 'What are you up to?'

It was the man who answered. 'We're going upstairs.'

'Oh no you're not,' she said. 'This is a decent house, this is. I'll not have any of those shenanigans under my roof!'

'I didn't come here for shenanigans,' the man said laughingly.

Mrs Evans thought she recognised his voice. She peered up at him through the smoke from her cigarette, but the brim of his trilby hat shadowed most of his face. He was smartly dressed, she could see that, and so was Carol, who was wearing a fur wrap and something silvery that shimmered in the dim light.

She's been to some posh club, Mrs Evans thought, and picked up this gent. Well, I'm not putting up with these film-star ways. Immoral. I knew it wouldn't be long before she was as bad as any of them. At least Patti never tried to bring any of her gentlemen friends back to her room.

'I don't know what you think you were doing bringing this man here,' she said, 'but I shall have to ask him to leave immediately. And you must find somewhere else to live, Miss Marshall. As soon as you can.'

'But that is exactly what Miss Marshall intends,' the man said. 'In fact, she's leaving right now. I've simply come to help her carry her belongings down. The taxi is waiting.'

'Helping her to move out?'

'If you look out of the door, you'll see the taxi,' the man said. 'And if you come upstairs with us, you will see that Miss Marshall's cases are packed and ready to go.'

Agnes Evans frowned. 'All right,' she said. 'But why now? Why in the middle of the night?'

'It's not that late,' the man said. 'We've come straight from the theatre. The original plan was for Miss Marshall to move out in the morning, but she told me she just couldn't stand another night here.'

Mrs Evans's indignation knew no bounds. 'There's nothing wrong with this place. I provide the best I can for my lodgers.'

Carol laid a hand on her companion's arm. 'Of course you do,' she said, 'and please don't think I'm not grateful. This was just the sort of place I needed when I first came to London, but now I have to move on.'

'In that case, I hope you intend to pay four weeks' rent in lieu of notice,' Mrs Evans said.

'I've already written you a letter giving notice, and I've enclosed a cheque for a month's rent,' Carol said. 'I've written my address in the letter so that you can forward my mail.

I was going to give it to you in the morning, but I decided that as I was all packed up, I might as well go.'

The man spoke again. 'We're very sorry to have disturbed you, Mrs Evans, but if there's nothing more you want to ask, the taxi is waiting.'

Mrs Evans remained where she was and watched them carry the bags down. Four cases and a posh-looking leather beauty box; that was more than the girl had had with her when she arrived. One battered suitcase and a string shopping bag, if she remembered rightly.

While the gentleman carried the luggage out to the taxi, Carol gave Mrs Evans an envelope containing the letter and the cheque. Mrs Evans opened it to check that the amount was correct. 'So you'll be moving in with him, I suppose.'

'Certainly not. I've found a flat of my own.'

The girl sounded so shocked that Mrs Evans was inclined to believe her.

'Carol,' called the man from the doorway, 'your carriage awaits you.' As he spoke, he jokingly doffed his hat and bowed like a character in a costume film. When he straightened up again, Mrs Evans recognised him immediately. Well, well, she thought, Paul Grainger. Carol Marshall certainly is moving up in the world.

Not long after Carol had finished work on *Salute the Brave*, she had started rehearsals for the Victorian murder mystery, *Dangerous Dreams*. As the female lead, this was a much bigger part than she had played before, and she found herself in a world of hair stylists, make-up consultants and costume fittings. She was also sent to a voice coach. The director, Max Preston, wanted to make sure that she could master the cockney accent of her character, Violet Gems.

Carol was good at voices. In everyday life she would watch and listen and reproduce someone's way of speaking almost perfectly. She loved her character's spirited attitude and the way she tried to better herself by copying the way the mistress of the house spoke – and sometimes making mistakes. This was an important point. For one day, when her lover's wife was already dead, she was forced to impersonate her, and got it terribly wrong.

Paul was perfect for the part of Brandon Lowry. He had the looks, the poise, and the figure to show the late-Victorian clothes to advantage. Carol would be eternally grateful to him for risking his own part in the film in order to save hers. She still had nightmares when she thought of what had happened in Monty Daniels' office.

The day after that, to her amazement, Ed Palmer had called to see her and told her that thanks to Paul the part was hers. Later, when he told her how much she could expect to be paid, she was astounded. Paul told her that she was worth every penny of it, and insisted that she come out with him to celebrate. Dinner at the Ritz, no less.

They began to be seen about town together quite often, and there were hints in the gossip columns of a romance between Paul Grainger and the promising film starlet Carol Marshall. It wasn't a romance as far as she was concerned, but Paul was easy company and for some reason he seemed to be determined to be charming to her.

Carol would have enjoyed the experience more were it not for the fact that no matter where they went or what they did, Paul could not get through the evening without a drink. There had been some embarrassing moments. Once, arriving at the theatre, Paul had fallen out of the taxi. People stopped to look. Carol got out and hurried to help him. 'Oh, look,' she said, 'your shoelace is undone.'

He gave her a grateful smile, and for once, he had ordered coffee in the interval instead of going to the bar.

Another time, as they were leaving Lenny's club, he

stumbled into a table and, grabbing the tablecloth as he went down, sent all the plates of food crashing to the floor. Lenny hurried forward with one of the waiters and they hauled him to his feet.

'I'll deal with this,' Lenny said to Carol. 'I advise you to leave him to me and go home. I'll call you a taxi.'

Only once had Carol been really frightened. They had been to Brighton for the day in Paul's Bentley. He had brought along a picnic hamper and a rug and they had sat on the beach enjoying the fresh air and sunshine. Carol had lain back and slept for a while, so she had not been aware of how much Paul had drunk.

On the way back to London, he started swerving from side to side of the road. At one point he narrowly missed ploughing into a family out on their bicycles. The car screeched to a stop and Paul sat behind the wheel, shaking with fright.

Carol realised that one of the bottles in the hamper must have contained vodka. She had picked up the studio gossip long ago that, like the famous American film star Joan Crawford, Paul drank vodka because he could pass it off as water.

Paul was so shocked by this incident that for a while he cut down drastically on his drinking. Sadly, this didn't last.

Paul and Carol became a regular item in the gossip columns. Ed was pleased.

'Once I would have been grateful that my new young hopeful was being seen out and about with a big star such as you,' he told Paul. 'But now it's the other way round. Being seen as the constant companion of this young, fresh-faced girl is good for your image – and may quell some of the rumours about your drinking. Gilbert Stern suggests that Carol is keeping you on the wagon and that you have enough sense left to listen to her.'

Gilbert Stern was a powerful gossip columnist who had a nose for the slightest whiff of scandal, and Ed was hoping fervently that he would not find out about Paul's visits to the back room at Lenny's club.

The harder Carol worked, the more she craved comfortable surroundings. As a small child, when her mother had been alive, their council house had been a haven of comfort, cleanliness and warmth. After her mother's death, when Hetty moved in, the house remained clean enough but the comfort vanished, leaving the rooms that had once known such happiness cold and dispiriting.

Now that money was no problem, she found herself a furnished flat in Richmond, which had the attraction of being near the river and also not too far from the studios in Twickenham. Paul helped her move in.

She had only been in her new apartment for a fortnight when Denise called at her old address. Carol did not find that out until much later.

In late November, Ed told Carol that her first film, *A Safe Bet*, was about to be released, and that the premiere would be at the Rialto in Seaton Bay.

Carol was dumbfounded. 'Why on earth would they have it in Seaton Bay?'

Ed shrugged. 'Probably a publicity stunt. You are expected to make an appearance.'

'I won't go.'

'You have to. It's part of the deal.'

'What deal?'

'When you won the Glamour Girl competition, you agreed to do any publicity the studio required of you.'

'I don't remember agreeing to that.'

'Your father signed the papers.'

'Did he read them?'

'No.'

'Didn't you tell him he should?'

'I mentioned it, but your stepmother's only concern was for him to sign the contracts as quickly as possible so she could get her hands on the money.'

'You paid them to sign the contract?'

Ed smiled cynically. 'I called it an advance on your earnings. I got the impression your father wanted to question me further but your stepmother just wanted to know how much they would get.'

'That doesn't surprise me in the least,' Carol said. 'What happens if I refuse to go to the premiere?'

'You would be fined – heavily.'

'I don't care.'

'And you'd get a name for being uncooperative. You can't afford that at this stage of your career. I presume you do still want a career?'

'All right. I'll go.'

'Paul's coming with you. He doesn't have to, but it was his idea. It will be quite an event in your old home town.'

'Do we really have to go tonight?' Kay said.

'You needn't if you don't want to,' Steve told her. 'I'll go with Muriel.'

'Why?'

'She asked me to.'

They stared at each other for a moment, and Kay must have realised that Steve was not going to change his mind. 'Oh all right,' she said. 'It might even be fun. A bit of a laugh, in fact. I think I'll phone Sarah and Jessica and see if they'll come along.'

Muriel could hardly believe her luck. Mr Blanchard called her into his office and told her that she was to cover the event at the Rialto. 'After all,' he said, 'you know Carol well, and you've proved you can write a good feature.'

'Thank you.'

'Will Miss Grayson be there?'

'Yes. She hardly ever goes out in public, but this is a special occasion for her.'

'I'll send someone along to take the photographs. It would be good to get a shot of Alice Grayson and Carol together. And speaking of photographs . . .' He paused. 'Does your brother still intend to follow up on that piece he did for *Picture Post*?'

Muriel looked at him uneasily. Mr Blanchard was a newspaper editor, and as such, he would probably appreciate Steve's work. But he was also Kay's father, and he must know that Steve's ambitious plans would upset his daughter.

'He doesn't really talk about it to me,' Muriel said.

'And if he did, you wouldn't tell me, would you?'

Muriel caught her breath, but then she saw that he was smiling. 'No, I wouldn't.'

She was about to walk away when something made her turn and ask, 'What do you think he should do?'

'I beg your pardon?'

'Steve . . . Do you think he should try his luck as a photo-journalist, or should he stay here and manage Latham's?'

Mr Blanchard gave her a keen look. Then he said, 'You don't really expect me to answer that, do you?'

'No, I don't suppose I do.'

Carol and Paul had taken the night train from London, and when they arrived at Newcastle, Paul suggested they should go to the Royal Station Hotel for breakfast. Carol felt dwarfed by the lofty Victorian architecture. She became even more perturbed when she realised they were attracting curious glances.

'People are looking at us,' she whispered to Paul.

'What do you expect? We're a handsome couple, and you look sensational in that camel coat. Casual but classy; couldn't be better.'

'The studio lent it to me, and also the dress I'm going to wear tonight. Oh Paul, won't it be wonderful when rationing comes to an end and I won't have to rely on borrowed or second-hand clothes?'

An important-looking man hurried forward. 'May I help you, Mr Grainger? Miss Marshall?' he said.

'Yes,' Paul said. 'We'd like some breakfast.'

Paul had the full breakfast, but Carol just picked at her tea and toast.

'Are you nervous about tonight?' Paul asked her.

'No. I'm nervous about going to see my father.'

When they had finished breakfast, the hotel manager called for a taxi. They had decided that rather than take the local train, they would travel in comfort. The weather was relatively mild for December, but by the time they were within a couple of miles of Seaton Bay, a thick mist had rolled in from the sea. The driver slowed almost to a crawl, and Carol looked out of her window as the grey swirls parted then coalesced again, giving a surreal view of the world.

When at last they pulled up outside her old home, Paul asked, 'Do you want me to come in with you?'

'No. Wait in the car. As soon as I've finished here, we'll go to Alice Grayson's.'

Carol got out of the car and the mist swallowed her up. Paul heard the click of the gate and the sound of her high heels on the garden path. Then the doorbell, and muffled voices. Carol hadn't told him much about her childhood, but it didn't take a genius to work out that it had not been happy.

He settled back in his seat and reached for the flask he kept in his inside pocket. He only allowed himself a mouthful. He wanted tonight to be a success. Ed Palmer thought he had offered to come to Seaton Bay with Carol in order to cash in on the good publicity surrounding her. That was partly the case.

But another reason was that it was getting a little uncomfortable for him in London. Lenny was growing impatient and had hinted that he might not be prepared to wait until the money started rolling in. The sooner *Dangerous Dreams* was in the can, the better.

'So you came,' Hetty said.

'Did you think I wouldn't?'

'To be honest, yes.'

The entrance hall was claustrophobic. Carol felt acute discomfort at being so close to the woman who had made her life a misery for so many years.

'To be equally honest,' Carol said, 'when I left here I had no intention of ever coming back.'

There was hardly any light coming through the small window set next to the door. Carol couldn't read the expression on her stepmother's face.

'Is my father in bed?' she asked.

'He spends most of his time there now.'

'I'll go up and see him. Alone. I don't want you to come.'

Albert Marshall was propped up amongst several pillows. He looked old and weak. Carol tried to hide her shock as she pulled up a chair and sat down.

'I was sure you would come,' he said. 'When I saw in the paper that you were to make an appearance at the Rialto, I told Hetty that no matter what had happened in the past, you would come to see your father.'

'What is it, Dad? What's wrong with you? Hetty's letters didn't make it clear.'

'I don't know how she could when the doctor doesn't know himself. He suspects it's the result of being gassed in the war – the first one. It's catching up with me and a lot of other old soldiers. He says he's got another patient like me and he sent him to see a specialist.'

'Why haven't *you* seen a specialist?'

'Hetty says we can't afford it. I mean, I know you've been sending money for us to live on, Carol, and I'm very grateful, but it's not enough for extras like that.'

'I'm sorry.' Carol took his hand. It felt dry and papery. 'I'll put that right straight away.'

'Are you sure? I mean, I don't want you to leave yourself short.'

Carol felt as though the narrow gap between the chair and the bed had suddenly grown wider. A huge gulf had opened up between the life she used to have and what her life had now become.

'I won't be leaving myself short, Dad. Believe me.'

She tried desperately to think of something to talk about. She suspected that memories of the past would be unbearable for both of them. So they sat in silence, taking comfort from each other's presence. Carol had not felt as close as this to her father for many years.

Hetty waited downstairs unwillingly. She would have preferred to be with them, because you never knew what Albert was going to say these days. She sat at the table smoking nervously. When Carol came down, she asked her if she wanted a cup of tea.

'No thank you. Just a quick word. Why didn't you tell me

you didn't have enough money for my father to see a specialist?'

'I thought you might be able to work that out for yourself.'

Carol stared at her for a moment, and then said, 'You're right. It's my fault, and I'm sorry. I'm going to increase the weekly allowance to ten pounds, and from now on my father is to have anything he needs. Tell them to send the bills to me. And I don't just mean medical bills. Clothes, books, a wireless for his bedroom, anything that will make his life more comfortable.'

'Feeling guilty, are we?'

'Why should I feel guilty?'

'For running off and leaving us like that.'

'If I hadn't run off, as you put it, I wouldn't be in a position to help in this way now, would I?'

Hetty remembered that it would be unwise to antagonise the girl. 'No, you're right,' she said. 'And ... and don't think I don't appreciate it.'

'Dad says you look after him well, and for that I'm grateful.'

'I do my best.'

'He's worried that it can't be much of a life for you.'

'Oh, I get along to visit my sister now and then.'

Carol was silent for so long that Hetty wondered if somehow she had heard something about these visits to her sister. And her sister's lodger, Joe.

But then she said, 'If ... when my father dies, I won't forget you. I'll see that you have enough to live on. Unless you get married again, of course.'

There was no more to say. Hetty went with Carol to the front door and stayed there as she got in the taxi and drove away. Then she went back inside and made a pot of tea and lit another cigarette. She had much to think about. If anything

369

happened to Albert, Carol was prepared to go on sending her money. Hetty wondered how much that would be. Ten pounds a week was a fortune, but Carol would surely reduce that amount when there was only one to provide for.

Well, well, Hetty thought. I'll have to wait and see. When the time comes, I'll have to decide what's best. To be a merry widow, or to marry Joe.

Chapter Thirty-One

When Carol and Paul arrived at Alice Grayson's house, they were met at the door by Denise's mother. Mrs Shaw, usually so cheerful and outgoing, was completely overwhelmed by Paul Grainger's presence, but she managed to invite them in and tell them that lunch was ready.

'It's salad and cold cuts,' she said. 'I've set up a table in her little sitting room. She likes it in there.'

Alice herself hurried out into the hall. 'Carol,' she said. 'You look marvellous. Every inch the star. I'm so proud of you. And you, Mr Grainger, I'm very pleased to meet you.'

'If you'd like to go and sit down,' Denise's mother said, 'I'll start serving the meal.'

Paul went ahead, and Carol lingered a moment with Alice Grayson. 'I'm so sorry it took me so long to write to you,' she said. 'But nothing was happening and I began to think they would send me home again. I didn't want to disappoint you.'

'Dear child, you should have known that you have my love whatever the outcome had been. I know this is a cliché, but you are like the daughter I never had.' Alice took her hand. 'Come along, Carol. There's no need to look like that. You're here now, and tonight we're going to celebrate.'

Carol, still emotional after her visit to her father, and moved beyond measure by Alice Grayson's generous greeting, was grateful to Paul, who took charge of the conversation, chatting to Alice about films both old and new, directors, actors and actresses of previous years and the performers to watch out for.

To Carol's surprise, Ruthie came in with the second course, a trifle. 'She comes along in her lunch hour from school,' her mother explained.

'We're coming to the Rialto tonight,' Ruthie told Carol. 'Denise said I have to write and tell her all about it.'

After the meal, Carol left Paul talking to Alice and went to sit in the kitchen to talk to Mrs Shaw and Ruthie. They told her how happy Denise was, how well she got on with her famous neighbours, and how she planned to have Ruthie over for a holiday. When it was time for Ruthie to go back to school she gave Carol a hug and said, 'I can't wait to tell the rest of my class that I've had lunch with Carol Marshall!'

After she had gone the house seemed much quieter. Carol returned to the sitting room to find Paul examining a copy of the local newspaper.

'What is it?' Carol asked.

Alice Grayson smiled mysteriously and said, 'Read it for yourself.'

Carol took the paper from Paul and read as she had been instructed. She looked up and said, 'A feature about you and me! And Muriel wrote it?'

'Yes, isn't it marvellous?' Miss Grayson said. 'Such insight; such style. I think that friend of yours will go far.'

'Oh I hope so,' Carol said. 'She certainly deserves to.'

'But now I'm feeling a little tired,' Miss Grayson said. 'And you, my dear, would you like to go up for a rest? Mr Grainger can stretch out here on the sofa if he wishes.'

Carol knew she would not be able to settle. 'Thank you but I think I'll go for a walk,' she said. 'To clear my head. If Paul wants to come, I can show him all the town has to offer.'

'Not frightened of being recognised?' Paul asked her as she slipped her coat on in the hall.

'We'll just be two figures in the fog. But even so, I'm going to turn my collar up and you're going to pull the brim of your hat well down over your face.'

'That will make me look like a gangster, but I'll do it if you'll be my moll.'

'Okay, buster,' Carol said, and they laughed as they set off arm in arm.

After a while, Paul said, 'Are you sure you know where we're going?'

'We're going nowhere in particular. I just wanted to walk and think.'

'Now she tells me. I could have had a nice snooze on Miss Grayson's sofa.'

'You can go back if you like.'

'I'd never find my way. Do you actually know where we are?'

'Yes, look.'

Paul turned in the direction she was indicating and saw that they were not far from a lighted shop window. Inside was a tasteful arrangement of mannequins dressed in what he assumed were the latest fashions.

'I used to work here, you know. In the French Salon.'

'Really?'

'Really. Does it matter?'

'It matters very much. It means we have something in common. Before Ed discovered me, I was selling high-class gents' wear in Simpsons of Piccadilly. You and I were obviously fated to meet one day.'

'I'm not sure if that makes sense,' Carol said. 'But come on.' She tugged at his hand.

'Where are we going?'

'Into the shop.'

Carol didn't know why she'd had this impulse to visit her old workplace, but it was too strong to resist.

The interior of the shop was quiet. Only a few customers had ventured out on such a day. Most of the shop assistants were tidying shelves or quietly gossiping. Few noticed as Carol and Paul hurried to the lift.

The first floor was even quieter. When they entered the French Salon, a slim, pale-faced young woman hurried towards them. 'Can I help you, madam?' she said. Then she stopped and stared. 'It's Carol Marshall, isn't it?'

Carol smiled and nodded.

'I don't suppose you've come to buy anything?' the girl said hopefully.

'No, I'm sorry. I just wanted to show my friend where I used to work.'

'Your friend?' The girl was staring at Paul, her eyes widening.

He tipped his hat back and smiled. 'Paul Grainger,' he said. 'I'm pleased to meet you ... ?'

'Moira.'

'Moira. Do you enjoy working here?'

'Yes, I do. Although I had been hoping to go to university.'

Carol saw the wistful expression in the girl's eyes and felt a pang of sympathy.

'Moira, are you looking after these customers properly?'

They all turned at the sound of the querulous voice, and Carol saw Miss Rawson emerging from her office.

'Yes, Mrs Wilmot,' Moira replied, and Carol remembered that Denise had written to tell her that old Rawbones had married her squadron leader.

'At least, they aren't really customers,' Moira went on uncomfortably. 'They've just come to ... come to ...'

'Miss Marshall wanted me to see where she used to work,'

Paul said. 'And I must say, this salon is as good as any you would find in London. I'm Paul Grainger, by the way, and I'm pleased to meet you.'

Carol shot Paul a grateful glance and then turned to see her old adversary's eyes widening as she stared at Paul. Remembering her manners, Mrs Wilmot turned to Carol. 'I never thought to see you again,' she said.

'We'll go now, if you like,' Carol said. She took Paul's arm and they began to move away.

'No ... wait. I ... I'm glad you came.'

'Are you?'

'When I look back, I think maybe I treated you too harshly.'

'No, you were right. I shouldn't have borrowed the dress.'

Paul raised his eyebrows, and Carol whispered, 'I'll tell you later.'

There was an awkward silence, and then Mrs Wilmot said, 'Gerald and I are coming to see your film tonight. We're both very pleased for you.'

'Oh ... good.'

Carol didn't know what else to say, but Paul came to her rescue. 'I understand there's going to be a bit of a crush in the foyer after the show. But if you and your husband are prepared to wait, perhaps we could have a drink together.'

'That's very kind of you, but we'll have to get home ... my mother, you know.'

'Well, if you can. And now Carol and I had better go and leave you in peace.'

As they walked towards the lift, they found Moira barring the way. Carol hadn't noticed that she had slipped away while they had been talking.

'The lift's out of order,' Moira said. 'You'll have to use the stairs.'

Something about the way the girl couldn't meet her eyes made Carol suspect that she wasn't speaking the truth, but she couldn't figure out why. The minute they began to walk down the grand old staircase, everything became clear. It seemed that the entire staff of Rutherford's, even Mr Rutherford himself, was waiting at the bottom. They began to applaud the moment they saw Carol and Paul, and to Carol's dismay, she saw that many of them were holding bits of paper.

'I think they want autographs,' she whispered to Paul.

'And we can't say no,' he whispered back.

Mr Rutherford, after making a little speech, kept order, and two queues were formed, with the top person peeling off and joining the end of the other queue just like in a country dance.

Carol was embarrassed to find that people she used to work with were treating her almost as if she were a stranger. Well, not a stranger exactly, just someone who didn't live in the same world as they did. When Eva Smithson from drapery reached the top of the queue, she leaned over and whispered, 'Are you and Paul Grainger going to get engaged?'

'Goodness, no. What made you think we were?'

'Well, you're always seen about together. Your pictures get in the papers. Go on – let me in on the secret.'

Carol smiled. 'Sorry to disappoint you, Eva, there's no secret. Paul and I are just friends.'

Eva grinned. '*Just good friends!* That's what they always say.'

'In this case, it's true.'

And it was, wasn't it? Carol glanced at Paul. He certainly liked to spend time with her, but nothing he had said or done had made her feel he was courting her. In fact they had laughed together at some of the stories in the newspapers. She was grateful for his friendship and indebted to him for saving her career, but she wasn't in love with him. How could she be, when she was still in love with Steve?

'We were just about to send out a search party,' Denise's mother said when they returned to Miss Grayson's house. 'Your pal Muriel is here. She says she has to interview you.'

'Muriel!'

Carol hurried through to Miss Grayson's sitting room. Muriel rose from her seat by the fire and greeted her smilingly.

A little awkwardly, they hugged each other. Then Carol introduced Muriel to Paul, and maybe she was just a little disappointed that her old friend didn't react the way most females did. She simply shook his hand and said that she was very pleased to meet him.

'I've read the feature you wrote,' Carol told Muriel. 'It's terrific! And now you're a fully-fledged reporter?'

Muriel smiled. 'Not quite, but today Mr Blanchard's giving me another chance to prove what a good journalist I am. I'll be covering tonight's event, but it will be a bit of a mêlée and I wanted to talk to you and Miss Grayson together without interruption.'

Muriel took her notebook from her bag, and Mrs Shaw said she'd go and make a pot of tea. 'Need any help?' Paul asked, and without waiting for a reply, he smiled at Muriel and headed for the kitchen.

Carol was touched by this thoughtful gesture. Paul Grainger was the real star here, and yet he was quite happy to allow Carol a moment of glory.

When Muriel was satisfied that she had enough information, she closed her notebook and put it in her shoulder bag, then glanced at her watch. 'I'd better go home and make myself glam. Don't want to give my dear sister-in-law another chance to criticise my style.'

'Kay's coming tonight?' Carol asked.

Muriel suddenly looked uneasy. 'Erm . . . yes. Kay and Steve.'

Both girls were subdued as Muriel took her leave.

'What was that about?' Paul had followed them into the hall, and he looked at Carol curiously.

Carol was too honest to tell him he was imagining things. 'Nothing much,' she said. 'It's just . . . well . . . Kay's not someone I'd like to meet again.'

'Are you going to tell me why?'

'I'd rather just forget about it.'

'Okay. But now we should get ready. And I suppose it will be ladies first for the bathroom.'

The cinema was crowded. Carol, Paul and Alice Grayson had been sneaked in through the back door and were greeted by Mr Benson, the commissionaire.

'Doesn't seem so long ago, does it?' he said. 'That night you and your pal came to see *Brief Encounter*. And now you're a film star and your friend is married to one.'

The manager of the Rialto, looking smart in his evening suit, invited them to wait in his office until the audience were seated. It wasn't long before Mr Benson returned and said, 'That's it, house full. We've had to turn people away, but they're waiting outside hoping to catch a glimpse of you when you leave.'

The manager explained that they would go on stage and he would introduce them to the audience. 'You'll say a few words,' he added, 'and then we'll play the film. Afterwards the plan is that you sign autographs in the foyer. Don't worry. You'll be safely inside the ticket office and Mr Benson will keep order.'

Alice Grayson was introduced first. She was wearing a full-length slim-skirted satin evening gown in her favourite eau de Nil. The bodice was encrusted with diamanté and the long sleeves came to a tapering point on the back of her hand. She wore a sequinned chiffon scarf the same colour as the dress to cover the scarred side of her face, and the marabou trim trembled as she spoke.

She took centre stage as if she had never left it, and her beautiful voice captivated the audience. Her speech was simple. She said that she had known Carol as a child and from the start had believed she had the talent to make a great future for herself. Then she stepped back and raised her arms to gesture to each side of the stage, and Carol and Paul walked on separately as they had been instructed.

Miss Grayson stood back and Paul spoke next. He said he was honoured to be in the company of Alice Grayson and that there must be something in the air in Seaton Bay to have produced two such beautiful film actresses. That got an appreciative laugh. Then he said that he was not the star tonight and that he had only come to support Carol. The audience applauded wildly, and then it was Carol's turn.

Carol crossed her fingers in the folds of her dress of smoky-blue chiffon and said how pleased she was to come home to Seaton Bay. She said that she owed everything to Alice Grayson, the teacher who had become her friend, and how grateful she was to Paul Grainger, who had come to support her tonight. She reflected later that it wouldn't have mattered much what any of them had said. The audience just wanted to have a glimpse of real-life film stars.

The three of them remained on the stage while a photographer from the local paper took photographs, then Mr Benson led them away.

The Rialto had once been a theatre, so Carol's party was shown to a box. Looking around, she was uncomfortably aware that the audience, as well as watching the screen, could watch them. Something caught her attention, and she looked across to the box on the other side of the auditorium to see Mrs Carshalton and Yvonne waving and smiling. She waved and smiled in return.

The curtains opened to reveal the screen, the lights dimmed and the show began. Carol's character, the cigarette girl, didn't make an appearance until about a third of the way through the film, and some of the audience became restive. When she finally did appear, there was a burst of applause and some wolf whistles.

'I can't watch this,' Carol said to Paul.

Sensing that she was about to get up and go, he gripped her hand and said, 'If you have to, just close your eyes, but don't you dare leave.'

And so Carol sat with her eyes closed throughout the screening of her first film.

'I know how you feel,' Alice whispered to her. 'I always found it difficult to watch myself on the screen.'

As the titles began to roll, Mr Benson came and spirited them away. 'I'll get you safely inside the ticket office before there's too much of a crush,' he told them.

Alice excused herself. 'They won't want my autograph, and besides, I'm very tired. The Shaws are going to come home with me in a taxi and we'll have a bite of supper together.'

In the warm, richly carpeted corridor, she embraced Carol, and Carol, close to tears, said, 'I promise I'll keep in touch.'

'Bless you, child,' Alice said.

From that moment the evening passed in a blur. The autograph books were pushed through the gap in the glass above the ticket dispenser. Some people just wanted Carol to sign her name, some wanted some sort of personal message, and soon Carol's hand was aching. Every now and then she glanced at Paul, who remained friendly and charming and totally in control. Thank goodness he hasn't had a drink today, she thought. He's like a different person when he's sober.

Mr Benson kept order throughout, and eventually the crowd began to thin. Carol became aware of a group of people standing apart. Muriel was with them. There were two girls she did not recognise, and Kay and Steve.

Muriel hurried over as soon as the last autograph had been signed.

'Congratulations,' she said. 'I had to tell you how much I enjoyed the film, but I've got to go now. Steve is waiting to take me home.'

As she spoke, Steve detached himself from the group and walked over to join Muriel.

'Hello, Carol.' He smiled uncertainly.

'Steve.'

'I enjoyed the film.'

'I'm glad.'

Carol could see her own reflection in the glass in front of her. She could also see Paul's reflection, and he was looking at her thoughtfully.

'Well . . . congratulations,' Steve said.

'Thank you.'

It seemed that neither of them had any more to say.

Kay walked over. 'Steve darling, we really have to go,' she said. 'It's been very amusing, but Sarah and Jessica aren't used to this kind of thing. Are you coming, Muriel?'

Kay linked her arm through Steve's and pulled him away. She had completely ignored Carol.

'Bitch,' Muriel said. 'I'm sorry.'

'Don't apologise. It's not your fault.'

'Well, I suppose I'd better go. I have to write up my piece before tomorrow morning.' She lingered for a moment. 'It's been great seeing you, Carol.'

'And you.'

After a tremulous smile, Muriel hurried after Steve and Kay.

'I can't thank you enough,' the manager told them as he ushered them across the foyer. 'This has been a memorable night for the Rialto. Mr Benson has put your bags in the taxi. It's waiting at the front door. I understand you're going to say a word or two to the fans who are waiting.'

'Keep smiling,' Paul said to Carol as they walked out of the cinema. 'This lot have waited here in the cold and they deserve a smile and a kind word from their own film star.'

'I think they may be waiting for you, not me,' Carol said.

'What makes you think that?'

'Look at them. They're all young and female.'

Carol was right. Although most of them asked for her autograph, it was Paul who was getting all the rapt attention. She stood back and watched how he dealt with his fans. She saw their adoring faces and knew that most of them would give anything to be in her shoes.

When the last autograph book had been signed, Mr Benson saw them into the taxi. 'I hope you'll come back here again,' he said to Carol.

'One day,' Carol said, vowing that that day would never come.

When the taxi pulled away, she breathed a sigh of relief. Soon they would be on the night train back to London.

Chapter Thirty-Two

When the train arrived at King's Cross the next morning, Paul persuaded Carol to come back to his apartment in Kensington. 'You're dead on your feet,' he told her. 'You need looking after.'

'What about you?'

'I'm tired too. Mrs Lambert, my housekeeper, will look after both of us.'

While Carol slept, Paul went to the small bar in the sitting room and made himself a vodka martini, a drink he had first tasted the last time he was in America. Then, easing off his shoes, he settled himself in an easy chair by the fire. He had much to think about.

While he and Carol were signing autographs in the department store, he had heard one of the girls asking Carol if they were going to get engaged. He sipped his drink and listened to the comforting sounds coming from the kitchen, where Mrs Lambert was preparing a meal for two. Domesticity. Did that appeal to him? It very well might. Perhaps he was getting just a little old for the rackety life he had been leading. He didn't want to become a laughing stock. But neither did he want to become a boring middle-aged married man.

For the sake of his image he needed a glamorous young wife. A woman whom every other man would envy him. And who would fit the role better than Carol? What a fabulous celebrity couple they would make. Just like Laurence Olivier and Vivien Leigh. Or Rex Harrison and Lilli Palmer. Or even Humphrey Bogart and Lauren Bacall. After all, good old Bogie had done wonders for newcomer Bacall's career.

He wasn't in love with Carol and he knew she wasn't in love with him. Sometimes, when she didn't think anyone was watching, she took on an expression of great sadness. Paul remembered the moment in the foyer of the Rialto, and how she had been at a loss for words when confronted with her friend's brother.

Was there a story there? Had she had her heart broken? Well, if that was the case, he must make her happy. He must start courting her in earnest; maybe play on her sympathy a little. Hopefully he would be able to convince her that marriage was the best thing for both of them.

When Carol woke hours later from an exhausted sleep, Paul told her that his housekeeper had left them a casserole warming in the oven and that by the time she'd showered he would have the meal on the table.

After they'd eaten, they cleared the table together, and then Carol walked over to the window in the sitting room, calling Paul to come and see the snow that had begun to fall. Soon it had covered the rooftops and the streets below and deadened the noise of the traffic. It seemed the most natural thing in the world for him to put his arm round her and hold her companionably close for a moment. Then he closed the curtains and they went to sit by the fire.

Paul put a stack of easy listening music on the record player, switched off the overhead light and sat down beside her. They listened to the music in companionable silence. He didn't attempt to draw her close. For the moment it was enough that she was comfortable just sitting beside him in the firelight.

★

Her flat was cold, and the first thing Carol did was to fill the kettle for a hot-water bottle. Paul had loaned her a travelling rug for the taxi, but the minute she'd stepped out into the night air she had started shivering.

She smiled at how unglamorous and far from film-starry she must look, and remembered what Patti used to say about her winceyette pyjamas. And tonight she had added an old cardigan and bed socks! This raised another smile, but as she sat up in bed with her cocoa, the full gamut of emotions evoked by her trip home to Seaton Bay gradually overcame her.

Finding her father looking so ill had shocked her. By the time she had left him, they had come to some sort of understanding. But it was an understanding without words. She knew that she loved him no matter how much he had hurt her by seeming to support Hetty. However, she thought she understood. He had been just as heartbroken as Carol when her mother died, and the only way he could cope with it was to find someone new.

Seeing Miss Grayson and Muriel had been wonderful. But the fact that she did not know when she would see them again was painful.

The worst moment had been when she had come face to face with Steve. Muriel had told her that he was coming to the premiere, but Carol hadn't expected him to seek her out. So when he came to speak to her, all her acting skills deserted her. The only comfort she could take was that he had seemed as dumbfounded as she was. She had actually been grateful when Kay had dragged him away.

She was sure Paul had noticed that something was amiss, but he just went on signing autographs and being charming. For that she was grateful. In fact she didn't know how she would have coped with the visit to Seaton Bay without Paul. He had been practical and kind and he had been willing to stand back and allow her her first moment of fame. And she couldn't even imagine what it must have cost him to remain sober. For Paul had his own problems.

She had been taken totally unawares when they had been sitting by the fire in his apartment and he had thanked her for putting up with him.

'Putting up with you?'

'When I'm with you, it all begins to make sense again,' he told her.

'What does?'

He smiled ruefully. 'Oh, I don't know. The world, I suppose.'

As he stared into the flickering fire, Carol thought he looked utterly desolate.

'Tell me about it,' she said.

Without turning to look at her, he continued, 'Seven days. For seven days after our ship went down we were adrift in the North Atlantic. We'd all suffered some kind of injuries but mine were the least severe. I watched my shipmates die, Carol. One by one I had to tip them overboard. By the time I was spotted by a convoy escort destroyer, I was the only one left.'

Still without turning to look at her, he reached for her hand and gripped it tightly.

Carol held his hand and waited until he sighed and turned to smile at her. 'Crazy world. Crazy things we do to each other, but when I'm with you I begin to feel I could be happy again.'

Now, as she lay with the bedclothes pulled up to her ears, Carol wondered if she was interpreting Paul's words and actions correctly. Was he telling her that she meant something to him, and more than that, that he needed her? And what of her own feelings? She loved Steve. Perhaps she always would. But Steve had chosen Kay. Surely that didn't mean that she should remain alone for the rest of her life ...

A couple of weeks before Christmas, Kay faced Steve across the breakfast table, the lines of her face taut with fury. 'I can't believe that you're not going to come with me to my parents' house on Christmas Day!'

'I didn't say I wasn't coming. I just said I would be late.'

She glared at him.

'Kay, I've got to do this. They'll be waiting for me.'

'But on Christmas Day!'

'That's the whole point. Several local families have invited German prisoners of war into their homes for Christmas dinner, and I'm going to be there to record the event.'

'German prisoners! The war has been over for sixteen months. Why haven't they all been sent back by now?'

'You know why. Some of them came here to help with the harvest; some have been working on bomb disposal. They'll all go home eventually, but before they do, it's important to record how former enemies are trying to make peace with each other. And Christmas Day is a wonderful opportunity to do that.'

'So you won't change your mind?'

'No.'

Kay's angry expression suddenly crumpled into misery. 'This is our first Christmas together.'

As so often these days, Steve was seized with guilt. 'I know, and I'm sorry, but we can have our own Christmas celebration later, here by our own fireside, can't we?'

'That's not the same as sharing it with my family.'

'Kay . . . you know plenty of people have to work on Christmas Day. Postmen, milkmen, bus and train drivers, doctors, nurses . . . I could go on. I'm sure all these people still celebrate Christmas no matter what time they arrive home.'

She looked up at him and scowled. 'The difference being that they have to work. You choose to.'

Kay rose and began to clear the table. Steve could hear her clattering the dishes about in the kitchen, and he knew that not only did she not understand but that she never would.

'Are you going home for Christmas, Carol?'

Paul and Carol were dining at Mario's. The atmosphere was lively, and from all the tables around them they could hear people making plans for the holiday.

'No. What about you?'

'I'll be staying in London. There's nowhere else to go. My parents are dead and I was an only child.' He paused and cupped one ear. 'Can you hear the violins?'

'Violins?'

'They always accompany the sad bits in a melodrama, don't they?'

Carol smiled. She liked Paul's ability to make fun of himself, even though she had come to believe this was a cover for real loneliness.

'So what will you do on Christmas Day?' Paul continued.

'Sit by the fire in my apartment, read the new books I've bought myself and eat lots of toast with hot sweet tea.'

'Are you serious?'

'Yes. What about you?'

'I've had an invitation to dine out, but I'm not really keen to go on my own.'

Carol, remembering the night she had come here with Patti, had ordered spaghetti bolognese, and so had Paul. When Mario himself brought the food to the table, he asked Paul what he would like to drink.

'Chianti,' Paul said. 'But just one bottle.'

After a delicious Marsala-rich zabaglione, they had coffee and the almond biscuits that came with it. Paul reached into his pocket and brought out a small jeweller's box. When he opened it, Carol caught her breath.

'Sapphire and diamonds,' Paul said. 'Sapphire to match your brilliant blue eyes and diamonds because you're precious. Well ...?'

'Is it ... I mean, are you ...?'

'Yes, I'm asking you to marry me.'

'Oh, but ...'

He smiled. 'I know. I've taken you by surprise. But you must admit, we get on well, and I've been a changed man lately. Surely you've noticed? You're good for me, Carol, and I believe I can make you as happy as you deserve to be.' He grinned. 'Do you want me to go down on one knee? Here in front of all these people?'

'No, please don't!'

Paul's smile was infectious, and suddenly Carol found herself laughing. For a moment the months of loneliness and heartbreak faded. Why shouldn't she take this chance of happiness?

To her consternation, while she had been thinking, Paul had left his seat and really had got down on one knee. The people at the surrounding tables were smiling and laughing.

'What is the answer to be, sweet maid?' he said like the hero of a medieval romance. 'Will you marry me, or are you going to send me away to die of a broken heart?'

By now, other diners in the restaurant were standing to see what was going on. 'Put the poor guy out of his misery!' someone shouted.

'Please get up, Paul,' Carol said.

'Do you accept my proposal?'

'Yes, I do.'

The other diners clapped and cheered, and Carol, carried along by the joyous atmosphere, began to believe that she could be happy again.

*

'I heard what happened in Mario's last night,' Ed told Paul. 'Very touching.'

They were sitting facing each other across Ed's desk. The windows were covered with sooty snow and the overhead light with its glass shade barely penetrated the shadows.

'Do you approve?'

'I don't know.'

Ed wasn't sure how he felt about the fact that Paul and Carol had got engaged. Part of Paul's attraction was that the female fans thought he was available. But on the other hand, if a male star remained unmarried for too long, the wrong sort of rumours got around. There were actors who much preferred the company of men who nevertheless married some poor woman to keep speculation at bay. As far as Ed knew, Paul wasn't homosexual, but there had been very few women in his life, so perhaps marrying Carol was a wise move.

It would be good publicity for Paul – good for his image. But what about Carol? She was very young. Should she tie herself down quite so soon?

'Do you love her?' Ed surprised himself by asking.

Paul reached into his pocket for his cigarettes and took his time lighting one. He picked a flake of tobacco off the end of his tongue before replying.

'As much as I can love anyone.'

'You're a cold-hearted bastard.'

Paul shrugged. 'Remember, I'm doing you a favour.'

'How's that?'

'We'll become a sought-after screen couple. You'll be able to ask for anything you like. Think of a number! You'll make a lot of money out of us.'

'There is that.'

'Thought that would make you happy. Now, I've got a wedding to arrange. Fancy being best man?'

When Paul had gone, Ed sat and thought and realised that he wasn't happy at all. Carol didn't know yet how good she was. Paul obviously did, and he'd made sure that he'd tied her to him before her star rose and she left him far behind.

He opened his top drawer, took out the bottle of whisky he kept there and poured himself a drink. He stared at it moodily. There was another reason he was unhappy, and that was that he couldn't bear to see Carol marrying someone who didn't really love her. She deserved much better than that.

Paul got a special licence and they were married at Caxton Hall on the Saturday before Christmas. Ed was the best man, and Paul's housekeeper and her husband were witnesses.

Ed had had a discreet word with his contacts in the press, so when the happy couple came out into the frosty sunshine, there was a barrage of flashing cameras.

'Carol!' someone shouted. 'Look this way!'

'Paul! Kiss the bride!'

Someone threw confetti, and the cameras clicked even faster.

When the assembled press gang were satisfied, the five of them went for a meal at Mario's. Then Carol and Paul went back to Paul's apartment. It was only then that Carol wondered at the morality of marrying one man when she was in love with another.

Chapter Thirty-Three

Early on Sunday morning, Bill Shaw was sitting by the fire reading the *Sunday People* when he looked up and shouted, 'You two! Get over here!'

'What is it, Bill?' Mrs Shaw asked. 'We're not at war again, are we? It's not the Russians this time, is it?'

'Nothing like that. Come and see for yourselves.'

Ruthie and her mother stared at the photographs showing Carol and Paul smiling through a shower of confetti. She was wearing a fur coat and a white pillbox hat with a half-veil. With one hand she held a bouquet of white flowers and with the other she clung on to Paul's arm as she smiled into the camera.

'Doesn't she look lovely!' Ruthie exclaimed.

'Married to Paul Grainger! Fancy that!' her mother said. 'I'll have to send this to Denise.'

Kay and Steve had gone to her parents' house for lunch. While Kay and her mother prepared the meal, Mr Blanchard and Steve read the papers. As a newspaper editor, Kay's father took all the national newspapers as well as the local ones. The story was in every one of them. Steve looked at the photographs.

Kay came in to summon them to the table and glanced at the paper over his shoulder. 'Clever, isn't she?'

'What are you hinting?' Steve asked.

'I'm not hinting anything. I'm merely stating a fact. Carol Marshall is a clever girl. That's one way to the top, isn't it? To marry a big star.'

Steve did his best to join in the conversation at the table and hoped he'd succeeded in hiding his anger. He wasn't angry with Kay. He'd accepted she would never change. He was angry with himself. His realisation that he loved Carol had come too late. He had allowed fate and a sense of duty to carry him along to marriage with Kay and he had let Carol slip away from him. He could only pray to God that Paul Grainger would make her happy.

After lunch, Mrs Shaw went to Alice Grayson's house to make sure she had managed to warm up and eat the meal she had prepared for her the day before. Miss Grayson was sitting by the fire with a cup of tea. Her newspaper was on the little table next to the armchair.

'So what do you think of Carol, then?' asked Mrs Shaw. 'Getting married to that gorgeous man.'

Miss Grayson smiled. 'Yes, he is gorgeous, isn't he?'

'You don't think she'll want to give up acting, do you?'

'No, I don't. It means too much to her.'

'And Mr Grainger? Do you think he'll want her to give up and stay at home and be a housewife?'

'I don't think so. I believe he will want them to work together.'

Once Alice was alone, she admitted to herself that there were two things worrying her. She had spoken the truth when she'd told Mrs Shaw that Paul would want to make films with Carol, but she wondered if he had thought it out. What would happen if Carol's career overtook his, as Alice was sure it would? Paul was used to being a star. Would his ego be able to stand it if his wife became a bigger star than he was?

The other worry concerned Carol alone. She looked happy enough in the photographs, but after all she was an actress, and a very good one. Alice sighed and tried to convince herself that she was imagining things, but she couldn't quite dismiss the thought that gorgeous though Paul Grainger might be, Carol wasn't in love with him.

On Christmas morning Carol and Paul exchanged gifts. She'd had no idea what to give him and had spent hours gazing into the windows of shops in the West End. Finally she had settled for the latest Omega gentlemen's watch, designed by Albert Piquet. She had never in her life spent so much money on one purchase, and now she held her breath as he removed the Christmas wrapping paper and opened the presentation box.

'Do you like it?' she asked nervously.

'Very much. I only hope my gift to you is as successful.'

He handed her a small package. The wrapping paper was gold and silver. It's more tasteful than the paper I chose, Carol thought anxiously. She opened the narrow velvet-covered case and lifted out a diamond and sapphire pendant, holding it up so that the gems sparkled in the light.

'Like it?' Paul asked.

'It's wonderful!' she gasped. 'Too much!'

'No, not too much,' Paul said 'Nothing is too much for my wife.'

Carol and Paul had their Christmas dinner at Lenny's club. The place was closed to all but a few special guests. There was a member of the House of Lords, a well-known broadcaster, a heavyweight boxing champion, a popular jockey, and two men who were introduced as Lenny's business associates.

Their wives and girlfriends were expensively dressed, and Carol was grateful that the film studio was prepared to lend her whatever clothes she needed. They intended to build her up as a star and they wanted her to look good whenever she was seen in public.

The meal was luxurious. You wouldn't think that food was still being rationed, Carol thought. Paul advised her not to question too closely where it came from. A different wine was served with each course, and after the meal most of the men moved on to hard liquor. Carol watched Paul anxiously but although he had more to drink than she would have liked, he didn't appear to be much affected.

He caught her looking at him and said, 'You're not going to be that kind of wife, are you? Begrudging a man a little indulgence now and then?'

He was smiling, but his tone was slightly querulous, and as she certainly didn't want to argue with him on Christmas Day, Carol said nothing.

After the meal, Lenny approached Paul and congratulated him on his marriage. Carol sensed a coolness between the men that she did not think had existed before.

'Still got big hopes for this film?' Lenny asked.

'Bigger than ever,' Paul replied. 'Don't worry.'

Carol wondered why Lenny should worry about the film they were making, but nothing more was said.

After a fairly mild spell in December, the weather worsened and the filming of *Dangerous Dreams* continued in what proved to be the coldest winter in fifty years. Work started at six thirty every morning, and on the drive to the studios they dressed as warmly as they could. Paul wore several jumpers under his sheepskin coat and Carol wrapped herself up in rugs. During the filming she wore a pair of slacks under her costume. She thanked her lucky stars that this was a period piece rather than a modern story where she would have to wear short skirts.

Then, as if the weather wasn't enough to deal with, there was an electricity strike, and the make-up girls and boys had to apply the cosmetics by candlelight. Fortunately there were generators to power the studio lights, and no matter how frozen and miserable people were, filming went on. Everyone pulled together, determined to overcome all difficulties, just like they had done during the war.

One day, when the strike was over and hot meals were being served in the canteen, Carol came across Ray sitting with Joan Summerfield. Although she was sure they had seen her, they didn't look up when she passed their table carrying her tray. On impulse she turned back to talk to them. Ray was dressed as a Victorian policeman and Joan as a kitchen maid.

'Hello, Ray,' Carol said. 'I'm pleased to see you here. Are you getting plenty of work?'

'I am. Apparently I look good in uniform. Soldiers, sailors, airmen and policemen. That seems to be my future.' He smiled suddenly. 'But don't get me wrong, it's better than driving posh people about in luxury cars.'

Carol looked at Joan, who was staring resolutely down at the table. 'And you, Joan?'

Joan looked up. 'You needn't pretend you're pleased to see me,' she said.

Ray put one hand over hers and pressed it warningly.

'Look, Joan,' Carol said, 'I think we got off to a bad start. I don't want us to be enemies.'

Joan looked surprised. 'Don't you? Really?'

'Really. If we're all going to go on working in this business, we ought to be pleasant to each other, don't you think?'

Joan pursed her lips and stared ahead mulishly.

Just then Paul entered the canteen, and Carol told Ray and Joan, 'Got to go, but no doubt I'll see you later.'

'Not if I can help it,' Joan muttered, and Carol gave up in

despair. She realised wearily that it was pointless to try and make friends with everybody. She would just have to accept that the more successful she became, the more likely she was to make enemies.

Paul was waiting near the door. 'I've managed to procure a two-bar electric fire for my dressing room. Take your meal there and I'll join you as soon as I have mine.'

A little later, with their trays on their knees, they sat huddled over the electric fire. Despite the two bars, the warmth didn't rise very far and the air remained cold. Both of them were wearing gloves, and Carol had tied a woollen scarf around her head to cover her ears. The hairdresser would scold her later, but she didn't care.

When Paul poured a generous measure of whisky into his cup of tea, he said it was to fend off the cold. Carol could hardly argue with that, but she only allowed him to pour a teaspoonful into her own cup.

'Spoilsport,' he said, 'but I'm not complaining. You're a good influence on me. My guardian angel.'

When he was completely sober, Paul was a kindly if not passionate husband. And fun to be with. He certainly liked to take Carol 'out on the town', as he called it, and seemed pleased when the press discovered where they were and demanded photographs.

He would look at the newspapers the next day with real pleasure. 'We look good together, don't we?' he had asked her more than once. 'A legendary screen couple. That is what we're destined to become. We'll make movie history!'

Carol wasn't so sure if that was what she wanted, but if it made Paul happy — Paul to whom she owed so much — she was prepared to go along with it.

Chapter Thirty-Four

March 1947

Steve had tried hard to combine his job at Latham's with his work as a photojournalist. Inevitably it meant that he spent less time at home. Kay had reproached him many times. He would reply that if he gave up working for Mr Latham, he would not only have more time to work on his features but also more time to spend with her.

'Mr Latham kept the job open for you. You can't leave him in the lurch like that,' she said.

'I wouldn't dream of leaving him in the lurch. I went to the employment exchange and I had a chap introduced to me. Jack Lawrence was a combat photographer in the army throughout the war. He saw the horrors of war close up. All he wants now is to make a home for his wife and family. He's the ideal person to manage Latham's.'

'But what you want to do would take you away from home.'

'I can't deny that.'

'What am I supposed to do while you're away?'

'I don't know, Kay. What do sailors' wives do? What do the wives of professional soldiers do? I wouldn't be away from home as long as some of those guys.'

'You're a beast, and I hate you!'

The argument would usually end with Kay in floods of tears and Steve feeling guilty as hell.

Picture Post had bought his Christmas Day feature about German prisoners of war and told him they would be interested in anything else he might send them. His first new project concerned the way people dealt with the overwhelming falls of snow. Before going to work in the mornings, he went out with the milkmen and the postmen and the newspaper boys. He photographed abandoned cars and trains stuck in sidings and buses that couldn't leave the depots. But even without public transport, people got to work somehow.

One evening he went to the casualty department of one of the local hospitals to record how they were coping with all the injuries caused by snow and ice. On the way home there was a fresh fall of snow and the bus driver had to negotiate near-blizzard conditions. The journey was excruciatingly slow.

After leaving the bus station, Steve trudged through the snowy streets. As he approached his house, he saw that there was a car parked outside and the lights were on in the lounge. When he opened the front door and stepped into the hall, he heard laughter and the murmur of voices.

Puzzled, he opened the door to the sitting room and saw Kay sitting by the fire and Rupert Penfold on the leather pouffe at her feet. Rupert was in the act of filling Kay's wine glass.

Kay looked up, saw Steve and scowled. 'For goodness' sake,' she said. 'Standing there with snow dripping all over the carpet. You might have had the sense to take your coat off.'

Furious to be spoken to like that in front of Penfold, Steve shouted, 'Never mind the bloody carpet! What the hell is going on here?'

'I say, old man, no need to shout.' Penfold rose to his feet and stood on the hearthrug smiling good-naturedly. 'We were just keeping the little lady company, you know.'

As Steve puzzled over the 'we', an arm rose from the sofa and waved. A moment later Jessica Harland sat up. The back of the sofa faced the door, so Steve had had no idea she was there. She glanced at him briefly and then got up. 'I sense we're not welcome here, Rupert,' she said. 'I think we ought to be toddling along.'

'Absolutely, old girl. That is, if we can get the motor to start.'

'Well if not, we'll just have to walk back.'

Steve remained silent until they had gone. When Kay had shut the door after them, she turned on him furiously. 'That was disgraceful,' she said. 'Treating my guests like that.'

Without waiting for a reply, she stormed upstairs. Steve took his coat and shoes off and wandered into the sitting room. He sat down by the fire. Despite the unpleasant scene, the warmth and comfort after his difficult journey home soon made him sleepy, and he lay back against the cushions. He was still there the next morning.

In mid-March, milder air brought the thaw, and this caused floods. These brought another set of problems, and Steve photographed marooned houses, flooded fields, and relief workers rescuing old and young alike and making sure that they were fed and had somewhere to sleep.

Not only had *Picture Post* bought these two features, but they'd offered him a job on the staff. It should have been a moment for celebration, but instead it caused Kay and Steve's final quarrel.

'London!' she said. 'You want us to go and live in London?'

'You might like it there, Kay.'

'No I wouldn't. I like living here. I've got my parents and my friends nearby. If we lived in London, when you went off on a job, I'd be all alone.'

'You'd make new friends.'

'I don't want to make new friends. I like the friends I've got already. There's no point continuing this conversation. I'm simply not going to listen.'

'You know if I were to stay here and work at Latham's for the rest of my life, I would find it very hard not to be resentful.'

'Why can't you be contented with what you have?'

'Kay . . . it's no use. This is not the life I want.'

'All right. Go if you want. But I'm not coming with you. And if you do go, you needn't bother to come back.'

Even though the weather was foul, Paul and Carol still lived what he laughingly called 'the high life'. The theatre, private parties, jazz at the Café de Paris, boxing matches at the Albert Hall, and dinners at Mario's. Wherever they went they were followed by press photographers, and some newspapers began to call them 'the Golden Couple of the Silver Screen'.

The waiting photographers would shout their names to get their attention.

'Paul! Carol! Over here!'

'Look this way!'

One night as they left a private party at the Ritz, the crowd of photographers was more unruly than usual, and Paul put his arm round Carol and drew her close.

'Would you move away please, Paul!' someone shouted, and this cry was taken up by one or two of the others. 'Let's see a bit more of Carol.'

A taxi was waiting, and Paul hurried Carol forward and pushed her inside without ceremony. Carol was surprised that he had reacted the way he had. They had been in no real danger. However, she sensed that he was annoyed and decided not to say anything.

As the month progressed, the weather grew marginally milder but there were frequent downpours. The rain had stopped, but the pavements were awash on the night of the premiere of *Salute the Brave*. This did not prevent a lively crowd turning up in Leicester Square. There were cheers as the stars arrived, especially for Phyllis Greenwood, who smiled sweetly and thanked everyone for coming. No one would guess how difficult she can be, Carol thought, and found herself admiring the older woman for her sheer professionalism.

Paul was greeted by the usual adoring female fans and was at his most charming. But before he had gone far along the rain-soaked red carpet, the crowd's attention turned to Carol. Paul glanced at her quickly, and then, despite the fact that some of the young women were still shouting for him, hurried into the cinema without her.

When Carol joined him in the foyer, he glanced down at her silver evening shoes and said, 'They're ruined.'

Perplexed, Carol looked down and saw that the dye from the carpet had stained them red.

'You should have worn black court shoes. Phyllis did,' he added.

Puzzled and hurt by his attitude, Carol responded with a flash of temper. 'Bully for Phyllis,' she said. 'I must remember to ask her advice in future.'

Just before the staff closed the doors, another car drew up and two women wearing headscarves, their slim figures heavily muffled in raincoats, got out and hurried into the cinema. Carol caught only a glimpse of their pretty young faces before the manager hurried them up the stairs that led to the circle and the boxes. When she took her seat in the stalls, she glanced up and saw that they were sitting in one of the boxes, although so far back that she could not see them clearly.

The lights dimmed, the curtains parted, and as soon as the film began, the audience was plunged into a dramatic tale of recent history. Carol sensed that although this might not be the greatest movie ever made, it would certainly capture hearts.

As the final scene faded, the entire audience rose and began to clap and cheer. Carol knew instinctively that the cheers were prompted not only by admiration of the stars of the film but also by patriotism and a shared sense of victory against all odds. When the lights came up again, she saw that many people had been openly crying. Curiosity caused her to look up at the box, but it was empty. The two young women had gone.

At the party afterwards, the excited gossip was that Princess Elizabeth and Princess Margaret had been in the audience, although nobody could say for certain and the manager wasn't telling.

Paul and Phyllis held court like a royal couple, and Carol, mindful of Paul's mood, endeavoured to stay in the background as much as possible. Eventually the groups of guests began to fragment and leave. By that stage, all Carol wanted to do was go home, so when she saw Paul coming towards her she was relieved.

But Paul did not want to go home. 'A few of us are going to keep the party going,' he told her, and seeing how eager he was to continue celebrating his triumph, she knew she couldn't deny him. She wondered if he remembered how snappy he had been with her before the film had started. Almost as if he had read her thoughts, he said, 'Was I cruel to you before? Never mind, I'll buy you another pair of shoes.'

Paul was enjoying being the centre of attention, and it wasn't until four o'clock in the morning that he seemed to wind down a little and decided that they should go home. Carol was relieved, because to her dismay, Paul hadn't refused an offer of a drink all evening. When they got home, however, he went straight to the drinks cabinet.

'Want to celebrate?' he asked her as he fumbled with the bottles and glasses.

'I thought we already had,' Carol said.

Paul wagged his finger at her and pretended to scold. 'I told you not to be that kind of wife,' he said. 'But suit yourself.' He shrugged and turned away from her.

Carol went to bed alone.

Steve hadn't been entirely enthusiastic about the assignment, but as the newest member of staff he could hardly refuse it. Fashions! How Muriel would laugh. In February, the French designer Christian Dior had presented his debut collection and it had been an instant success. Dior had sensed that the public were ready for a new style after the war. After years of privation, women wanted some excitement.

Even though rationing was still enforced, the new look had begun to appear on the streets of London. Soft shoulders, waspy waists and full flowing skirts. Steve accepted that this was social history. His editor had instructed him to attend the premiere of *Salute the Brave* in order to photograph the rich and famous, and knowing that Carol would be there, he had had mixed feelings about attending.

Because of the rain, he persuaded the manager of the cinema to allow him to stand in the foyer and photograph the guests as they arrived. He'd taken some good shots. First of guests whom he recognised from the society pages, and then of the film people. Phyllis Greenwood looked stunning in a full-skirted strapless white dress with bold patterns of what looked like palm leaves. She was happy to smile and pose for him.

The next person to enter the cinema was Paul Grainger, followed soon afterwards by his wife. Steve caught his breath. Carol was more beautiful than ever, in midnight-blue satin. He had already decided to step back into the crowd so that she wouldn't see him, but he needn't have bothered. Unlike Phyllis, she wasn't smiling. In fact she and Paul seemed to be having an argument.

They hurried by before Steve had recovered enough to take a shot. Watching her vanish through the doors into the warm darkness of the auditorium filled him with anguish. Somehow he didn't have the heart to work any longer tonight. He left the cinema and caught a taxi home.

Home was a basement flat in a large house in Redcliffe Square. The cavernous rooms must once have been the domestic quarters in the days when the house had been occupied by one rich family. Now every floor of the house had been divided into as many separate dwellings as possible, and many of the tenants seemed to Steve to be the flotsam and jetsam washed up on the shore after the war. Disorientated people, discarded people, ex-servicemen who would never be the same again but who were nevertheless trying to make a new life for themselves. Times were hard, but despite this, London was an exciting place to be. Even if you were living on your own.

When Kay had realised that he really was going to leave Latham's, she had told him once more that he need not come back and had decamped to her parents' house while he packed his clothes and prepared to leave. There had been an uncomfortable interview with her father.

Mr Blanchard had told him that if he was deliberately deserting Kay then he must do the decent thing and sign over the house to her. Steve had not until that moment thought of it as desertion, and he was shocked. He had agreed to sign the house over and also to send her maintenance.

'You can't expect Kay to go out and get a job just because you've decided to leave her.'

'Of course I don't,' Steve had told him. 'But I hope you understand that I wanted her to come with me. It's Kay herself who has decided to stay.'

At this point his father-in-law's attitude had softened a little. 'I know that, Steve, and I'm sorry it's worked out this way. But I'm her father and I love her, and no matter what I might think, I remain firmly on her side.'

They had parted as not exactly friends but as men who understood each other.

If Steve had expected the meeting with Kay's father to be difficult, he'd had no idea how much worse it would be with his own parents. His father had given him a stern talk about the duties and responsibilities of a married man and his mother had declared herself disappointed and heartbroken.

The evening before he left home, Muriel came round to see him. 'They'll get over it,' she told him. 'Just give them time. When they see how much happier Kay will be without you, they won't think so badly of you.'

'Thanks a lot!' Steve said.

'No, I mean it. She *will* be happier. You were never right for each other. Kay wants a different sort of man entirely, and I predict it won't be too long before she finds one. She'll be okay. It's you I worry about.'

'Why?'

'Because you've already let your best chance for happiness slip through your fingers, haven't you?'

There was a long pause while brother and sister looked at each other solemnly. Then Steve had sighed and said, 'Perhaps I have.'

When Carol got up the next morning, she found Paul asleep on the sofa, an empty glass in one hand resting on his chest. He had loosened his tie and taken the collar stud from the front fastening of his formal shirt. The collar, still attached at the back, was askew. He looked like the classic picture of a drunk in a movie. Despite the amount he must have put away, he still looked handsome, but Carol could see the future in the slight puffiness around his eyes.

She took the glass from his hand, eased off his shoes and covered him with a rug. She washed and dressed, then made herself a cup of tea and sat in the easy chair watching him. Eventually he opened his eyes, and after a moment or two of disorientation was able to focus on her. He yawned and smiled.

'Quite a night, wasn't it?' he asked her.

'Yes, it was quite a night.'

'Have the papers arrived?'

'Yes.'

'Let's look at them.'

The reviews were good. The cinematography was judged to be outstanding. Paul and Phyllis were praised for their performances and Carol was mentioned as someone to look out for. The brief scenes between her character and Paul's were said to be poignant and maybe even a little more moving than the scene where the brave husband and wife were reunited at the end of the war.

'Phyllis won't like that,' Paul said. 'You'll have to watch out. Might be a few problems there.'

Carol knew he was right, but it wasn't Phyllis's jealousy she was afraid of. She was confident that she could handle whatever that led to. The problem was Paul himself. No matter that he thought them a great team, he was used to getting all the attention. There had already been signs that he didn't like it if Carol got too much of the limelight. She realised that the more serious issue might be that her growing success would damage her relationship with Paul.

Chapter Thirty-Five

If the winter they had just lived through had been one of the coldest on record, the summer was proving to be one of the hottest. Londoners took their sandwiches into the parks at lunchtime, boated on the Serpentine or swam in the lido. During the day, Steve got some wonderful shots of people who were learning to be carefree again. At night he went to the dogs.

Greyhound racing was all the rage, and he knew he'd get a good feature out of it. He photographed the punters and the bookmakers, the queues at the tote where seasoned gamblers lined up with their forecasts, and he went up to the club area to take shots of the track.

As well as the hard-working people determined to have a good night out, Paul had learned that criminals frequented the dog tracks. Petty criminals such as pickpockets and dangerous men like the guys who bet big money and whose winnings depended on the dogs being doped. Steve had heard that in one race every dog except one had been doped so that the outsider won. The people who administered the dope were usually kennelmaids who had been bribed handsomely.

He realised he was beginning to attract attention, and fearing that he might be mistaken for a nark, he learned to be discreet. He also learned a lot about London's teeming underworld. He knew this would make a fantastic feature, but it would be a risky undertaking.

Dangerous Dreams premiered at the beginning of July. London was hot and dusty, and members of the St John Ambulance Brigade moved amongst the crowds outside the cinema, helping those who had succumbed to heat exhaustion.

There was no doubt in anyone's mind that the film was going to be a smash hit. After the premiere there was a party at the Ritz. Many of the guests were important figures in society or in the world of entertainment whom Carol had never met before. Nevertheless they treated her like an old friend.

She and Paul were separated, carried away by different crowds of people, but each time she glimpsed him she could see how elated he was – and how much he was drinking. She was standing talking to Ed when they heard a burst of laughter. They turned to see that Paul had fallen over and was being helped to his feet by a portly gentleman in heavy-framed spectacles.

'For God's sake!' Ed exclaimed. 'That's Gilbert Stern, the gossip columnist. Paul couldn't have chosen a worse moment to make a fool of himself.'

Ed left Carol and hurried over to Paul. Whatever he said seemed to have some effect. Paul didn't have another drink and he was subdued in the taxi on the way home. Once there, he allowed Carol to help him undress and go to bed. He soon fell asleep. Carol, still in her evening clothes, made herself a cup of cocoa and sat down at the small kitchen table. Tonight should have been a triumph not just for Paul but for her as well. She knew Paul couldn't help it, but he had spoiled it for her. She stared down at her cocoa and pushed it aside. Hours later, she was still sitting there.

As predicted, the reviews of the film the next morning were good, but Carol was dismayed to find that she seemed to have top billing. 'A Star is Born!' one of them began, and went on to praise her performance at length before mentioning Paul. He was described as being as handsome and charismatic as ever, but the reviewer suggested that perhaps it had all become too easy for him and no matter what part he played, he remained himself, Paul Grainger. The review went on to say that nevertheless Carol was lucky to have met up with him so early in her career.

Carol breathed a sigh of relief when she read this, but when she watched Paul read the same piece and saw his scowl she knew that the final compliment hadn't been enough to make up for the mild criticism.

Worse was to follow on the day Gilbert Stern's column was published. People often said that the gossip columnist's pen dripped pure poison. Many a reputation of the rich and famous had been ruined, and this time he had not spared Paul. The film was mentioned briefly before Stern went on to write about the party and how Paul Grainger seemed determined to sink his success with an excessive intake of alcohol, but how he was lucky to have such a beautiful and loyal young wife whose own acting talents were obviously going to take her far.

When he read this, Paul threw the paper down angrily and stormed out of the apartment. Carol heard the revving of a car's engine and went to the window. She looked down to see the Bentley pulling away and veering down the street erratically, taking the corner in a wide wild swerve.

He was only away for a couple of hours, but Carol lived through a hell of anxiety and fear. When she heard the car pull up and the door slam, she prepared herself for an angry scene, although she knew that she had done nothing wrong.

To her intense relief, Paul didn't even mention what had gone before. But he did look a little shamefaced. 'Why don't we go out for a meal tonight?' he asked. 'We'll go to Mario's. And don't worry, we'll get a taxi.'

Mario treated them like royalty and offered them a bottle

of the best champagne – on the house. Paul told him he didn't need alcohol tonight because they were still intoxicated by the success of the film. Carol saw how hard he was trying to please her, and realised to her dismay that the strongest emotion she had for him was pity. She felt responsible for him.

The food was as good as ever, but they were hardly left any time to enjoy it. People kept coming over to the table to congratulate them. Instead of finding this trying, Paul was enjoying the attention until Lenny appeared unexpectedly.

'Hello, Paul,' he said. 'Long time no see.'

Paul's smile vanished and Carol could have sworn that he looked frightened.

'Mind if I join you?' Without waiting for an answer, Lenny took a vacant chair from the next table, swung it round and sat down. 'I hear the film is going to be a smash hit,' he said.

'That's right,' Paul replied.

'So I guess you'll be coming along to see me soon?'

'Well . . . it may take a while.'

'Not too long, I hope?'

'I assure you, you have nothing to worry about.'

'But I'm already worrying, Paul. I'm investing heavily in a new venture, so I trust you won't let me down.'

Lenny left without another word, but on the way out he stopped to speak to Mario. 'Slimy little bastard,' Paul said. 'He must have sent word to Lenny that I was here. They're all in it together, you know.'

They left soon after that. In the taxi on the way home, Paul was subdued.

'What was all that about?' Carol asked.

'Oh, nothing. Lenny's just pissed off because we haven't been along to the club lately.'

'What did he mean about not letting him down?'

'Well, you know, he likes to show me off and impress people.'

'So why did you stop going there?'

'Give it a rest, Carol,' Paul said. 'I'm dead beat. We can talk about this some other time.'

Carol lay awake for hours trying to make sense of what had happened. The night seemed to be the hottest yet, and she pushed the bedclothes aside and went to the window to open it. As she stood there, a flash of lightning tore the clouds apart and she waited, holding her breath, for the thunder. When it came, it seemed to be directly overhead. She had never been superstitious, but she could not help thinking it was a presage of trouble to come.

'What have you done now?'

Hetty stared in despair at the cup lying on its side on the carpet and the tea stain spreading over the sheets she had only changed that morning.

'I'm sorry, Hetty. It just slipped from my fingers.' Hetty didn't miss the flash of fear in her husband's eyes.

'Never mind. If you can just shuffle yourself on to the chair, I'll have the bed changed in a jiffy and I'll make you another cup of tea. It's a good job we can afford to send our linen to the laundry, isn't it?'

She gave him what she considered a reassuring smile. She knew she would have to control her growing impatience or Albert might say something to Dr Eddlestone next time he called. Carol had arranged for the doctor to visit at least twice a week, and Hetty was pretty sure he would be sending reports to Carol of her father's progress.

Progress! Hetty thought as she went downstairs to make another pot of tea. The only progress Albert Marshall is making is towards the grave. And as far as I'm concerned, he can't get there quick enough. Carol had promised to send money to make sure her father was being looked after properly, and at first Hetty couldn't have been more pleased. Money for doing nothing, she had thought. She hadn't realised that as Albert grew more ill he would need so much looking after.

She was a prisoner in the house these days. It was weeks since she had made more than a flying visit to her sister's, and she could sense that Joe was getting impatient with the situation. Carol had also told her that she would look after her financially after her father passed away. Unless she married again. It hadn't taken Hetty long to work out what to do about that.

Joe and his gang would be moving on to another town soon. She would tell Carol that she wanted to move because of all the sad memories, and she would go with him. Although no one except her sister would know that. They could even get married and just not tell anyone. Hetty reckoned there was no way Carol would be able to find out. But meanwhile she would have to curb her frustration and keep the old bugger upstairs happy.

Dangerous Dreams was breaking all records, and Paul's recent moods seemed to vanish once the money started going into their bank accounts. Carol wondered whether that was what had been worrying him. Surely not. He'd been a star for years, since before the war; he couldn't have been short of money, could he? He certainly didn't live as if he was hard up.

One night Paul told Carol that he was going to Lenny's club. 'You needn't come along,' he said. 'I won't be long.'

He could see that she was puzzled, but she didn't object, and he guessed that she was probably glad to have a relaxing night at home.

'Welcome, stranger,' Lenny said, and gave one of his lopsided smiles. 'The fact that you're here must mean that you have some good news for me. Why don't we go to my office?'

Paul followed Lenny to a room he had never entered

before. Two burly minders stood at the door as if on guard duty, but they nodded politely enough to Paul as Lenny opened the door and led the way inside.

Once there, Lenny closed the door and went to sit at his desk. Paul glanced round. As they were below ground level, there were no windows, and the room was harshly lit by a light without a shade. Apart from the desk, the only other piece of furniture was a large safe. He waited for Lenny to invite him to sit down, but the invitation was not forthcoming.

'You've got something for me?' Lenny asked.

'That's why I'm here.' Paul took a fat envelope from his inside pocket and tossed it on the desk. 'I can tell you, it raised a few eyebrows at the bank when I asked for this much in cash.'

Lenny opened the envelope and counted out the money. 'Where's the rest?' he said.

'It's all there. Three thousand pounds, that's exactly what I owe you.'

'What about the interest?'

'What do you mean? There's no interest due on gambling debts.'

'What made you think that was so? I'm afraid there is. I want another six hundred quid.'

Paul was stunned. 'That's twenty per cent.'

'That's right.'

'But that's criminal!'

Lenny burst out laughing. 'Of course it is, Paul. Who do you think you're dealing with? Now, surely a big star like you can afford another six hundred quid. And if you've been overspending, why not ask that pretty little wife of yours to help out?'

'I'm not asking Carol. And I'm not paying up, either. Gambling debts aren't enforceable, so you can whistle for it.'

Paul turned to leave and Lenny laughed. He followed him

to the door and said to the two goons, 'Mr Grainger is leaving now. I'd like you to take him out the back way and show him what happens to people who don't do as Lenny tells them. But leave his face alone.' He laughed. 'Got to protect my investment.'

Steve's investigations at the dog tracks had led him to believe that a group of underworld characters were in the process of forming a syndicate that would take over and control the tracks. A few names had been mentioned, and one of them was Lenny Costello.

The other names meant nothing to him, but Costello owned a famous nightclub. Outwardly he was law-abiding, but it was rumoured that he ran an illegal gaming den in a back room of the club. Steve suspected the reason he got away with it was because some of the men who gambled there were powerful figures of the Establishment.

Tonight he had decided to try and get into the club, become a member if he had to, but the doorman had turned him away. Steve had left his camera at home, obviously, but he wondered if, because of his investigations, he had been recognised as a person to be wary of.

He was about to turn away when he heard muffled groans. They were coming from an alleyway just a little further down the street. Thinking that it might be some trick to catch an unwary Good Samaritan then rob him, he approached the entrance cautiously. Once there, he stared into the gloom and saw the figure of a man stumbling towards him.

As the man emerged into the brighter light of the street, Steve just had time to recognise Paul Grainger before he fell at his feet.

Carol was sitting reading when she heard Paul's key in the lock. A moment later she heard voices. Paul had brought someone home. Then she heard him stumble and groan, and thought it more likely that someone had brought Paul home and that that person would be Ed. She hurried through to the hall, and stopped and stared in shock. It wasn't Ed who was holding Paul up; it was Steve Douglas.

She was aware that she was almost rigid with shock. And then she began to shake. Paul, seeing how distressed she was, jumped to the wrong conclusion.

'I'm not drunk,' he said. 'In fact I'm completely sober. I just had a little accident, that's all. This kind chap found me and brought me home.'

'Look,' Steve said. 'I think we ought to get him to bed. I'll help him if you like, and you should go and have a cup of hot sweet tea.' He gave a wry smile. 'That's what they do in the movies, isn't it?'

Carol began to awake from her trancelike state. 'I should help him,' she said.

'No.' There was almost a note of panic in Paul's voice. 'You go and have a cup of tea like a good girl. This chap will tell you all about it later.'

Paul groaned in agony as Steve helped him to undress. When Steve saw the bruises on the other man's body, he was horrified. 'Do you think you ought to go to hospital?' he asked.

'Can't afford to. Can't afford the gossip. The scandal. If I think I need medical attention, my agent knows a doctor who'll be discreet.'

'And of course you can't tell the police, can you?'

Paul climbed into bed and Steve covered him with the bedclothes as if he were a child. 'No. I can't tell the police.'

'Was it a gambling debt?'

'Something like that.'

'And are you going to settle it?'

'What's it to you?' Paul suddenly sounded querulous.

'Because if you don't, they might harm Carol.'

Paul looked at Steve and his eyes widened. 'You're right, of course. It was a matter of principle for me, but that doesn't matter if it's going to put my wife in danger. I'll settle the debt. But before you go, tell me something.'

'What's that?'

'I know who you are, don't I?'

'I don't see how.'

'I saw you in the cinema that night when Carol and I were signing autographs. What are you doing in London?'

'I work here now.'

'And should that worry me?'

'I don't know what you mean.'

'Yes you do.'

'No, you needn't worry. I don't think Carol wants anything to do with me.'

'Good. Now if you don't mind, please just tell her that I tripped over and fell badly. I don't want her learning the truth.'

Chapter Thirty-Six

For Steve, it seemed surreal to be sitting at the kitchen table drinking tea with Carol. She had asked what had happened to Paul and he had told her that he had fallen outside Lenny's club. He wasn't sure whether she believed him.

'But what were you doing there?' she asked.

'Working – sort of.'

'I don't understand.'

'I work for *Picture Post*. I'm doing an investigative piece about London's . . . London's nightclubs.' He stopped himself in time before he told her that it was London's criminal fraternity he was investigating, and that Lenny Costello was almost certainly one of its more dangerous characters.

'So you live in London?'

'I thought Muriel might have told you. You do write to each other, don't you?'

'Muriel never mentions you in her letters. Why should she?'

'Why indeed.' He shouldn't have been surprised at how much that hurt.

'How did your family feel about you leaving Latham's?'

'They weren't pleased. Neither was Kay. She refused to come with me.'

Carol was silent. They stared at each other wordlessly, and Steve was suddenly gripped with a powerful urge to reach over and take hold of her hands. To tell her how much she meant to him and what a fool he'd been not to realise that until it was too late. But that would have been totally inappropriate. Her husband was sleeping in the next room and Steve himself was a married man, even if Kay was now talking about divorce.

'I suppose I'd better go,' he said.

'Yes.'

'Will you be all right?'

'Of course.'

She led the way to the door of the apartment, and in the narrow hallway, Steve felt all his senses stirring at her proximity. He caught his breath when she turned to look at him, but she merely regarded him levelly for a moment before opening the door. He stepped out into the foyer.

Suddenly he couldn't stop himself saying, 'Carol — are you happy?'

Again that cool gaze. 'Of course,' she said. 'Good night, Steve. Thank you for bringing Paul home.'

Steve had no idea whether she felt as bereft as he did.

Carol closed the door and stood leaning her forehead against it, closing her eyes. So Steve was in London. She tried to tell herself that she didn't care, but the hollow feeling within her laid bare the lie. She wondered if he'd had any idea how shocked she had been to see him standing there with Paul — and how much it had cost her to keep her feelings under control.

Sitting at the kitchen table she had asked him about finding Paul and then gone on to chat as if it were perfectly normal to have him there, in such domestic surroundings, talking like old acquaintances when once she had hoped for so much more.

She pressed her hands against the door to steady herself and realised they were icy cold. And yet her forehead was hot, as were the tears that were burning against her eyelids. When she opened her eyes the tears spilled out and she rubbed them away angrily with the back of her hand.

It's just shock, she told herself; shock at seeing Paul so injured – my husband. Uneasy guilt carried her to the bedroom to see how he was. Steve must have put out the light for the room was dark. Carol stood in the doorway and the light from the hall fell across the bed revealing his sleeping form.

She took a step towards him and was greeted by the usual aroma of alcohol and cigarette smoke. Suddenly Paul moaned and flung an arm across the bed. Carol eased a pillow from under his arm and rolled up the eiderdown. She left the room quietly and, as she made up a bed on the sofa, she convinced herself that it was because she didn't want to disturb him.

The next morning Paul refused to talk about what had happened to him, but he was so obviously in pain when he moved around the flat that Carol guessed that it been much more than a mere fall. She had almost decided that Paul must have annoyed one of the dangerous characters he liked to mingle with in Lenny's club and had been beaten up. Lenny, who used to protect him, seemed to be an enemy now.

So she was surprised and anxious when a few days later Paul said he was going to the club again. This time when he returned it was as if some burden had been lifted from his shoulders.

'No need to worry now, Carol,' he said cryptically. 'No need to worry.'

He seemed to be really happy, and started talking about their golden future again. But his cheerful mood didn't last long.

The next morning, before Paul was up, Ed Palmer telephoned and told Carol that she was being considered for a part in a Roman epic to be shot in Italy.

Carol was bemused. 'What kind of part is it?' she asked.

'The female lead. A young Roman aristocrat who falls in love with a gladiator.'

Carol laughed. 'Sounds like nonsense to me.'

'It is nonsense, but it's high-quality, expensive, Technicolor nonsense, and if you make a success of this, it could be your ticket to Hollywood.'

Carol caught her breath. 'Hollywood?'

'That's what I said. Are you excited?'

'Of course. And what about Paul? Is Paul to be the gladiator?'

There was a silence. Carol suddenly felt afraid.

'They don't want Paul,' Ed told her.

'Why not?'

'Two reasons. They can't afford to engage someone who might jeopardise the schedule because of his drinking. And secondly, the opinion is that his drinking is beginning to affect his looks.'

'But he's still so handsome. Surely make-up . . . ?'

'That's true. But that doesn't tackle the underlying problem, does it?'

'No. What if I could persuade him to stop drinking?'

'Forget it, Carol. You and I both know that's a lost cause.'

Before Carol had time to respond, she heard a click on the line, and a moment later Paul burst into the room. He must have been listening on the extension in the bedroom. He grabbed the receiver from her.

'You bastard!' he yelled. 'You've made a fortune out of me and now you're arranging to quietly drop me because you've found someone else to fill the coffers.'

Carol could not hear what Ed's reply was, but suddenly Paul thrust the receiver back into her hand and shouted, 'Tell him! Tell him you wouldn't dream of being in the film unless there's a part for me.'

'Is that you, Carol?' she heard Ed say. 'Don't listen to him.

They won't have Paul whatever you say, and if you turn down this part now, you'll regret it for the rest of your life.'

'What are you waiting for?' Paul shouted. 'It's not so difficult to get the words out, is it? If you remember, I did the same for you. You would never have got the part in *Dangerous Dreams* if I hadn't told that fat bastard Monty Daniels that if he wouldn't give it to you then he couldn't have me.'

'Carol − I'm coming round,' Ed said.

'What did he say?' Paul asked.

'He's coming here to see us.'

Paul grabbed the receiver again. 'No you're bloody not. Or if you do, you won't find me here. I'll leave Carol to tell you what she's decided.'

He slammed the receiver down and stormed over to the drinks cabinet.

'Paul . . . no . . .' Carol began.

He ignored her and poured himself a large glass of vodka. He raised it mockingly. 'Here's to my wife. My loyal little wife!' he said.

Carol began to cry.

'Cheer up, Carol,' he said. 'You're going to be a big star. That's what you want isn't it? No matter who you trample over on the way up.'

Draining his glass he pushed past her and went into the bedroom, emerging only minutes later with his clothes pulled on roughly and his hair uncombed.

'Where are you going?' Carol asked.

'Out.' He grabbed the bottle of vodka and took his car keys from the table. Then he left, slamming the door behind him.

Carol hurried after him to find that the lift was already descending. She took the stairs and ran down as fast as she could, but by the time she reached the street door, Paul was already driving away, the wheels sending up huge sprays of water from the roads flooded by the recent downpours. She stood and watched him go in despair, then went back to the apartment and phoned Ed. She told him not to come round as she had a lot to think about and she would give him her decision later. Then she sat down in the hall and waited for Paul to return.

Carol knew even before she opened the door who she would find there. The young policeman looked at her nervously, and his companion, a policewoman, said, 'Mrs Grainger?'

Carol nodded and stood back to allow them to enter. 'Is it about Paul?' she asked.

'I'm afraid so.'

'What is it? I mean . . . is he . . . ?' She looked at the policewoman beseechingly.

'Mrs Grainger,' the young woman said, 'I think you'd better sit down.'

In the days that followed Paul's fatal crash, Carol felt completely numb. She couldn't even weep. Ed spared her the identifying of the body and he also managed to arrange the funeral without the press finding out the time or the location. Later, when she looked back on that period of her life, her memories were like a series of film clips playing on the screen in her mind.

The first scene was in a neglected, dusty church. The supporting cast was small. Just the priest, a handful of mourners, and the undertaker's men. But there was one surprise appearance. Carol had expected to find only Ed Palmer and Paul's housekeeper, Mrs Lambert, and her husband, so she was startled to see a heavily veiled black-clad woman slip into the pew at the other side of the aisle just before the funeral service began.

She succumbed to wild imaginings. Was this a woman from Paul's past? An abandoned lover, even a wife? When the brief ceremony had ended, the woman came to walk by her side as they followed the coffin to the newly dug grave. Carol found herself trembling violently when the woman took hold of her arm.

'I'm sorry, Carol, have I frightened you?' the woman said. Carol recognised the voice of Lorna Lane.

'Why are you here?' Carol asked. 'And how did you know where to come?'

'I told Mr Palmer I wanted to see you. He understood.'

'But why?'

'I feel guilty. I was partly responsible for thrusting you into this outlandish new world. I know what it did to me. I ought to have befriended you.'

The leaves of the trees were dripping from the recent rains but the sun was shining and the air felt as though it had been washed clean. In a movie it would still be raining, Carol thought, and the skies would be black and threatening. But instead her husband was to be buried on a beautiful sunny day.

When Paul's coffin had been lowered into the grave, they left the gravediggers to their sombre task and made their way back to the waiting cars.

'I'm not coming back with you,' Lorna Lane said. 'But I want you to know that you can call on me whenever you need to talk. Promise me you will?'

'I promise.'

The next scene in Carol's personal movie was back at Paul's apartment. She found she couldn't think of it as hers, or even theirs. Mrs Lambert had prepared a small buffet, and she and her husband joined Ed Palmer and Carol. They all stood around awkwardly, not knowing what to say.

When the Lamberts had gone, Ed told Carol that he was going to retire. 'I'll probably live abroad. I'm not sure where.

But don't worry,' he said. 'There will be more than one agent willing to snap you up. Will you trust me to guide you?'

'I suppose so,' Carol said listlessly, and it was only then that she began to weep. She wept for Paul, for all his talent gone to waste, destroyed by his own insecurity and pride. She knew he had never really loved her, but also that she herself had been to blame for their hollow sham of a marriage – two lonely people pretending to be happy. Where had it all gone so wrong?

She decided to sell the apartment and move back to her flat in Richmond for which she had gone on paying rent. Mrs Lambert was upset, but Carol told her that if she wished she could come and work for her. The housekeeper agreed, and then set to cleaning and tidying the apartment. Mr Lambert helped to pack up Paul's clothes. Carol told him to keep what he wanted for himself and to donate the rest to the Salvation Army. The estate agent told her that he would deal with any prospective customers so that she could move out as quickly as possible.

On her last evening in the apartment, just after Mrs Lambert had gone home, the doorbell rang and Carol, thinking the housekeeper had forgotten something, opened the door to find Denise and Muriel standing there. The shock stunned her into silence.

And then she broke down completely and found herself sobbing in Denise's arms, while Muriel shooed them inside and declared that if she could find the kitchen she would put the kettle on.

'Why are you here?' Carol asked shakily when they were sitting at the kitchen table with cups of tea.

'Surely you don't have to ask,' Muriel replied. 'I read about Paul's death in the newspapers and made arrangements to come as soon as possible.'

426

'And you, Denise?'

'It was in the American papers too, but Howard said Paul would have been upset at what was actually said.'

'Why?'

Denise smiled ruefully. 'The headline I saw said, "Carol Marshall's husband killed in auto crash." '

'Oh.' Carol stared bleakly into her cup of tea. 'That makes me feel more guilty than ever.'

'Why on earth should you feel guilty?' Denise asked. 'I mean, you didn't ask him to go out and smash himself up, did you?'

'Denise!' Muriel admonished.

'No, it's all right,' Carol said. 'And it's nothing I said to Paul; at least I don't think so. It's difficult to explain.'

'Why don't you try?' Denise reached across the table and took Carol's hand.

Carol told her friends how much she owed to Paul, how grateful she was and always would be, and how her dream of success had almost turned to ashes when she realised what it was doing to Paul.

'He should have been big enough to take it,' Denise said.

'But he wasn't,' Muriel said, 'and Carol, you'll just have to accept that.'

The atmosphere in the tiny kitchen was uncomfortably stuffy, and Denise thought longingly of the air-conditioning system in her home in California. She rose to open the window, and immediately closed it again when she was met by a blast of hot dusty traffic fumes.

Muriel suddenly said, 'Is anybody hungry? I know I am.'

'Oh ... I'm sorry,' Carol said. 'I don't think there's much left in the pantry. I'm moving back to my flat in Richmond tomorrow.'

'We could go to my hotel,' Denise said. 'I could treat us to a slap-up meal.'

'Where are you staying?' Carol asked.

'Brown's,' Denise replied. 'I'd never heard of it, but Howard said it was the oldest and the best hotel in London. He's going to join me en route to Italy.'

'Italy?'

'They're going to be shooting some big Roman epic there. Howard's already lined up for the part of a Roman bigwig. He's pleased as punch, because apart from the fact that we'll be able to spend some time in Italy together, he thinks he'll look good in a toga.'

'So you're going too?' Carol asked.

'Sure am. Howard's far too attractive to young beauties for me to leave him on his own!'

The three of them laughed and the mood lightened.

'Incidentally,' Denise said, 'Howard says that rumour has it that you've been offered the part of his daughter, the beautiful Aurelia. Is that right?'

'Yes, I have.'

'And you are going to accept, aren't you? I mean, you're not going to let what happened, tragic as it is, ruin your career?'

'Yes, I am going to accept. I'd already decided. But even if I hadn't, I couldn't refuse now, could I? Not when I know that you and Howard are going to be there.'

'So are we going out to dinner?' Denise asked.

'I'm not sure,' Carol said. 'I've been lying low since . . . since Paul died. I might be recognised, and I don't think I could stand it if something got into the newspapers about my being out on the town again so soon.'

'Such is the price of fame!' Muriel said. 'Let me have a look in this pantry of yours.' A moment later she said, 'Not bad. There's a lump of fruit cake, a box of crackers, and some cheese in the fridge. I think we could make do with that.'

'And better still,' Carol said, 'I think there may be one bottle of wine left in the drinks cabinet.'

'Great,' Muriel said. 'We can celebrate in style.'

'What are we celebrating?' Carol asked.

'Are you getting married?' Denise asked.

'For goodness' sake, you're as bad as Steve,' Muriel retorted. 'No, it's much better than that. I'm no longer the office dogsbody. Mr Blanchard has promoted me. I'm a proper reporter.'

'That's wonderful!' Carol said.

'It's great. I'm really pleased for you,' Denise added warmly.

'And furthermore,' Muriel continued, 'I don't intend to stay in Seaton Bay all my working life. A few years' experience on the local rag and then it's Fleet Street, here I come!'

The three of them talked until the early hours, and when Denise said that it was maybe time for her and Muriel to get back to the hotel, Carol asked them to stay. They had helped her just by being here, and for the first time in weeks she was beginning to believe she could rebuild her life and reclaim her hopes for the future.

Chapter Thirty-Seven

Steve had read in the newspapers of Paul Grainger's fatal accident and had not been surprised when Muriel phoned to say that she was coming to London. 'Denise is coming too,' she told him. 'She phoned all the way from America.'

'Do you want to stay here with me?' Steve asked his sister.

'Thanks but no thanks. I'll be staying with Denise at her hotel. She insisted.'

After the call, Steve was in an agony of indecision. He couldn't bear to think of what Carol must be going through. Should he go to see her and offer sympathy and support? But if he did, he knew it would be impossible to conceal his true feelings. And how could he tell her he truly and deeply loved her when she was mourning the death of her husband?

The morning after their feast of cheese and crackers, Denise and Muriel helped Carol move back to her flat in Richmond. Several letters had been delivered just before Carol closed the door for the last time, but she stuffed them in her bag to deal with later.

'This is super!' Muriel said, looking around the tasteful but comfortably furnished flat. 'It's just the sort of place I hope to have one day.'

Carol had brought none of Paul's furniture with her,

so it didn't take the three of them long to unpack her personal belongings. Denise suggested they should go for a walk by the river and find a nice restaurant for a bite of lunch.

Not long after that, Denise went back to her hotel. She had to pack her things because she was leaving for Italy the following day. Muriel had been planning to go to Steve's apartment for another day or two, but Carol asked her to come and stay with her, and Muriel agreed happily.

It wasn't until later that night that Carol remembered that she hadn't dealt with her mail. Most of it was business correspondence that she could hand over to Ed, but two letters were personal.

The first one she opened was from Alice Grayson, expressing her sympathy and telling her that she would always be prepared to help in any way she could. The second one was from Dr Eddlestone, her father's doctor.

'What's the matter?' Muriel asked when she saw Carol's face.

'Here, read it.' Carol handed the letter to her friend.

Muriel read it and looked grave. 'What are you going to do?' she asked.

'I'll have to go and see him.'

'I'll come with you.'

The next morning they caught an early train from King's Cross. The journey was very different from Carol's first journey down. This time there was no bag of sandwiches and packet of crushed biscuits. They had breakfast in the first-class restaurant car and went back there later for coffee.

'This is the way to travel!' Muriel said. 'I could get used to this. I'm ever so grateful that you upgraded my ticket.'

'Well it would have been really silly, wouldn't it, for you and me to sit whole carriages apart!'

When they arrived at Newcastle just before lunch, despite Muriel's protest at the expense of it, Carol got a taxi. They arrived at Dr Eddlestone's house just as he was finishing morning surgery and he saw them straight away.

'I'm glad you came, Carol. I didn't want to tell you everything in the letter. It's ... it's delicate.'

'You said you were worried about my father's condition. Is he dying?'

'I'm sorry if you jumped to that conclusion. No, he's not dying – at least not for a while yet. Not if he receives proper care.'

'And you don't think he is?'

'I'm afraid not. I'm not sure that he's getting all his medication and ... oh dear, I don't know how to tell you this, but there are unexplained bruises.'

Muriel gasped and Carol was aware of a cold fury building up inside her.

'Have you asked him about these bruises?' she said.

'I never get the chance. Your ... ah ... your stepmother never leaves me alone with him.'

'I'm going to see him now. Would you come with me?'

'If you wish. But before we go, I'd like to make a suggestion.'

Muriel said she would wait for Carol at Miss Grayson's, and Dr Eddlestone took Carol to her old house in his car. When Hetty opened the door, she looked at Carol's expression and her eyes widened with alarm. She recovered quickly and put on a sickly smile.

'Home for a visit?' she said. 'How nice. I was really sorry to hear about your husband,' she added as an afterthought.

'I've not come here for a social visit. I've come to see my father.'

'I'll take you up.'

'There's no need. I know the way. Dr Eddlestone and I will see him together.'

Hetty knew it was over. She should have been more careful. But for months now Albert had been enough to try anyone's patience. It was like looking after a baby. Not that Hetty had ever looked after a baby; she had made sure of that. She supposed she should have guessed that that nosy old doctor was suspicious and that sooner or later he would write to Carol. And now goodness knows what Albert would be telling them when she wasn't there.

The longer they stayed upstairs, the more nervous Hetty got. They wouldn't call the police, would they? She didn't think she'd done anything to warrant that.

By the time Carol walked into the room, Hetty had worked herself up to a state of defiance. 'Well,' she said. 'Had a nice little talk with your father, have you?'

'Yes, I have.'

'So what's he told you?'

'That you've neglected him. That you've bullied him. That you've wished him dead.'

'That's ridiculous. I never said anything like that.'

'You didn't have to. My father may be ill, but he's not stupid.'

'So what are you going to do?'

'Dr Eddlestone has arranged an emergency bed in the hospital for tonight, and tomorrow my father is going into a convalescent home. You need never see him again.'

'And that will salve your conscience, will it? First of all you pay me to look after him, and now you're going to put him in a home.'

'Yes, I blame myself. I should never have trusted you to care for him. As for the home, he'll have the very best of care for as long as he needs it.'

'And you'll be visiting him there, I suppose?'

'Whenever I can. You probably don't need telling that I'll stop sending the money orders, and as I presume you don't want to say goodbye to my father, I'd like you to leave the house until we've gone.'

Hetty pulled on her coat and went out, slamming the door behind her. Who the hell does Carol think she is, giving me orders as if she was the bloody Queen? What am I supposed to do now? Go back to the laundry? Not likely. Albert in a home and me back at work? I can just imagine the sly looks and the backbiting! Hetty thought.

In her rage she had hardly noticed where she was going, and she pulled up short when she realised she was at the corner of her sister's street. Her anger turned to fury. What a let-down Joe had been. To think she had once believed that she and her sister's lodger might have a future together, when all the time he'd been married. She only found this out when his job in Seaton Bay was finished.

'I'll write to you,' she'd said.

'Better not,' he'd replied. 'The wife wouldn't like it.'

'Wife?' She had stared at him unbelievingly.

'That's right. My next job's near to home so I won't have to take lodgings.'

'You lying, cheating bastard!' she'd yelled.

'Now wait a minute. You're no angel. You've been cheating on poor old Albert and taking money from his daughter at the same time.'

Hetty had raised her hand to strike him, but he'd caught her arm and gripped it so fiercely that it hurt.

'Listen Hetty,' he'd said. 'We've had a good time together, so let's part friends, shall we?'

'Damn you to hell!' Hetty had screamed as she pulled her arm free and stormed off. She had never seen him again.

And now? Hetty took a cigarette from the pack in her

pocket and lit up. She narrowed her eyes and squinted through the smoke. Well, at least she'd had the sense to put some money by. That ungrateful bitch Carol could hardly take it back from her. Maybe she should leave Seaton Bay. Find a job in another town. It would be better than staying here and facing the questions and the gossip.

That's it, then, she thought. As soon as Carol and that meddlesome old doctor have got Albert out of the house I'll pack my things and leave. She sighed. I don't know what else I can do.

Carol remained in Seaton Bay until her father was settled in the convalescent home. She stayed with Alice Grayson. Muriel called after work each day, and Denise's mother and Ruthie were delighted to see her.

Soon it would be time for her to return to London and prepare for her trip to Italy, but on the Sunday, when Muriel was off work, they went for a walk on the beach together. The sun was bright, but the cool air told them that summer was nearly over. A brisk wind from the sea worried the crests of the waves and tossed spindrift into the air. The only other people on the beach today were dog-walkers and a lone fisherman.

They were both quiet until Muriel suddenly said, 'Do you realise we haven't walked on the beach together since we were kids?'

'Yes, I know.'

'We should have brought a picnic. Sandwiches and hard-boiled eggs and fizzy pop.'

Remembering the last time they'd picnicked on the beach, Carol smiled. 'I don't suppose you want to paddle, do you?'

'The sea will be freezing! But why not?'

They laid their coats on the marram grass on the sand dunes and took off their shoes and stockings.

'It's more complicated than when we were kids, isn't it?' Muriel said. 'Do you think we should tuck our skirts into our knickers?'

'You can if you like,' Carol said laughingly, 'but I think I'll just risk getting wet.'

The sea was too cold to paddle for long, so to warm themselves up they ran along the shoreline almost as far as the lighthouse. The sea, the sun, the wind and the bracing air revived Carol's spirits and she was laughing when they turned round to run back. She pulled up short when she saw someone standing where they had left their coats.

'Why is he here?' she asked Muriel.

'Because I told him where you were.'

'Some friend you are!'

'Yes, I am your friend, Carol. That's why I phoned him. And please don't pretend that you don't want to see him.'

'But . . . but he's married . . . married to Kay.'

'Not for much longer. She's divorcing him for wilful desertion. She wants to marry a guy called Rupert Penfold. He's got a job as estate manager at Woodford Hall. Can't you just see Kay lapping up the lifestyle!'

More slowly now, they returned to where they had left their coats. 'Hello, small fry,' Steve said.

'Small fry yourself,' Muriel bantered. 'Now turn your back while we ladies put our stockings on.'

When they were ready, Muriel gave Carol a swift hug and said goodbye, then walked away, leaving them looking at each other wordlessly.

It was Steve who spoke first. 'Can we start again, Carol?' he asked.

'Start again?'

'Can we pretend that the last year never happened? Pretend that I've just come home and found you waiting and realised what a lucky guy I was?'

'I don't know, Steve. I don't know if I want that now. Life moves on.'

'Well, here on the beach, let's turn the clock back. I don't blame you if you're angry with me. But for God's sake give me a chance to put things right.'

Suddenly any anger and hurt that remained drained away. The love she had always had for him almost overwhelmed her and filled her with longing. He must have sensed the change, because he reached out for her. She held back.

'We can't change everything, you know,' she said.

'What do you mean?'

'I'm not the same person I was when you first came home. I have my work, now. It's important to me. I won't give it up.'

'I wouldn't expect you to. I have my work too. Right now I'm in the middle of an investigation into the London underworld. As you can imagine, some of the characters I'm after are camera shy to say the least.'

'Isn't that dangerous?'

'Don't worry, I've learned to look after myself.'

Carol looked at him gravely then said, 'I'm sure you have.'

'Our life together will be complicated,' he said. 'But I promise you, it will never be boring!'

He closed the distance between them and took her in his arms.

As he lowered his head to kiss her, Carol said, 'Wait a moment.'

Steve groaned. 'What now? Why the smile?'

'If this were a movie, the background would fade to a romantic haze, the camera would circle us, the waves would be heard crashing on the shore and the music would start to play.'

Steve laughed. 'But we don't need any music, do we? We only need each other.'

The Promise

Benita Brown

*In his last moments he offered up a prayer to the Almighty.
'God, keep my daughters safe from harm . . .'*

Marion Brookfield is just eighteen when she makes
a promise that will change her life for ever. When
her father, a journalist, is murdered by a vagrant, she
vows to put aside her own dreams and care for her
younger sister Annette.

Orphaned and penniless, the girls believe they have
found a refuge when charming businessman Victor
Bateman proposes to Marion and they move into his
luxurious home.

But Marion's friend Daniel Brady is conducting his
own investigation into Henry Brookfield's death. He
learns the journalist was closing in on the ruthless
head of a child prostitution racket when he was killed.
And now his precious daughters may not be so safe,
after all . . .

Praise for Benita Brown's powerful novels:

'I didn't want to put it down . . . A must for Catherine
Cookson lovers' *Coventry Telegraph*

'Real heroines, genuine heartache . . . What more
could you want?' *Northern Echo*

978 0 7553 3476 6

headline

The Dressmaker

Benita Brown

'Mrs Winterton, Melissa has the makings of a fine dressmaker, better than I could ever be. I want you to look after her . . .'

Emmeline Dornay's dying wish is for her daughter Melissa to have a home. But when the funeral is over, Melissa discovers that her future looks bleak. Wealthy Lilian Winterton *will* honour her promise and put a roof over Melissa's head, but only if she can earn her keep.

As an unpaid seamstress in the grand Winterton household, Melissa is ignored by the family and mistrusted by their servants. And when scandal occurs and the blame lands unfairly at her feet, she is thrown out on to the streets. Left with nothing but her needle and thread, Melissa finds her dreams are in tatters. But can the rags of her life be sewn into riches . . . ?

Praise for *Fortune's Daughter*, longlisted for the Romantic Novel of the Year Award 2007:

'If Catherine Cookson were alive, she'd be giving Benita Brown a pat on the back for this' *Northern Echo*

'A wonderfully evocative tale' *Lancashire Evening Post*

'A romantic tale of rivalry and deceit' *Newcastle Upon Tyne Journal*

978 0 7553 3474 2

headline

Fortune's Daughter

Benita Brown

Daisy Belle, a gifted singer from the Tyneside backstreets, is devastated when her baby daughter Rose goes missing. Little does she know Rose has been stolen and given to a wealthy woman who, tricked into believing she's an orphan, adopts her and renames her Rosina. Worse still, it was all arranged by Daisy's ruthlessly ambitious agent, Jack Fidler.

Years later, when tragedy strikes. Rosina runs away to join a theatrical troupe and her natural talent for singing soon wins the hearts of the crowds. But this brings her into direct competition with one of the northern music halls' established stars, Daisy Belle – and back into the path of Jack, who is determined to destroy her . . .

Longlisted for the Romantic Novel of the Year Award 2007

Praise for Benita Brown's popular sagas:

'You won't be able to put it down' *Yours* magazine

'A splendidly powerful and touching saga' *Newcastle Evening Chronicle*

'A wonderfully Dickensian flavour . . . Everyone in the book is alive and believable' *Historical Novels Review*

'A must for Catherine Cookson fans' *Wiltshire Times*

978 0 7553 2328 9

headline

Now you can buy any of these other bestselling books by **Benita Brown** from your bookshop or *direct from her publisher*.

FREE P&P AND UK DELIVERY
(Overseas and Ireland £3.50 per book)

A Dream of Her Own	£6.99
All Our Tomorrows	£6.99
Her Rightful Inheritance	£6.99
In Love and Friendship	£6.99
The Captain's Daughters	£5.99
A Safe Harbour	£5.99
Fortune's Daughter	£6.99
The Dressmaker	£5.99
The Promise	£5.99

TO ORDER SIMPLY CALL THIS NUMBER

01235 400 414

or visit our website: www.headline.co.uk

Prices and availability subject to change without notice